P

Before becoming a full-time writer Bernard Cornwell worked as a television producer in London and Belfast. He now lives in Massachusetts with his American wife. He is the author of the hugely successful *Sharpe* series of historical novels.

Penguin publish his bestselling contemporary thrillers *Sea Lord, Wildtrack*, *Crackdown*, *Stormchild* and *Scoundrel*, and also his myth-imbued Arthurian romance, *The Warlord Chronicles*, which consists of *The Winter King*, *Enemy of God* and *Excalibur*.

For more information about Bernard Cornwell's books, please visit his official website: www.bernardcornwell.net.

BERNARD CORNWELL

REDCOAT

PENGUIN BOOKS

PENGUIN BOOKS

Published by the Penguin Group
Penguin Books Ltd, 80 Strand, London WC2R ORL, England
Penguin Group (USA) Inc., 375 Hudson Street, New York, New York 10014, USA
Penguin Group (Canada), 90 Eglinton Avenue East, Suite 700, Toronto, Ontario, Canada M4P 2Y3
(a division of Pearson Penguin Canada Inc.)
Penguin Ireland, 25 St Stephen's Green, Dublin 2, Ireland (a division of Penguin Books Ltd)
Penguin Group (Australia), 250 Camberwell Road, Camberwell, Victoria 3124, Australia
(a division of Pearson Australia Group Pty Ltd)
Penguin Books India Pvt Ltd, 11 Community Centre, Panchsheel Park, New Delhi – 110 017, India
Penguin Group (NZ), 67 Apollo Drive, Rosedale, North Shore 0632, New Zealand
(a division of Pearson New Zealand Ltd)
Penguin Books (South Africa) (Pty) Ltd, 24 Sturdee Avenue, Rosebank, Johannesburg 2196, South Africa

Penguin Books Ltd, Registered Offices: 80 Strand, London WC2R ORL, England

www.penguin.com

First published by Michael Joseph 1987
Published in Penguin Books 1993
1

Printed in Great Britain by Clays Ltd, St Ives plc

ISBN: 978-0-141-04982-3

www.greenpenguin.co.uk

Redcoat was conceived
and nurtured by
IRVIN KERSHNER,
a Patriot, to whom the book
is now gratefully dedicated

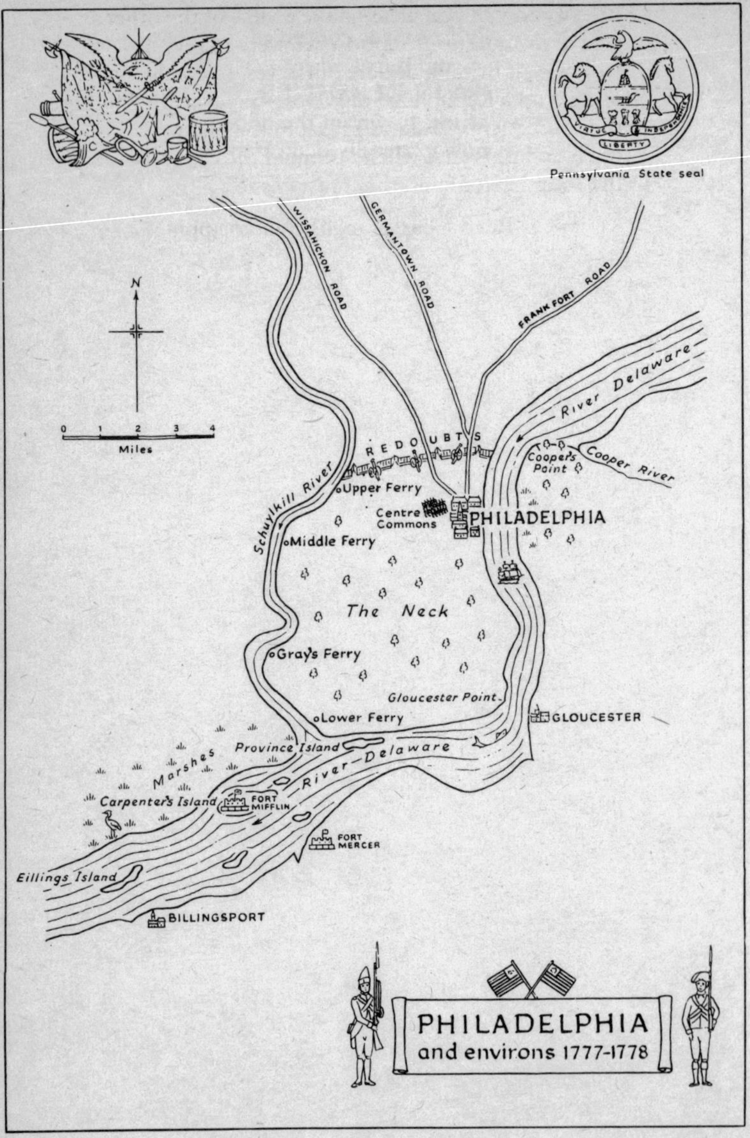

Pennsylvania State seal
VIRTUE
LIBERTY
INDEPENDENCE
WISSAHICKON ROAD
GERMANTOWN ROAD
FRANK FORT ROAD
N
0 1 2 3 4
Miles
River Delaware
REDOUBTS
Schuylkill River
Upper Ferry
Cooper's Point
Cooper River
Centre Commons
PHILADELPHIA
Middle Ferry
The Neck
Gray's Ferry
Gloucester Point
Lower Ferry
GLOUCESTER
Province Island
Marshes
River Delaware
Carpenter's Island
FORT MIFFLIN
FORT MERCER
Eillings Island
BILLINGSPORT
PHILADELPHIA
and environs 1777-1778

"Let us now, if you please, take a view of the other side of the question. Suppose we were to revolt from Great Britain, declare ourselves independent, and set up a Republic of our own – what would be the consequence? I stand aghast at the prospect – my blood runs chill when I think of the calamities, the complicated evils, that must ensue."

Revd Charles Inglis, Philadelphia, 1776

PART ONE

ONE

The Bloodybacks stole through warm darkness to the killing.

A hidden moon silvered chasms of cloud and offered a wan glow which silhouetted the jagged spikes of pine tops on the western horizon. The eastern sky was unclouded; a pit of blackness studded with the clean brightness of stars. The paths beneath the trees were dark, utter dark, a blackness in which long files of men cursed softly.

The sun would rise to bring the steamy, breath-stealing heat of the full day; yet even now, in the night's small hours, there was a close, stifling warmth that made the men sweat beneath their thick woollen coats. Red coats. The men were soldiers; six companies of Redcoats who followed their leaders through a wooded defile towards a tavern, a crossroads, and the enemy.

A stream made its homely sound to the south, the wind rattled pine branches, while the night hordes of insects drowned whatever noise the nailed boots made on the dry and fallen needles. A whispered order was passed down the files of men. They stopped and crouched.

Private Sam Gilpin's hands were slick with sweat. His body prickled with the heat. A horse whinnied.

It had to be an enemy's horse, for the Redcoats had come on foot. Even the General was on foot. The sound told Sam that the enemy must be close, very close, and, despite the cloying warmth, he shivered suddenly.

His musket would not fire. None of the soldiers' muskets would fire, for they had been ordered to unscrew the dog-heads and take out their flints. A musket without a flint could not spark the powder, so it could not fire a bullet, but nor could a careless man stumble in the dark and fire a shot which would warn the enemy.

The Redcoats had come in the warm darkness, in silence, and the enemy was close.

"Follow!" Again the order was a whisper. Sam's company was led off the path into the blackness beneath the trees. Each man tried to walk silently, yet twigs snapped, dry pineneedles crunched together, and once a brass-bound musket butt crashed loud against a pine trunk.

The sound made the men freeze, but no warning shout came from the enemy lines. Sam wondered if the enemy was waiting, awake and ready. Were their muskets loaded, flints drawn back, cocked to blast flames and smoke and death into the trees? His heart pounded heavy with the fear of a soldier before the killing. Sweat stung his eyes. It was hard to breathe the resinous air. The file moved again and Sam saw the smear of a red glow to his left and he knew it marked the enemy encampment.

"Down!"

Sam stopped, crouched. The redness was the remnant of a camp fire. There were other dying fires visible through the trees. The glowing embers revealed the shapes of dark buildings. Again a horse whinnied, but Sam could see no movement around the fires.

"Bayonets! Bayonets!" The order was a hoarse whisper.

Sam tugged his bayonet free of its scabbard. He had sharpened the blade to a wicked point in the dusk; now he slotted it over his musket's muzzle and twisted it into place. The grease that kept the bayonet free of rust was sticky on his palm. All around him he could hear the scrape and click of blades being fixed and it seemed impossible for the enemy not to hear, but still there was no shout or musket flash. Sam took a leather lace from his ammunition pouch. He tied one end around the blade's shoulder, and the other he lashed to the musket's sling-swivel. Now no enemy could seize and wrench the blade away, nor, twisting the bayonet free of dead flesh, would he lose the weapon to a corpse.

There was fear in Sam, but also exhilaration. He feared letting his comrades down, he feared Captain Kelly's disappointment or Sergeant Scammell's scorn, he feared his own fear, yet he also had the fire of a young man's pride inside him. They were the red-coated Bloodybacks, the kings of the castle, cocks of the dungheap, and soldiers of the King, and in a moment they would be unleashed like rough-pelted hounds to tear and savage the King's enemies.

Footsteps sounded to his right and Sam saw the tall dark shape of Sergeant Scammell pacing along the company's front. "You're not here to fucking dance with the buggers, you're here to kill the fuckers. You hear me?" Scammell's voice was a mere whisper, but still fearsome. Few men in the company liked Scammell, but even those who hated him were glad of his presence this night, for, in the confusion of battle, the Sergeant displayed a chilling efficiency. The embers of the enemy's camp fires reflected dull red on the steel of Scammell's seventeen-inch bayonet.

Sam fingered his own greased blade. It was a three-sided bayonet, channelled to release blood so that the blade would not stick in flesh. It was not a weapon for cutting, but for stabbing. "Go for their bellies or throats," Scammell was whispering. "Don't tickle the bastards, kill them!"

Captain Kelly and Ensign Trumbull had their sabres drawn. The two officers stood at the edge of the trees, staring at the enemy. Kelly was tall, quiet, and liked by the men. Trumbull was thirteen, a schoolboy given an officer's coat, and despised. Sam saw the small twitching of the Ensign's sabre blade and knew the boy was nervous.

Sam's twin brother was also nervous. "You'll stay close, Sam?" Nate asked.

"I'll stay close," Sam offered the reassurance, just as he always offered reassurance to Nate. On nights like this, back home in England, the brothers would sometimes crouch in the Squire's coverts where, while Sam eagerly anticipated the sport, Nate would inevitably fret about mantraps and gamekeepers. Sam had always led, and Nate followed, but this night their prey was more deadly than the Squire's deer.

Sam watched the enemy's dying fires. Perhaps in England the hearth of his parents' cottage was similarly fading as it waited for morning's rousing. Captain Kelly had told Sam that the sun rose earlier in England than it did here, but Sam did not understand the concept, and so he imagined that it was at this very moment that his mother's cockerels would be ruffling themselves to wake the world and his father's dogs would be twitching in their sleep beside the kitchen fire. Then he wondered what the village girls would think of Sam Gilpin if they could see him now, face dirty, gun in hand, waiting for the order to attack the King's enemies. That thought stilled his nervousness and made him smile.

"I wish they'd start," Nate muttered beside him.

The night sky's edge was touched with a hint of grey to pale the brightness of the eastern stars. It was the false dawn. The land was still black. The enemy horse whinnied again and Sam heard its hooves trampling hard ground, and he wondered if, around the dying fires, he could see the humped shapes of men asleep. The inevitable fears, bred of waiting, began to make him edgy. Had they no sentries? The enemy should have picquets on the forest edge. Perhaps they were waiting. Perhaps they had cannons in the darkness by the houses and, in an instant, the great muzzles would explode flame and scraps of shot to tear men's bellies to bloody shreds.

Sam licked dry lips and flirted with the fear of what was about to erupt in the night. Captain Kelly, before they marched, had said this was the enemy's rearguard, left to harass the British advance, and the Redcoats plotted to destroy the rearguard, not with fire and bullet but with the seventeen-inch blades. Sam feared that, instead, they would march like sheep to the slaughteryard.

"Go, go, go!" The order, when it came, was soft. Somehow Sam had expected the blare of trumpets, the unfurling of great silk colours, the panoply of pride to drive a soldier on to death.

"Move!" Scammell was hissing at the men. The officers were out of the trees now, walking in the small moonlight that seeped between the rifted clouds. Sam followed. To his left, beyond the track, he could see the lines of soldiers coming like ghosts from the trees. The Redcoats appeared black in the darkness, but the pale breeches and white crossbelts seemed bright, though not as bright as the long blades that glinted in the night.

The ground was rough grassland; tussocky and uneven. The men advanced in three ranks which were made ragged by the dark and by their eagerness to close on the sleeping enemy. Except they might not be sleeping. Sam, in the leading rank, watched for the dim glow of a linstock that could touch fire to a cannon's charged barrel.

A dog caught the scent of unwashed strangers on the small wind and barked. One of the humped shapes by a fire stirred and sat up. The steel-tipped lines advanced, their boots noisy in the grass, their breathing hoarse.

The dog's barking became frantic. It woke another dog that bayed at the moon, and the sound stung the advancing officers to throw stealth to the wind. "Charge! Charge!" The second word was drawn out like a banshee's howl of death.

And the men, unleashed, cheered. Their nerves, made tight by apprehension, threw them on. Sam's fear disappeared to be replaced by the elation of danger. No enemy cannon crashed fire and death. No muskets blazed from the dark. The enemy sentries slept, and the Redcoats had achieved surprise.

The first of the enemy died in their sleep.

Others woke to see the bright surprise of blades above them. The bayonets stabbed down. Sam, coming to the first fire, aimed at the white of a sleeping man's throat. He thrust down, and the blade went clean through the soft tissue to impale the earth beneath. Blood splashed Sam and turned the white skin of his enemy's face black. More blood, fountaining from a slit artery, hissed in the dying fire.

Redcoats were going past Sam now, blades thrusting down. The enemy were scrambling out of their blankets, but too late. They died with blades in their bellies, in their ribs, in their necks. The British were surging on through the waking encampment, and their sound was a surly growl of effort punctured by the butcher's chop of steel in flesh.

Sam twisted his blade free of the soil. His victim's body flopped up as Sam tried to drag the bayonet out of the torn neck and he had to stamp on the dying man's chest to rip the steel free.

Sam was in the rear now and, his spirit soaring with the joy of battle, he ran to the skirmish's front, careless of where his brother might be. He saw two of the enemy running to a stand of muskets and he caught one, tripped him, kicked the man in the jaw, then stabbed the second in the small of the back. The enemy screamed, arched, and tried to grip the blade that was twisting in his kidneys. The man's open mouth bayed at the dying stars, then he fell, dying, screaming, but his screams were drowned by the other screams and by the triumphant shouts of the Redcoats.

Sergeant Scammell was not shouting, just killing with his usual efficiency. Captain Kelly's sword was reddened to the hilt. Ensign Trumbull was screaming like an excited girl, whirling his sabre, shouting orders that no one noticed.

Muskets sparked to Sam's left.

"Incline left!" Captain Kelly's voice was strangely calm. "Form! Company will advance at the double! Steady, lads!"

Perhaps half the company obeyed, the rest were too busy with death.

"Charge!" Sam saw the huddle of enemy break before the threat of the blades. One man, perhaps an enemy officer since he carried a sword, screamed defiance and made a lone attack upon the Redcoats. His sword cracked against a parrying musket barrel, then Sergeant Scammell's blade grated on the enemy's ribs, the man gasped, sobbed, and two more blades thrust him down to ragged ruin. The rest of the enemy ran, disappearing into the forest. Another enemy, white shirt bright in the night, flung himself on an unsaddled horse and galloped away.

The killing seemed to end as swiftly as it had begun. A moment of triumph and savagery, then the shouts of officers and sergeants brought the killers to discipline. Grinning Redcoats, strangers, were around Sam now. The light companies of six different regiments had marched to this attack, and nearly all had wet bayonets. A Highlander, his belted plaid sopping with blood, killed a wounded man with a short vicious slash of a knife, then crouched to search his victim's clothing for coins and food.

Picquets were set, flints were put in folded leather pads and screwed into dog-heads. A handful of prisoners found at the tavern were prodded into the field. The Redcoats forced laughter for the relief of survival.

Dawn flooded the land with a grey light which showed a field littered with torn corpses. Blood on blood. A dog licked at blood. The prisoners, all in shirts and trousers only, stared in horror at the bloody bodies that lay twisted in the pale grass. One man vomited. Another wept. Others faced their captivity with bitter, proud faces.

The clearing about the tavern buzzed with flies coming to the killing ground. One of the enemy, killed as he ran, had fallen into a dying fire. His hair and scalp had burned away to his blackened skull. A Redcoat was pulling off the man's good linen breeches.

Nate found Sam. Nate's bayonet was unblemished. "Like pigsticking," he said in a kind of wonderment.

Sam was resharpening the tip of his blade with a stone. He saw his brother's unused bayonet. "I'm surprised you didn't run with the buggers."

"Not on my own, I wouldn't." Nate crouched by Sam and surreptitiously pulled his bayonet through a sticky patch of bloodied mud to make it look as though he had fought as hard as his comrades. He watched for Sergeant Scammell as he made the deception, but Nate's persecutor was far off. "But I am going to run," Nate said obstinately.

Sam nodded towards the dead. "You'll end up like them."

"We'll all end up like them," Nate said, staring at his sticky bayonet, "unless we run."

The heat was rising to the thick hateful swelter of daytime. The corpses would stink if they were not buried soon, but first they must be plundered. The enemy dead were stripped of clothes, searched for coins, and their teeth were wrenched out to be sold to the men who made false-teeth for the wealthy. Other Redcoats sat and broke apart the dry bread and thick hanks of salted beef that were breakfast.

Ensign Trumbull came from the tavern with a trophy. It was an enemy flag; one of the new standards that had appeared on the battlefields this summer. Trumbull swung the flag around his head in triumph. Nate watched the epauletted boy. "Pisser," he said savagely.

"You'll be a pisser if you run," Sam spoke with harsh affection to his twin brother. "They'll catch you. If you're lucky they'll flog you." Sam pointed his cleaned and sharpened bayonet towards Nate. "But they'll probably kill you."

"They won't catch me."

Sam drained the last of the tepid brackish water from his canteen. He tried to count the dead, but gave up at a hundred. No Redcoats had died. The flies buzzed. The first staff officers were arriving on horseback to see the night's carnage that had turned the field around the tavern into a shambles. The laughter of the newcomers was loud.

One of the staff officers took the enemy flag from Ensign Trumbull and, wheeling his horse, rode with the banner towards his companions. He passed close to Sam and, as he did, so the new sun flecked the horizon with a dazzling brilliance to slant one long lance of brightness that struck the enemy flag and made it luminous. Sam, momentarily shadowed by the great flag, flinched from the glow of its thick red and white stripes that carried a circle of white stars on a blue upper quadrant. Then the officer went and Sam blinked as if to rid his eyes of the flag's gaudy dazzle.

The Bloodybacks had come in the night and taken steel to the sleeping Yankees. Now Sam Gilpin, Redcoat, lay on the grass and slept.

TWO

In the small hours of the morning of Friday 19 September 1777, Jonathon Becket woke to the startled belief that the world was ending.

It was a forgiveable mistake for, on the previous Sunday, the Revd MacTeague had preached on the Second Coming and thus, when the lights flamed sudden in the night streets and screams woke people from their beds, there were many Philadelphians who believed, like Jonathon, that the bright-winged millions of God had come to cleanse the world of sin.

Trumpets sounded and hooves echoed in the city's long straight thoroughfares. Citizens fumbled with tinders and steel to discover that it was only the first hour of the day, yet the commotion was like that of the Apocalypse. Children cried, and flames made lurid patterns on housefronts where shutters were thrown back as people leaned out to shout for news.

The news proclaimed that the city was not threatened by the world's ending, but by the British army. Horsemen had been glimpsed crossing the Schuylkill at the Upper Ferry. The Redcoats were coming, and Philadelphia panicked.

The truth, which was lost in the night's alarm, was that a rebel cavalry patrol had been searching the river's western bank and had been mistaken for the invading British, and so the Patriots fled in the darkness.

Men who were delegates to the rebel Congress hastily threw their papers and valuables into travelling cases. The Liberty Bell was already gone from the State House, and the papers of the State Library and the money from the Public Loan Office had been sent to hiding in the western valleys of Pennsylvania. And now the Patriots, the architects of revolution who had argued and fashioned the Declaration of Independence, followed.

Coaches were harnessed and brought to house doors. Furniture was wrestled down street steps and laden on to wagons. Women cast anxious glances westward, fearing to see the red coats come into the flamelight. Philadelphia had been appointed the home of the revolution, the capital of the new American nation, and its godly citizens feared that the coming of the enemy would be like the descent of the Philistines on to the Children of Israel; soldiers greaved in brass, bearded and terrible, would come for their revenge, and so the whips cracked in the dark and the children wept.

There was terror and haste, yet not every citizen feared the Redcoats. There were Loyalists in Philadelphia, Tories who were eager for the restoration of British rule, and in their Loyalist houses the apprehension of the British coming was mingled with a prayerful relief that at last the rebel Whigs were being ousted. Abel Becket, whose warehouses dominated the city's wharves, was one such Loyalist who, in the night's alarum, barked orders to his house servants. "Lock the back gate! Put torches in the yard and by the street steps! Lively, man!"

He was a tall man with cropped black hair that was usually disguised by a neatly curled white wig. He was thin, and the passage of fifty years had made his face haggard, but his eyes still showed an almost youthful intelligence. Abel Becket was a merchant, and, just as his guile had steered him through the treacherous shoals of recent political debate, so his wealth had allowed him to survive the thin years of rebel rule in the city. He had traded with rebels, for there had been no other choice in the last three years, but the trading had given him no pleasure, and little profit.

"Upstairs, miss! Upstairs!" Abel Becket despatched a frightened kitchen maid to the upstairs parlour where Mrs Becket waited with prayer book and bible. As the girl went up the staircase, so Jonathon Becket, hastily dressed in black, limped down to the hallway where Abel Becket made his preparations for the British arrival.

"Uncle!" Jonathon dragged his right foot, swollen and twisted like some leather-clad monstrosity, behind him. "What's happening, sir?"

"The British are crossing the Schuylkill. The rebel scum are running, and God alone knows what mischief they'll fetch on us in their panic." There was an exultation in Abel Becket's voice, not in anticipation of mischief, but because he was seeing the defeat of the rebels.

"Who's at the warehouse?" Jonathon asked.

"I've sent for Woollard."

"I'll go, sir."

"It isn't safe."

For answer Jonathon pulled back his coat to reveal a pistol's butt protruding from his belt. For a second Abel Becket was torn between the safety of his nephew and the fate of the expensive goods stacked in the warehouse. Cupidity won, and he dragged back the bolts of the front door. "Go carefully."

"I will, sir." Jonathon hid the pistol, then hobbled into a scene that was almost as astonishing as his waking vision of the Second Coming. Like a hive brutally kicked apart, Market Street was in chaos. A wagon was being whipped away from the opposite pavement. The wagon was loaded as high as the hay barges that came down the Delaware in late spring; beds and cupboards, tables and chairs, chests and cases, all were lashed crazily high on the wagon's bed, but, as Jonathon watched, a spinet jerked loose from the hastily knotted ropes, bounced on the backboard, and shattered in a splintering discord on the hard-rutted mud. A carriage, its four horses being flogged to speed, bumped a wheel over the broken fragments of inlay and ivory. No one seemed to notice in their desperate hurry to escape.

Jonathon plunged eastwards through the crowds. He heard snatches of hectic conversation. British cavalry was said to be plundering the Northern Liberties, Hessians had started burning Southwark, while the Redcoats were drowning those citizens who attempted to escape across the Delaware. The crowd reacted to each rumour by flowing in a new direction to escape the imagined threat. On the corner of Second Street, where most of the carriages and wagons were being funnelled north towards the Frankfort Road, a preacher was shouting that men should repent, that God would spare the city if enough righteous men would bear witness, but the man's cries were drowned by the rumble of wheels and the neighing of frightened horses. Jonathon, his face showing the pain of walking, struggled through the chaos.

He had been crippled at birth twenty years ago when, to his mother's screams, he had been dragged into the candlelight with a twisted right leg that would never grow into full strength. His mother had died, but Jonathon, to his father's astonishment, had lived. There were times when people even forgot that Jonathon was crippled. His leg might be twisted and club-footed, but Jonathon had ever refused sympathy. If he could not run, then he could ride a horse as well as any man and better than most. He might limp when he walked, dragging the foot in a dipping gait, but he stood tall and had his family's thin and handsome looks.

Now, amidst the panic, Jonathon was jostled by the crowd, and once he fell heavily into a shop doorway, but he pressed doggedly onwards. Not every Patriot could find a wagon or coach to carry them clear of royal revenge, and Jonathon, as he neared the city's wharves, found himself part of a flood of refugees who sought the Delaware's ferries that could take them to New Jersey. A small child, screaming and lost, shrieked its despair from a doorway in Front Street and Jonathon lifted the girl high into the glow of a bracketed torch and bellowed for someone to recognize the child. His voice stilled the crowd momentarily. "Whose child? Whose child?"

A woman fought back against the tide of families and reached for the girl. Jonathon cut the woman's thanks short, and turned instead into an alley which cut down to the wharves. The doors to his uncle's warehouses, he saw, were still padlocked and inviolate, but the big flat-bottomed shallop which was tied to Abel Becket's quay was swarming with men who, unfamiliar with the boat's rigging, hampered the crew's effort to set sail.

"Stop!" Jonathon had worked four years on the waterfront and had a voice that could carry to a ship in the river's centre.

A man, wrestling with the complicated spring which held the shallop against the river's current, recognized the limping figure in the flickering torchlight. "He's a Becket. Ignore the bastard!"

"The British are coming . . ."

"Hurry!"

Their voices rose in a tumultuous and fearful babble. Women and children, their faces wan in the light of the shallop's lanterns, huddled about the main mast. More crewmen, wakened from their tavern beds, hurried down the quay.

"I said stop!" Jonathon dragged the pistol from his belt, pointed it high into the sky, and pulled the trigger. The gun hammered the night and the jolt of its recoil rammed down Jonathon's arm. The men on the boat, appalled by the sudden noise, stared at him. Jonathon, as the echo thrown from the warehouse walls died across the river, spoke calmly. "That shallop is to carry gunpowder to General Washington's army. The powder's been paid for. If you want to take the boat, then you take the powder with it. I've just come from the city and there are no British there yet. If they do come, then you can cast off. But if you don't take the powder, then the British will capture it and use it against you." He pushed the pistol back into his belt. "Besides, that boat's unballasted, so you'll all drown unless you put some weight into her."

Jonathon's last words, or perhaps his voice which was so calmly confident, persuaded the refugees. Jonathon kept his authority over the reluctant men by giving quick and confident orders. The lanterns with their treacherous flames were moved fore and aft. Planks were rigged from quay to shallop, then the vast barrels were rolled out of the warehouse, across the quay, and lowered with a slung whip into the hold. Each barrel held four hundred pounds of best gunpowder, all of it captured from a British merchantman taken the previous autumn by a privateer from the Chesapeake Bay. Jonathon had bought the powder, then resold it at a fair profit to the rebel army. It was to rescue the precious cargo, and keep it from the British, that Jonathon had come into the hectic night.

The barrels rumbled over the stones, then down the planks, and no Redcoats appeared to interrupt the work. Instead, a huge hulk of a man with shoulders humped like a plough-ox lumbered down the quay and demanded to know who had authorized the lading.

"I did." Jonathon had been standing in the shadows on the shallop's deck, but now, with his odd sideways gait, he shuffled back to the quay.

Ezra Woollard's anger was checked as he saw his master's nephew limp into the light. "Does your uncle know you're doing this, Master Jonathon?"

"He sent me."

Jonathon's reply was equivocal, and Woollard, sensing the evasion, scowled. "Why give the bloody stuff away?"

"Because it's paid for."

"But if the British come, Master Jonathon, we can sell it to them as well. Two payments for the same goods?"

"The Congress has paid for it, and the Congress shall have it." Jonathon was tall, but he seemed dwarfed by the massive Woollard, Abel Becket's wharfmaster and foreman. Like Woollard, Jonathon worked for Abel Becket, but in a few months Jonathon would enter into his inheritance and become a part-owner of the Becket business. Until then Ezra Woollard treated Jonathon with a careful mixture of contempt and respect that made clear the foreman's resentment that, in time, this crippled young man would become his master.

"Or would you be sending the powder away," Woollard asked snidely, "because your sympathies have been turned by a woman?"

Jonathon did not rise to the taunt. "You're standing in my way, Mr Woollard."

"Oh, my lord!" Woollard gave an ironic bow, then stepped back to watch the last barrels being trundled across the quay's cobbles. The crowds by the ferry piers were lessening and the flames of the torches were being dimmed by the first faint grey of dawn. The shallop's captain thanked Jonathon. "I almost lost my ship. Thank you."

"You almost lost the powder."

"And that's more precious these days. I don't know when I'll see you again, Master Becket, but God bless you."

The heavy shallop warped into the stream and, its sails unleashed, caught the dawn wind to carry its burden northwards. Jonathon, as he watched the boat's wake glimmer silver against the dark water, felt a sudden weariness as heavy as the cargo he had just saved from the British.

Woollard was gone. Jonathon locked the warehouse, then, for a moment, he stared hopefully across the river; but whatever he wished to see did not appear and so he turned his back on the water. His right foot dragged as he walked. There were times when he hated the sound of the foot's scraping, when he despised himself for the twisted mockery of a leg, but he hated others to offer pity or even to notice that he was not whole.

The streets were quieter now. The Patriots had fled, and the Loyalists, sensing that the British army was not to come after all, explored the dawn-lit city to see who had stayed and who had gone. The Tories had always outnumbered the Whigs in Philadelphia, and Jonathon realized, with a shameful pang, that his city would welcome the British occupation.

He limped to the corner of Market and Fourth where he climbed the steps of a tall stone house. The shutters were open, indicating that the household was awake, so Jonathon hammered on the door. He yawned, then glanced westwards as if expecting to see red coats where the city's streets faded into the countryside. Nothing moved there. The only sounds in the city now were the crowing of cocks and the lowing of cows waiting to be milked. There had been a time when dawn in Philadelphia had been a cheerful cacophony of church bells, but the rebels had taken all the bells to be melted down for cannons. Jonathon turned to the door and banged the brass ring again.

The door opened as he knocked. "My God, you're early!" Martha Crowl grimaced at the bright and slanting sunlight. "I haven't seen the dawn since my wedding night, and I prayed then never to see it again. Do come in, dear brother."

Jonathon stumped behind Martha to her upstairs parlour. "I half expected you to have left."

"And leave all these pretty things to be mauled by a Redcoat?" Martha gestured about her parlour that was, indeed, filled with pretty things. A Venetian looking-glass surmounted a mantel of white marble, on which stood a gilded clock flanked by candelabras of delicately fluted silver. Martha's lawyer husband had bought paintings from Europe; fine paintings of ancient cities and Arcadian landscapes, and he had purchased furniture from the finest cabinetmakers in London. Thomas Crowl had been a man of taste and refinement, and, Martha liked to say, a man considerate enough to die early so that Martha, at twenty-six, was already a widow of fortune. Crowl had also, in addition to his wealth, left Martha with a daughter, Lydia, who was now six years old. "She didn't wake up," Martha said, "God knows why. Would you like some tea?"

"Please."

Jonathon sat as Martha crossed to the bellpull. She was as tall as her younger brother, and had the same narrow face which some thought too bony to be accounted beautiful, but Martha compensated with a natural elegance. Her hair, like Jonathon's, was jet black, but this morning was hid beneath a mob cap. She turned back to her brother. "You look quite filthy."

"I've been loading eighty barrels of the finest cylinder charcoal powder, saving it from the British."

"Who never arrived," Martha said drily. "Perhaps they won't come at all now?"

"Not if General Washington can stop them."

"He didn't last week, did he?" The British, advancing cautiously from their ships in the Chesapeake Bay, had been met by the rebel army at Brandywine Creek, where, once again, General Washington had been outflanked and defeated. It was the old story. Only at Trenton, in the previous winter, had General Washington won a battle. A thousand Hessian prisoners had been paraded through the city as proof, and the sight had raised the

Patriot hope that, at last, their general had discovered the habit of victory. In that hope they had cheered the army on its way to Brandywine, then, a week later, stood in silence as its men, wounded, defeated and sullen, trooped back.

The Loyalists had been elated while the Patriots felt despair. Martha and Jonathon shared the despair for, though their uncle was a Tory and a Royalist, Martha had married a Whig, and Jonathon had avidly followed the impassioned debates within the city and chosen the rebel allegiance. Now it seemed that allegiance was to be tested because, for the first time since the fighting had begun, the British were coming to Philadelphia.

Martha surreptitiously watched Jonathon massage his right thigh. "Hurting?"

"I walked further than usual. There wasn't time to saddle a horse."

"Poor Jonathon." Only Martha could offer him pity, for, since his birth, she had been his closest companion. Marriage had taken her from his home, then their father had died and Jonathon had become a ward of their uncle, but the closeness of brother and sister had never faltered. Jonathon was no longer a crippled boy who needed protection, but the habit was ingrained into Martha.

The tea came. Jonathon was sitting on the window seat, staring ruefully at the shingled and tiled rooftops. "Last night was shameful. I never thought to see people so degraded."

Martha half smiled. "You are stern, brother."

"It was undignified!"

Martha shrugged. "I've no doubt that the British flight from Boston was every bit as shameful."

Jonathon gave a swift smile to acknowledge the consolation, then leaned back against the folded shutters. "Do you think we can win?"

"You're not usually in the habit of asking foolish questions, unless you believe I've been given the gift of prophecy?"

Jonathon flinched with not pain but sudden anger. "I just can't bear to think of them coming here! Strutting up our streets! Flaunting themselves in our houses! Mocking our people!"

"If they come at all." Martha did not sound hopeful, but it was a time for Patriots to clutch at straws. "I heard they might go south, to Baltimore?"

Jonathon seemed not to hear. He was still staring at the

rooftops that were sharp-edged against what promised to be another cloudless sky. "I can't bear to stay and see them gloat."

"It will be hard," Martha agreed.

Jonathon turned towards her. "So I'm leaving."

Martha went very still. Her brother was a dark silhouette in the window, but she did not need to see his face to know what a stubborn expression it would show. "Leaving?"

"I've been useful so far," Jonathon's words were suddenly febrile. "I'm a good trader! I've served the Congress well! I've supplied the army with hides, pig-iron, flints, and powder, but the British are coming! If we trade now it will have to be with the enemy. So my usefulness is at an end. If I stay here I have to take British gold and sell to British traders, and I can't do it! I won't do it!"

"You're too proud to do it?"

"If you like, yes."

Martha still watched her brother's silhouette. "So what will you do?"

"I can ride!" Jonathon slapped his right leg. "I agree I can't march, but I ride as well as any man, and all a cavalryman needs to do is ride and fight." He smiled at his sister. "I'm going to volunteer."

"Oh, you can ride!" Martha said scathingly. "But suppose the horse gets shot? What will you do? Hop away from the enemy?"

Jonathon laughed. "If I have to, yes."

"You're a fool!" She stood and walked away from him. "Good God, Jonathon! You're a fool!" She turned on him. "Or is this Caroline's doing?" Jonathon offered no answer and Martha, irritated by his calm, snapped at her brother. "You can't marry her!"

Jonathon smiled. "As it happens, I haven't asked her to marry me."

Martha, more emotional than her brother, felt her irritation growing. "Can she read?"

"Fluently."

"You know Ezra Woollard wanted to marry her?"

"And she said no." Jonathon was keeping his answers mild. It was a habit that annoyed some people, for under even the most extreme provocation he held his temper and always sounded reasonable.

Martha, on the other hand, could sound most unreasonable.

"She's a tradesgirl! She lives across the river! She sells me vegetables!"

"And I'm a tradesman." Jonathon laughed. "But the answer to your original question, dear sister, is that Caroline has tried to dissuade me from leaving the city. She thinks like you."

"That's something in her favour," Martha said acidly. "My God, haven't you done enough? The army needs whole men, not cripples!"

Jonathon still did not rise to her provocation. "They need men."

"I won't let you do it." Martha walked back to the window seat. "If you go away to fight, you'll lose your inheritance, and all our father's work will be for nothing! Ezra Woollard will take the business. Abel likes him! And Uncle Abel hasn't a son to leave anything to! Is that what you want?"

"I think I want what you want, liberty."

"God help us!" Martha stared into her brother's dark and amused eyes. "I'm sorry I called you a cripple."

"But it's true. I lurch about the city for the amusement of small children. It's something I've got used to doing. But now I want to be a soldier."

Martha sat beside him. "Suppose I offer you another and even better way of fighting against the British?"

"Tell me."

Martha hesitated a second, as though seeking the right words that would keep her brother from his foolishness. "I'm staying in the city because it's my home, and it's Lydia's home, and I can't bear to think of us being harried about the countryside by a pack of Redcoats. So I'll endure them, but I'll fight them! I'll entertain them, Jonathon, I'll give them wine and music, and I'll listen to their jests, and all the time I'll be listening. You can do that! If you trade with the British, you'll become intimate with them. They'll trust you. They'll tell you things. And you'll see things on the wharves! What troops arrive and how many? Those are the things we have to tell our army, and it's a far more useful task than pulling a trigger!"

"Maybe."

"Not maybe! Of course it is!" Martha sought for another reason to make Jonathon stay and, in her desperation, used an argument that would fly in the face of all she wanted for her brother. "And Caroline will stay. You'll be close to her!"

Jonathon was silent for a few seconds. He watched the skeins of smoke drift from the kitchen chimneys, then sighed. "If I stay here in comfort I shall despise myself."

"No one will blame you!"

"Because of this?" Jonathon tapped his right leg.

"Because of that, yes!"

He smiled. "But I know, sister, and you know, that I can do almost anything another man can do. And if another man can fight, and risk his inheritance, then I can fight and risk mine. No one would blame me if I didn't, but I'd blame myself!"

"You're a fool." Martha stared through the window. "The British aren't here yet, and the Loyalists aren't crowing their victory, so will you wait? That's all I ask! Just wait!"

"So you can dissuade me?"

"So that I can persuade you that by staying you can do more damage to the enemy than by going, that's why!"

"I'll wait," Jonathon said. "I wasn't planning to leave immediately, so you've time to harass me."

"It's not harassment." Martha closed her eyes. "I've lost my mother, father, and husband. Am I now to lose you?"

"God's already played his joke on me," Jonathon said deprecatingly, "and I doubt he plans worse."

"You think you'll live for ever?" Martha asked bitterly.

"I think," Jonathon said calmly, "that I'd like another cup of tea."

Thus Philadelphia, fairest of cities on the American coast, waited for the beat of foreign drums. The Redcoats were coming.

THREE

"'Talion!" The sergeant-major's voice could be heard three fields away, "'Shun!"

Seven hundred right boots thumped on to the dry pastureland, followed by an utter stillness in the ranks. Ten companies were on parade, formed into three sides of a square, and in each company the tallest men were on the flanks, the shortest in the centre, so that the long battalion line rose and fell and rose and fell like a well-clipped ornamental hedge. Sergeants, canes ready, prowled behind the battalion. The sun sparked from belt buckles and musket fittings.

The sky was cloudless and the day had an oppressive, humid heat that itched beneath the men's thick red woollen coats. Sweat glistened on their faces.

Facing the paraded battalion, where the fourth side of the square should have been, was a tall tripod made of split rails. The apex of the tripod was eight feet above the ground, looking for all the world as if it waited for one of the cumbersome Flaunders cauldrons to be suspended from it. But no cooking fire was lit beneath this tripod; instead, a soldier, stripped to his dirty breeches, was lashed by wrists and ankles to the newly split wood. A plank, torn down from a chapel in the nearby village, had been nailed across two of the staves so that the victim could not bend his naked back away from the lash. No leather pad covered the man's kidneys, a sure sign that his officers wanted him to die in this hot American evening.

Two men watched from a hundred yards away. They were not in the battalion on punishment parade, and thus were free to express opinions that could have doomed them to the same fate as the prisoner. "What he did wrong," Private Nathaniel Gilpin said, "was getting caught."

"What he did wrong," Sam Gilpin corrected his twin brother,

"was to run. Daft as lights." Most of Sam's uniform was piled on the grass and now he pulled the black spatterdashes from his ankles and took off his boots. Like the man pinioned to the tripod, Sam was stripped to the waist, but Sam faced no punishment. Instead, he rolled up his breeches, waded into the small stream and, whistling as he worked, began to scrub down Captain Kelly's mare, Cleo. The horse stood quietly. Sam Gilpin had always been good with animals. Good with every living thing, and too good, his mother said, for the army, but seventeen-year-olds are blessed with certainty and Sam had broken his mother's heart.

His brother Nate seemed obsessed by the flogging. The drums sounded across the field as the two boys with the whips whirled the lashes twice about their heads before bringing the thongs slashing down on to the victim's back. Nate flinched with each stroke. "Must bloody hurt."

"Of course it bloody hurts! It's meant to, isn't it?" Sam ignored the flogging. He was happy working with horses; a reminder of the world he had left behind when he took the red coat three years before. He was twenty years old now, tall, with a cheerful, quick face. His hair, now whitened by flour paste, was naturally golden and drawn back to a stiff queue. "Don't watch it!" He was brushing the dust from the horse's flanks, seeing how the shine of the coat was growing back. Many of the officers' horses had died during the terrible, heat-savaged voyage from New York. The fleet, for reasons that no soldier would ever know, had lingered for days in the long, sun-reflecting swell as the food turned rancid and the flux fouled the ship's bowels and the horses, driven mad by heat and thirst, kicked their stalls to bloody shreds so that they had to be shot. These few weeks on shore had worked wonders for the survivors.

Sam touched the long scar on the mare's haunch and noticed she did not quiver. The wound was healing well. A rebel bullet had gouged her pelt at Brandywine Creek, but Sam had made a poultice of old bread and cobwebs which had worked its usual miracle. He stroked the mare's nose. "Tough old thing, aren't you, Cleo? Ain't a Yankee who can kill you, eh?"

"Oh, Jesus." Nate was watching the blood stream down the victim's white breeches. The man jerked and twisted in his bonds as the alternating lashes landed, while, after each stroke, the boys drew the whips through smeared fingers to free the leather thongs of blood and gobbets of flesh. "Poor bastard."

"Don't watch!" But just as Sam said it, the victim spat the leather wedge from his mouth and gave a wavering, horrid scream that pricked the mare's ears back and made Sam turn despite his distaste. Men from other battalions, men bivouacking in the spread of fields either side of the dirt road, flinched because of the foul, despairing scream. Sam shuddered. "They should just shoot him."

"He shouldn't have got caught, should he?" Nate said.

"He shouldn't have run. Asking for trouble, running." The man was a deserter, recaptured. To desert the army was the unforgiveable sin, and the sin most savagely punished.

"I'll do it properly," Nate grinned. He was darker than Sam, but they shared the same mischievous face. Tall, country-bred boys who had been the Recruiting Sergeant's dream; only now Nate had a dream of his own. He wanted to desert. He wanted to run because he was certain that, somewhere beyond this humid coastal plain, there was an American paradise where crops grew without effort, where the apple trees were so heavy with fruit that boughs broke under the succulent weight, and where, most important of all, Nate could be alone with Maggie. There was no hunger in Nate's American paradise, no touching the forelock to the Squire, and no red coats. No sergeants, no floggings, no spatterdashes, no leather stocks, no slashing canes and mornings thick with vomit and children crying in the night. No army.

"They'll catch you," Sam did not believe in Nate's paradise, "and they'll flog you till your ribs are bare. Don't be a bloody idiot, Nate." He looked at his brother with a mixture of fondness and pleading. They had always been close, were close still, but Sam could not bear the thought of his brother running into chaos and pain. "Don't even think about it!"

"Three could do it better than two, Sam."

"They'll catch you and flog you and I'll bury you. Don't be a goddamned bloody fool!" Sam's affection for Nate made his voice angry. He turned away and untangled the mare's mane. He remembered the pleasure he used to take from grooming the great plough-horses on high days back home.

Three heifers, thin and mournful, were driven to the stream's edge thirty yards away. Behind the animals and their butchers came a straggle of the battalion's wives and children. Muskets were cocked, aimed, and three shots sounded flat and harsh in the hot humid air. The three heifers shuddered and crumpled heavily on to the grass. One of the beasts still bellowed, then was chopped through the spine with an axe blow. The hooves of the others kicked feebly as the four butchers unsheathed their knives. Blood spilt like water and the children laughed to see it. The women, their own knives drawn, crept close like wild animals to snatch for flesh. One of the butchers backhanded with a wet axe to drive them back. A brindle mongrel bitch snarled, and the thick smell of new blood made Cleo whinny and Sam's nostrils wrinkle.

"Beef tonight." Nate forgot the flogging for a moment. "Be a change from bloody pork. Maggie's there."

"Leave her alone, Nate!"

"She won't leave me alone." Nate stared towards the butchers who were now tossing the livers and kidneys into a wooden bucket as delicacies for the officers' mess. "She's seen me."

"For Christ's sake, Nate!" Sam led the horse a few yards upstream, as if to take his brother away from the girl's gaze, but a fallen willow trunk barred any escape in that direction. The smell of newly lit cooking fires came from the battalion lines while, in the next field, the flogging went on, mercifully silent again. The man had been sentenced to one thousand lashes of the six-thonged cat. A group of officers, their uniforms bright in the evening sunlight, checked their horses to watch the deserter's agony.

Sam concentrated on his work. It was not his job to look after Captain Kelly's mare, but all the battalion's officers knew that Sam Gilpin did a better job than their own servants and so were happy to pay him a shilling or so to groom and doctor their beasts. He wiped Cleo's eyes and nostrils with a wet rag, then heard the telltale splashing in the water just beyond the patient mare.

"Nate!" Maggie smiled in nervous greeting. Her skirts trailed in the water which, reflecting the late afternoon sun, made ripples of light on her thin, sun-browned face. Nate embraced her, careless of who might be watching. The girl looked over Nate's shoulder and smiled at Sam. "Hello, Sam."

"Mrs Scammell," Sam acknowledged her presence very formally.

"I got you this." Maggie had a bloody scrap of oxtail that she offered, not to Nate, but to Sam. It was Maggie who had put the idea of desertion into Nate's head, and Maggie who knew that Nate would not run without his brother. Maggie was for ever trying to persuade Sam to join them, but Sam was not unhappy in the army. Sam had discovered he could fight as well as the next man, he liked the horses, and he reckoned he could avoid the punishments.

He refused to take the oxtail. "Give it to your husband, Maggie."

"I never church married him!" She was suddenly vehement.

"Don't need to, do you?" Sam knew his words were making his brother miserable, but Sam had always been the stronger of the twins and considered it his job to look after Nate. "Now go away, Maggie! You want to have Nate flogged? Look, girl!" Sam pointed at the triangle. "It ain't pretty, is it?"

But Maggie would not look at the blood-soaked man. She drew Nate into the shelter of the mare's flank where they were hidden from the battalion's bivouac in the meadow. Flies buzzed at Sam's sweat-soaked chest and face as the lovers twined sad arms and stared at him as if capable strong Sam was the person who could answer their dreams and take them away from the army.

And Sam could understand Nate's obsession. Most of the women who followed the battalion were drudges – diseased and ugly, with tangled, matted hair and foul, reeking mouths – but Maggie was somehow different. Her brown hair was greasy and lank, but it framed a wistful, appealing face that made men want to protect her. She looked, Sam thought, ever on the point of tears, but also as if a single kind touch or loving word would light her face with happiness.

Which happiness Sam wished for Maggie, but in New York she had chosen Sergeant Scammell, and the sergeant was a jealous man. "Why don't you wait for him to die in battle?" Sam had asked them. "Then you can marry Nate legal!"

"I want to go home," Maggie would say.

Her home was in Connecticut. It was of Connecticut that Maggie spoke when she filled Nate's head with her dreams of paradise, of a place where the apples grew so thick that there was scarce room for leaves on the trees, where geese waited to offer their meat to the table, and where the water ran pure as crystal. Maggie had run from that paradise once and gone to New York where she had become a shilling whore in the Holy Town where the brothels did their business. Now she had fallen for Nate and wanted to go home. "They'll give you fifty acres each," she pleaded. The oxtail hung at her side, dripping blood on to her skirt. "Fifty acres, two sows, and a hog. They promised it!"

"Promises are easy," Sam said.

"They will, Sam!" Maggie clung to Nate and stared at Sam with big, bruised-looking eyes. "They got it down on paper, didn't they?"

"You can read?" Sam asked brutally.

"They promised!" Nate said fiercely, like a child.

The rebels had indeed promised the land and the hogs to any man who ran from the British army, but Sam doubted if the land would be worth a thimble of spit, and reckoned the hogs would be fevered if they existed at all. His guess was that Nate's paradise would have more serpents souring its apple trees than ever the first Paradise did. So Sam would not run with them. "But if you do run," he leaned against the mare's flank, "then do it proper! Don't just go in the night. You'll get caught. You'll end up like that poor bastard!" He gestured towards the flogged man who now hung from his leather bonds. Blood dripped to the field.

"I will do it proper," Nate said sullenly.

"You're daft as lights! You never did anything proper! Have you got any ordinary clothes? You can't bugger about in a red coat, Nate. One side or other will have you. You need proper clothes, you need some money, you need to know where you're going. You have to have somewhere to hide the first two days till the cavalry's gone. Have you thought of any of that? Have you?"

"You have," Nate said stubbornly.

"Aye, but I'm not running," Sam said firmly, then dipped his brush in the water to scrub at the mare's pelt.

"Oh, that's grand." The voice came from a tall man who must have crept like a stalker through the willow shrubs and who now stepped on to the trunk of the fallen tree. He stood, legs apart and face shadowed by the peak of his silver-fronted tricorn hat, staring at Maggie and Nate. He was a big man, strong chested and flat bellied, who wore a brushed uniform on which the buttons were polished to a gleaming sheen. A handsome man, too, with a kind of power in his face and voice that cowed other men. "Kiss the girls and make them cry, is that it, Nate?" The sergeant, despite his clean boots, jumped into the stream and walked towards the lovers.

Maggie twitched her arm from Nate's elbow and raised the oxtail in a pathetic attempt to placate Sergeant Michael Scammell. "I got this for you."

"Fuck that." Scammell whipped at the scrap of meat with his metal-topped cane, sending it spinning into the long grass beside the stream. He brought the cane whistling back, slicing it hard over his wife's cheek. "Now piss off, Maggie! And wait for me. Move!" He screamed the last word as though he ordered a whole battalion to his bidding.

Maggie, terrified of her husband, scrambled from the stream.

Scammell watched her go, then turned back to face Nate. "You want to do something about that, Private Gilpin?"

"We was only talking, Sergeant."

"Shut your face!" The cane flicked out, scoring down Nate's jawbone. "If I smell you on her, Nate Gilpin, I'll cut your liver out and push it down your bloody throat. You understand me?"

"We was only talking."

"Only talking!" Scammell moved with a sudden vicious speed to hook Nate's ankles with his right boot and elbow him down into the stream. Scammell had no physical fear. At Brandywine, when a trapped rebel company had threatened a desperate charge to escape, Scammell had plunged into them with a musket and bayonet and Sam remembered the cold efficiency with which this man had killed. A good man to have at one's side in a battle, but not a man to have as an enemy.

Now Scammell stood above Nate and put his cane beside Nate's face, turning it. "See that?" A body, soaked in blood and with tatters of skin hanging from its spine, was being carried away from the flogging triangle. The man had died beneath the lash. "You see what happens, Nate Gilpin, when you aggravate your betters?"

"Yes, Sergeant."

The cane rapped Nate's face back so he had to stare up into Scammell's tough, knowing eyes. "I'll have you on a bloody triangle and I'll flog you myself!" Scammell hissed the words at Nate. "If you so much as look at my bloody woman again, Private Gilpin, I'll have you on a flogging charge and I'll have the skin off your fucking back. You hear me?"

"Yes, Sergeant."

"The girls like you, don't they? Handsome Nate!" Scammell's face suddenly twisted in a shudder of anger and he slashed with the cane again, once, twice, opening cuts on Nate's cheek and forehead. Then the Sergeant stepped back. "Get up and piss off." The scorn of the stronger man for the weaker was absolute.

Nate scrambled out of the stream and Sergeant Scammell watched him go, then sat himself on a branch of the fallen willow. He wiped a smear of blood from the cane's tip. "Are they planning to run, Sam?"

"Not if I can help it, Sarge."

"That's not what I bloody asked, is it?"

Sam looked at Scammell. Other men hated this tall, confident sergeant, but Sam was not so bothered. He recognized Scammell's virtues which, though harsh, kept the company safe in battle, and, by treating the big sergeant with a fearless honesty, Sam had found he was treated fairly in return. "They're not going to run, Sarge."

"They must be bloody brain-sick." Scammell sounded genuinely puzzled. "Do they think I don't notice?"

Sam did not like to say that his brother was in love, and that lovers were always brain-sick. "Nate was always daft, but he doesn't mean any harm, Sarge."

"He means to have my whore!" Scammell's eyes were oddly unsettling, perhaps because they suggested that he could snap into a sudden violent rage at any moment. "Maggie's a whore, but she's my whore. If anyone's going to sell her, Sam, it's me. Not your brother."

"I told him that, Sarge." Sam had hated watching Scammell cut his brother's face, but to have offered brotherly assistance would have been to invite a flogging on a charge of striking a superior officer. The knack of the army was caution, and Sam reckoned he had that knack pretty well mastered.

Scammell opened his pouch and took out a tuft of red wool. "For you."

Sam took it. The tuft was about three inches long, tightly woven, and dyed a brilliant red. "What is it?"

"Put it on your hat. We're all going to wear them, Sam." Scammell laughed. "Remember that other night, when we stuck those bloody Yankees? The bastards are whining now, aren't they? Saying we was unfair. We should have woken them up before we killed them. So the lily-white bastards have said they'll take revenge and we're going to show them who to aim for, Sam. Wear it to show them who did the damage. They say we're murderers, so we'll be proud of it. The buggers will think twice the next time they see the red hackle on the hats, won't they?"

"I think they will." Sam was oddly pleased, reckoning that the red badge was a mark of honour. He tossed it on to the bank beside his stiff black tricorn. "I'll sew it on tonight, Sarge."

Scammell still sat on the willow branch. "I watched you the other night, Sam. You were good."

"Yankees were asleep," Sam said in a modest disclaimer of the praise, yet the sergeant's approval was oddly pleasurable. It gave Sam status as a fully-fledged soldier, one who could join the small élite of hard men who, with Scammell's approval, formed the heart of the company.

"You're a good lad, Sam, so don't spoil it."

"Spoil it, Sarge?"

Scammell scooped a handful of water to his mouth, then stood. "If Romeo and Juliet piss off, Sam, I might reckon it was your fault for not keeping an eye on your brother. You understand me? And then I might get unhappy with you. So watch him, and there won't be no trouble."

"He'll be all right."

"Or he'll be dead." Scammell climbed on to the bank. "We're Bloodybacks, Sam, and we stay Bloodybacks till we're wounded or dead. There's no way out, none." Scammell picked up the oxtail from the grass. "We took the oath, Sam, and we're here till they push us under the daisies. Tell your brother that." He nodded a curt farewell, then strode towards the turf bivouacs.

Sam brushed the mare's docked tail a last time, then flopped into the stream to cool himself. Fires sent the smell of cooking into the sky to mingle with the camp stench of thousands of unwashed men and women that was now so familiar to Sam that he did not even notice it. He found himself looking forward to the coming meal, to the conversation about the fire, and to the small laughter of comrades. He knew Nate's foolishness could risk that small happiness.

Because, for a Redcoat, there was no paradise; only the army, the smoke of battle, and the pride of a red hackle that proclaimed a man's expertise at the slaughter. Sam had taken the King's Shilling, and in return he had promised his life. Sam would be a Redcoat till death, and be bloody proud of it too.

FOUR

The ridges faded into a far distance, each ridge dark with trees, yet each ridge more faintly limned until, at the western horizon, the hills melted into the shimmer of pale sky. In the valleys between the ridges there were farms, roads, even small towns, yet from this vantage point the landscape seemed virgin. "Like Britain," Sir William said, "when the Romans came."

"Not the happiest simile, perhaps?" Lord Robert Massedene ventured. "You remember they left, sir."

"So they did." Sir William spoke absently. To the south-west, and evidently drawing his attention, there was a smudge of smoke in the cloudless sky, but the smoke was too distant for any of the horsemen to tell what burned. A forest fire? A house? They feared something worse, but none was willing to express the fear aloud.

The horsemen were on a bare hill. Beneath them, curling about the hill's base towards a ford, an earthen road was stirred into a choking dust by marching men. Battalion after battalion, trudging with the mindless step of weary men, followed their mounted officers towards the day's bivouac. Guns, their bright barrels dimmed by the dust, spewed up yet more dust that settled on the high wagons of sutlers and engineers. The army's women and children straggled along the road's verges. The day was hot with the steamy, breath-stealing heat of the American summer, and the horsemen knew how the marching men would be sweating in their thick woollen uniforms.

A red-coated horseman spurred along the road, scattering the camp followers until, seeing the bright uniforms above him, he turned his horse to the slope. The horse's hooves spurted small plumes of dust from the dry ground.

The man, a captain, curbed his sweating mare beside Sir William. "No news yet, sir."

Sir William had been made hopeful by the horseman's evident haste, but he showed no visible regrets at the lack of news. "You look hot, John!"

"It's a damnably hot country, sir. God knows why we fight for the bloody place."

"For their own good, I suppose." Sir William turned back to the west and continued his fruitless search of the heat-hazed landscape.

Sir William was a burly man, heavy in his saddle, with a dark coarse face which went ill with the gaudy lace and shining braid of his senior rank. The face suggested a man of little thought and choleric temper, but in truth Major-General Sir William Howe, Commander-in-Chief of His Majesty's Army in North America, was a lazy, placid, and most genial man. A kindly man, known as Good-Natured Billy to his friends and aides, but a man capable of a country squire's coarseness when, as rarely happened, his wrath was provoked. He turned back to the newcomer. "The Rangers left this morning, John?"

"Yes, sir." Captain John Andre, aide-de-camp to General Grey, confirmed that the Rangers had indeed ridden into the endlessly ridged landscape that shimmered in the heat.

"I suppose watching won't help." Sir William swung himself from his saddle, then groaned as a stab of pain pierced his spine. Sir William's father had suffered dreadfully from a pained back, and Sir William feared the same affliction, but this twinge happily passed swiftly. "You can eat with us, John?"

"That's why I hurried, sir. Your table puts General Grey's to shame."

"I'm serving mere commons today, John, but you're most welcome!" Sir William liked John Andre, and would dearly have liked to make the young man into one of his own aides, but he dared not poach from another general. That was irritating, for Sir William needed another aide now that the army was strung along the winding Pennsylvanian roads, rather than crammed into its New York garrison where messages could be so quickly acknowledged.

Sir William, as the horsemen dismounted and their servants fetched food and wine to the hilltop, strolled to the eastern edge of the hill and gazed at the gentle hills and deep woods that stretched to a far river plain made faint by the haze of heat. "A remarkable landscape," he said happily.

Captain Lord Robert Massedene knew how fond his master was of all things American. Some country chapel with rotting boards and a sagging roofline could elicit Sir William's admiration simply because it had had a lick of new limewash and thereby demonstrated the triumph of diligence over adversity. Massedene knew how senseless it would be to express his opinion that the landscape was really rather commonplace. "Magnificent, sir."

Sir William peered at a glint of silver which glimmered on the far plain. He supposed the bright gleam to be the River Delaware. "Shouldn't we be able to see Philadelphia from here?"

"Unless we landed in the wrong place." Lord Robert Massedene was twenty-two, and the son of one of Sir William's friends, which had made his appointment as an aide to Sir William a matter of tactful necessity, though Sir William had never regretted the enforced choice. Robert Massedene was short and stocky, with a boyish round face that bore a cheerful and indomitable grin. He was a younger son, doomed by primogeniture never to inherit wealth, and had chosen instead to earn his living by the sword which hung from silver chains at his waist.

"The city's to the right, sir." John Andre joined the two men and pointed to where, in the hazed distance, Philadelphia was hidden by a swell of wooded ground.

Sir William stared into the shimmering landscape. "Music," he said suddenly. "Music!"

The young aides, who were as fond of Sir William as he was of them, smiled at this sudden and inexplicable enthusiasm. "You want us to sing to you, sir?" said Lord Robert jokingly.

"If you insist, Robert, but I was thinking more of Philadelphia." Sir William turned to see how his servants were progressing with the preparation of dinner. "We must have music in the city. I want to see people happy. It must be a glow in dark times, a winter of joyfulness." Sir William spoke with a fervour that contrasted with his usually placid disposition. He was a distant cousin of the King, yet he hated the royal policy and had, when the rebellion began, sworn never to fight against the colonists he so admired. Impecunity had changed Sir William's mind, for he needed the commander-in-chief's salary to pay his manifold debts, yet, even above his appointment as commander-in-chief, he valued his appointment as Peace Commissioner. He yearned for peace and believed the prize would come with Philadelphia.

John Andre smiled. "But there won't be any joy in the city, sir, till we've taken the river forts."

"We'll take them, John." Sir William seemed to dismiss the problem of clearing away the rebel forts that barred Philadelphia from the sea, and which would stop British ships bringing supplies into the city. "Is there a theatre in Philadelphia?"

"There was four years ago, sir, though the churches wanted it closed."

"We could have a winter season of the drama, you think?"

"Your second-in-command," John Andre said slyly, "would suggest you hung Mister Washington first?"

"My Lord Cornwallis would," Sir William was not above a gentle mockery of his own, "but even My Lord knows you can't conquer a wilderness. Look at it!" He gestured westwards towards the receding and fading ridges. "It goes to the world's end! No, our best hope is to prove that the rebels have nothing to fear from us, nothing at all! We shall seduce them with success and dazzle them with benignity, isn't that what you told me?"

"I was ever eloquent." Andre, half Swiss, was an elegant and clever man who knew how to amuse his elders. "Ah! Salmagundi! Chicken! I see we shall not starve today."

The soldiers slogged along the road while, above them, Sir William and his military family dined. Besides John Andre there were three other aides, as well as Sir William's Hessian interpreter, and his private secretary. Hamlet, Sir William's dog, was pampered by all of them; fed the choicest meat and tempted with water flavoured with wine. The horses cropped at the hill's thin grass and the servants waited out of earshot. It was a gentle scene, only lacking ladies to give it domestic charm, yet it was spoilt for Sir William by the worries that constantly made him search the western view.

John Andre, knowing just what disturbed Sir William, essayed reassurance. "It'll arrive today, sir."

"You said as much yesterday, John." Sir William, the food forgotten, gazed westwards. "If Mister Washington did but know it, we can scarce fight a battle!"

"We've ammunition enough for one victory," Lord Massedene said soothingly.

"So Mister Washington can afford to lose one more battle, then gain a famous victory immediately afterwards!" Sir William absent-mindedly caressed his dog's ears. "Unless he's given up after the last drubbing?"

"Mister Washington," Andre said, "is like a man with a headache who constantly seeks a brick wall against which to hammer his skull. No, sir. He'll turn up again. He yearns for military glory."

"If he turns up today," Sir William said, "he'll get it! We're an army without balls!"

The aides smiled at the coarse jest which was, in all sadness, nearly true. Sir William's army, ever manoeuvring itself closer to Philadelphia, was fast exhausting its stocks of musket cartridges. It was not battle which had depleted the men's cartouches, but fear. Each night, marooned in the vastness of the American wilderness, the picquets became nervous. They fired at phantoms, and in minutes whole battalions were woken, had seized their muskets, and were joining the fusillade of crackling and sparking shots that flayed the empty night with noise and lead. Orders and threats had failed to stem the waste.

It was a waste of fearful cost. Each paper-wrapped cartridge had to be brought from Britain to New York, and thence in smaller ships to the Chesapeake Bay, from where it was dragged in wagons over the ragged roads. Cartridges were like gold, yet each night the infantry hammered the empty darkness as though they possessed an inexhaustible supply. Threats to flog the offenders had not worked, for a whole army offended and Sir William's only hope now was the arrival of a convoy of wagons loaded with the precious ammunition.

The convoy was late.

Somewhere in the dark trees, somewhere in the mysterious landscape, the ammunition convoy was lost. The Queen's Rangers, tough Loyalist horsemen who were born to this empty land, had gone to search for the convoy, but Sir William feared that they, like the cartridges, might have been ambushed. He did not express the fear, for risk of tempting fate, but every officer on the hilltop knew it anyway.

"We managed without ammunition at Paoli's Tavern, sir," John Andre said lightly.

"I fear the Yankees won't always oblige us with sleeping sentries," Sir William said.

Thomas Evans, Sir William's principal servant and given a freedom with his master because of his exalted position, climbed to the hilltop. "We ought to be going, Sir William."

"You're concerned for my safety, Tom?" Sir William twisted,

causing another spasm of pain in his back, to look down the hill's eastern flank. The army's rearguard was marching past. "You can clear the plates, Tom, but we're going to wait for a few moments before we leave."

They waited, though prudently mounted, and every officer knew why they waited. Sir William wanted the solace of the convoy. He wanted to see the heavy wagons, swollen with cartridges beneath the roped tarpaulins, lumber into view. It might not be the Commander-in-Chief's task to wait for such a menial thing as a supply convoy, but no officer knew better what disaster threatened if the wagons did not arrive.

"We really should be going, sir," Lord Robert said nervously. The army was safe enough wherever it stood, but once it had vacated ground, the rebels mysteriously flowed back to occupy the land.

"Another minute, Robert." Sir William stared fixedly to where the road disappeared into the deep shadow of trees.

And where, quite suddenly, a green-coated horseman appeared.

John Andre's hand instinctively went to the hilt of his sword, while Tom Evans dragged a cavalry carbine from his saddle holster. Major Zeigler, Sir William's Hessian interpreter, spurred forward to place himself between the Commander-in-Chief and the strange horseman, but Sir William waved the German away. "It's all right, Otto. He's a Ranger!"

Andre's hand left his sword, and Evans's carbine went back into its holster. More green-coated horsemen appeared, all Americans who fought for their King, and behind them, a blessed vision, came the wagons which the Rangers had sought. Sir William's face, that had been drawn with worry, cleared. "God's still an Englishman, eh?"

Then the elation drained from the watching horsemen. God might be an Englishman, but He had sent only three wagons. The tarpaulin of the third was scorched, while all three were guarded by Hessian troops who walked like men who had struggled through the valley of the shadow. This was not the convoy, but rather the remnants of the convoy.

A red-coated officer walked his horse with the Hessian infantry. He stared up the hill, saw the bright uniforms of the staff officers and, with a weariness that was visible from the summit, climbed into his saddle. He spurred the horse up the hill, but the mare was desperately tired and could only walk.

No one on the hilltop spoke. The approaching officer proved to be a lieutenant, his handsome face made dirty by sweat and powder stains. When he took off his hat to salute Sir William he revealed fair hair that was matted to his skull. His red coat, which had the facings and turnbacks of an unfashionable line regiment, was stained with blood and scorched by fire. Among the staff officers' pristine uniforms, with their golden aiguillettes and looped frogging, the shabby lieutenant seemed like a man from another world. A soldier.

"Lieutenant Vane, sir," he reported to Sir William.

"Do you know who I am?"

Vane nodded wearily. "Yes, sir."

Sir William's usual affability had faded at the sight of the shrunken convoy. "Are you here to tell me, Lieutenant Vane, that there are only three wagons?"

"Yes, sir."

Sir William rarely showed temper, but in the face of Vane's calm words the temper threatened. "What did you do with the rest?"

Vane stiffened. "I did nothing, sir. The convoy was not my responsibility."

There was a pride in Vane's voice which, though his tone was respectful, nevertheless edged his words with a defiance that no usual lieutenant would dare use to a commander-in-chief. Vane rubbed a sleeve over his forehead, smearing powder stains and sweat into his matted hair. "Fifty wagons left the Head of Elk, sir, but they were ambushed ten miles out. The rebels drew the escort to the north of the road, then sent horsemen from the south." Vane's voice was suddenly bitter. "They hamstrung the draught animals and burned the wagons, sir."

Sir William instinctively glanced towards the smudge of smoke on the horizon. He tried to imagine the exploding wagons and the screaming horses and the blood and horror on a forest road, then he was assailed by thoughts of the crisis he had feared. How was he to fight without ammunition?

"There weren't many rebels," Vane interrupted Sir William's thoughts, "but one burning wagon set fire to another, and we could only save three."

"We?" Howe looked back to the lieutenant.

"My servant and I, sir." Vane gestured towards a Redcoat who waited at the foot of the slope, then, with immense weariness, the lieutenant explained how he came to be with the convoy. "We were returning to the army, sir, and were ordered to march with the escort."

"Then where's the escort commander?" Sir William asked. "Shouldn't he be making this report?"

Vane, after the smallest shrug, spoke with a seeming reluctance. "Major Woodward deemed it wiser to return to the Chesapeake Bay, sir."

"He . . ." Sir William paused. "Go on, Vane."

Vane seemed embarrassed. "I believed the army's need to be extreme, sir, so thought it best to bring the three wagons. The Hessian company volunteered to make the journey with me." Vane straightened in his saddle. "I'd like to commend their bravery to you, sir."

Major Zeigler, the Hessian interpreter, preened himself at such news of German valour, while every other officer on the hilltop stared at Lieutenant Vane and thought of what he was choosing not to report. Doubtless Vane had argued with Major Woodward, and doubtless Vane had disobeyed orders in insisting that the remnant of the convoy should be taken onwards, and doubtless Vane had displayed a reckless bravery. A lieutenant had defied a major, then brought his tiny force through the dark woods and past the small farmsteads where the men with their deadly rifles lived. A full battalion was needed to escort any convoy through such terrain, yet this lowly lieutenant had come through with a handful of men because he knew how desperate the army's need for ammunition might be.

Now, with sweat running down his face to make rivulets through the dust and powder stains, Vane waited in the sunlight as though he expected a reprimand. "I'm sorry it was only three, sir."

"It would have been none without you!" Sir William said warmly.

John Andre, seeing the black stains on Vane's face that were caused by the exploding powder in a musket's pan, and knowing that no officer ever fired a musket unless the danger was terrible, spoke gently to Vane, "Did you have to fight to bring your three wagons through, Vane?"

"Yes," Vane frowned as though trying to recall the incident. "It was last evening, but it was hardly serious."

"Hardly serious?" Sir William asked.

"They were merely vagabonds among the trees, sir. I thought they should be unsettled before they understood how weak my force was." Sir William's officers imagined the muskets and rifles flaming from the trees, and the small band of soldiers trapped about their wagons. Vane spoke slightingly of the event, but his modesty only made the feat more impressive.

"Vane." Lord Robert said the name musingly. "There are Vanes in Northamptonshire, are there not?"

"I wouldn't know. My family was in trade." Vane made the embarrassing admission with a touch of his previous defiance.

"Was?" Sir William asked gently.

Vane hesitated. "My father died, sir. I used my inheritance to buy a commission."

It was evidently not a very successful investment, for Vane was already in his middle twenties when a richer man might expect to be a captain at the very least. But it was evident that Lieutenant Vane could not afford to buy his next promotion. His mare was a poor horse and his uniform was a threadbare coat. He could not purchase the captaincy, but nor could an unconnected tradesman's son expect the patronage that a nobleman's relative might enjoy. Vane was an ordinary officer from an ordinary regiment facing the ordinary tedium of a soldier's career. Except, in these last two days, Vane had proved himself as brave as any man in the army.

"How long have you been in America?" Sir William turned his horse and, to his aides' relief, at last led his party off the hilltop.

Vane followed Sir William. "Since December, sir."

Sir William beckoned Vane to ride on his right flank. "You were at Brandywine, then?"

"Indeed, sir." Vane's voice sounded warm at the memory of that recent battle in which the rebels had been pushed out of the path of the British advance. "I was ordered to escort our wounded back to the ships afterwards. I feared that by doing so I might miss the next engagement, sir."

Sir William smiled at the enthusiasm. "You enjoy soldiering?"

"Indeed, sir."

"I'm glad you chose it instead of trade, Lieutenant! 'Pon my word I'm glad! Three wagons are better than none, eh?"

"But not so good as fifty, sir."

"No." Sir William, reminded of his problems, fell silent until the horsemen reached the road and could spur after the three wagons. Vane's servant, carrying a musket, trudged in the dust. Sir William smiled at Vane. "Your man can meet you at headquarters? After supper?"

"Indeed, sir." Vane was perhaps too tired to show any astonishment at being invited to eat with the Commander-in-Chief. He gave the instruction to his servant, then caught up with Sir William who was wondering aloud how he was to fight without ammunition.

"More will come," Major Zeigler said.

"But Mister Washington might come first." Sir William spurred past the convoy, calling his praise to the Hessian troops who were as dirty and tired as Vane. "I've threatened to flog any man who fires without orders," Sir William complained when he had overtaken the wagons, "but it doesn't work! Flogging rarely does work."

"Because it isn't done hard enough." Major Zeigler had taken Vane's place at Sir William's right hand.

Sir William, grimacing at the Hessian's words, turned in his saddle to find Vane. Sir William's question, when he asked it, did not truly seek an answer, but was merely an indication that Sir William wanted Vane to feel welcome. "How would you stop the picquets blazing away my ammunition, Lieutenant?"

"I'd make the battalion officers pay for every wasted cartridge out of their own pockets, sir."

"Good God." Sir William curbed his horse in his enthusiasm. "It's a splendid notion! Touch an officer's pocket and you harness his obedience, isn't that so, my lord?"

Lord Robert Massedene agreed it was so.

"My God, Vane! I have all these clever aides and not one of them thought of . . ." Sir William's voice faded away, then a broad smile came to his face as a notion, which, in its own way, was as splendid as Lieutenant Vane's, came to him. "You deserve a reward, Vane."

"For doing my duty, sir?"

"But duty is so rarely done well." Sir William was at his happiest when he could make others happy and now, within his gift, was the priceless patronage that an officer like Vane lacked so badly. "I have a mind to make you my aide-de-camp, Vane."

Vane was astonished into incoherence. The horses had stopped and he was surrounded by Sir William's military family into which, by one word, he could gain privileged admission. Instead he stared at Sir William and, at last, managed to stammer a response. "But you don't even know me, sir!"

"I know you're brave! I've discovered you're not without clever notions! What more do I need to know?"

Vane seemed overcome. This was fortune beyond an officer's wildest ambition, and, offered it, he seemed overwhelmed by amazement.

Sir William, seeing Vane's expression, was delighted. "It's not such a great thing, Vane. You're more likely to die in battle as an aide! Isn't that so, John?"

Andre, who was enjoying Vane's confusion, smiled at the Lieutenant. "Welcome to the marble, Vane."

"The marble?" Vane looked dazedly at the elegant Andre.

"Your tomb in Westminster Abbey," Andre explained. "For now you are on the path of glory."

"If you accept," Lord Robert observed drily.

The words startled Vane into acceptance. "I do, sir," he said to Sir William, "and am honoured beyond any thanks I can give. I shall do my utmost to prove worthy, sir."

"I'm sure you will." Sir William was warmed by the man's response. A gift had been given, and very properly received. "But you can't be a lieutenant, Vane! That won't do at all, oh no! My colonels don't take lieutenants nearly seriously enough. I'll gazette you captain this night."

"Sir." It was all Vane could say. Promotion, more pay, patronage; all had come to him on a rutted road that had been kicked to dust by a passing army.

"And I can't go on calling you Vane, either. What did they christen you?"

"Christopher, sir." Vane said.

"Christopher, eh?" Sir William glanced at his new aide. "Do we call you that, or Kit?"

"Kit will do very well, sir."

"Or Kitten?" Lord Robert suggested mischievously.

Vane turned and stared into his lordship's eyes. For a second there was a chill in the hot day. "I'm never called that. By anyone."

Massedene saw how pale Vane's eyes were. "No offence, Captain Vane."

"Shall we go, gentlemen?" Sir William, who had missed the brief exchange, smiled at his young men. The Commander-in-Chief might be short of ammunition, but he had Philadelphia within his grasp, a new aide, and a belief that peace was but a few weeks away, and so Sir William, Good-Natured Billy, was a happy man.

FIVE

On the Sunday after the patriots had fled Philadelphia, the Revd Donald MacTeague, for the first time in over three years, publicly read the prayer for the King's Majesty as a part of divine service. Martha Crowl, dressed for Matins in her widow's black, stood in protest as the first syllables of the prayer were uttered. Every eye in the church watched as she picked up her bible, prayer book, and parasol. The Revd MacTeague's voice faltered. Martha took her daughter's small hand. Some parishioners in the crowded church waited for a thundering denunciation, but the minister was silent as Martha banged her pew door shut and stalked loudly down the centre aisle. The six-year-old Lydia, evidently enjoying her mother's defiance, smiled at her Uncle Jonathon who, tempted to join his sister, smiled back.

A few moments later there was another shiver among the congregation when MacTeague read aloud the text which he had drawn from the fifteenth verse of the final chapter of the Book of Joshua. "Choose you this day whom ye will serve!" He paused there, as if daring any of his other parishioners to choose as the Widow Crowl had chosen. None did and MacTeague went on to extol the manifold blessings that would accrue to the city when the British arrived; busy wharves, full warehouses, the return of good English coin and the confidence of the mercantile world. These, MacTeague said, were God's gifts that would be brought by the King's forces.

At dinner, following the service, Abel Becket vented his embarrassment at Martha's display. "She disgraces our family!"

"By the consistency of her opinion?" Jonathon asked.

"Do you defy me, sir?" Abel Becket paused, carving knife in hand, to glare at his nephew.

But Jonathon had long learned that the best way of dealing with his aunt and uncle was by an equable honesty that could neither be denied, nor challenged. Jonathon lived as a ward in his uncle's house and had become an adept at avoiding the disagreements that had made other houses in the city so unhappy. He smiled. "I merely asked a question, sir."

The knife plunged back into the leg of pork. "If she finds the city inimical, she should leave!"

"Or at least worship with the Presbyterians," Hannah Becket said. "They're all rebels! I hear they plan to fire the city before the British arrive."

It was a time of such rumours, bred by uncertainty, because the British had still not come to Philadelphia. It was reported that the rebel army still attempted to block the British advance on the city, though few Loyalists expected George Washington's defiance to succeed. The news of the British victory at Brandywine Creek had been followed by a story of mayhem at Paoli's Tavern and Philadelphians who in these past years had suffered Whigs at their supper tables now proclaimed that they had never, for one instant, doubted the return of the royal writ.

"We shall say grace," Abel Becket announced when the leg was carved.

Jonathon bowed his head as his uncle thanked a beneficent and almighty God for the favours of a full table and a promising harvest. Abel Becket enjoined God's protection on the family, His blessing on the food, and then, instead of his customary amen, added a further plea. "And we beseech thee, O Lord, for the success of Thy royal army and we pray Thy blessings on its men and their commanders. Amen."

"Amen," said Hannah Becket.

There was a pause. Both uncle and aunt waited for Jonathon to echo the word, but Jonathon kept silent.

"Amen," Abel Becket said again, then, as though there had been no embarrassment, remarked that the weather had suddenly turned unseasonably cold.

"A sharp winter, I don't doubt," Hannah Becket said.

Thus, again, conflict was avoided, yet Abel Becket dreaded the moment when it would sully his hopes for the future of his trade. Jonathon was the only heir, yet Jonathon, he feared, was no Tory. And Abel Becket, in his deepest convictions, was a fervent Loyalist. Liberty, to Abel Becket, was a word conjured by the lawyers to rouse the mob, and, should the ignorant win, and the King's writ be expelled from America, it would bring ruin to a seaboard. For how could thirteen colonies, on the edge of the known world, hope to trade without the protection of a greater power?

And trade, Abel Becket believed, would bring America greater blessings than any slogan. Trade brought money, and so Abel Becket prayed for the arrival of the British and the opening of the seaway. He had even gambled on British victory for, in his warehouse, Abel Becket had hoarded a great stack of sawn black walnut, ready for the day when it could be sent to the London market for real coin. The Philadelphia furnituremakers had begged to buy some of the precious timber, but Abel Becket had spurned their depreciated rebel paper dollars. London was the town that mattered, the town with gold, and the town that could make Philadelphia strong again.

Yet, if the trade was to come to the city, then first the rebel forts on the Lower Delaware would have to be taken. The next morning, standing on his wharf, Abel Becket watched two large shallops that, under grey sails, beat into the cold north wind. Both boats had been rigged with small bow-cannon, and both were crewed by armed men. "Look at them!" Abel Becket spat his derision into the breeze. One of the ships bore a scarlet flag on which the Tree of Liberty had been sewn, while the other carried the new rebel flag of striped red and white. "It looks," Abel Becket said scathingly, "like a clown's pantaloons unfurled."

The boats had come from the rebel forts. One of the craft, the one with the striped flag, fell away in the wind so that it was driven close to the jutting wharf where Abel Becket stood.

"Are they come? Are they come?" A man, making a trumpet with his hands, shouted the question of the moment across the choppy water.

"They'll come!" Abel Becket shouted back.

Beside him, obsequious as ever in his master's company, Ezra Woollard chuckled, "And they'll run you off the river, Johnny Lyle!"

"Go to hell, Ezra!" The insult was followed by a wave of the hand before the shallop bore up into the wind.

Becket watched it go. "You say they're obstructing the river?"

"They're sinking pontoons at Billings Island, sir."

"You've got details?"

"And maps." Woollard followed his master back into the warehouse, past the great baulks of walnut and past the fragrant bales of linseed that would sail for Ireland. Yet nothing could sail before the British came and the forts were taken.

Ezra Woollard, safe in Abel Becket's private room, put his plans of the rebel defences on the table. "I was thinking," Woollard said, "that these should reach the British."

"Indeed." Abel Becket's agreement was whole-hearted.

"They're north of the city now. It won't be a difficult ride."

"I can spare you." Becket stood by his window which looked down into Water Street. "God knows but there'll be no business till the city's safe."

Woollard smiled. "I was thinking, sir, that maybe I wouldn't be the best messenger."

Becket turned. "No one knows the river better than you."

"And I can write my knowledge down, sir, but I'm not a smooth talker. And the British are gentlemen, are they not? And they might despise a common man like myself?"

Becket offered his foreman one of his rare smiles. "Not so very common, Woollard."

"But I'm no hand at dealing with gentlemen." Woollard's humility came hard, for, as a young man and not so long ago, he had prospered as an independent merchant in Philadelphia. He had made his fortune as a dealer in New Jersey tar, and it sometimes seemed that there still clung a sulphurous reek to him.

Woollard's tar business, that had grown from one leaky shallop bringing barrels from New Jersey to the Delaware's shipwrights, had been broken by the British naval blockade. There were not enough ships being built on the river, nor needing repair, and Woollard had only been saved from bankruptcy by Abel Becket. The older man had paid the debts of the ailing tar business and made Woollard into his foreman. It was a good bargain, for Woollard had the skills of a trader and the physical force of a man toughened by a hard trade. His round face was scarred and pitted, his hair was coarse and thick, his body bulky and strong. In rescuing Ezra Woollard, Abel Becket had found himself a most effective foreman.

"Are you suggesting," Abel Becket asked, "that I should ride to the British myself?"

"You'd be better at persuading them than myself, sir. But I was thinking of Master Jonathon."

"Ah." Becket went back to the table and sat. He stared at the plans of the rebel defences. "I don't think he'd make a willing messenger."

"I heard," Ezra Woollard said slyly, "that Mister MacTeague preached from Joshua 24, verse 15, yesterday?"

Becket's dark eyes looked up at the foreman. "He did."

"So Master Jonathon must choose."

"Jonathon is my nephew." Abel Becket was dressed in his customary black, with an old-fashioned black Steinkirk about his neck, and the sombre clothes added an odd force to the warning note in his voice.

"And it's not for me to interfere in family affairs," Woollard said blithely, "but it seems to me, sir, that the British will be in a position to reward some families in this city, and to punish others. They'll bring trade, but they'll not give trade to merchants whose loyalty isn't absolute." He paused, as if to give his master a chance to protest, but Becket stayed silent.

"And they could hear, sir, how Master Jonathon hurried eighty barrels of fine powder out of the city the other night! They'll not like it!"

"It was paid for."

"With paper, not coin that they'd have given us." Again Woollard paused, but again Becket stayed silent and the foreman knew that he was expressing the fears of his employer. "And, with respect, sir, his sister doesn't help. It just seemed to me, sir, and with the greatest of respect, that Master Jonathon must be made to display a proper loyalty."

Becket frowned. "I've no doubt, in time, that he'll do just that."

"Not if what I hear is true."

Woollard paused, and Becket could not resist asking the invited question, though he gave it a scornful twist. "Waterfront gossip, Woollard?"

"He's sweet on Caroline Fisher."

Becket frowned at the news, then grimaced as he saw a personal motive for the revelation. "Whom you once wanted to marry?"

"That was before I knew of her levelling views, sir. She's a rebel, and fervent! Now it's none of my business, and I'll cease my talking as soon as you tell me to, sir, but it seems to me that if Master Jonathon can be forced into showing a proper loyalty then Caroline Fisher will scorn him as quickly as she can."

Becket, troubled by the information, stood again and walked restlessly back to the window. "Jonathon's never mentioned her to me."

"He wouldn't! He'd be ashamed!"

Becket watched two carts sidle past each other beneath his window. One of the drivers, carrying a load of dried fish, expertly flicked his whip at a small boy who tried to filch a free meal. "Jonathon's young," he said, almost to himself, "and the young like to flirt with dangerous views. But he's good!" He turned back to Woollard. "He's as talented a trader as you or I, Woollard! That deal for ticken, how much did we make? A thousand dollars?" Becket smiled. "It's that leg. They feel sorry for him and don't know that he's a better man than they'll ever be!"

"So we mustn't lose him, sir. We mustn't let the likes of Caroline Fisher and, begging your pardon, sir, Mrs Crowl, turn his head to nonsense! Make him choose." Woollard gestured at the plans that lay on the table. "Send him to the British, sir, and no one will doubt his loyalties after that." He paused, and he saw the doubt on Abel Becket's face, and Woollard knew that the merchant was contemplating the possibility that Jonathon would rebel against the order and thus provoke the confrontation that so far the family had avoided.

Woollard chuckled. "Master Jonathon's not such a fool as to quarrel with his bread and butter!" He made his voice confiding, almost reassuring. "He's a good lad. He just needs his mind made up for him."

"Maybe." Becket still stared into the street. "Caroline Fisher?"

"A slut, sir, if you'll forgive the word. She needs a good whipping. Not that it's my business, but I'd hate to see a girl like that taking all the profits from your hard work." Woollard shrugged. "Forgive me for saying too much, sir, but it's all in our interest if the British favour us. And if you want me to ride north with the papers I'll gladly do it."

"No." Becket, his mind evidently decided, turned back. "Leave them."

"Sir." Woollard bowed his head then clattered down the stairs to the counting house where the empty desks showed how trade had suffered in these last years. Three clerks only worked where once a dozen had scratched at their ledgers. The clerks held their breath till the foreman had gone, but Woollard's mind was not on mere clerks; instead he considered the fate of a business that he had a mind to own, and to which end, but for the most respectable and justifiable of reasons, a cripple must be forced into a decision. Jonathon must choose.

SIX

Opposite Philadelphia, on the Delaware's eastern bank, was marshy land that rose to low sandy ridges that were thickly wooded. It was poor land, yet from this Caleb and Anna Fisher had made a farm.

The farm lay south of where the Cooper River joined the Delaware and its poor soil had been enriched by its proximity to Philadelphia where, in the echoing covered market, Caleb sold melons, cucumbers, pumpkins, squashes, mulberries, apples, cherries and chestnuts. His wife churned milk to butter, made cheese, and baked broad high-crusted pies that were carried across the river for sale.

The reward for their work was a weather-boarded house of warm snugness. The main room was a huge kitchen, off which there was a small parlour where, each winter morning, Caleb Fisher read the scriptures. In summer he sat on the back porch to make his private devotions. There were two bedrooms, both in the attics, and a cabin for the black slave family that provided the farm's only workers. Caleb's neighbours had helped build a towering barn beside which a grove of sycamores shaded the yard where chickens pecked. It was not a rich farmstead, nor a grand one, but to Caleb and Anna it was a palace.

"The Lord's been good to us," Anna liked to say, even though she had lost three children in infancy. Her only surviving son had grown up and married. Then he too had died, with almost all his family, in one of the dreadful fires that sometimes swept the small wooden houses built on Philadelphia's margins. One baby had survived that fire; Caleb and Anna's grandchild, who had lived ever since on the farm and who had become dearer to her grandparents than any other person on earth. So dear that Anna sometimes forgot she had not given birth to Caroline herself.

There were those, both in the small New Jersey river settlements and in Philadelphia across the water, who thought the girl had gone wild. She should, they said, have been married long before. Caroline was eighteen now, four years past marriageable age, yet her grandparents made no move to force her into wedlock. They had even supported her refusal to wed the rising Woollard when his young business looked set to make a fortune. Some thought Caleb and Anna would not let Caroline go because they needed her help about the land, but others, who knew the Fishers better, understood that Caroline had her own thoughts on marriage. It would come, but in her own time and of her own choice.

And there would be choice, for she was a girl who caught the eye of men. Her golden hair was lightened by the sunlight to a gleaming paleness that contrasted oddly with her tanned skin from which a pair of blue eyes challenged a disapproving world. She could ride like a boy, milk a cow like a dairymaid, and handle a river shallop like a waterman.

It was the shallop that made Caroline noticed, for, as her grandfather grew older, it became her duty to take the farm's produce over to the city's quays. A bright-haired girl sailing a boat with such skill was bound to provoke attention. Like all the river sailors, she wore a knife at her belt to cut at tangled rigging, but there was something about her face that suggested the knife could be used for more than slashing ropes.

Not all the farm's produce went to the market. Caroline carried the choicer fruits and firmest cheeses to her special customers, among whom was Martha Crowl, and it had been at the widow's house that Caroline had first met Jonathon. She had first seen the clubbed foot appear on the kitchen stairs and she had felt a pang of pity for the boy. He had limped beside her as she returned to the wharf and they had discovered that each was orphaned, and that each was a Patriot living in a Loyalist house.

Caroline's grandparents' loyalism was not like Abel Becket's, who held the creed as a matter of fervent belief. Anna Fisher remembered seeing the old King before she sailed to America. "A grand man, he was! A grand man!" Caleb swore that Anna had never seen the King at all, but only some grandee passing through her Yorkshire village, but Anna insisted that the King of England had smiled at her, and that one smile had kept her loyal for nearly sixty years. The rebellion, in Anna's sturdy view, was all the fault of the Philadelphia lawyers. "I never did trust a lawyer, it was lawyers who tried our Lord and Saviour, and lawyers who chopped off good King Charles's head, and all the lawyers ever cared about was their own pockets. Have you ever known a poor lawyer?"

Caleb believed a Christian should be ruled by a king, because, just as land needed water or a calf milk, it was natural. To him the rebellion was a fuss across the river, nothing more.

But Caroline had never seen a king, and she crossed the river to hear the city's debates, and the rebellion seemed a fine thing to her. She had been born in the colonies and her espousal of the Patriot cause was as instinctive as was her grandparents' more ancient loyalty. To that espousal she added the passion of the young who believe the world can still be changed for the better, and Caleb and Anna accepted her enthusiasm, knowing that it would be as futile to try and check the Delaware's spate in full flood as to try and change their granddaughter's mind. Caroline, like Jonathon Becket, would be a rebel.

They had known each other for a year, and their meetings had always been in the city. Jonathon would waylay Caroline on the wharf and insist on carrying her baskets to market. Sometimes he would limp with her through the shipyards to the north of the city and he would tell her which shipwrights used bad timber and which thinned their tar; sometimes they spoke of the rebellion and Jonathon would list what supplies he had found for the rebel army that week, and how his sister made up the profit above the meagre payments the Congress would allow so that his uncle would be content to sell to the hated rebels. Always Caroline knew that this charming, eloquent, and wealthy young man was trying to tell her that he was in love. Why else would he inflict the pain of the long walks on himself?

"He'll be rich," Anna Fisher sometimes teased Caroline.

"A rich merchant."

"Nothing wrong with money, child."

Caroline had grimaced. "He'll have to live in the city, won't he?"

"If that's where the money goes, and it usually does."

Once, when Abel and Hannah Becket were at a church meeting, Jonathon had taken Caroline around their house and she had seen the quiet, solid wealth of the family, and it had scared her. The table had been set for a supper, and Caroline had never seen so much cutlery, or so many plates, or such shining glassware, or so many spermaceti candles that cost nine dollars a tierce. "We use tallow," she had said defensively.

"So do we, upstairs."

"I make them myself," Caroline had said, "starting by killing the sheep."

"You don't!"

She had looked almost challengingly at Jonathon. "You've never killed a sheep?"

"Lord, no!"

Caroline could not imagine how a person could live in such ignorance of country necessities, nor, when she was truthful, could she imagine herself living in a city.

Yet, if Jonathon had his way, and his way could be as forceful as it was amusing, she would live in a city. He had not offered marriage, but he would, and Caroline did not know how she would respond. She admitted to herself that there was something flattering in his attention, and the dragging foot invited pity, but Caroline almost feared the moment when Jonathon would demand her response.

Then, in the last week of September 1777, on a Tuesday evening, Jonathon came to Caroline's house for the very first time.

He arrived in the sunset. At first, as Caroline watched the strange horseman come down the track from the plank bridge across the Cooper River, she did not recognize Jonathon, but then he lifted his hat and smiled. "Watching the sunset?" he asked as he reined in beside her.

"I'm deciding what cattle we'll keep." Caroline nodded towards the cows that grazed on the marshland by the river's edge. "The wind's taking their milk early this year." She looked up at the sky. "There's a bad winter coming."

"You think so?"

"I know so." Caroline saw how, on horseback, Jonathon lost his crippled appearance. The right stirrup, to encompass his clubbed foot, was made twice as large as a normal iron, but he sat straight and tall, and she sensed how hard it must be for Jonathon to walk when he could ride so well. "You want the horse to drink?"

She ducked through the fence and led the mare round to the cattle trough by the milking barn. From here, when her face was hard by the warm flanks of the cows as she milked them, Caroline could see the glorious sight of the city across the river. In high summer, on still days, the spires and roofs were reflected as cleanly as if the steel-flat water was a mirror. In spring the tiles and shingles lost their starkness as the poplars on the streets came into new leaf, while in winter the snow gave the city a shining glory. Now, in the turn of summer to fall, there was a golden darkness to the city that was accentuated by the absence of masts from the quays.

"You've come a long way." She wiped the sweat from the mare's flanks.

Jonathon, secretly wishing she had shown more enthusiasm for his arrival, slid from the saddle. "I left the city at nine this morning, crossed at Davie Logan's, and here I am."

He had ridden miles to the north, crossed the Delaware, then ridden the long miles back on the New Jersey bank, and Caroline, who had learned the hard way that work should be done economically, shook her head in amazement. "What's wrong with the usual ferry?"

"Everything. I didn't want to be seen."

"By whom?"

"Anyone who might stop me." Jonathon said it to mystify her, then smiled. "And I wanted to see you. Can we talk?"

Caroline took him towards the river where there was a small rise of pale grass on which they could sit. She seemed to be in a daze, as though she knew what was about to be said, and what she ought to say in return, yet at the same time it was all so unexpected and unsettling. "You've run away?" she asked Jonathon.

"I'm not sure if that's an exact description. Perhaps I've been driven away? Expelled from Eden." He gestured across the rippling water to where, beyond the silhouetted city, the sun was sheeting the western sky with a wash that melded from a fierce crimson gold to a delicate pale pink.

"Driven away?"

"I was asked to deliver these to the British." Jonathon fumbled in a pouch at his belt and produced folded papers that he showed to Caroline. Then, as she looked through the sheets, the words poured out of him. How his uncle had demanded his loyalty, and how Jonathon had not liked to refuse his uncle directly because it would have seemed ungrateful after all the years of kindness, and how Jonathon had always feared that this break with his guardian must come, and how, rather than provoke a terrible argument with his uncle, he had decided to let Abel Becket believe that he was riding in obedience to deliver the treacherous papers to the enemy.

He was as full of words, Caroline thought, as a preacher man. "But you're not going to deliver them, are you?"

For answer Jonathon took the sheets from her and tore them into scraps. "I shall have to write to my uncle and tell him I disobeyed. I suppose that's a cowardly way of doing it, but it seemed for the best." He scattered the scraps into the wind. "There! All Woollard's work in vain."

"Woollard?"

"The repulsive Ezra!" Jonathon laughed. "But I'm free of them all now! And I couldn't stay there! I couldn't watch the British gloat over us." He seemed to shudder at the thought. "No, there's only one thing to do now, and that's fight them."

Caroline watched the scraps of paper blow in the small wind that blew towards the great furnace glow that blazed on the western horizon. "What will your uncle do? When he finds out?"

"I think he'll be angry."

"Will you lose your inheritance?"

Jonathon smiled. "Does that matter?"

"Not to me. But to you?"

And again Jonathon launched himself into words as eloquent as any Caroline had ever heard from a pulpit. The lawyers and the politicians spoke of liberty with the same glib ease that the preachers spoke of repentance, but Jonathon could invest the word with a heart-touching fervour. He believed that the British were a corrupt and tyrannical race who had betrayed the fine ideals of their own people in America. The time had come when the Patriots must defend those ideals. To Jonathon this was not a war about stamp tax, or about threepence on tea, but a war about God's own country where honest men could make a new heaven on an old earth. There would be no more Placemen from London, sent to live in the great houses and take their unearned salaries from honest folk, but instead there would be a good people on a good soil, America, and what was an inheritance against that great ideal?

Caroline listened to the wondrous words and, because she dealt in realities more than in ideas, she asked a flat question when the words ended. "And what will you do if you lose your inheritance?"

"I'll farm." Jonathon teased her and was rewarded by a shocked look of disbelief. He laughed. "I can become a lawyer, maybe a politician? Just so long as we're free, and just so long as you're waiting for me when I come back from battle."

He had spoken casually, but no less earnestly because of it. Caroline had known, as soon as she had recognized the strange horseman, that Jonathon had come to demand a decision of her. She had expected it for so long, but it still surprised her that he wanted to ride to war with her colour pinned to his lance. She was suddenly swept by a great pity for him. How could a cripple live in the harsh world of gunfire and sabre blades and blood?

"You want me to wait?" She said it to gain time in which to think of her answer.

"It's more than I deserve," Jonathon said. Caroline, as she thought, stared at the shivering reflections on the wide river, and Jonathon stared at Caroline. Her looks did not match the refined and elegant delicacy of the city, which so prized a fashionable paleness that the Fisher farm sold lemons, cucumbers, and tomatoes to be made into poultices for blanching the skin. Caroline's was a wilder and rougher beauty that some men might have thought coarse, but which had enslaved Jonathon. "It's more than I deserve," Jonathon repeated, "but I even dare to want you to do more than wait for me."

Caroline knew what that further question was, and she did not want to face it now, not under the great glow of the dying sun in an evening when emotions were already charged too high for good sense. She frowned. "You shouldn't be going at all . . ."

". . . I cannot stay."

Caroline turned on him fiercely. "God gave you other skills. Can you sit in a saddle all day? Do you have the strength for that?"

"I did today."

"You walked the horse. Imagine galloping and turning, twisting and fighting!"

But Jonathon was stubborn. "I can do whatever I have a mind to do. God gave me that strength, and it will be enough."

"I pray so." Caroline stared again towards the dark and intricate skyline of the city that was punctured by church steeples and by the needle-sharp spire of the State House where lawyers had fashioned the Declaration of Independence, and where some of those lawyers, young enough to fight, had then packed their papers and said they had done enough for the revolution and would return to their estates. While Jonathon, out of his passion, would ride where they feared to go.

She looked at him again. "Have you got food for the journey?"

"It can be bought."

"I'll make something." She took refuge in practicality. "And you can sleep here tonight. There's a bed that folds down in the kitchen for strangers."

Jonathon sensed her evasion and, quite gently, he took her right hand. "I don't care where I sleep, but I do care that you'll wait for me."

Caroline knew she had deflected the greater question, and she could not deny him the answer to the lesser. She nodded, "I'll wait," and, as soon as the words were said, she saw that he had implied assent to both questions, for his happiness was as golden and huge as the swelling and sinking sun on the western edge of the world. He held her suddenly, pressing his face to her hair, holding her as if he would never let her go. "I'll wait," she said again, but this time unprompted, a gift of her own wild and free will.

While, across the river, the first lights of the city glowed soft and yellow behind windows to shake their reflections on the wide, hurrying river. On the far bank, in merchants' houses and in the smaller tenements on the city's edge, life went on in its commonplace way, but Jonathon felt as though he had leapt from darkness into light, and from confusion into the glorious promises of love. He was a Patriot, and he would fight for his country against the Bloodybacks and their Hessian mercenaries, and he would fight for this girl whose love he would earn and keep for ever.

Jonathon, forsaking trade, was a rebel at last.

SEVEN

The company's evening parade was held on a patch of worn grassland close to the wood and turf bivouacs that were the men's homes. Sergeant Scammell harangued the Light Company. "Listen to your uncle Scammell and don't you dare bleeding laugh or I'll skin your bloody arses." He paced menacingly down the front rank. "We are short of ammunition. Therefore you are not to fire your bleeding muskets. You understand? You are only to fire your muskets if you get an order to fire your muskets. Not from a corporal, but from me. If any of you bastards fire without a bleeding order I'll have the skin off your backs!" Scammell's disgust at such an order was obvious, but the force with which he delivered it made the men nod nervously. The sergeant whirled round and pointed at Corporal Dale who, under Scammell's command, would lead one of the night picquets. "What are you not to do, Corporal?"

"Fire."

"Unless. . . ?"

"You tell us to, Sergeant."

"Good boy. If you see a rebel then pat him on his woolly head and tell him to fuck off. It's all bloody mad, but this is the bloody army. And that goes for all of you!" He glared at the other men in the company who, like Sam, were not on guard duty this night. "Hands off your muskets or I'll skin your backs! Picquets! To me!"

The duty picquets trailed disconsolately behind Sergeant Scammell to mount their night guard where the cultivated fields gave way to the thick, dark woods. The men who remained in the bivouac crouched about their fires, drank their ration of rum, and glanced enviously towards a small house where refugees from the nearby village of Germantown had taken shelter. "There's women over there." Liam Shaughnessy, a thin man who had been coughing blood in the last week, nudged Sam's arm. "You want me to hold one down for you, Sam?"

"It's all right, Liam, I can manage."

"Nate can manage, can't you?" Shaughnessy laughed, and the laugh turned into a foul grating cough. He spat into the fire, then grinned at Nate. "Scammy's on duty all bleeding night. You should tuck yourself in with Maggie."

"What would you know, Liam?" Nate hated to hear men talk so familiarly of Maggie.

Shaughnessy gave an evil grin. "He sold her to the Colonel last night, that's what I heard. Two shilling, Nate!"

Nate twisted towards Shaughnessy, but Sam pushed his brother back to the turf. "Shut up! Both of you!"

"I'll give the Irish bastard a kicking!" Nate pushed against his brother's restraining arm. Shaughnessy had pulled his bayonet scabbard round on its shoulder sling and grinned wickedly as if inviting the attack.

"For Christ's sake, calm down!" Sam glared at his brother. "You cause enough trouble as it is."

"It's only a doxie," Shaughnessy said. "And there'll be a lot of doxie in Philada, won't there now?" Few of the men could pronounce the city's name, or even cared to try. "There'll be crack by the yard! Just waiting for us, Sam." The delights of Philadelphia formed a constant and hopeful thread in the company's conversation; it being generally agreed that a soldier's dreams would be fulfilled there in the form of shelter, food, warmth, and a plenitude of women.

Sam snapped a fence rail and threw it on to the fire. A vagary of wind blew smoke into his face. He coughed. "If we ever get to Philadelphia."

"We'll get there," Shaughnessy said. "Then kiss the girls, we will." He laughed.

Sam glanced towards the small house, no bigger, he thought, than his parents' cottage where he had last seen his mother. He remembered, with a pang, how proud his mother used to be. "He's quick," she would say of Sam, though when the seven-year-old twins joined the stable staff at the big house as ostlers' boys, the head coachman used to say that Sam needed his reins looped beneath the rings. Only lively, stubborn, and troublesome horses had reins looped low so that the bit could be levered into a twist against the horse's mouth. Nate had never needed such curbing.

Nate had always looked to Sam as his leader except on the day, three years before, when Nate had seen the red-coated soldiers following the drummer boy and Nate had been dazzled by their jackets and by the recruiting sergeant's practised patter. Until then Nate had always been the shy twin. But now, for the second time in his life, but this time in a foreign field where the dusk shadowed the far trees, Nate needed his reins looped deep below the rings.

Nate needed curbing because he still dreamed of desertion. "A corporal in Captain Courtney's company ran today. They haven't caught him yet."

"They won't if he's clever." Liam picked a shred of beef from his teeth.

"They catch most of them," Sam insisted.

"Nah!" Nate was scornful. "The army just tells you that, don't they? They want you to be scared! Most go to the Yankees! More pay and no floggings!" He spoke as passionately as any Methodist seeking souls. "And you're not in their army for life! You don't even have to join if you don't want to! You can just take the land they give you!"

"Who says?" Sam challenged.

"It's a fact! Everyone knows!"

Night was falling. All around Sam the presence of the army was betrayed by cooking fires that lay across the darkened folds of ground like a fallen blanket of stars. A rain began to fall, hissing on embers and drumming on tricorn hats that bore the proud red hackles of killers. A dog limped past Sam's fire and sheered away from a soldier's blow. Somewhere a child cried, then was cuffed into silence. The cavalry horses whinnied from their far lines. The picquets, fearful for the punishment which would follow if they opened fire, were quiet at the encampment's dark edge.

"And when the Yankees lose," Liam Shaughnessy lit a clay pipe with a burning twig from the fire, "they'll round up all the deserters and hang them. No thank you, Nate. Isn't worth it, nor is it."

"I'm going to run," Nate said stubbornly.

"You always talk about it," Liam sneered, "but you never will."

"I will." Nate still dreamed of Maggie's paradise beyond the horizon. "You'll be jealous. I'll be tucked up with a girl and you'll be sweating on a march somewhere."

"I'll be flogging you." Shaughnessy laughed.

Nate ignored the Irishman, turning instead to his brother. "Would you flog me if I ran, Sam?"

"I'd knock your bloody head off, you silly bugger." Sam said it lightly.

"I mean it, Sam." Nate stared earnestly at his brother. "Would you?"

Sam rubbed his face. "I said how I'd look after you, brother, and so I will. You stay with me, and there'll be no call for a flogging." He looked at his twin and saw the unhappiness on Nate's face. "For God's sake, Nate! Liam's right. There'll be girls in their hundreds in Philadelphia! Just waiting for us. Everyone says so. They're loyal. They want us to come!"

"It's Maggie," Nate said simply.

"Bugger Maggie." Sam was tired of holding his brother's reins. He looked away to see an American youth, scarce more than a boy, who was nervously exploring the battalion's bivouac. Liam Shaughnessy, suspecting that the boy was after some of the company's food, growled a belligerent challenge.

The boy shied away from the harsh words. He wore ragged brown trousers, a cast-off torn coat, and had an odd, wide-brimmed hat above his long hair. An old pistol was thrust into his rope belt. He gestured uncertainly towards the lights across the fields as if to suggest that he were merely on his way to the village.

"You want something?" Sam spoke just a little too gruffly, playing the soldier, but his voice was a kindness compared to Liam's, and the young man looked relieved. "The guns," he said pathetically.

"You want to see the cannons?"

"Yes." The boy jerked his head towards the small house. "I'm from there." He offered the information as though it would soften the Redcoats' hostility.

Sam pointed towards the village. "Guns are in the market place, lad. Ask nicely now. You don't want your head blown away by a nervous sentry, do you now?"

The boy, who was merely curious about these strange red-coated creatures who had appeared during the day, seemed grateful for Sam's few words which, if not altogether friendly, were not downright hostile either. He grinned again, then wandered uncertainly onwards, weaving a cautious path around the knots of resting men. A fight suddenly broke out in Captain

Phillip's company. Two drunken men were clawing and scratching while their comrades made a loud, jeering ring about them. The sight made the young American nervous, and he stopped, unsure whether it was safe to proceed.

Sam lay back, careless of the rain. "What will you do," he asked Nate, "when the rebellion's over and they're looking for all the runners?"

"Big place." Nate gestured towards the dark. "Can't search everywhere, Sam. And there's a living to be made here. Land's good. No bleeding officers. No sergeants."

"There's nothing wrong with Captain Kelly," Sam said loyally, "and Scammy's all right if you stay upwind of the bastard." A musket fired from the field's far edge, then another. "Jesus, Nate, I don't want to see you hung or shot."

Nate dropped his voice so that only Sam could hear him. "Maggie's got some civilian clothes, like you said. She's hidden some food, too, and got some money. We're going to do it, Sam, we're really going to do it!"

"Don't be a fool."

"We're going to do it! This week!" Nate was whispering urgently. "Like you said, Sam? Proper clothes, bit of money, and hide from the bloody cavalry for two days. What the hell's happening?" Nate suddenly twisted round to stare north. The muskets, which had been ordered to stay silent because of the shortage of ammunition, were firing again.

Sergeant Scammell's voice, far out on the edge of the encampment, shouted fierce, but then the muskets blazed again in the snapping crackle of volley fire.

"Buggers are here!" Liam Shaughnessy scrambled to his feet and ran towards the stand of muskets. Other men, stirred by the sudden shots, rolled out of their shelters and grabbed their guns.

More musket fire stabbed the darkness from the picquet line. Tongues of flame leapt towards the dark woods at the edge of the encampment. Someone whooped a howl of delight and the first shots from the camp itself crashed loud in the night. This was an antidote to boredom, an irresistible opportunity, and men stood in the firelight, pulled their triggers, then reloaded eagerly to fire again. The American boy, startled by the sudden commotion, stood helplessly amidst the excited men who ran past him to flay the night with musketry.

"Cease fire! Cease fire!" sergeants shouted in the twilight, but the firing was infectious. Up and down the line, spreading to neighbouring battalions, the muskets flamed towards the trees. The picquets, far out, would be cursing and crouching as the heavy lead balls whipcracked overhead to crash among the leaves.

"Stop firing! Stop firing!" An officer's voice shouted behind Sam.

Sergeant Derrick, the Light Company's second sergeant, slashed his cane down on a man's musket, then another. "Cease fire! Cease fire!"

Slowly, fitfully, the firing died. Occasionally it would flare up again, crackling like burning thorns in the distance, but the officers and sergeants, roused from their sleep, gradually beat order into the men and drove them back towards their fires. Other officers galloped from the village angrily demanding to know which picquets had fired and upon whose orders.

Corporal Dale's picquet had fired, and done so without orders, and Sergeant Scammell, the guard sergeant, was rousted back to the lines where, in a voice loud enough to be heard in the next battalion, he swore it was the neighbouring troops who had first fired.

Lieutenant-Colonel Elliott, his face red from an evening's drinking, knew that the battalion's officers were threatened with a fine for this night's work, that the guard sergeant would be reduced to the ranks, and the men flogged. He did not care about the flogging, but he cared about one of his best sergeants and about his own pocket. He drew Scammell to one side where the two men bent their heads together.

"He's getting a right roasting," Liam Shaughnessy opined.

"They said any sergeant who fired without orders would lose his stripes!" Nate laughed. "Imagine Scammy back in the ranks?"

The laughter died as Sergeant Scammell about-turned and marched with a grim face towards the company. "Get in your beds, you scum! And put those muskets in the stands!" His hard face sought a victim and settled on the young American boy who, bemused by all the firing and fuss, still grinned half-wittedly beside Sam's bivouac. "You! What are you doing here?" Scammell pointed his metal-topped cane at the farm boy.

The boy seemed incapable of speaking, so Sam, who had not even fetched his own musket, spoke for him. "He wanted to see the artillery, Sergeant."

Scammell, amazingly, smiled. "The artillery! You want to see the cannons, is that it, lad?"

"Yes, sir." The boy nodded.

"You should have said! Come on then, lad. I'll show 'em you. And I'll give you a bite to eat. You're hungry, I dare say?"

"I am." The boy, perhaps fifteen or sixteen years old, lapsed into embarrassed smiles under the Sergeant's unexpected friendliness.

"What's your name, lad?"

"James, sir."

"Well, come on, Jimmy-me-lad! Rare big guns, we've got."

Sam watched the Sergeant lead the boy away and supposed that the hapless James would be blandished into joining one of the loyalist regiments. And quite right too, in Sam's view, for why should the Americans not fight to put down their own trouble-makers?

Sam, once the excitement of the evening was over, crawled into the shelter of his bivouac, laid his head on his hat, and closed his eyes.

He woke in the cold, wet, silver-grey before dawn. The reveille had not yet sounded, but already a few shadowy figures moved through the mist; women remaking the cooking fires or bugle boys rubbing the sleep from their eyes. Sam yawned, tried to sleep again, but immediately he closed his eyes it seemed that the bugles split the air with their racket. Sergeant Derrick, a vast-bellied and affable man, must have been ready for the reveille for he was fully dressed, cheerful, and rousting through the shelters. "Let's be having you bastards! Up and shine! Sam! Nate! I want you two! Fetch some axes! Lively now!"

Derrick wanted timber cut. It seemed an unnecessary chore to Sam, for there were plenty of fence rails still to be stolen from the fields, but Derrick insisted and so the brothers, axes over their shoulders, followed the Sergeant out of the bivouacs towards the misted woods where the dawn made the shadows mysterious and grey. "Maggie still giving your brother trouble, Sam?" Derrick asked.

"Like an itch, Sergeant."

Derrick laughed. "She's daft, that one. I told Scammy not to trouble himself with her, but she's a pretty thing. Makes a man jealous, that does. I had a woman in tow once." He shrugged, then hefted his musket as they approached the dew-wet bushes at the wood's edge. "No rebels here." He said it cheerfully, but was plainly nervous. He cocked the gun, and the click of the pawl dropping into place seemed unnaturally loud.

"Start here, Sarge?" Sam gestured towards a birch tree that grew at the very edge of the woods.

"Too wet." Sergeant Derrick stared around the trees. "Over here, boys." He prowled the wood's margin, walking as carefully as a poacher who fears a spring gun or steel-jawed trap. It seemed to Sam that the big Sergeant was searching for something other than timber to be cut and, after just a few slow paces, Derrick found it. "My oh my! Look at that, lads!"

Sam had to edge past Nate to see what had caused the Sergeant's evident relief.

A corpse lay in the long grass. It was a boy dressed in a torn coat and baggy trousers belted together with a length of frayed rope. A floppy, wide-brimmed hat lay a couple of feet from the dead boy's head, while, next to his outstretched right hand and fallen into the grass, was the pistol. The boy's long hair was bright with dew, and in his skinny throat was a red-filled, ragged-edged hole. It was the same boy who had edged so shyly towards Sam's fire the night before, the boy who had only wanted to stare at the soldier's big guns. "A Yankee Doodle Dandy," Sergeant Derrick said softly, "with a bullet in his gullet."

In the dawn's grey light Sam could see that the boy's pistol had no lock, and that the iron bands which fixed barrel to stock were rusted and loose. The pistol could never have been fired. The gun was nothing but a toy to a growing boy too interested in soldiers.

"That ain't a rebel," Nate said fiercely.

"Now, boy! Watch it!" Derrick grinned confidingly, but Nate would not heed.

"He was called James! He was with Scammell last night. He was talking to us! Just before the firing!"

Sergeant Derrick stood very close to Nate. "Listen. That is a rebel. He was shot last night after firing at our picquet. That's what happened, Private Gilpin, and that way none of our lads fetch a skinning, none of our sergeants loses his stripes, and none of our Jack-puddings has to pay a fine. Do you understand?"

"But – "

Sergeant Derrick struck Nate's face a stinging, skull-ringing blow. "You didn't hear me, son! It's a rebel. He was attacking us, so the fucking picquet did the right thing. Or do you want a kicking? Is that it, Nate Gilpin? You want the sergeants to have a mill with you?"

Sam looked past Derrick. The boy looked oddly peaceful. His hands were curled into fists and his legs slightly drawn up. There was something horribly pathetic about the rope belt about his waist. A fly crawled towards the bloody hole. Sam supposed Scammell had stabbed the boy with a bayonet to make it look like a bullet hole. Blood had drenched the torn jacket and flecked the grass. "He wasn't a rebel, Sarge." Sam's voice was tentative, so unlike his brother's passionate denouncements.

Derrick turned on Sam. "Of course he wasn't a bloody rebel! I know it, you know it, and Nate knows it, but the bloody army doesn't know it!" The Sergeant glared at the brothers, and Sam understood that, because Scammell had seen them talking with the boy after the firing, it was important that they keep their mouths shut. Sergeant Derrick, who was popular, must have been deputed to square the Gilpin brothers. "The silly buggers say we're not supposed to fire," Derrick went on, "but they can't blame us if we were attacked, can they? So here's the enemy!"

But Derrick had hit a streak of stubbornness in Nate. Somehow Nate believed that if only Sergeant Scammell could be humbled, then Maggie would be free. "I talked to him," Nate said staunchly. "Sam did too, didn't you, Sam?"

Sam said nothing.

Nate pleaded with his brother. "Sam?"

Sam shrugged. "He could have been spying on us, couldn't he?" Sam knew instantly he had done wrong, that he was condoning murder, but he wore a red hackle now to show that he was one of the élite men who had taken the blades to the enemy at the tavern. Sam had earned Sergeant Scammell's praise, and Sam did not want to lose that approbation. And how could Sam and Nate, mere privates, take on the certainty of the sergeants and officers who would insist that this pathetic corpse was a rebel soldier?

Sergeant Derrick grinned at Sam's answer, then went to the field's edge where he waved his arms and hollo'd towards the nearest picquets. He turned back to Nate. "You heard your brother, Nate. He's a rebel."

Nate bent down, picked up the floppy brimmed hat, and covered the dead boy's face. "He was only a kid. He weren't never a rebel, never!"

"Don't be so soft! He's a Yankee! They smile to our faces and shoot us in the back an hour later!"

Sergeant Derrick grabbed Nate's shoulder and turned him so quickly that Nate lost his footing and stumbled into the grass beside the dew-covered corpse. Derrick bent over him. "One word from you, Nate, and I'll tell Scammy you were under the blanket with Maggie last night. You can understand that, can't you? I'll say you were laughing at him and rogering his woman. He'll skin you alive, Nate, he'll give you a belting like you never had." Derrick prodded the stiff corpse with his musket. "He's a rebel and this way no one gets hurt by the staff! No flogging, no demotions, no fines. Everyone's happy!" Derrick laughed suddenly. "Except his mother, of course, but she won't miss the little bastard. Bloody Yankees breed like rabbits. Now, get up, lad."

The battalion's officers arrived, and after them came a staff officer mounted on a big black horse. The undergrowth was trampled around the boy's body as a ring of uniformed men stared in triumph at the puny corpse. Sergeant Scammell, chin shining from an early shave, proclaimed that the body was proof that the picquets had indeed been attacked, and therefore justified in returning fire.

"There." Lieutenant-Colonel Elliott, vindicated, looked up at the staff officer.

"Damned lucky for you, Elliott!" The staff officer asked to see the boy's weapon and Sergeant Derrick picked the broken pistol out of the grass.

"It got damaged, sir," Derrick said confidingly.

For an instant, a suicidal instant, Sam had the urge to step forward and proclaim that the American boy had been innocent, that he had been with Sam when the shooting started, and Sam's right foot actually moved involuntarily forward, but then he caught Scammell's gaze: the Sergeant's eyes were as hard as stones and filled with a promise of dreadful violence. Sam froze.

The staff officer fingered the weapon's rusty hoops, clear evidence that the pistol had not been fired in months. He smiled. "Dangerous men, these Yankees." He threw the broken toy far into the undergrowth. "One armed rebel," he said, thus finishing the matter.

"Just good shooting," Elliott beamed. "And alert picquets, wouldn't you say?"

"I'd say you're off the hook, Elliott. I'll tell the General." The staff officer wheeled his horse and spurred away. The hooves made small, bright fountains from the wet grass.

There was a murmur of relieved laughter from the ring of men, then Elliott nodded at Scammell. "Bury him before his bloody mother finds him. And well done, Sergeant."

"Thank you, sir."

Later, after the boy had been tipped into a shallow grave at the trees' edge, Nate shook his head. "You're a bastard, Sam. He was a kid, and you know it!"

"And it was our word against Scammy's, and Derrick's, and the Colonel's! You might want a skinned back, Nate, but I don't!"

"It was murder," Nate said. "Murder." He stared almost in horror at his twin brother. "You could go home and tell mother what happened? Could you? You could boast about that?"

"Don't be so bloody daft!" But Sam was troubled. After the boy had been buried and his grave had been disguised with year-old leaf mould, Sam had seen Scammell putting coins into Derrick's hand. He knew murder had been done and that an innocent was dead, but this was the army and Nate's squeamishness would win no wars. Yet his brother was right, and Sam knew it, and he wondered why right and wrong became as blurred as the mist which still lingered on the pastures. "I'm sorry," he said finally and with undisguised misery.

Nate put his arm on Sam's shoulder. For the first time ever it seemed as if Nate were the stronger of the two brothers. "You want to get out, Sam," Nate's voice was troubled, "before they change you."

"I'm not changing."

"You'll be like Scammy," Nate said. "You've got to get out, Sam, before they twist you. Come with Maggie and me."

But Sam did not respond, for there was nothing to be said and nothing to be done. Because he was a Redcoat.

EIGHT

The British were coming. It was certain now. George Washington's army, attempting to stay between the Redcoats and Philadelphia, had been outmanoeuvred and left adrift, so nothing now stood between the city and the British. Indeed a message had already come, brought by the first Redcoat to appear in the streets, which requested the citizens of Philadelphia to stay within their doors while the troops arrived. The message, sent by the British Commander-in-Chief, had only increased alarm among the ladies of the city. If General Howe warned honest folk to stay indoors, then surely the danger must be dreadful?

The preceding twenty-four hours had been truly fearful. There were rumours that arsonists equipped with barrels of tar and other incendiaries had been infiltrated into the city. When the British came, it was said, Philadelphia would be torched, thus preserving the pride of the rebellious Americans who could then claim their capital had not been taken.

To prevent the arson, Loyalists had formed watch-parties and searched the city. Abel Becket and Ezra Woollard had led one such group, probing into the dark, empty corners of the warehouses behind Water Street, then breaking into the vacated houses of the Patriots to make certain that no incendiarist lurked in the cellars. Neither an arsonist nor a tar barrel had been found, but in the night two drunken men had boasted they had tinder and steels ready, and so the rum-soaked pair had been locked in the New Jail on Walnut Street.

The morning of the British arrival dawned cloudy and wet, but rifts appeared in the clouds, sunlight shone across the river, and the Loyalists interpreted the clearing rain as a symbol of hope. The crowds, despite the request that citizens should remain indoors, gathered early, stretching from the Northern Liberties to the city's centre. The British, it was clear, would be welcomed to the rebel capital not by a handful of stubborn Loyalists but by crowds that would number in the thousands.

Jersey Loyalists crossed the river by ferry, and across their path went a shallop with a single girl at its helm. Caroline Fisher also went to Philadelphia, though not to cheer. A weak sunlight cast long shadows as she moored the shallop and climbed to the wharf. The wharf-master who usually guarded her craft was missing, evidently gone to join the crowds pressing towards Second Street. To avoid the crush Caroline went south along the quays, then cut into the city along the narrow path by Dock Creek.

"Hey!" The voice came from behind her. Caroline, who was used to being accosted, ignored it. "Caroline!" The call was more peremptory this time, and was followed by pounding footsteps that made her turn to face her pursuer.

It was Ezra Woollard, grinning and heavy, and dressed in clothes so ill cut that he might have been a Quaker. He slowed, still grinning. "Come to see the Redcoats?"

Caroline's face showed the disgust she felt for her former suitor. "There was a time when you'd have shot at them, Ezra."

"Maybe I still would." Woollard was breathing heavily from his pursuit of Caroline. "But there's more to a man's loyalty than what you see on his face." If Woollard hoped to pique Caroline's curiosity by coyness, he failed, for she showed no interest in pursuing his hint. Woollard offered her a quick smile. "Been a long time, girl."

"I hadn't been counting the days."

"You wouldn't, would you? Been too busy with Master Jonathon, haven't you?" Woollard laughed to see the flicker of anger which rewarded his words. "He came to see you last Sabbath, didn't he?"

"I don't have to tell you – '

"Come on, girl!" Woollard interrupted her, "I heard from Davie Logan! The cripple crossed the river twice, and where the hell else would he be going? So where's he gone now?"

Caroline was hatless and her hair was bright in the dank shadow of the warehouse that edged the creek. She glanced sideways, but Woollard's closeness had trapped her against the brick wall. She looked defiantly into his face. "He went to deliver your message to the British, Ezra. All your careful plans. I know what your loyalty is."

"You know nothing, girl." Woollard betrayed neither surprise nor dismay that Caroline should know of his treachery. Instead, stepping a half pace closer to her, he shook his head. "Jonathon never bloody got to the British, did he?"

"Don't curse to me, Ezra."

"Don't lecture me, girl!" There was no trace now of the obsequious subservience with which Woollard treated Abel Becket. Woollard was a hard man, and he was determined to discover what had happened to Jonathon. Five days had passed since the boy had ridden from the city, and in those five days there had been no news of him. Ezra Woollard was certain that, had Jonathon ridden to the British army as his uncle had ordered him, some news would have come to the city by now and so, with Jonathon's whereabouts still a mystery, Woollard had followed Caroline to snatch this chance of discovering the truth. "He's gone to General Washington, hasn't he?"

"What is it to you, Ezra?"

Woollard smiled. "If he's gone, then there's a chair to be filled, isn't there? His uncle's getting on, ain't the young man he used to be. So if it isn't to be Jonathon, who knows?" He let the question linger. "Tell me where he is."

"I told you where he went." Caroline twisted away from the big man, but Woollard reached out and plucked her back. This morning Abel Becket, with other prominent merchants, was waiting to surrender the State House to the British, and Woollard would have liked to take some firm news to his employer. He wanted to tell Abel Becket that Jonathon had forfeited his share of the business, but Caroline, whom Woollard was certain knew the truth, was contemptuous and defiant.

Woollard pinned her against the wall with his left hand, while his right threatened to strike her face. Water lapped in the creek behind him, carrying its stinking load of ordure between the muddy margins that were littered with dead rats. "I want to know where he is, and you know. So you tell me, girl, or I'll have you in front of the magistrates this morning and we'll see how you like a taste of the Correction House."

"The Correction House!" Caroline was scornful.

"I've got some Hambro Line missing from the warehouse. I might just discover it on your boat! Who are they going to believe? You or me?"

Caroline pushed against his rigid left arm, then, in sudden

submission, she leaned on the wall and sighed. "Do you really think someone as badly crippled as Jonathon can fight?"

Woollard frowned. "So if he ain't with the rebel army, girl, where is he?"

Caroline shrugged in resignation. "He went to Frankfort."

"Frankfort?" Woollard's surprise turned into a sudden gasp as a slice of pain shot through his left arm. The arm, stung as if by fire, jerked back and Caroline slashed with her knife again, this time towards his eyes and Ezra Woollard ducked and twisted away from the blade. It was then that Caroline, unable to resist the temptation, pushed him with her left hand and watched as he teetered, arms flailing, then fell, bellowing, into the fetid mud of the creek. Water spewed up, Woollard's hat fell off, and the girl's mocking laughter echoed from the high dark walls.

Caroline did not wait. She crossed the drawbridge over Front Street, then turned up past the City Tavern bedecked with bunting to welcome the Redcoats. The crowds, whom she had tried to avoid, blocked her path still, and now, far away, she could hear a sudden thumping in the air; a rhythmic, pounding sound that punched at the sky. Thin over the thumping came the sound of instruments. It was a band playing "God Save the King".

Caroline glanced behind her, fearing the apparition of a mud-drenched pursuer, but there was no sign of Ezra Woollard. She laughed at the memory of his flailing fall, then tried to push between the people who stood thick on the pavements by Christ Church.

"Get back, girl," someone growled. Then the street erupted into a huge cheer and Caroline, sidling through the press of bodies, saw the first horsemen riding by. They were all Americans; Philadelphians who had ridden to guide the British home.

For the British had come at last. They thumped and strutted their bright way between the houses, and were cheered for their arrival. Bands played, officers' horses caracoled elegantly, while their riders doffed plumed hats towards the prettier women. When one officer, more handsome than the rest, bowed towards a fair-haired beauty leaning from an upper window, the crowd erupted into cheers and laughter. "God save the King!" someone called aloud, and the cry was taken up along the whole of Second Street, gaudy with British flags. A general, looped with golden aiguillettes, rode amidst his aides. His name was whispered along the pavement. It was Lord Cornwallis, sent by Sir William Howe to take possession of the city. Caroline thought he rode like an insolent conqueror into an enemy capital.

The thronged pavements went silent a moment later as a company of Grenadiers goosestepped past. At their head, pacing magnificently, a sergeant led a black bear on a silver chain. At times, prodded by its keeper, the bear reared hugely on its back paws and flailed the air. Behind their prancing mascot the soldiers were helmeted in mitred shakos faced with brass, while their faces had huge, thick moustaches that were waxed into upturned tips. They had silver buttons on yellow waistcoats and silver cords hanging from the shoulders of their dark blue jackets. Short golden-hilted swords hung from white leather straps by their hips. Their muskets had scarlet slings and fittings of gleaming brass. Meaty white-breeched thighs rose in the grotesque march before the gaitered boots slapped down into the mud.

"Hessians!" a voice near Caroline said, and the hiss went through the crowd. The Hessians seemed so demonic. Behind them came a Hessian band playing a doom-laden march. Caroline, appalled by the sight of such men, tried to console herself with the memory of the Hessian prisoners, taken from Trenton last Christmas, but even that could not take away the fearfulness of these moustached veterans who seemed so huge and magnificent and capable. Their tread seemed to shiver the very street, and Caroline thought with despair of the volunteers who made up General Washington's army. What chance did Jonathon have against these automatons? For Jonathon had volunteered, and was now in the rebellion's service. The letter Caroline carried had confirmed it.

Behind the Hessians, mounted on mud-flecked horses, came a troop of the Queen's Rangers, American Loyalists all, dressed in their plain green Hussar uniform with their black plumes and cresset badges. Many had relatives in the crowd and they laughed, waved, and blew kisses towards the women.

A louder cheer greeted a group of British cavalry officers dressed in fur-edged pelisses, embroidered sabretaches, and loops and buttons and froggings of brightest gold, and even Caroline reluctantly thought she had never seen anything so splendid in all her life.

"God save the King!" the woman in the window called aloud, and again the cry echoed through the city to startle pigeons up from the shingled roofs.

Caroline remembered how, just weeks before, the crowds had cheered General Washington's army when it marched through the city to give battle to these men. Now, though, it seemed the cheers were louder, and the thought shamed her. She edged away, as if she could blot this procession from her mind, but a jangling, rumbling, and thunderous sound made her turn back to watch again. The great guns were passing, deadly machines of brass and wood and iron, with vast blurring wheels that spewed mud high into the air, and with carriages hung with dangling buckets and coiled chains. The mouths of the cannons were stained a deep, ragged black; evidence that these machines had fired and, Caroline presumed, killed. She felt a sudden despair for Jonathon. How could such a gentle boy live in a world where these guns ruled? Yet she also felt a surge of pride in him, so much so that, to her surprise, the tears welled up in her eyes.

Then gasps sounded from Caroline's right, and she looked, expecting some new marvel of the British army, but instead found herself staring at the first true horror of the day. The camp followers had come, and the crowds fell into a silence as they understood for the first time just what guests were being fetched into their city.

Women with insolent eyes stalked beside wagons heaped with grimy bundles. Grinning, filthy children eyed the crowd. A toothless hag riding a wagon cackled towards the well-dressed spectators. One woman had a baby at her bare breast, while another woman, fat as a barrel of salt cod, waddled hugely down the centre of Second Street and, in mockery of the officers ahead, waved at the onlookers. She had a goat tied to her belt, while behind her, like some parody of the days before the flood, a ragged flock of cattle, goats, sheep, and razor-backed hogs was herded by urchins with long staves. A woman with bleeding sores on her face limped behind, and next to her a laughing Negress who had none of the subservience a Philadelphian would expect of the servant race. It was a circus of beggars come to town, the effluent of the slums parading like conquerors. The women were guarded by Redcoats who marched at intervals on either side of the convoy, but every watcher in the street wondered what would happen when this rabble was released upon Philadelphia's kindly streets.

It was only when the camp followers had gone, and the sound of the bands was fading down Chestnut Street, that Caroline could cross the road and run down Market Street. She twisted into an alley, let herself into a backyard, and thence down a flight of stone stairs to a basement kitchen where Jenny, Martha's black maid, looked surprised to see her. "It's not market day, Miss Caroline!"

Caroline opened her bag and brought out a crumpled and sealed letter. "That's for Mrs Crowl, Jenny. It's important."

Jenny wiped her hands on her apron. "What a day! You heard the din of the soldiers? Thumping away!"

"I watched them march in."

"It'll break the mistress's heart." Jenny took the letter. "You want to wait, Miss Fisher? There's tea in that pot."

Caroline waited as Jenny took the letter upstairs, then, to Caroline's surprise, the black woman returned to say that Mrs Crowl would like to see her in the upstairs parlour. "It's up the stairs and first door you see," Jenny said. Then, seeing Caroline's nervousness, she offered an explanation, "She'll be glad of company on a day like this."

But when Caroline reached the elegant and beautifully furnished parlour, she found that the Widow Crowl already had company in the form of the Revd Donald MacTeague who, teacup in podgy hands, turned in some astonishment as Caroline arrived. Such girls, he thought, should not be invited into the parlours of society, but Martha Crowl had ever favoured flamboyant behaviour, and the Revd MacTeague was too much of a gentleman to make any comment. He stood, gently disposing of the six-year-old Lydia who had been trying to crawl on to his lap. "It's Miss Fisher, is it not?"

"Indeed, sir."

"I have enjoyed your grandmother's most excellent pies, indeed I have. You watched the arrival of the legions?"

"I did."

"Such a happy day! Such a happy day!" MacTeague sat again, then tilted the teacup to drain its dregs. He smiled benevolently at the ragged girl who, he guiltily thought, was rather beautiful in a hoydenish sort of way. "I thought I would offer my protection to the Widow Crowl." He thus explained his presence to Caroline, then bowed to Martha, who, in a wide-skirted dress of lilac silk, sat in the window with the unopened letter beside her. Martha's black hair was piled elegantly, and decorated with silken bows. She looked calmly fashionable, dressed as if for a ball rather than in mourning for a city lost.

"The Revd MacTeague," Martha said drily, "is concerned that I might be killed by the vengeful British. In which case he would lose my pew-rent."

"You jest, dear lady!" MacTeague was pained. "I come on a Christian duty, nothing more!"

Lydia was standing by a window and now turned excitedly to her mother. "Is that a lobster?"

"Yes, my dear. They're best boiled." Martha stared at a lone red-coated soldier who wandered down the far pavement and stared in awe at the high houses of stone and brick. Martha sighed. "It must have been like this when the Goths descended upon Rome. Or was it the Vandals? The Huns, perhaps?"

"On the contrary." MacTeague had placed his cup upside down on its saucer; the polite indication that he wished for no more refreshment. "This day more closely resembles the retaking of Rome from the barbarians. It is the restoration of lawful authority and I rejoice in it."

"More lobsters." Lydia was delighted with the word. "We have to boil the lobsters."

MacTeague offered a pained smile, while Caroline, made nervous by the elegance of the room and the presence of the unctuous priest, hovered nervously by the door. Martha, however, with what Caroline thought was a peremptory gesture, indicated that she should sit on the sofa beside the hearth.

"So!" said MacTeague, trying hard to keep up the flagging conversation and looking at Caroline, "you ignored the warning to stay indoors, Miss Fisher?"

"Yes, sir."

"An egregious warning, I thought, though doubtless kindly meant. We are in no danger from our friends, and certainly a fatherless child and a widowed gentlewoman have nothing to fear!" He raised a hand in vague blessing over Lydia's head.

"There weren't many of them," Caroline blurted out.

"Many of whom, child?" MacTeague asked.

"British. Hessians."

MacTeague smiled. "They haven't sent their full power, dear me, no! Most of the army remains at Germantown, I'm told. Mister Washington is loitering to the north so Sir William awaits to do battle there. Our prayers will support him."

"Yours might," Martha said, "but not mine."

"Dear Mrs Crowl," the priest murmured, then twisted in his

chair to look down into the street where an elegant group of officers strolled as unconcernedly as though walking down London's Strand, 'it seems we are not in any danger. May I assume that my protective duties have been adequately discharged?"

Martha smiled gratefully. "Most honourably discharged, sir."

MacTeague stood. "We may disagree about earthly things, dear lady, but about the more important matters, I trust, never." He bowed to Martha, then, less formally, to Caroline. "If you need me, then summon me! Good day, ladies."

"He wants," Martha said when the priest was gone, "to ingratiate himself with our conquerors. I think MacTeague fancies himself to be the first Bishop of Philadelphia." Martha spoke scornfully, then critically examined Caroline who, till now, she had only glimpsed delivering vegetables and fruit to the kitchen downstairs. The widow's face betrayed neither approval nor condemnation; instead, looking away, she picked up the letter. "I presume, from the handwriting, that it's from Jonathon?"

"Yes, ma'am. It came this morning."

Martha slit the letter open with an ivory-handled knife, then unfolded the crumpled paper. She seemed to take a long time reading her brother's words.

Caroline waited. Lydia, bored with watching the strangely dressed men in the streets, crossed the room and stared solemnly into Caroline's face. Caroline smiled nervously, and the invitation was sufficient to make Lydia climb on to the sofa.

Martha laid the letter down. "Did Jonathon write to you as well?"

"Yes, ma'am."

Martha sighed. "He shouldn't have volunteered."

"No."

"It isn't as if there aren't enough two-legged men in America to fight without Jonathon being sacrificed!" The words were said angrily, but, immediately they were spoken, Martha shook her head in rueful sadness. "However, I suppose I'm proud of him."

"I think you should be," Caroline said defiantly.

"Uncle Jonathon?" Lydia had heard the name and now sought news of her missing uncle.

"He's become a soldier, dear," Martha explained. The letter said that Jonathon had been appointed an aide-de-camp to a cavalry commander called Colonel Jackson Weller. Jonathon explained in the letter that the appointment was not due to any virtue inherent in himself, but rather because he had brought the rebel army a good horse, saddle, and bridle. Martha tried to explain to Lydia what an aide-de-camp was, then, failing, ordered the child to go down to Jenny in the kitchen. "I have to talk to Miss Fisher, my dear."

After Lydia left, Caroline felt even more nervous. Martha picked up the letter once more. "Jonathon says he's going to marry you."

Martha's voice had been cold. "Yes, ma'am."

"If he is," Martha said with a flash of annoyance, "then for the Lord's sake stop calling me ma'am. You make me sound ancient!"

"I'm sorry."

"Forgiven." Martha again examined Caroline. "I must say my poor brother has an eye for a certain sort of beauty. Do you want to marry him?"

Caroline shrugged. "I said I'd wait for him."

"Which doesn't answer my question." Martha stood and, in a susurration of silk, crossed the floor to stand close to the sofa. "Are you going to marry him?"

Caroline felt offended by the questioning, and was driven to a sulky defensiveness. "I know his family doesn't wish for that."

Martha seemed amused. "Why on earth should you think that?"

Caroline gestured at her thick, heavy skirts and plucked at her blue ticken jacket. Compared with the luxury of the room and the lavishness of Martha's clothes, she felt poor and negligible, and her gestures spoke it all without needing words to point the contrast.

Martha turned away from the girl. "My husband's family disapproved of me, most strongly. I was not wealthy enough, though God knows I brought him a large enough portion. They wanted Thomas to marry some spineless child from Virginia who'd have brought him eight thousand acres of tobacco land. They'd have preferred an English bride, I suspect, with English land, but they were willing to compromise for the lesser reward. But they were not happy with me. I was definitely shoddy goods."

Caroline was not certain why she was being told the story. "But your husband defied his parents?"

"Clearly he did." Martha said it a little too sharply, then shrugged. "I'm not sure he was very wise, for we were not well suited. I was too self-willed for him. I suspect you're self-willed?"

Caroline made no answer, and Martha, who had crossed to the window again, turned to look at her. "But I married Thomas for his money. I wanted to be rich, you see. I never wanted to be thought shoddy again. Is that why you want to marry Jonathon?"

"He wants to marry me."

"And Jonathon has a way of getting what he wants. It's the leg. He uses it to blackmail the world." Martha laughed softly. "He'll be very uncomfortable as a soldier."

Caroline was nonplussed by the sudden change of subject. "I'm sure."

"He's rather like me in some ways," Martha went on as though Caroline had not spoken. "He likes his comfort. He's been used to it, you see, and I suppose he deserves it because it can't be easy dragging that lumpen foot about. I can't see him giving up the city for the farmer's life, can you?"

"No."

"And you look, if you'll forgive me, unsuited to the city?"

Caroline thought she would rather face Ezra Woollard in a stinking alley with a knife in her hand than face this needling examination. She was determined to bring it to an end with bluntness. "You're saying we shouldn't marry?"

"I would never be so impertinent!" Martha said, quite forgetting that she had told her brother exactly that. "You marry whom you wish, and Jonathon will marry whomsoever he wishes. I don't believe in liberty, Miss Fisher, just to deny it to my brother. But I've been a kind of mother to Jonathon since the day he was born, so can I be forgiven some slight curiosity as to the girl he wishes to make my sister-in-law?"

"Yes." Caroline was confused and miserable. She felt she was being blamed for a proposed marriage that was pursued with far more enthusiasm by Martha's brother than by herself.

Martha had turned to stare haughtily down at a mounted British officer who talked with a girl on the opposite pavement. "I don't oppose your marriage," she said in an oddly strained voice, "because if I do I might lose Jonathon. Isn't that so?"

"I don't know." Caroline decided the acceptance, though grudging, was better than opposition.

"And I have yet another reason for desiring your friendship." Martha still stared down at the officer who flirted with the girl. "I imagine that it will be hard to send letters to men in General

Washington's army now that the Revd MacTeague's friends have arrived?"

It was another confusing tack in the conversation, but one Caroline felt far more able to cope with. "I would think so."

Martha turned. "But you live across the river, so you can do it safely?"

"I would think so, yes. So long as the British don't garrison Cooper's Point."

"Why should they?" Martha, with a true Philadelphian's arrogance, implied there was nothing worth capturing in New Jersey. "Can you send more than letters?"

Caroline frowned. "More than?"

Martha paused, then explained. "I'm asking whether you could send information to General Washington's army. Information that I might hear and would wish to pass on."

For the first time since she had entered the room, Caroline smiled. "I'd be proud to do that."

"That's why I stayed in the city. Oh, I wanted to protect these things!" Martha waved a negligent hand at the silverware and gilded mirrors and varnished paintings. "But I can do more for our cause by sending news out of the city than I ever could by fleeing from it. And you can help me."

"I'd like to," Caroline said.

"Then, dear Caroline, you must consider yourself as a welcome guest in this house. You are, after all, my prospective sister-in-law." Martha smiled and held out both hands towards Caroline, who, quite flummoxed by this last sudden change in Mrs Crowl's demeanour, hesitantly stood and crossed the room. Martha, to Caroline's astonishment, kissed her. "Don't make him unhappy." The words were whispered fiercely.

"I won't."

"And I won't be your enemy." Martha drew Caroline to the window. "For we have enemies enough in the city now, without quarrelling amongst ourselves." Martha stared down at the British officer and tears ran down her face. She cried because the enemy had truly come and the future suddenly seemed so bleak.

"It's the shame of it," she explained her tears, "the shame of it." Because Philadelphia, without a shot being fired in her defence by its citizens who had, indeed, welcomed their conquerors with a fawning adulation, had fallen.

NINE

Captain John Andre, an elegant and fastidious man, stood in the window of the farmhouse that had been sequestered as Sir William Howe's Germantown headquarters. He was watching the red-coated infantry camped in the pastures nearest to the house; men who, in their search for firewood and comfort, had wrought such sad destruction on what had once been a lovely orchard. Andre thought what a plague such soldiers were; a contagion of evil, twisted, squat dwarves; the hopeless, the failures, the dregs, the creatures no one else wanted; a tribe of toothless, poxed men with their lumpen, cackling women and their filthy, sly-eyed children. King George's army. "Soldiers," he said abruptly, "are such graceless creatures."

Christopher Vane, working at a table, smiled. "Did you join the army to remedy that, John?"

"I joined the army because I was disappointed in love. Most of us do. We're an army of the damned led by jilted lovers." Andre turned towards the tallboy where Sir William's decanters were kept. On his way he gave a glance of mock horror at Vane's industriousness. "Do you have to work so hard, Kit? You make the rest of us seem positively idle."

Vane smiled, but said nothing. He sometimes perceived the other aides as nothing but lounging praetorians, elegant and privileged, all-knowing and supercilious, but it was an opinion he took care to hide lest it soured his determination to prove himself worthy of the kindness that Sir William had shown him. Even now, two weeks after his sudden promotion, Vane could be startled awake by the sheer pleasure of his new captaincy and, as recompense to his patron, no aide worked harder than Vane in these dull, cold dog-days of early autumn; days in which Vane discovered that, as an aide to a commander-in-chief, he could command other men's respect. Colonels of regiments who, just weeks before, would have disdained Vane's acquaintance, now sought him out because he could secure them favours from the General.

The troops, like most of the aides, idled. Lord Cornwallis, the Second-in-Command, had been sent to occupy Philadelphia with a small force, while the main army camped around Germantown to guard the approaches to the city. It was believed that George Washington, smarting under the loss of the rebel capital, might attempt to recapture the city, though many in the army believed, like John Andre, that Washington would do nothing. "Why should he? All he has to do is name another city as the rebel capital. Philadelphia counts for nothing!"

"America's largest city?" Vane suggested in mild disagreement.

"It's a smaller town than Bristol," Andre said scornfully, "with far too many churches and a paucity of taverns, despite which my hosts insisted that it was the New Jerusalem. It seemed impolite to disabuse them."

"You've been there?" Vane was surprised.

"Before the fighting, yes. Billy has great hopes for it, but for the life of me I can't see why the rebels should lose heart just because we've taken Philadelphia." Andre, having poured himself a glass of rum, looked over Vane's shoulder and showed immediate alarm because Vane was working through the commissary accounts, a record of all the headquarters' expenditures for horses, food, lodgings and necessaries. "For God's sake," Andre said, "don't be too efficient."

"Because Sir William's stealing money?" Vane smiled. "I suppose every general does it, and all I'm doing is hiding it a little more efficiently."

"Good God," Andre stared with grudging admiration at Vane. "You are ambitious!"

"Is there anything wrong with that?"

"One should never admit to it."

Vane shrugged. "My father lost most of his money before he died, my family is sliding into obscurity, so my only hopes of advancement lie in working hard." He regretted the words as soon as they were spoken, feeling that they revealed his naked self to a man who might be a rival. In truth, Andre, a frequent visitor to Sir William's headquarters, was the friendliest of all the elegant young men who inhabited Vane's new world. It was Andre who had taught Vane that Sir William's nickname was Billy, and who now explained that Billy needed the extra money for his expensive American mistress. "Lizzie will be here as soon as the city's safe, and then you'll hardly see Billy at all. He's besotted."

"Is she pretty?"

"More beautiful than an angel. Intelligent, too, which is a most unfair conjunction. Her husband's been fobbed off with a job in New York."

"Is Billy married?"

Andre wondered if he detected a prudish note in Vane's question. "Not so long as he's in America."

"Ah." Vane closed the account books as footsteps sounded in the passageway outside. It was dusk, a time when the aides, after recovering from their languid dinner, liked to gather in contemplation of supper. All except Vane were bored, fretted by the necessity to linger in the countryside while the urban delights of Philadelphia were so close. Lord Robert Massedene, heading straight for the decanters, first pronounced his blessing on the room, then offered Vane a glass of claret. "I went to see your new horse, Vane. Very impressive."

"He's fast." Vane's duties demanded two horses, and so he had borrowed money to buy a magnificent black stallion with three white socks and a white blaze. Vane had also borrowed money to buy his new uniform complete with its golden aiguillettes.

"I'm sure he's fast," Massedene allowed, "but a little young, perhaps?"

Vane felt immediately defensive as though, in criticizing the stallion, Massedene was attacking Vane himself. "Young?"

"He ain't nagged properly, not for battle," Massedene said firmly. "One cannon shot, Vane, and that stallion will get the shivers. Cling to your old mare in battle, and find a good man to nag the stallion. Just a word of advice."

It was a word of advice that irritated Vane, an irritation that was made more acute by his knowledge that Massedene was right. The stallion was a nervous beast that Vane had no intention of riding in battle until it was properly trained, and thus he found Massedene's assumption of his ignorance to be gratingly patronizing. He disliked Massedene. Vane resented that the younger man should have such an effortless career, fuelled by his noble birth, while Vane, who perceived himself as an abler man, must struggle for advancement.

The dislike was accentuated by their opposing views on almost every aspect of the rebellion. Lord Robert Massedene, like John Andre, only wished to see the rebellion ended, and did not much care how that culmination was achieved, so long as there was peace. Vane, like the Hessian interpreter Zeigler, believed that republican sentiment in America could only be stamped out by a military victory.

It was an argument that continued at that night's supper. Major Zeigler, coming late to the table, reported to Sir William that a schoolmaster from one of the Pennsylvanian German settlements had come to the Hessian lines and reported that the rebel army was planning to attack the following morning. They would march through the night, the schoolmaster had said, and attack at dawn. Lord Robert Massedene airily dismissed the man's claim. "Washington won't dare attack us. One more licking and his men will desert in their thousands!"

"I think you're wrong." Vane rather surprised himself by offering the contradiction. So far he had been a listener rather than a partaker in such discussions.

Massedene waited with a decanter of port poised in his hand, then shrugged. "Don't leave us in suspense, Vane."

"If our reports are right," Vane struggled to hide his distaste for the pug-nosed Massedene, "the rebel army outnumbers us for the first time. So I think Washington will attack."

"Ah! Reports!" Sir William, presiding over his young men, chuckled. "We had a very reliable report once that the armies of the Lord had been observed descending on a mountaintop in Massachusetts. I believe they had golden wings and carried muskets of jasper? I'm never sure about these reports, Kit."

Vane, uncertain whether he was being rebuked, held his ground stubbornly. "I still believe Mister Washington will attack, sir. He has to win a victory to restore his men's morale."

"As he did at Trenton last year." Andre made the sly dig at Otto Zeigler who, like all Hessians, still smarted at the memory of that Hessian defeat.

"They surprised us!" Zeigler said defensively. "We were drunk. Every German is drunk at Christmas."

Sir William smiled. "At least he can't surprise us here." Sir William made the statement with a satisfaction born of his precautions. He had doubled the army's picquets and, thanks to the happy arrival of three convoys of ammunition, those picquets could now blaze into the night with impunity. Sir William, thus comforted, fondled his dog's ears.

John Andre trimmed a candlestick. "I hate to disagree with you, sir, but I think Mister Washington has to attack. *Pour encourager les crapauds.*"

"Whenever you drop into French, John, I suspect you of spiflication," Sir William said.

"He'll fight, sir, to draw the French into the war."

Sir William shook his head. "I don't deny that the French would like to embarrass us, John, but why should King Louis encourage republicanism?"

"And why would the French risk another whipping?" Zeigler asked.

"Because the French have short memories," Andre said happily. "Every defeat only encourages them to believe in their own invincibility. It's a trait they share with Mister Washington."

There were appreciative smiles, then Zeigler opined that the French would not enter the war unless it was already won for them, and the rebels stood no chance of winning. They had no capital and soon General Burgoyne would slice New England away from the rest of the colonies and the rebellion would wither on the vine.

"But the mere threat of French intervention," Andre said, "might persuade London of the need to make peace."

"Or victory," Vane said.

"Just peace." Sir William smiled at Vane. "We can't win a military victory, Kit. Everyone recognizes that. The army's only here to force the rebels to the negotiating table."

Vane looked in astonishment at Sir William. "We can't beat them, sir?"

"Don't sound so forlorn! Of course we can't! My dear Kit, we had to abandon Boston to find the forces to take Philadelphia. It takes five thousand men to garrison a city and another five thousand to scour the countryside about that city for food, so we only have sufficient men to hold three cities, perhaps four, in all this gaping wilderness. Then we have to garrison Canada and the Floridas. Dear me, no. It would take a hundred thousand men to defeat the rebellion, and who'll pay for that, eh? You think the House of Commons will vote the taxes? I assure you they will not, at least not as long as I'm a member of the House!"

Sir William's other aides smiled at the shock on Vane's face. "So you see, Kit," Andre leaned across the table to pour Vane more port, "the colonists, if they did but realize it, can get everything they want at the negotiating table."

"Except their independence," Massedene added.

Sir William still watched Vane. "My dear Kit, I fear you'll have to accept the mathematical logic of war. Our army is too small to take a continent."

"War can't be about mathematics, sir." Vane, piqued by the defeatism he heard and perhaps emboldened by the port which circled the table so freely, was suddenly fervent. "It's about men and morale and weather and spirit! God, sir, we're British! We're the best goddamned pirates the world ever saw, and we're worrying about the French? About a nation of dancing masters? Or about the colonists' sensibilities? There would be no colonies without us. The colonists are like children squawling at their nurse!"

"Hear, hear!" Zeigler broke the embarrassed silence that followed Vane's impassioned words. "Break some heads and make some orphans. That'll empty their damned bellies of spleen."

There was laughter at such Germanic bombast, then Sir William wondered whether Mister Washington had similarly belligerent advisers, and Zeigler demanded that the schoolmaster's report be taken seriously, and Massedene reminded Sir William that a butcher had brought in a similar tale two days before which had turned out to be false, and Sir William ended the discussion by stating his firm belief that, if the rebel army were marching to the attack, the cavalry patrols would discover it. "So we shall ignore a schoolmaster's tittle-tattle," Sir William suggested, "and play a hand of whist instead."

More port was opened, the cards broken out, and the candles guttered down to smoking stumps before Vane stumbled up the stairs to the linen store that he shared with Major Zeigler as a bedroom. A stomach ache woke Vane just before dawn and drove him into the garden where he squatted by a quince tree that was wreathed in a new and thickening fog. The whiteness sifted by the house, mingling with the greyness of dawn to hide the chimney pots. A cook whistled in the kitchens, and from the side path came the homely clanging of water pails.

"Sir! Sir! Are you there, sir?" It was Vane's servant, Private Smithers, who liked his privileged new life as a headquarters' servant.

"Quiet, you rogue! I'm dying." It occurred to Vane that the morning was quiet, at least of musket fire. God damn all schoolmasters.

"Eggs, sir?" Smithers, coming from the house, grinned down at his master. "Two eggs for breakfast, sir? Bought them off the gunners."

"Who stole them, you fool, but I thank you anyway." Christopher Vane, who was partial to fried eggs, overcame his initial liquor-induced revulsion. "Fry them and I might be restored to life."

A rattle of musketry, muffled by the whiteness, sounded from the north. It was hard to tell how far away the gunfire was, but it faded after a few seconds and Vane assumed that the picquets had merely cleaned out their musket barrels by the quickest expedient. He stood, buttoned his breeches, and groaned as a pang of agony lanced through his head. He was remembering the interminable bottles of port of the previous evening, wondering if he would ever learn moderation.

Sir William's servant appeared in the garden with a full chamberpot. "Good morning, sir!"

Vane, knowing that to be greeted so cheerfully by Tom Evans was a sign of acceptance in Sir William's military family, groaned dramatically. "It's a foul morning, Evans."

"Be all right with a tot of rum inside you, sir." Tom Evans tossed the pot's contents on to the lawn, then frowned as another fusillade muttered and cracked. "They're a bit frisky this morning?"

"It's the fog. It unsettles people."

Hamlet, Sir William's dog, came wagging into the swirling mist, barked for Vane's attention, then happily went off to explore the new smells around the once-pretty garden.

Vane bent to the pump and splashed his face with water. The musketry died, then splintered again, this time reaching a crescendo of noise that was sustained like thunder. Vane stood, water dripping from his face, and stared helplessly northwards into the fog. He could scarce see the shapes of trees thirty yards away.

"Kit! Kit!" Sir William's voice called from an upstairs window.

"Sir!" Vane ran into the house. "Smithers! Smithers! Leave the eggs. Saddle the mare!" He raced upstairs, buttoned his jacket and buckled on his sword. He could not find his pistol and cursed as he searched among the fallen blankets, but finally found the weapon inside a spare boot. Otto Zeigler gaped from his tangled blankets on the floor. "What's happening?"

"Either the picquets have gone mad or it's an attack. My hat? Oh God, oh fuck! My hat!"

"Here." Zeigler had been using it as a pillow.

Vane seized the hat, threw himself through the door and collided with Sir William who was still buckling on a sword as he made his way to the stairs. A messenger, smeared with mud, had already found the General who, oddly calm in the panicked atmosphere, checked Vane's haste with a raised hand. "Go to the Beggarstown outpost, Kit. Find out what's happening. I'll join you there."

"Yes, sir."

Smithers was still tightening the girth of Vane's mare. He cupped his hands for his master to use as a mounting stirrup. "Orders, sir?"

"I'm going to Beggarstown. Bring me some food if you can."

Lord Robert, jacket unbuttoned and hat in his hand, ran towards the stables. "You were right!" he shouted, but Vane had no time to reply. Instead, he raked his heels back and turned his horse's head towards the long, poplar-edged drive. The mare's hooves spattered great gobs of mud from the road as Vane scattered troopers from his path.

He sawed on the reins at the Skippack Road and spurred northwards. The market place milled with confused troops, none accoutred for battle, and Vane shouted at them to get out of his way as he headed up the main street in the ever-thickening fog.

He galloped past the Chew House, the northern limit of the British billets, then spurred on towards the incessant crackle of musket fire that came from the heavy picquet line. He felt for the watch in his waistcoat pocket and found it missing. He cursed, but guessed it was around five in the morning. A dog raced out of the Meeting House yard and yapped at his mare's galloping heels, then, sudden and heart-stopping, a musket ball whiplashed from the blind fog to crack past Vane's face. A wounded Redcoat, trailing blood from a shattered thigh, crawled back down the road. The first signs of battle.

Vane galloped past two more wounded men dragging themselves to safety then, dimly to his right, he saw a company of Redcoats formed in front of a grove of trees. He swerved off the road, jumped a flooded ditch, and galloped to the company's rear. The men were in their three ranks, as tightly locked together as the pieces of a child's jigsaw puzzle. "Fire!" their Captain shouted and a volley stabbed smoke and flame into the fog. The skunk stench of burnt powder assailed Vane's nostrils. "What's happening?"

"Rebel skirmishers, sir!" a sergeant at the rear of the company answered. A captain was giving the firing orders, as calmly as though he stood on a parade ground at home. The men, their faces already blackened by the flashing of powder in the lock pans by their faces, bit open new cartridges. They had scraps of red cloth in their hats as marks that this was one of the Light Companies that had taken part in the action at Paoli's Tavern two weeks before.

"What rebels? Where?" Vane's question seemed suddenly superfluous, for a flicker of musket balls slashed into the ranks. A corporal screamed and went down, another man pitched back with a hole in his forehead.

"Close up! Close up!" The sergeant ignored Vane.

"Present!" the captain shouted. "Fire!"

Another British company, beyond the road, was still in skirmish order, the men picking targets in the fog and firing from a kneeling position. Vane wrenched at his reins and spurred his horse back to the road.

The fog was obscuring understanding, and Christopher Vane knew that his job as an aide-de-camp was to help his master comprehend the battle. Thus he went forward towards the enemy and ahead of the foremost British troops. He had no idea if he was supposed to go so far forward, but he was intent on doing all that Sir William had asked and more. Captain Vane, plucked from regimental obscurity, would prove himself to be the best aide that any general could wish for.

He walked the mare forward, always ready to screw the beast around and slash back with his spurs. Foot by nervous foot he advanced, and Vane could feel his horse quivering in apparent fear. Her ears were pricked, reacting to every hissing bullet in the grey, wet fog. Vane wondered if the horse fetched her nervousness from him, but then decided that even to think of the question was proof that he was not afraid. Once more the odd, calm joy of battle, which he had first known at Brandywine, surprised and pleased him. He felt brave, immortal, blessed by a charmed life; but then a sudden swirl of wind lifted the fog and, in the momentary gap, he saw the brown, red-faced uniforms of the rebel army. The enemy troops were in open order, but Vane had an impression, nothing more, of a mass of men further back marching beneath a gaudy banner. There were flecks of white in their hats.

Then dawn's silence gave way to angry noise and flurry. A bullet drove a splash of mud up beside the right shoulder of Vane's horse, and another bullet hissed behind his head as he turned, kicked back, and let his mare gallop him away. Rebel taunts followed him, but Vane had done his job and seen the enemy. He galloped past the British skirmishers and saw a knot of mounted men spurring up the road. They were Sir William's other aides. "The General?" Vane shouted.

"Over there!" A dragoon major pointed towards the company Vane had first visited, and Vane swerved in that direction. The company had shaken into loose order to make itself less of a target, but so much fire was now pouring from the dark, smoke-thickened fog that the men were giving ground and taking cover in the trees.

"Form up! Form up!" Sir William, showing a rare flash of anger, was behind the retreating men. "It's only a scouting force. We don't run from scouts! Form up! Captain! Form your men, if you please, sir! Let me see firmness!"

Sir William saw Vane, waved, then suddenly a cannon ball fired from the rebel front smashed into the branches above the Commander-in-Chief's head. Twigs, leaves, and scraps of wood showered down as Sir William's horse reared and twisted. Another cannon ball tore open a Redcoat's chest, splaying his ribs as clean as if a butcher had used a filleting knife.

"Not a scouting party, sir! They're formed and in force." Vane shouted to Sir William who, smothered in fallen leaves, brought his horse under control. "I saw them, sir. Coming straight down the road!" Musket balls hummed around them, clipping at leaves, hissing, whipcracking, and thumping clean splinters from trunks.

"Back!" Howe shouted it at the man who, a moment before, he had ordered to stand and fight. "Back! Inform your flanks, sir! Form on the Meeting House!"

"You must go, sir!" Vane tried to seize the bridle of Howe's horse, but the General jerked away. He was staring into the dirty, grey, half-light of the fog-shrouded dawn as the Light Company filed hurriedly towards the rear.

"My God, this is rich, Kit!" Howe was oddly elated as he watched the first rebels appear in the fog. Their bayonets were the brightest thing in all the dawn, brighter even than the scraps of white paper they all wore in their hats. Sir William, who liked all things American, was predictably impressed by his enemy. "They come on damned well, Kit, damned well! Don't they look well?"

Vane tried to place himself between the General and the enemy, but Sir William insisted on an uninterrupted view. Vane finally seized the bridle and turned the General's horse by main force. "Back, sir, I do beg you!"

The British outpost line was in full retreat now. The wounded were being dragged towards the village, while the dead were left where they had fallen. On either side of the road, colours high, the rebels advanced with bared bayonets.

Howe let himself be drawn back out of the enemy's sight. "I'll form Musgrave to hold those rogues up! You fall back with these fellows. Keep an eye on the flanks!" Sir William lightly punched Vane's upper arm. "I wish you joy of the day, Kit!"

"And you, sir!"

Sir William smiled and, bearing a charmed life in the bullet-ridden gloom, spurred away with his entourage, passing a single horseman who, riding toward the enemy, smiled in relief when he saw Vane.

"Breakfast, sir?" It was Private Peter Smithers, Vane's servant, who was mounted on Vane's new horse, the young and expensive black stallion with its three white socks and bright white blaze. Smithers held out two slices of bread between which he had put the fried eggs. "Breakfa – " He could not finish the word because a rebel cannon ball, fired blind into the fog, had taken off his head as neatly as if a headsman had swung an axe. One second Smithers was grinning with pleasure, and the next there was a glossy fountain of blood and a stub of white bone amidst the astonishingly scarlet flesh.

Smithers brains spattered across Vane's face as the breakfast fell into the mud. The blood, spurting lower, drenched Vane's white breeches, then the headless corpse thumped on to the mud in which the egg yolks had spilt bright yellow. The nervous young stallion, frightened by the smell and by the crack of bullets, reared high with eyes white and teeth bared.

"Jesus Christ!" Vane stared aghast at his servant's headless trunk. "Peter? Peter?" He had the insane urge to dismount and comfort the dead man, then he looked up to see the stallion bolting into the fog bank. Christopher Vane thought of the money he had borrowed and he turned the mare to follow his terrified stallion, then a rebel shout of triumph, too close behind, made him rake back his heels and turn the mare's head towards safety. Damn and damn and damn. The loss seethed in him, galled him, and was made worse by the thought that a damned rebel might find his expensive stallion. He turned in the saddle as he galloped away, smeared the grey jelly from his eyes, and saw the faces of his enemies' success. They seemed to jeer as they advanced, then a swirl of the drifting vapour closed down once more.

The enemy had come from the fog in the dawn, and between them and Philadelphia was nothing but a bewildered army who had been surprised. Mister Washington had his battle.

TEN

Martha Crowl was woken by the distant crackling of burning thorns punctuated by a deeper percussion that seemed to softly punch the chilly and vaporous air. It was the far-off sound of battle; the thornlike crackling was musketry, and the deeper throbs were artillery. The sound made Martha pull on a woollen robe and run downstairs to the kitchen.

Jenny shook her head. None of the servants had any news, except a stablehand who said he had heard that the British were attacking the river forts.

"Not to the north, they're not," Martha said. "The sound is coming from the north, isn't it?"

She went to her front door, opened it, and saw that her neighbours were also standing on their steps listening to the far-off sound. A troop of cavalry, part of the city's garrison, clattered north on Fifth Street while Redcoats were marching on Fourth; all going towards the sound of the guns and evidence that whatever had happened was alarming enough for Sir William to have summoned help.

Cheered by that thought, Martha went back into the house, dressed, and took breakfast with Lydia, who wished to know if the percussive gunfire meant that the lobsters were being roasted. Martha pretended to misunderstand the question, insisting that Lydia read from her primer instead. The lesson was interrupted by a hammering on the front door, a hammering so insistent that Martha jumped with alarm and wondered if the British had at last come to arrest a prominent Patriot.

Instead it was her uncle, Abel Becket, dressed in his customary black, but with a face made pale by anger. Jenny showed him into the upstairs parlour where, without any greeting, he thrust a letter towards Martha. "Did you know?"

"Good morning, dear uncle. Say good morning, Lydia."

Lydia gave a curtsy. "Good morning, great-uncle."

Abel Becket, faced with the child's courteous innocence, managed a calm response. "Good morning, child. Did you say your prayers?"

"Yes, sir." Lydia, whose black hair was twisted in curling papers, smiled at her great-uncle. "I prayed that the lobsters would be roasted."

"You did what?"

"It doesn't matter," Martha said hastily. "Would you like some tea, uncle?"

Abel Becket refused, instead demanding to speak privately with his niece, then waited impatiently as Jenny was summoned to take Lydia down to the kitchen. "Did you know?" he again asked angrily when the child, clutching books and rag dolls, was gone.

Martha carefully poured herself some tea. She wore a morning dress and a lace-fringed mobcap over her dark hair. She took her time with the strainer and teapot, trying to compose herself, for, though she was not her uncle's responsibility, nor, indeed, had she ever lived beneath Abel Becket's roof, his anger frightened her. "If you mean, did I know about my brother, yes. Has he written to you? I told him he should."

Her calm words seemed to fluster Becket who, the crumpled letter still in his hand, paced to the window which vibrated in sympathy with the guns' hammering. "He may be your brother, girl, but he is no longer my nephew."

Martha shrugged, as if she did not care.

Becket threw the letter across the room. "Read it!"

"I think I know its contents, uncle. Are you sure you won't have tea? The leaves were smuggled past the British blockade so have an added piquancy?"

Becket ignored her provocation. "Jonathon tells me, ma'am, that after prayerful consideration he has no choice but to fight for the traitors! He then suggests that I buy his inheritance and give the proceeds to you!" He paused, as if to underline the outrageousness of the request. "I will not reply, but you may, Martha, you may. You will tell him that he has forfeited his rights, that he is a traitor, and that I will pay no money to traitors. He has no inheritance!"

"The law," Martha said carefully, "may not agree."

"Do you think," her uncle asked passionately, "that the law will forgive a rebel? If he even lives to attempt to secure its forgiveness?"

Martha heard the distress in her uncle's voice. She knew how proud he had been of Jonathon's aptitude for commerce, and knew how hurt he must be by his seeming rejection. "If the rebellion succeeds," she said calmly, "the law may not forgive the Loyalists."

"Succeed!" Abel Becket pounced on the word. "And if it did, Martha, just what kind of country would it breed? Have you ever thought of that? For one moment, in all your heady nonsense, did you ever think what disasters the lawyers would fetch on us?"

"Liberty?" Martha suggested sweetly.

"Liberty!" The word stung Abel Becket into fury. "Were we so unfree before the rebels stirred? How many warehouses has liberty filled? We made money here. Men made fine farms and built good roads and made houses like this! Were you so unfree, my girl, when you moved into this house? It was built by work, not by mouthing fine words. And where will our work be without England? Will France offer us markets? Spain? Must we indenture ourselves to Popish states in the name of liberty?"

Martha wondered what had turned her uncle, who had once been a man of nimble amiability, into a man ridden by faction. She shrugged. "There was a time when you were as fervent for the colonists' rights as any man. You signed the protests, you refused to trade in tea, you marched against the Governor. Yet now you're one of them. I don't understand, truly." Martha spoke gently, but she could have accused him of harsher ills. She could have reminded Abel Becket how, in the years of rebel rule in the city, he had supplied the Continental Army and taken the rebels' money and never once showed the courage that had put other Loyalists into prison for daring to express their views. "Why do you risk ruin for a foreign king?"

Abel Becket stared at his niece as though he doubted her sanity. "You understand nothing," he said finally, "nothing! I protested against restrictions on trade, and I would protest again if it were necessary. But I did not, nor will I ever, fight for some dreamer's madness called independence. Life is commerce. We work to live, to put food on the table and a roof over our heads. We live, we work, and we worship God!" He spoke now with a fervent intensity. "I know more of this world than you. I know the British. There is corruption and sin in London, God knows, but there are also godly men and traders who could buy this city and every city in America besides! Are we to set up as their rivals? Are we, out of jealous men's pique, to defy all authority for that?" He gestured towards the sound of the guns. "Your head's been turned by fools who think the death of our young men will buy them a vote! A vote for what? To make lawyers rich?"

"To give us our freedom?" Martha suggested.

"You have never been unfree, never! Freedom is wealth, my girl, nothing else! Wealth comes from trade. Trade feeds you, clothes you, and keeps you and your daughter out of the slums and in the luxury you've never worked for. And trade is London!"

"And we must be ruled by London to trade with London?" Martha asked drily.

"If London won't trade with us, then we are nothing. Nothing! My God, why can't you understand?"

Martha did suddenly understand one thing, and it occurred to her with the peculiar force with which a younger person sees a weakness in an elder who, hitherto, has always seemed so sure and strong. She understood that her uncle was frightened. He had nailed his colours to the royal mast, and now the guns could mean a rebel victory. "Poor uncle, I shall say a word for you if your friends lose today."

"I don't need your pity!" Abel Becket was stung by her kindness. He stooped and plucked the letter from the carpet. "What I do ask of you is family loyalty. I wish you to write to your brother and enjoin him to give up this madness! Tell him he's been encouraged to foolishness, but that he can relent. He pays attention to your views."

"Not always." Martha, noting that her uncle's threat had decidedly softened, shrugged. "He doesn't take every piece of advice I give him, uncle. I told him he shouldn't marry the Fisher girl, but it's clear he intends to."

It was also clear that Jonathon had not informed his uncle of his proposed marriage. "That slut?" Abel Becket erupted.

Martha wished she had not mentioned the girl's name. "So he tells me."

"He's mad! He has to marry someone of advantage!" Becket took two frustrated paces, then turned again. "She's nothing!"

"I'm beginning to be fond of her, and I assure you she's no slut." Martha frowned suddenly. "Did Ezra Woollard sink her shallop?"

Abel Becket was disconcerted by the sudden question, but his face clearly showed that he knew nothing of the sunken boat.

"On the day the British arrived," Martha explained, "Caroline Fisher's shallop was holed with blocks of masonry thrown from the wharf. She believes Ezra Woollard did it."

"The girl's talking nonsense."

"The boat was certainly sunk! I had to buy her another."

"Then you're a fool. You think money's to be thrown away like old bones?"

Martha smiled sweetly. "How am I to communicate with my friends beyond the city if I have no one able to cross the river? Or how am I to write to Jonathon?"

"You write to him." Abel Becket put the letter on an inlaid table. "He listens to you. So write to him and tell him that he is to return immediately! Immediately! Or else he is not a member of this family, and he forfeits all hopes of me if he disobeys. You tell him that!"

"If he believes in victory," Martha demurred, "I doubt he'll listen to such threats."

"Then tell him that his victory will make a crippled country, and what future will a lame boy have in such a broken world?" Abel Becket gestured towards the windows that suddenly shook under a renewed attack of gunfire. "You've sent your brother to die for nothing!"

"Jonathon is doing what he believes to be right."

"He's diseased, ma'am, diseased. His head's been turned by the ignorant prattle of foolish women. Tell him to return. Tell him to abandon the madness! Tell him I will forgive him, but only if he returns instantly, because I will not share the profits of my labour with a rebel. Nor will I have my family's reputation fouled by rebel allegiance."

Martha smiled. "Do I foul it?"

"You are a woman, and a woman is not held accountable for her whims. Now, ma'am, will you write to your brother?"

Martha picked up the crumpled letter, smoothed and folded it, then held it out to her uncle. "You must tell him your own message, for I will not. I don't believe he should be fighting, but nor can I recommend him to abandon a cause in which I believe," she paused, seeking to soften her refusal, "however whimsically. Write the letter, uncle, and I will guarantee its delivery."

Abel Becket refused the proffered letter. "You won't help wean him from this insanity?"

"How can I, if I share it?"

"Then I shall account you responsible for his destruction. Good day, ma'am." Becket snatched up his hat. "I doubt we have further business." He slammed the door as he left, leaving their former affections torn. They were enemies.

Martha went back to the window and tried to read a message in the soft pummelling of the guns, but she could not tell from such dull sounds who gained the day. She listened and she grieved for her family which, just like the seaboard itself, was riven, not just by rebellion, but by civil war.

ELEVEN

Sam's reveille was the blistering crack of gunfire in the dawn, followed by urgent shouts as sergeants ran through the bivouacs. No one knew what was happening, but that it was more than nervous picquets firing was made obvious when the great ear-thumping crash of cannon fire began.

There was no time for any breakfast, only a milling confusion as men struggled into their packs, boots and belts, then fell into rank. Some of the battalion's women came running to the parade with scraps of bread and flasks of rum for their men. Small children cried, scared by the cannon's thumping from the clinging fog.

Maggie came timidly towards the company. "Nate's over here, darling!" Corporal Dale called aloud to provoke laughter, but Sergeant Scammell, busying himself at Captain Kelly's side, did not hear.

The girl smiled shyly towards Nate, but did not approach him. Instead she held out a cloth-wrapped bundle that the Sergeant snatched from her as he paced towards the company.

Nate watched his enemy approach, then leaned confidingly towards Sam. "We're running today," Nate whispered.

Sam looked at his brother in amazement. "It's a bloody battle. Don't be a fool."

"She's going to hide over by the woods. I'm going to join her. Easy in a battle, isn't it? No one knows what the hell's happening."

"If Scammy gets killed today she'll be yours, anyway," Sam said.

"The Yankees can't kill Scammy," Nate said.

"They're killing someone. Right bloody row they're making."

A staff officer sped past, then a flurry of orders turned the battalion towards the north and, in columns of companies, they marched up a mud-slick road in the fog. The staccato fury of the musketry never ceased to Sam's left. He tried to gauge what was happening in the blanketing, distorting fog, but it was impossible to tell.

The battalion wheeled right into a rough pasture where two light galloper guns were deployed. As the battalion was brought to a halt, and faced front, both guns fired. They kicked back with shocking force, digging their trails into the mud so that the wheels bucked off the ground as the vast gouts of grey-white smoke thickened the fog. Then, though there was no reply from the north, nor any indication of what effect the two cannon balls might have had, the crews limbered up the guns, whipped their horses, and slewed back towards the encampment.

Captain Kelly, mounted on his mare Cleo, rode to a point fifteen paces ahead of the company. "Load." His voice was quite soft, almost apologetic. Sam took out one of the thick, paper-wrapped cartridges and bit the bullet off. The black powder was gritty and saline on his tongue. He lifted the musket's frizzen and put a pinch of powder into the pan, closed the lid, then upended the musket on to its butt so that he could pour the rest of the powder down the barrel. He stuffed the crumpled paper after it, spat the bullet into the muzzle, then drew out the long, brass-tipped rammer that he thrust hard down the barrel to compact bullet, paper and powder in the breech. The rammer went back into its hoops, and he brought the musket up for inspection. Scraps of powder were left on his lips.

Sergeant Scammell, looking wolfishly pleased at the thought of action, tugged at Sam's flint, flicked the frizzen, then moved on to Nate. "You'll look after your brother, Sam?" He stared into Nate's eyes as he spoke to Sam.

"Yes, Sergeant."

"We don't want to lose our little lover boy, do we?"

Scammell laughed, walked on, and Ensign Trumbull who, at thirteen, was the youngest officer in the battalion, paced down the face of the company. "Let's hope we can use the bayonets, Sergeant Scammell."

"Indeed, sir. Nothing like the spike, sir!" Scammell gave an exaggerated salute to the youngster, sweeping his hat off until it touched his right thigh. Ensign Trumbull seemed oblivious to the mockery. The men grinned.

Captain Kelly's mare staled steaming urine on to the grass as the Captain stared gloomily into the fog and put a pinch of snuff on to his hand. Sam could hear the percussive hammer of the big guns firing, but there was no indication of where they fought, or which side had deployed them. The Captain sneezed.

"We fixed it," Nate whispered again. "Maggie found this place, you see, where we can hide?"

"Don't be a clod!"

"No! I can find it! You can come, Sam!"

Sam turned and stared at his brother. "I don't want to come, Nate. I don't mind it here! There's worse things than being a soldier."

"This ain't a bleeding parish meeting!" Sergeant Derrick shouted from behind the company. "Keep your bloody tongues still."

Another staff officer, this one mounted on a grey horse, galloped mysteriously past the battalion's front and was swallowed into the fog. "Stand easy!" Captain Kelly called. He brought out a watch, clicked the lid open, then yawned hugely.

Lieutenant-Colonel Elliott trotted his horse to Kelly's side and the two officers bent their plumed heads together. Their sudden laughter was oddly comforting to Sam. It was only when action threatened that all the battalion's officers showed themselves; most of the time the men were left to the care of sergeants, but the presence of the officers seemed to brace the battalion for what might come. And Kelly was a decent man to follow, quick with his praise and always ready to give a man the benefit of the doubt.

"What's happening, Sergeant?" a man called George Cullen, one of Scammell's cronies, called out to the sergeant.

"You think Mister Washington's told me, George? How the hell do I know?"

Sam borrowed a stone from Liam Shaughnessy and obsessively sharpened the tip of his bayonet. He felt strangely confident. He believed he had earned the red hackle that he wore so proudly. Before, at the battles around New York and at Brandywine, he had been scared of the enemy, but now he felt that the enemy might be even more scared of him. He was not entirely fearless; no bravery could protect a man from a cannon ball or a well-aimed rebel bullet, but Sam felt as good as any man he might face this day; even better, for he wore a red hackle. Around him the usual small jests sent ripples of laughter up and down the ranks. A man in the next company, suffering from a hangover, vomited, while another man seemed to shake uncontrollably. But Sam felt good. Sam felt like a soldier.

Elliott turned his horse. "What will you do to them, lads?"

"Kill them!" The replies were ragged.

Elliott cupped his hand to an ear. "I can't hear you!"

"Kill the bastards, sir!" Scammell shouted, and the men first cheered, then took up the shout.

Elliott laughed at their defiance. "They're rebels, lads, and they need a lesson taught them. You're going to do it! You're going to show them how real soldiers fight! You're doing it for your King! For good King George, and for those, lads, those!" Elliott pointed to the heavy silken sheets of the battalion's colours that had been drawn from their leather tubes and unfurled to the damp air. The sight of the fringed colours made the men cheer once more, and Sam suddenly felt surrounded by the fellowship and love of his comrades. He forgot Nate's plans to desert in the chaos of battle, for this day Sam knew that the Redcoats were unbeatable and he prayed for the enemy to appear from the fog so that the Bloodybacks could prove again that there were no soldiers on God's whole goddamned bloody earth who were better at the slaughter of their enemies.

Sam's spirit was fired, his musket loaded, and he was a Redcoat who could not be beaten. Sam was ready.

A huge cheer sounded to Jonathon's right. It was a regiment of Virginians, flayed to ardour by their colonel. They fought, the Virginian colonel said, for liberty, and to make widows weep in England. This day they were going to humble the damned English; they were to kill the fribbles and fops and send the skipjackets home in shameful defeat. "For what are you?" the colonel shouted.

"Americans! Americans!"

"So kill the bastards! Kill the bastards! Kill the bastards!" And the Virginians took up the cry like a great yell of defiance that challenged the clinging fog.

Jonathon was lost, confused, excited, and terrified. None of his competence as a merchant could help him in this, his first battle. He was not entirely sure that this was a battle, though Colonel Jackson Weller, who had appointed Jonathon as his aide, said it was, and the other officers spoke excitedly of the massive attack General Washington had planned this day. For the first time ever the Continental Army, reinforced with the States' Militia, outnumbered the enemy. The Patriots would advance in four great phalanxes to strike at the British line and the British, Weller had said, would not know where the Americans came from. As soon as General Howe thought he had found the main attack, another would slice in from another road and, in just a few hours, the lobsters would be carved, cooked, and served as a delicacy for General Washington's delectation.

"We're going to win, Johnny!" Jack Weller had said, and Jonathon had agreed, but now, in the fog, he could not make head nor tail of what was happening.

He knew that Colonel Weller's men had the task of keeping the two most easterly American columns in touch with each other. As the columns advanced, so the horsemen would zigzag between them, but the fog made what had seemed like a simple duty into a terrifying mystery. Neither column was in motion now, though somewhere on the battlefield there was action, for Jonathon could hear gunfire that seemed to come from the east. The sound was a great rumbling and tearing noise that quickened Jonathon's heartbeat and seemed to catch the breath in his dry throat. He was imagining the horror of great guns smashing his already-crippled body with roundshot.

"Remember all I told you, son?" Sergeant Spring walked his horse to stand beside Jonathon's and leaned over to tap the drawn sabre in Jonathon's hand.

"I think so, Sergeant."

Spring was a fatherly man and an expert horseman who was also a Methodist preacher. He hated Colonel Weller's swearing, chided Colonel Weller's drunkenness, prayed earnestly that Colonel Weller's womanizing might be forgiven, and followed the Colonel with an avid loyalty. Sergeant Spring was said to have killed six Redcoats in a single skirmish after Brandywine. "He said a prayer over each one, didn't you, Spring?" Weller teased his sergeant.

"They're the Lord's children, even if they are English."

"They're the spawn of skunks and hogs," Weller said, "and every one I kill makes me feel better."

Now, on the verge of battle, Sergeant Spring put away his New Testament and smiled at Jonathon. "Are you prepared?"

"Yes," Jonathon lied. The truth was that his mouth was dry, his stomach churned, and a muscle in his good left leg flickered uncontrollably. His clothes were dirty, damp, and uncomfortable, his thighs were chafed to rawness by a night in the saddle, and his unfamiliar sword slings kept snagging on a torn edge of his saddle. He wanted to vomit, he wanted to empty his bowels, but he was keeping up a bold appearance.

Sergeant Spring, who had learned about young men going fresh into battle, recognized the bravery. He leaned over and took Jonathon's sabre into his own hand. "Use the edge, son, not the point. Hack with it, don't spear with it, and let your horse do the work."

Jonathon was grateful for the reiterated lesson. "Yes, Sergeant."

"And keep your weight off your right stirrup. You don't want to tumble by leaning too far." The advice was the sole and tactful reference to Jonathon's twisted leg. "If you can't reach the enemy, then go for a closer man."

"I will."

Spring smiled and handed back the sabre. "And don't chop your horse's ears off, son."

"No, Sergeant." Jonathon was suddenly terrified he would do just that. He had been feeling strangely guilty about the mare, wondering if he would be accused of stealing it from his uncle, but Colonel Weller had said that horse-thieving was a small transgression in a man who fought to steal a whole country from the tyrant.

And this day, God willing, Jonathon would strike a blow against that tyrant, and his battle shout would be, not Liberty, but the name of the girl he loved. Caroline had written Jonathon one letter which he had combed for a sign of affection. He had found that sign in her last words where, once more, she promised to wait for his return. So now Jonathon rode for her, and the memory of her had given him courage in the damp discomfort of a horse soldier's life.

It was a life in which Jonathon had never worked so hard, been so sore, slept so briefly, nor been so happy. His leg had been an obstacle to those who had given him advice in Philadelphia, but here, among the fighting men, it did not seem to matter. If he was slow in reaching the horse lines he was mocked good-naturedly, but no one called him cripple, or wondered why he had volunteered for the fight. He was accepted, and today he would reward his comrades' friendship by showing that a wealthy young city boy could fight as well as any man.

"Johnny! Johnny!" demanded Colonel Jackson Weller, galloping from the fog.

"Sir?"

"You know where Forrest's scoundrels are?"

"Yes, sir."

"That's more than most people do." Weller was scribbling with a lump of charcoal on a sheet of paper. "They're militia, so the buggers probably can't read. Ignorant country bastards, they are, but don't tell them I said so." He turned the paper over and kept writing.

Jonathon waited. His awe of Weller had increased in the last few days. The Colonel was a huge man, bigger even than Woollard, with a battered face and a grating voice, and a mischievous temper that could also make men cringe in fear of his displeasure. Gossip said that Weller had been a wastrel and a gambler before the rebellion had found a use for his restless energy. Today Weller wore a brown leather jerkin with the red sash of his rank about his waist. His hard-planed face was shadowed by a brimmed hat which bore the scrap of white paper which, in the confusion of uniforms and homespun, was the Patriots' mark for the day. He finished scribbling and held the paper out to Jonathon. "If Forrest can't read, tell him to advance anyway. Straight up the draw, then slant towards the village. Tell him, then come back here."

"Yes, sir."

"And Johnny . . ."

"Sir?"

"I want you by my side today. A good man beside me makes me feel better."

Jonathon, whose face had been drawn with worry all morning, suddenly laughed. "Yes, sir!"

He wheeled the roan mare and trotted to the west. Somewhere behind him a rebel band of flutes struck up the Jacobite "White Cockade" as a taunt to the enemy's Hanoverian monarch. Then, with a shout, and beneath their great flag, the Virginians went forward and Jonathon, riding in the fog, was determined that on this day of battle he would become a man worthy of the girl who waited for his return. He would fight, he would conquer his fear, and he would strike a blow for the cause; not with the point, but with the edge. For this day, with God's blessing and in defence of a God-given liberty, Jonathon would become a soldier.

TWELVE

Just as Sam thought that his battalion was doomed to wait forever in the white, dispiriting fog, Colonel Elliott turned in his saddle and signalled with his sword arm to Captain Kelly. The Captain's sabre rasped out of its scabbard. "Light Company! Skirmish order! One hundred paces only!"

Sam was in the Light Company; the skirmishers who had the honour of first meeting the enemy. Their job was to act as a screen for the remaining nine companies; a screen which tried to unsettle an advancing enemy with aimed musket fire. The enemy would try to defeat the skirmishers with light troops of their own, but, as Sam and Nate went forward together, no enemy was visible in the fog.

"Far enough!" Captain Kelly had ridden forward with the company. Ensign Trumbull, on foot, repeated the command to halt in his breaking and squeaky voice.

Sam knelt. Ten paces either side of him were other men, while, staggered back between the front men were their partners. Nate, Sam's partner, would advance after Sam had fired. Nate's loaded musket would offer protection as Sam reloaded. And so they would fire, turn and turn about. The other nine companies, waiting invisible in the fog behind, would never spread out like this, but would stay in their three tightly locked ranks to pour out massed volleys of musketry.

Captain Kelly walked his horse along the skirmish line. He grinned at Sam. "Awful morning for a battle, Sam."

"Yes, sir."

They talked horses for a moment, chatting as calmly as though this were the English countryside and they were waiting for the hounds to start a cub from a covert. Nothing stirred the mist before the skirmish line. "Well, look after yourself." Kelly nodded at Sam, then turned his mare towards the west from whence the battle sounds still came.

"We're in the wrong bleedin' place," Liam Shaughnessy, the advance man of the pair to Sam's left, grumbled.

"Keep your eyes skinned and your tongues still!" Sergeant Scammell shouted.

Ensign Trumbull, strolling in front of the line and cutting at poison ivy with his sword, stopped close to Sam. "It's Gilpin, isn't it?"

"Yes, sir." Sam said.

"Very good, very good." Trumbull said pointlessly, then walked on towards the right flank where the ground dropped away to a wooded valley that was merely a vague shadowy blur in the fog. The ensign's uniform was too big for him, bulky and tight-belted. He looked like a child in his elder brother's clothes.

"We're in the wrong bleedin' place," Liam said again. "We should be over there, killing the bastards." He gestured towards his left, where the village and the source of the musketry were both hidden by the fog.

"We should be at home," Nate said. "When did you last drink a drop of decent ale? Spruce beer's like horse piss."

"You'd know, Nate, wouldn't you now?" Shaughnessy laughed.

Sam stared into the gentle, white fog. He put the brass butt of his musket on the ground and leaned on its barrel like a shepherd resting on a crook. He felt for his sheathed bayonet, found it in place, then fingered the lump of his lucky musket ball in his top pocket. The ball, spent by its long passage, had struck his crossbelt on Long Island and thumped harmlessly to earth. He had picked it up and kept it close to his heart ever since. He recalled that battle, then thought of Brandywine; both had been fought in full light, not in this clinging fog that was more like the fumbling darkness about Paoli's Tavern. He suddenly wished there was artillery close to the battalion. He remembered how the British cannons had flayed the enemy lines at Brandywine.

"You all right, Sam?" Nate asked.

"You're still here, then?" Sam grinned at his brother.

"For the moment."

"Don't be a fool, Nate. I'll miss you."

"Then come with me."

Ensign Trumbull was idling away his time, slashing at the ivy and dreaming a boy's dreams of military glory. He hoped he looked suitably fearsome in his over-large uniform, but he felt very puny compared to the massively impressive Sergeant Scammell. Trumbull hacked at another ivy leaf and stared towards the underbrush in the small wooded valley where he saw, among the wet leaves, men in brown uniforms who carried bayonet-tipped muskets. There were white scraps in their hats. Trumbull could only stare at them for a moment in shocked disbelief, wondering if he was dreaming. "Sir?" His voice came out as a childish croak. He turned towards Major Kelly who was an indistinct shape in the fog. "Sir?"

No one in the Light Company heard him. The men stared to their front while, from their right flank, brown-clothed men with white papers in their caps broke into a charge.

"Sir!" Trumbull's third effort came out as a despairing screech.

"Right flank, incline! Close!" Scammell's shout pumped warm panic in Sam's chest as he glimpsed the enemy coming so sudden from the misted valley.

"Fire!" Scammell's shout twisted Sam half right. He raised the musket, pointed it, and pulled the trigger so that the brass butt gave its mule kick to his shoulder and the flaming scraps of powder burnt his cheeks.

"Close on me!" Scammell, as ever, was superbly calm in battle. The skirmishers had been surprised and outflanked, but Scammell was coping as though the attack were merely an inconvenience.

Ensign Trumbull flicked up his sword, it was hammered aside, and a tall man skewered the boy with a bayonet. The ensign screamed, then another bayonet was rammed into his throat and the Americans seemed to flood over his body in their eagerness to attack the company's exposed flank.

"Rejoin! Rejoin!" Captain Kelly galloped towards the danger, pointing back towards the main battalion that would greet this attack with a numbing volley. "Go! Go! Go!" His bugler, left alone in the mist, sounded the retreat.

A musket ball hit Cleo. The mare screamed, blood frothed at her lips, and the Captain kicked his feet from the stirrups as the horse reared, twisted, and fell.

Nate grabbed Sam and pulled him back. "Run, Sam!"

"Move!" Scammell, still calm in the panic, was shouting at the Light Company, but the shouts of the rebels were closer. They seemed to Sam to be screaming like fiends. He ran, worrying that his musket was still unloaded, but suddenly the fog ahead of him, in which the battalion appeared like a dull red wall, blazed with a flickering of myriad flames, tongues of fire, and the musket volley crashed around Sam's ears and the sound of the volley was like a beat of thunder in his skull.

"Jesus!" Nate, unscathed by the volley, sheered away. There were American light troops between the skirmishers and the battalion now and Sam, suddenly confused, ran away from both. He thought he heard Scammell shout at him, but all Sam's confidence had evaporated in the sudden mêlée. He could hear the rattle of ramrods in barrels, he could hear screams of wounded men, and he heard an American officer shout that these men wore the red plumes. Sam, driven away from his battalion by the suddenness of the rebel attack, ran blindly in search of any shelter.

Another crashing volley behind, more flames, then Sam saw a rail fence and he dived for its scanty cover and began reloading his musket. More of the Light Company, shorn away from their comrades, took refuge by the fence. Liam Shaughnessy was there, swearing and spitting blood. Nate grinned nervously while Sergeant Derrick, panting from his exertions, cursed the confusion.

Corporal Dale led another half-dozen men to the fence. "Kelly's dead. They got him with bayonets."

"We'll all be dead if you don't get your head down." Derrick snapped.

Sam spat a bullet into his musket and rammed the charge down the barrel. He skinned his fingers on the pan as he primed it, then cocked the gun. He could hear the volleys crashing between the two bodies of troops, and he could hear the screaming, the terrible screaming of wounded men.

It had all happened so suddenly. Sam had imagined seeing the first figures in the fog, then fighting as he had been trained before the bugle ordered him back to the waiting battalion which would blast the enemy away with its practised volleys. Instead, in a sudden paroxysm of violence, the Yankees had hooked in from the fog and now Sam was bereft, isolated, and lost in a frightened huddle on a strange battlefield. Captain Kelly's horse, that Sam had tended so lovingly, was beating its hooves on the ground as it lay dying. Men, bleeding and dying, lay crying in the fog.

"Right mess, innit, Sam?" Sergeant Derrick, his breath back, was wild-eyed and scared.

"What are we going to do?"

"Take those hackles off, that's what we do." Derrick pulled off his hat and ripped the red wool away. "All of you! I'm not going to be slaughtered for a scrap of bleeding wool! Get 'em off!"

The men, crouching frightened by the fence, obeyed. Sam ripped off the red wool, the sign of his pride, and hurled it into the pastureland. "Right, lads!" Sergeant Derrick seemed calmer now that the distinctive marks were gone. "We wait for those Yankee bastards to move, then we go round the right flank to find the battalion."

"Behind! Behind!" Corporal Dale, voice rising in panic, twisted to face north.

Sam writhed round, the fear sudden at his chest, and saw more brown-clothed men in the fog. It was a new enemy skirmish line that advanced on the right flank of the first attack. He put the musket to his shoulder, then heard hooves to his right and saw the shapes of mounted men hammering in a sudden gallop.

"Run!" Sergeant Derrick bellowed in panic.

"Fire!" Sam shouted the word. "Fire, fire, fire!"

Perhaps six men instinctively obeyed Sam. They made a rough line, they shouldered their muskets, and they pulled their triggers. The brass bruised Sam's shoulder and the lock spat burning powder into his right eye. Smoke blossomed, stinking like filth, and through its screen, and through the wet fog, Sam saw a horseman throw up an arm, slump, then fall sideways from the saddle. A trumpet was screaming in the morning, hooves were like drumbeats from hell, and the bright surprise of drawn sabres sliced into the Redcoats.

"Run!" Shaughnessy was ten yards ahead, sprinting, as Sam seized Nate's arm and dragged him to the right. The horses crashed past. There was only a handful of horsemen, but they split the panicked skirmishers apart like wolves snarling into a flock.

Sam twisted away from the crashing hooves. He stumbled, and the fall saved his life. A sabre hissed by his head, missing by a handsbreadth, he rolled, and heard the horrid, terrible, meaty-wet chop of a blade striking home.

"Nate!"

"I'm here!" Nate was flat on his face, cowering from the drumming hooves.

"Mother!" The word, pathetic and awful, came from Sergeant Derrick, falling, blood sudden from a savage wound in his shoulder; his despairing cry turned to a scream as another sabre whipped its razor edge across his big belly.

The volleys still crashed in the fog behind, the horsemen wheeled from their threat, and now, from the north, the second battalion of rebel troops marched from the fog. Men ran from its ranks with bayonets raised.

"Don't!" Nate screamed it, holding up a hand to ward off the threatened killing blow.

"Get up!" the rebel snarled. The American had a thin, tanned face which seemed to Sam as hard as dried leather.

Sam and Nate stood. Other survivors of the Light Company were also taken prisoner and, like Sam, they were being stripped of weapons, ammunition, food; of anything that might be useful to the rebels.

"Move!" The leather-faced rebel jabbed his bayonet into Sam's ribs. "Move, you bastard!"

Sam stumbled over the pasture. Behind him there was a rebel cheer that melded into a sudden, stunning volley and Sam heard a Yankee officer with a voice like the avenging angel order the charge. But Sam could do nothing. Sam was a prisoner. He was shaking. The rebels were nervous, their fingers tight on triggers, and Sam hurried to obey their orders. Sergeant Derrick lay lifeless, his guts spilt blue on the field and his torso sheeted with bright blood. Liam Shaughnessy was bleeding from the belly, gasping, dying. The smell of blood was thick as smoke.

"Sit, you bastards!"

There were ten prisoners from the Light Company. They sat. The firefight in the fog blazed for a few moments, then suddenly died. There was shouting, the screams of the wounded, and the barking of commands. One man was screaming for Jesus over and over until his voice was suddenly chopped short and, afterwards, it seemed very silent in the pasture. Then, out of the fog, shambling in a dispirited and defeated mass, more captured Redcoats were pushed towards Sam's group.

"Jesus!" Nate, appalled that so many should be taken, stared at them. The newcomers told of the battalion fighting the first enemy, then being surprised by the second attack from the left flank. Most of the battalion, behind its volleys, had fallen back before the rebel charge, but a good sixty prisoners had been taken. They were stripped of their weapons and ammunition, then ordered to take off their boots.

A dozen Americans were ordered to stay with the prisoners. The guards were grinning and confident men who chewed tobacco as they ordered the Redcoats to collect the wounded and drag the dead into a heap. Sergeant Derrick's guts were scooped on to a red coat and dragged away. Liam Shaughnessy suddenly jerked like a hooked fish, and died.

A dismounted American horseman, perhaps an officer if the red sash about his waist indicated anything, prowled around the prisoners. He carried a drawn sabre, and he was staring at each captured man as if seeking a face he would recognize. His own face looked as hard as weathered wood. He stopped by Sam and Nate. "You two! Put some boots on and come here."

The brothers, apparently chosen at random, were taken fifty yards up the road to where the Americans had gathered their own wounded by the roadside. One man was breathing bubbles of blood and would die soon. Another, with a bullet in his groin, rocked to and fro on his haunches and wept silently. A third, wearing riding boots and with an empty sabre scabbard at his hip, lay white-faced on the grass. His breath was coming in short, moaning gasps. His right thigh was a mess of blood that had been staunched by a twist of rope tightened about his leg at the groin.

"Look after them," the American officer said. "If that leg starts to bleed again, tighten the rope."

"Yes, sir." For a moment Sam had thought the American was planning to execute him and Nate with the drawn sabre.

"Keep him warm. If he wants water, give it to him." The officer dropped a canteen on to the grass, then untethered a horse he had tied to the rail fence behind the wounded men. He swung himself easily into the saddle. "I'll be back. You keep him alive, you bastards, or I'll crucify you both! You hear me?"

"Yes, sir," Sam said. Then, as the officer spurred his horse into a gallop, Sam turned to the American who, he saw, could be no older than himself. The wounded man had a thin, pale, handsome face and long black hair. He was trying to sit up and the pain was making him cry out.

"It's all right," Sam said. "It's all right. Calm now." Sam had always been a genius with sick horses, and now he found he had the same ability with this wounded boy who, eyes flickering, looked first with alarm at his red-jacketed comforter, and then seemed to relax.

"Here," Sam said, "I'll pull you up. Slow now." He eased the boy up and propped him against a fence post. One of the

American guards wandered close, saw nothing to trouble himself, and turned to watch the larger mass of prisoners.

Sam wet his right hand with water and rubbed it over the wounded boy's face. It did not seem at all odd to be giving help to an enemy. "You're going to be good as new," Sam said. "It's only a bullet hole!"

The American gave a weak smile. "My first."

"I've never had a bullet in me," Sam said. "Like as not never will now."

"Battle," the American said. "My first battle."

The man who bubbled as he breathed suddenly hiccuped, gagged, then his face rolled to one side and an obscene eruption of blood spilt from his mouth. He was dead. The second man was unconscious now, moaning, while Sam's American had tears of pain on his cheeks.

"Come on now." Sam wiped the tears away. "You don't want to cry in front of an Englishman!"

"Lobsters," the boy said.

"Lobsters?"

"That's what they call you. We call you." The American boy's breathing was easier now, much easier. Sam saw how good the boy's clothes were: a coat of the finest wool weave, a linen shirt, and a thick, leather sword belt.

"Are you an officer?"

"I don't think so." The boy grinned weakly.

"You should know, shouldn't you?" Sam teased him.

"I was an aide."

"I should call you sir," Sam said, trying to keep the boy's spirits up.

"Jonathon," said Jonathon Becket. "My name's Jonathon Becket."

"Like the archbishop, eh?" Sam said.

"He died," Jonathon said weakly.

"Don't be soppy," Sam said sternly. "I'm Sam, that's Nate. We're twins. I was born first, and I got all the brains." Sam was suddenly glad that this was not the horseman who had fallen to his panicked volley. Sam had seen that man lying dead, so Jonathon must have been hit by another bullet fired elsewhere in the misted confusion. "You ain't too bad," Sam said with rough comfort. "Leg's torn up a bit, but the bone's not broken."

"He's a doctor." Nate grinned at the American boy. "Joined the army 'cause he couldn't stand the sight of blood."

Jonathon laughed, and it made him flinch with sudden hurt. "It hurts, Sam. It hurts."

"You shouldn't join the army if you can't take a joke." It was the oldest jest of soldiers, but it worked. Jonathon opened his eyes and gave a smile.

"You're going to be all right." Sam was staring at Jonathon's wounded leg, and he saw beneath the blood that the leg was twisted and that its foot, encased in a grotesque boot, was clubbed. God help the rebels, Sam thought, if they were sending cripples to war. "I've seen worse wounds," he said to encourage the American.

"That was on horses, Sam." Nate said chidingly.

"I mended a horse that speared itself on a fence post once," Sam said, "and I had it trotting like a winner in a month! I'll have you on your feet, Yankee." He saw Jonathon shiver and so Sam took off his thick woollen coat, his red coat, and draped it about his enemy's chest to keep him warm.

"My first battle," Jonathon said. He looked as if he were about to cry, not with pain, but with the shame of failing so signally in his very first battle.

"You'll have other battles," Sam said.

"Not if I lose the leg."

"What are you talking about? That wound's nothing!" Sam's scorn was both kindly and truthful. "I reckon you must be an officer if you're making a fuss about a little scratch like that!" Sam knew the wound was far worse than a scratch, but Sam also saw how his enemy was needing this comfort, and was, indeed, clinging to every word with a desperate hope.

Jonathon seemed to laugh. "It wasn't much of a leg to start with."

Sam smiled. "It was the one God gave you, Yankee, so you might as well hang on to it. You'll fight again, Johnny. I'll have you on your feet, I'll have you fighting, even if it is for the wrong bloody side. I promise it!"

Sam had made a promise while about him, in the smoke thickened fog, the rebel army marched on.

THIRTEEN

Captain Christopher Vane had begun to believe that God intended great things for him; why else would providence have let him survive the first hours of a battle in which he, Christopher Vane, had seen things that before this day had only dwelt in nightmare?

He had watched the advancing rebels savage at the retreating Light Infantry. No prisoners had been taken as the attack flooded down Germantown's main street, for the memory of the night attack at Paoli's was still fresh. Men chopped and stabbed and skewered with bayonets. Vane had seen the enemy's bared teeth, heard the hiss of their breath and the grating of their bayonets on ribs. He had seen a Redcoat begging for mercy and watched the man pinned to a tree with such violence that his killer's bayonet had bent in two. Vane, spurring his mare forward, had slashed his sabre across the American's skull, then, in the macabre dance of death, Vane had slithered away from the man's battle-crazed comrades whose dawn attack threatened to drive clean into Philadelphia itself.

A musket ball had plucked at the skirts of Vane's coat, another had thumped on its hide-stiffened shoulder and had ripped off an epaulette, while a third had drawn blood from the back of his hand. He stayed with the retreating Light Infantry, obeying Sir William's instructions, and twice he had fended off bayonets with his sabre, the second time riposting with such speed that he had taken the American in the eye and sent the man reeling and clutching at his face. He had shot two men with his pistols. The world had become a small, stinging circle of fog in which men panted, screamed, shot, stabbed, and died. Time was chaos in which Vane was once again astonished by the exultation of battle. Each moment was a challenge, and each danger survived a victory.

"Move yourself, sir, move over!" the voice bellowed at Vane. "Move, sir, damn you, move!"

Vane turned in his saddle and was astonished to see a British battalion drawn in tight formation across the road with their three ranks of muskets aimed at his horse. He spurred to the battalion's flank, clearing it just as their first massive volley pulsed smoke and flame into the fog.

"Who are you?" he shouted at a lieutenant.

"40th, sir!"

These, then, were the men Sir William had placed to check the rebel thrust, and Vane felt a fierce joy as the battalion went into the deadly rhythm of platoon fire. Now, instead of single volleys, each half-company fired separately, immediately after the half-company to their right, so that the muskets spat in unending ripples of flame down the long front. The men worked with an apparently soulless precision. They fired, reloaded, rammed, fired, reloaded, rammed, and the only untoward movements were the flickers as red-coated men fell backwards from the enemy's fire.

"Close up! Close up!" the sergeants shouted, and the men, with scarce a glance at the wounded who were either dragged backwards or thrown forwards, shuffled again into their locked formation without breaking the tempo of their work. The front rank knelt on their right knees, the centre rank stood behind with each man's left foot hard against the right foot of the kneeling man in front, while the rear rank locked their right boots against the centre rank's left feet.

The muskets pumped smoke to thicken the fog through which, their blood roused by imminent victory, the Americans charged. They paid for their temerity. This was not Light Infantry, scattered in a skirmish line, but a drilled, formed battalion that could hammer bullets in a rhythm of death that would spew gouts of blood into the muddy street.

"Close up! Close up!" A sergeant dragged a wounded Redcoat from the line and threw him, bleeding, to the rear. A bandsman dropped his drumsticks and ran to help the casualty.

The battalion's colours of heavy, fringed silk jerked from bullet strikes. Sergeants armed with wide-bladed halberds guarded the precious flags. "Steady!" the colonel shouted. "Well done! Well done! Steady now, lads!" He pushed his horse between two files of men to stare into the smoke-fouled fog. "Cease fire! Cease fire! Load!"

The battalion went silent. Those men with unloaded muskets bit into cartridges. Ramrods rattled and scraped in barrels. Enemy fire still spat through the fog, and men still twisted and jerked back, but the platoon fire had repelled the first rebel attack. The colonel, studiously ignoring the musketry that was aimed at his gilt-bedecked coat, drew his sword. "Fix bayonets!"

"Fix bayonets!" the sergeants echoed the command.

The Americans had withdrawn into the smoke-pearled fog to regroup. Now, with a cheer, they made a fresh and spirited charge. Vane heard them before he saw them. He heard the cheering and the slop of boots in mud, then, in the whiteness, he saw the rebel ranks coming at a run. Their ordered ranks, denied the practice of their red-coated enemies, had shaken into a looser formation, but their outstretched bayonets looked foully businesslike.

"Wait!" the colonel shouted. "Wait, my boys! Wait!"

The American cheer seemed to rise into a howl of blood lust and hatred that rang until, just as it seemed to Vane that the 40th's colonel had left his volley too late, the sword flashed down and the command was shouted into the sky. "Fire!"

Seven hundred muskets flamed together in one terrible stinging volley that threw the attacking line into ruin. Vane saw men fall and jerk like bloodied puppets. "Front rank rise!" The colonel was standing in his stirrups now, sword raised. "Battalion will advance! On my word!" The sword pointed forward. "March!"

The shining halberds swung down and the Redcoats went forward, not in a loose running mass like the rebels, but with a ponderous and deadly efficiency. Wounded rebels were silenced with bayonets. Not a Redcoat cheered, not a man shouted, not a man broke the slow, blade-tipped and silent advance. The surviving enemy did not wait to contest the charge, but edged warily backwards.

"Halt! Reload! Front rank, kneel! Wait for my word!" The colonel waited as the ramrods rose and fell. His sword went up. "Rear ranks only!" The blade seared down. "Fire!" Another full-throated, heavy volley coughed and flamed, this one slashing into rebel ranks already disordered by the 40th's murderously disciplined fire. This was infantry work at its awesome best, but it was not enough. The colonel, his front quietened for a moment, trotted round to his right flank where he saw Vane. "You're Kit Vane, aren't you?"

"Yes, sir."

"Glad you became an aide?"

Vane laughed. "Yes, sir." He was exulting in it.

Colonel Musgrave watched his two rear ranks finish their reloading. "Buggers are turning my left flank. Nothing I can do about it." He peered into the opaque whiteness. "The bloody Yankees have got their tails up this morning, haven't they?"

Vane smiled. "Indeed, sir."

"So I'm going to earth." Musgrave gestured towards a substantial, brick-built house behind him. "Cram the lads in there and invite 'em to dig us out. Perhaps you'd tell Sir William?"

"Of course I will, sir."

Colonel Musgrave, his wig in place and his white stock impeccably tied, stared northwards. "I suspect this is their main lunge, Vane. I could have sworn I saw Fat George. Ugly bugger, and he sits on a horse like a pregnant fishwife, but he's brave enough." Musgrave took out a snuff box, opened the lid, and offered a pinch to Vane. "But after that little lesson I suspect they'll bring up their cannon, don't you? So I think the house is the best thing. Try and relieve us when you can."

"Of course, sir." Vane refused the snuff, then twisted in his saddle. "You think they've got behind us?"

"No doubt about it. You'll have an exciting ride, Vane. Death or glory, eh? Good luck." Musgrave laughed grimly, then cupped his hands. "Left flank, incline to the rear! Smartly now!" He shook his head proudly. "They're good lads, Vane, the very best, but it's time I got them tucked up safe. You'll give my compliments to Sir William?"

"I will, sir."

"Tell him he owes me a pipe of port if the 40th live through today." Musgrave, instead of retreating in front of the rebels, planned to turn a brick house into a fortress. He might be trapped there and ground to mincemeat, he might be forced to surrender, or he might make his name as the man who checked a victorious enemy attack.

A half-mile behind the house, the Commander-in-Chief waited in the centre of his main defensive line at the southern edge of Germantown. Sir William fidgeted with his watch, then cast an irritated glance at the fog which showed no sign of lessening. Sir William wondered whether Mister Washington was also irritated by the weather, then was besieged by the irrational superstition that somehow, perhaps by prayer, the Americans had arranged for this fog to blanket the battlefield. The Americans were very fond of prayer, it was one of their few habits that rather irritated Sir

William. He had been amused by Christopher Vane's pungent observation that, for a people which put such stock on reason, the Americans' dependence on prayer was quite illogical.

John Andre, horse lathered, galloped from the fog, saw Howe, reined in, and let his horse slither to a quivering stop. "General Grey's compliments, sir," he paused to quieten the nervous horse, "and Luken's Mill is still in our hands."

"Thank God."

"But he needs men, sir. The outposts were badly cut up. We put Elliot's battalion in support, but he lost a good few men."

"God help them," Howe said, and suddenly realized that, like his enemies, he was adopting the habit of prayer.

And prayer was needed for, if Sir William's fears were right, then this battle was already lost. Slowly, as vaguely as the fog that surrounded him, Sir William was piecing together a picture of his battlefield, and it was not pretty. American columns were advancing down at least three roads, and the fog made their progress almost impossible to measure. At any moment Sir William feared an eruption of musketry behind him, for he might already be surrounded.

Yet, though Sir William had once sworn never to fight against the Americans, neither did he intend to lose to them. They might hold the initiative now, but Sir William was no mean commander. The flanks, he decided, must be staunch. The right flank, deeply wounded by the rebel attack, was demanding reinforcements, but Sir William refused the request. This battle would be decided in the heart of the field, and Sir William would fatten the centre of his line and hope that the rebel onslaught did not come before he could assemble the men who must first withstand the assault, then counterattack. Sir William fretted for the arrival of men from the city's garrison and pulled in the reserves from his flanks. He also saw the concerned faces of his entourage and, in search of some touch of normality that would calm their fears, he twisted in the saddle to look for his servant. "Evans?"

"Sir?"

"Is Hamlet safe?"

Tom Evans, mounted on one of Sir William's spare horses, held up the General's dog. "Quite safe, sir."

"Good man. As long as he's safe we can't lose, eh?" Forced laughter sounded as Sir William turned back. In front of him a battery of artillery pointed down the wide, fog-shrouded main street, but the waiting barrels were still masked by red-coated infantry that sniped at enemy skirmishers flitting past like phantoms in the whiteness. Then, between those enemy skirmishers, and riding like a man set to win a fortune on a steeplechase, came a single red-jacketed officer. His horse, hooves spewing mud, had bared teeth and white eyes. The British cheered him and John Andre, standing in his stirrups to watch, suddenly laughed. "God, but he's having a high time!"

"That's Vane?"

"That's Kit, sir."

The fog closed behind Vane who, hat awry and epaulette torn by a bullet, slowed his mare first to a canter, then to a trot. He bowed left and right to the Redcoats who cheered him, then, face beaming with the delight of the day, he took off his hat to Sir William. "Good morning again, sir! They've pushed Musgrave aside."

"Have they now?"

"But he thinks this is their main lunge. He's fairly sure he saw Mister Washington with them."

"Our intrepid George is never far from the main action, is he?" The scrap of information was useful to Sir William, for it confirmed his suspicion that the struggle in the village would decide the battle, but it was small comfort. He had nothing like enough men assembled yet to check a determined thrust. "And Musgrave?" Sir William asked.

Vane turned in his saddle to stare down the village street. "He's gone to ground in a large house, sir."

"They'll march straight past him." Sir William said it gloomily, for he had been relying on the 40th to blunt the rebel attack. "Did Musgrave hold them at all?"

"He gave them hell for a while, sir."

"Let's hope they need an hour to reform." It seemed a vain hope on which to pin victory, but it was the only hope Sir William had at this moment.

Vane, who had ridden and fought amidst horrors all morning, was yearning for an acknowledgement of his achievement from Sir William. He thought that praise was coming when the Commander-in-Chief noticed Vane's bloodied uniform, but, before Sir William could utter a word, a spent musket ball fluttered between the two men. Sir William frowned like a man irritated by a wasp, then twisted as a yelp sounded from behind. Tom Evans had been struck by the ball. It had only bruised him, but the shock was sufficient to make him release Hamlet who, barking and brisk, scampered towards the enemy.

"Stop him!" Sir William shouted. "Stop him!"

There was a maelstrom of gunners and Redcoats diving at the dog which barked, swerved, then ran free into the fog. It disappeared.

"Christ on his bloody cross! Can't you do anything right?" Sir William wrenched his reins round. "God damn it, Evans!"

"I'm sorry, sir." Evans was massaging his bruised shoulder.

"God's teeth! You bastard!" Sir William's temper was an awesome thing. The dog had been a gift from his Boston-born mistress, and the loss of it struck sore. It also tempted fate because of Sir William's jest that had tied the dog's safety to the battle's outcome. Soldiers were notoriously superstitious, and Sir William's glib remark had invited disaster. Christopher Vane, who had never seen Sir William's rare anger before, was appalled by the force of it, then he wondered if it was really prompted, not by the dog's loss, but by Sir William's knowledge that only one thin and unsettled line of troops lay between George Washington and victory.

The General brooded behind the guns while his aides waited further back. John Andre frowned at Vane's breeches. "Are you hit bad?"

"Someone else's blood," Vane said shortly, and the thought of his dead servant reminded him of the bitter loss of his young stallion. "Billy makes a kerfuffle over a lost dog and I've lost my spare horse." Vane said it angrily as he and Andre dismounted by the gun limbers. "A hundred guineas gone in the fog!"

"I'm sorry."

"A hundred guineas! I shouldn't have bought the damn thing. And I lost my watch!"

Andre could not help laughing at Vane's distress. Britain was on the brink of losing a battle, perhaps losing thirteen colonies, and all Vane could worry about was a horse and a watch. Then Andre saw he had offended Vane and was immediately penitent. "I'm sorry, Kit, truly."

"Not as sorry as I am. And I didn't get breakfast!"

"We can remedy that, at least." The gunners had a mess of lentils and salt pork standing on a limber and, in return for Andre's silver, happily allowed the two officers to spoon their fill from the lukewarm pot. Somewhere to the west troops moved indistinctly through the whiteness; British troops moving forward, hurrying to block the place where the rebel forces were expected at any second and in overwhelming force. From behind came the sound of hooves and Vane and Andre turned to see a mud-spattered Lord Robert Massedene gallop from the mist.

Massedene spoke with Sir William, then trotted back to his fellow aides. He slid stiffly off his horse. "We're bringing every spare man from the city. God knows if they'll be in time. Is that food?"

Andre offered his lordship a bow. "Good morning, Robert."

"Morning, John." Massedene nodded curtly at Vane. "You look as if you've been in the wars, Vane?"

Vane's reply was checked by a sudden eruption of sound from the north. Cannons and musketry combined in a hellish crescendo, yet their murderous work was hidden by the fog. It was the noise of carnage, but who died and who won was impossible to say.

Massedene, who had been sent in urgent summons for reinforcements from the city's garrison, turned to stare into the fog out of which came the sound of cannonade and musket fire. "My God, is it that bad?"

"I rather think Mister Washington has wrong-footed us." Andre spoke very quietly. "It's going to be mildly desperate, I think."

Massedene stared northwards. "How many of them?"

"God knows." Vane, determined not to show any tremor of concern in front of Massedene, imitated Andre's insouciance. "They're as thick as penny whores round a barracks' gate."

"I never lingered in such places," Massedene said carelessly, "but I'll take your word for it."

Vane, knowing he had been slighted, looked angrily away and saw that the sun had become a pale disc. The mist was clearing, and the rebels held the war's outcome in the palms of their powder-stained hands.

And all the despised George Washington needed to do was squeeze.

FOURTEEN

The horse, empty stirrups flapping, trotted jauntily out of the fog.

It was a young horse; a black stallion with a distinctive white blaze and three white socks. It saw the prisoners and swerved away with its handsome head tossing in mane-swirling elegance. One of the guards whooped and ran towards the stallion. The beast avoided him easily. Other guards, seeing the value of the fine, glossy horse, ran to help. Sam thought they were like children playing a boisterous game.

"They're Virginians," Jonathon said. He grinned as the stallion thudded northwards into the fog to escape the loud and clumsy pursuit. "I'm not. I'm from Philadelphia."

The ebullient guards, their prize lost, wandered back to the prisoners. The wounded American with the bullet in his groin lay curled on his side with blood seeping down his trouser legs. "Nothing I can do for him," Nate said helplessly. Musket fire still sounded through the fog. The prisoners sat silent.

"Are you from London?" Jonathon asked Sam.

"No."

"There was a time when I dreamed of nothing else but going to London." Jonathon suddenly hissed with a stab of pain.

"I've never been to London," Sam said. "Wanted to, but never did." Jonathon turned his head to stare with some amazement at an Englishman who had never been to London, but Sam just shrugged. "Long way from my village." Sam wondered how long it would be before he saw home again, if ever he would. He was thinking of all the tales he had heard around camp fires; tales that told of dreadful prison camps where the British starved and died of the fever or bloody flux. "What happens to us now?"

"I don't know." Jonathon gave a rueful shrug. "I've only been in the army eleven days."

"That was clever of you," Nate said, but not unkindly.

Sam turned as a new bout of firing erupted in the south, then another in the west. It was impossible to tell what was happening, but he had an idea that the fog was slowly clearing. He could just see the black stallion, head erect, perhaps seventy yards to the north. He guessed the animal was frightened and wanted reassurance, but then a thicker waft of fog hid the horse again.

"Jesus!" A lance of pain streaked up into Jonathon's groin and belly. He shifted. Sam had bandaged the wound with a dead man's torn shirt, then released the tourniquet. Jonathon, feeling the throb of the torn flesh, hissed in agony. "I'm going to lose the leg."

Sam scorned such pessimism. "No! You'll be dancing again!"

Jonathon tried to laugh and sobbed with pain instead. "Do I look like someone who ever danced?"

"So what's wrong with having a hobble?" Sam looked at the leather-clad clubfoot. "Has it always been like that?"

Jonathon felt oddly complimented that Sam's acceptance of his foot was so matter-of-fact. "From birth."

"Must be bloody useful for kicking the lights out of people you don't like." Sam saw that the pain was still flickering up from Jonathon's wound and, because he had nothing better to offer, he uncorked the canteen of water. "Pity it isn't good ale, eh? I miss the ale. Good, thick ale."

Jonathon wanted distraction from the pain. "Go on."

So Sam found himself talking about home. About Parson Harvey who shot rooks from the church tower with a blunderbuss, and about the sound of the hunting horn drifting over cold fields in winter, and about Plough Monday when there was a great feast up at the Hall.

"Did you have a school?" Jonathon asked.

"Parson's wife made us learn letters, but not much." Sam had learned the really useful things from his father. How to shoe a horse and how to stop an earth so a dog fox, coming home with a full belly on a January morning, would be up and about for the gentry to hunt. How to spot a steel-trap, set to snatch a man's leg in a pheasant wood, and how to take a cock pheasant with a throwing stick. How to loop a pike, or lime a singing bird for the London market, and how to spot a good ratting terrier in a litter. "I had a rare terrier," Sam said wistfully. "Could take a dozen rats in an eye-blink!"

"And girls?" Jonathon asked.

"He never snapped at girls," Sam grinned. "We had girls. Summer nights! Back of the wheatfields." His homesickness made his voice plaintive.

"Why did you join the army?" Jonathon asked in some astonishment.

"My daft brother dared me to." Sam punched Nate's shoulder. He remembered how Nate had come running home with news of the bright gold the army was offering to recruits. "The sergeant showed me, he did." Nate had said. "Guineas! I bit one! And in a year you can be an officer. There was a captain there, all glittery, and he was only a farm boy a year back! The sergeant said so!"

Nate and Sam had been seventeen then, and they knew with all the certainty of youthful hope that there would be gold, and Sam was sure there would be more than gold, that he would strut through a market place with silver loops hanging from a braided jacket and with a pretty girl on his arm. Such a future seemed better than the bawling, echoing stables where in winter the ice made a skim on the stones and in summer the flies filled the air like a midden.

"This bloody fool dared me," Sam said wistfully to Jonathon. Nate had offered the dare, and so the twins had run to the town and taken the King's Shilling and discovered the promised bounty was spent on boots, brushes, stockings and flour to the hair. "It bloody hurt, that!" Sam laughed.

"What hurt?" Jonathon asked.

"Your hair, see?" Sam turned to show the American boy the thick pigtail that hung stiff behind his head. "You have to grow it first, then they pull it back. Christ, but they pull! You can't close your eyes, it's so tight! Honest! Then they smear it with tallow, twist it round a leather pad, and fill it with flour. It's called a queue."

"Called other things too," Nate grinned, and Jonathon, seeing the thick, plump shaft of whitened hair, laughed.

"The stock was the worst," Nate said with the perverse pride of a man describing a hardship endured. He tapped the stiff leather collar. "It put scars on your neck in the beginning, it did." Their first lesson as soldiers had been how to stand straight and unmoving as the leather stock abraded the skin under the chin into two bloody welts that slowly calloused into hard, white ridges. Then they had learned to march in the high-knee, boot-thumping step, how to fire their big, clumsy muskets, and how to stand in the battle line while death whipped at them.

They slept two in a bed, head to toe, and the barrack rats would chew their flour-stiffened queues at night. They ate the slops the King gave them. They were beaten, whipped, snarled at; they spent their small money in alehouses that no decent man would dare enter and were expected to take their pleasure on whores that no other man would touch, and they knew it was for ever, for the only escape was through wounding or death. Sam had broken his mother's heart. If he had not been a fool, his mother said, and if he had kept his wits about him, he could have become the Squire's chief coachman and worn the triple-caped coat. Instead he had thrown it all away for a dare. He shrugged now. "Why did you join?" he asked Jonathon.

"Because I want our side to win," Jonathon said. "Because tyrants in London will make us slaves."

"You're as daft as him!" Sam gestured at his brother. "No one's enslaving you! I've never heard such gammon! Slaves! You're the buggers with slaves, not us. No cuffy slaves in England, no white ones neither! Us enslave you? You're daft as lights!"

"You should go and tell George Washington!" Nate grinned at his brother. "He'd probably stop fighting if you had a quick mutter. What do you know about it, Sam?"

"I'm English, and I'm bloody proud of it," Sam said belligerently.

"So'm I," muttered Nate, "but I'm still buggering off." He looked towards the rebel guards who, bored with their duty, now sat on the ground and stared southwards.

"Don't," Sam said. He could not bear to think of losing his brother. "Please, Nate."

"Maggie, Sam, Maggie." Nate's answer was laconic. "I promised. She's waiting for me, and I'm going whether you like it or not! Better than being a bloody prisoner, Sam!"

"You want to desert?" Jonathon had been listening to the conversation.

Nate grinned. "It is my ambition, my good Yankee, to find somewhere to live in America. My loyal brother here is nervous, but not me. Nathaniel Gilpin has had enough of King George's army, and if you asks me, Sam, we should both now, very formally, resign our red coats and run like hell."

Jonathon laughed. "You should."

"Well, Sam?" Nate asked.

"And you get liberty!" Jonathon said with the true passion of a young revolutionary.

"I've got liberty!" Sam said in blithe disregard of his predicament. "And he ain't interested in liberty. He's got a girl."

"A Yankee girl," Nate said to Jonathon with sudden enthusiasm. "She's waiting in a spinney over there. She's pretty as a picture!"

"So's mine," Jonathon said warmly. "She's called Caroline." There was a sudden burst of musket fire to the south, where the Virginian regiments had marched, and the fire rose to a continuous splintering sound that suggested hard and brutal fighting. Men were dying in the thinning fog. Somewhere to the west a house was burning, its flames made pale by the mist.

The black stallion had come closer again. "If you get me on that horse," Jonathon said to Nate, "I'll come with you. I promise I can get you past our lines."

Sam turned to see the stallion quivering just forty yards away. Its nostrils were dilated and its eyes showed white. It was the stance of an animal ready to flee at the smallest provocation.

Nate looked at his brother. "You could catch it, Sam. He can do anything with horses!" This last was to Jonathon. "I'm not half as good." Nate turned back to Sam. "You can do it, Sam! Will you?"

"Just so you can run away?" Sam was scornful.

"Sam, please." Nate was suddenly serious. "I can't take it, Sam. Scammy kicks the lights out of Maggie, he's going to kill her. And I want her, Sam. I want to be with her! She's gone over there." He pointed to the east where, in the shifting pearl skeins of fog, the far woods were a dark blur. "And I can find her!"

"I'll help you!" Jonathon said forcefully. "I only need a horse."

Sam stared at his brother. "Nate . . ."

"It's my life, Sam!" Nate was suddenly angry. "We ain't tied by chains, you and I. You be a soldier, Sam! You be the best goddamned soldier you can ever be, but let me be what I want to be!" Nate's eyes were glistening. "Sam, please!"

Sam hesitated. Jonathon, who had watched the brothers as they argued, pulled back his jacket to reveal, next to his brass-hilted pistol, a purse hanging from leather straps. "I need a horse," he said to Sam. "And I'll pay you if you fetch it."

"I thought you were wounded," Sam said.

"I can ride, even if I can't walk." Jonathon frowned. "Please, Sam?"

"You're both mad," Sam said, but he stood and, ignored by the guards, ducked through the fence rails.

"You need help?" Nate asked.

"Not with horses," Sam said scathingly.

He walked very slowly towards the handsome black horse. It was scared. Its muscles twitched beneath the glossy, mud-flecked skin. Sam immediately recognized the value of this high-strung, well-bred beast that must have cost some officer a small fortune.

"Easy, boy! Easy!" Sam stopped twenty paces from the stallion. It must have belonged to a British officer for it had the royal cipher embroidered on the tail of its dark blue saddle cloth. "It's all right, boy, all right. Nothing to fret about. Only Sam coming for you." Sam talked the soothing nonsense as he walked closer and closer to the trembling, white-eyed stallion. Its ears pricked and its front right hoof pawed at the ground. "Haven't seen a horse like you for years! Good boy, now, good boy. Easy. Easy. Easy." Sam plucked a handful of grass and, still talking, held it out to the beast. He let the stallion smell him. "Good boy, now, good boy." The horse, still quivering, stepped towards Sam who, very gently, reached with his free hand for a ring of the bit. He took it, then let the horse take the grass. "Easy, boy, easy, easy."

He soothed the stallion, rubbing its flanks and letting the nervousness flow out of it. It had been lost in the fog, terrified by cannon and musket fire, and now it trembled as Sam rubbed it down. "All right, boy. Let's see how you go, shall we?" Sam took the saddle horn in his left hand and pulled himself on to the stallion's back. The horse shivered, its ears pricked back again, but Sam knew how to soothe nervous animals. "Good boy, good boy. Easy now." He touched its flanks with his heels and the stallion, obedient to his touch, walked forwards.

The noise of battle seemed to be all around Sam now, louder than it had been all day, but he was riding this magnificent horse and, for a few seconds, he forgot his predicament. There was just a pure pleasure in being in the saddle.

"Sam!" Nate called. The rebel guards were watching Sam now and one of them put a musket to his shoulder, but the range was too great to try a shot. Sam kicked his heels back. He could ride back to his own lines. He could forget Nate's madness and go back where he belonged. No prison camp; instead, merely by riding southwards, Sam could regain the battalion's warmth and comradeship.

He turned the horse southwards.

A miracle was coming from the mist.

Redcoats.

Lines of Redcoats. Redcoats marching beneath their colours to take victory where they had tasted defeat.

Sam stared.

Ahead of the advancing line were the skirmishers and Sam recognized Sergeant Scammell at their fore. Sam grinned. The handful of prisoners had also seen their salvation. They stood and cheered as their guards fled.

"Sam!" Nate's scream was despairing, frantic.

"You're too late!" Sam shouted. He stood in the stirrups and waved at the advancing battalion. Some of the skirmishers fired at the fleeing guards and one of the Americans span in the field, fell to his knees, then pitched forwards. A bagpipe skirled suddenly, fierce and blazoning, revealing a Highland regiment on the road's flank.

"Sam!" Nate was leaning on the fence, frantically gesturing for Sam to bring him the horse. "Sam!"

"We've won, Nate! We've won!" Sam's exhilaration soared. "We've bloody won!"

Sergeant Scammell was waving now, shouting incomprehensibly at Sam, and the sight of his hated enemy made Nate turn and run. He ran northwards, running away from the Redcoats, running to the freedom that had haunted his dreams in the weeks since the army had come ashore in Chesapeake Bay.

"Nate!" Sam shouted, then twisted the stallion's head round. "Nate!"

But Nate was fleeing. Nate had tasted a moment's freedom and he wanted more. He took off his red coat as he ran and threw the heavy woollen garment down as though it would slow his bid to reach the paradise he sought.

"Private Gilpin! Halt!" Scammell, leading the skirmishers and far ahead of the battalion, shouted at Nate.

Nate, boots sticky in the thick mud, floundered on.

Sergeant Scammell pulled back the cock of his musket. He put the brass butt to his shoulder and aimed down the crude sights.

"Put it down!" Jonathon Becket, lying by the roadside fifteen yards from Scammell, aimed his pistol.

But Sergeant Michael Scammell feared no wounded rebel boy. "Stop!" he shouted.

"Sergeant!" Sam shouted the word.

Scammell fired.

The flint fell on frizzen, sparked to the pan, and the gun bucked back in its cloud of smoke.

Sam saw the powder flash in the pan, then the gout of flame-driven smoke from the muzzle and he was turning, shouting, screaming, but Nate was arching his back and in the very centre of his spine a great smear of red spread on his dirty grey shirt.

"Sam!" It was a scream like a man on the edge of hell. Nate was on his knees now, still trying to go forwards, but falling. "Sam?"

The range must have been thirty yards. A long shot for a musket. Fifteen yards was no great distance for a pistol, but Jonathon's shot, fired from an enfeebled hand, went yards wide. Sergeant Scammell walked up to the boy, stared down with eyes like agate, then ground his boot's heel into Jonathon's wounded thigh. Jonathon screamed.

Nate twitched face down on the road. Blood soaked his shirt. His fingers scrabbled for purchase as his head turned towards his brother. "Sam? Sam?"

"Nate!"

Sam had kicked the horse onwards. He jumped the fence, reined in, and slid out of the saddle. He let the horse run free. Loyalist cavalry had appeared in the pasture beyond the fence, and some were on the road ahead, but Sam saw none of them. He only saw his brother. "Nate?"

"Sam." Nate was crying now. The sobs became great pangs of agony in which Sam could hear the word Mother again and again.

Sam lifted his brother, turning and cradling him. "Nate?"

But Nate could not hear. Nate bent his back like a man broken on the wheel and his scream pierced through the fog in terrible agony before the blood, flooding up his windpipe, choked it off. Sam, holding his brother as though he could put his own life and strength into Nate's body, felt the terrible jerk as the scream ended.

Blood spilt like water and there was silence. Nate's eyes glazed. There was no movement, except in the fingers of Nate's left hand which slowly, slowly curled. He was dead.

"Nate?" Sam asked. "Nate?"

His brother's head was tilted back from Sam's left arm. Blood trickled down the dead face to mat Nate's hair.

"Nate?"

A shadow fell over Sam. Sergeant Scammell had seized the black horse's bridle and now, standing above Sam, he looked down on the dead boy. "He was running, Sam."

"You murdered him."

"He was running!" Scammell snapped the words. "Now get your red coat on before I say you were running, Sam Gilpin!"

Sam laid his brother in the mud. He stroked Nate's cheek once, feeling the stickiness of blood, then stood. "You murdered him."

"He was running."

"You murdered him!"

Scammell stared coldly into Sam's eyes. "Be careful, Sam."

"Bastard."

Scammell's hand flicked out to strike sense into Sam, but Sam's world had changed. Everything had changed. "Bastard!" He hit Scammell one huge blow; a blow that snapped Scammell's face round and made the Sergeant release the horse.

Sam seized the reins. Scammell had lost his balance, but was trying to unsling the bayonet-tipped musket from his shoulder. Sam kicked the Sergeant in the belly, then, blinded by tears, he pulled himself on to the stallion's back.

There was madness and tears and a sorrow fit to fill a world in Sam. He heard shouts. The field was a blur of red coats, of flags, of thinning smoke and tears. He saw his brother's dead face, and then he kicked back his heels as if he would ride the black stallion to the world's ending.

The stallion took Sam away from the smoke and the red coats. Scammell shouted in rage behind, but Sam did not hear, for Nate was dead and all the King's horses and all the King's men were like dust in the eye for Sam now. He was a Redcoat, and his brother, with all his dreams of paradise beyond the hills, was dead. And Sam, riding to nowhere, wept.

FIFTEEN

Bands played. The fog was a cacophony of brass and drums, jingling-johnnies and flutes, all punctuated by gunfire and accompanied by the unending musketry.

The sound jarred Sir William's ears as he waited for his doom to burst down the village's main street. The enemy skirmishers, harbingers of British defeat, increased, yet moment succeeded moment and no American columns appeared beneath their lifted banners. Artillery fired, but no roundshot bounded towards Sir William. It almost seemed as though George Washington's forces conducted a private war in the cloaking whiteness.

"You don't think . . ." Sir William heard himself beginning to express the hope of victory, then checked the tentative words lest he tempted providence.

The mist thinned and paled to reveal a chaos of men. The wounded dragged themselves for succour, the dead lay where they had fallen, while the living had the wide- and empty-eyed look of those who must still endure death's lottery. Yet in the chaos, drawn by Sir William's will, there was the shape of a counter-attack ready to advance. Sir William looked at his watch, snapped the lid shut, and nodded. "Put the hounds to work."

The colours of three regiments were heaved into the sky. Officers calmed horses and sergeants filled their lungs. "By the right! Quick march!"

Sticks fell on newly tightened drumskins. The attack, lurching and ponderous, advanced. Trumpets extolled them to victory, galloper guns protected their flanks, and the great fringed squares of silk led them towards the cauldron of noise where the rebel strength lay.

George Washington had held victory in the palm of his hand, but let it go.

In the centre of the field, where the rebels could have broken Sir

William's defences, Washington had turned aside to attack the house where Musgrave's 40th had gone to earth. Rebel cannon-balls bounced from brick and masonry walls to be answered with jeers and musketry. The dead thickened in the garden and orchard, and the dead were all rebels.

Outside the village, where men marched to support the central fight, the fog brought fratricide. Two rebel regiments, each mistaking the other for enemy, opened fire. Rebel slaughtered rebel, and on their flanks, like an avenging torrent, the red-coated counterattack drove home.

Murderous volleys tore the rebel lines to bloody shreds. The attack drove mercilessly on. Bereft of orders, lost, defeated, the Americans gave ground, and the retreat turned into flight.

God wore a red coat that day.

The American centre had nearly snatched victory, but faltered. The right had struck a Hessian-defended ravine, and halted. The rebel left had driven deep into the British lines and captured the bivouac area where the chance of plunder checked their advance as surely as any Redcoat volley. Their officers had tried to roust them onwards, and wondered when the promised support would come from the centre or the left. It did not come, and the Virginians were stranded.

Captain Christopher Vane rode towards that embattled flank. He met a brigade major who offered him a flask of brandy and gestured towards the sod bivouacs that studded the gardens and fields. "Fully of Virginians," he said cheerfully. A rifle bullet, fired by a rebel sharpshooter, whiplashed between the two officers. The major would not give the enemy the satisfaction of appearing to notice the threat. "They're trapped."

"Trapped?"

"We've sent two battalions to their north. Ten minutes, Kit, and they'll have to surrender." The major raised the brandy flask in a toast. "I give you joy of the day."

"Indeed!" Vane felt the exhilaration of victory as Redcoat volleys scoured the edge of the bivouacs. The lead balls thumped into turf huts and spurted embers from the cooking fires that had been abandoned in the dawn. The Virginians, who had fought so deeply into the British line, were being crammed into a small tight scrap of hell where the bullets thudded and the smoke thickened. Around them, making a new fog with powdersmoke, the Redcoats and Hessians fired. They had faces smeared black with powder, and blackened lips drawn back from snarling teeth as they killed and went on killing. Men tore their fingernails as they clawed at flints. They loaded and reloaded, pouring death into a shrinking circle. Musket fire came back from the rebels, but the American fire was drowned by the slaughtering, vengeful musketry of the victors.

The rebel fight ended when Hessian cannons, charged with the canister that broke apart like birdshot from the bucking muzzles, opened fire. The smoke billowed in vast clouds towards the camp where bivouacs were shattered into scraps of turf and wood and screaming men. From somewhere in the fog-shrouded horror a voice shouted for the Germans to hold their fire.

The guns, that had hammered five yards back with each killing shot, fell silent. The smoke, thick as gruel and stinking of blood, drifted with the shredding fog. A white shirt, pathetically torn, waved from the rebel ranks.

"I think that'll serve!" the major said cheerfully. "You care to join me, Kit?"

They rode forwards, swords sheathed, and from all around the bivouac other officers trotted towards the rebel regiment. The Virginians' colonel, surrounded, outnumbered, and bereft of the support his general had promised, helped his officers tear their flag to small shreds which they burned on a Hessian fire. Some of their men wept for the shame of it. Others smashed their muskets on the ground, breaking the butts so the weapons could not be used against the Patriots. Others, the wounded, just bled and suffered.

"Captain Vane!" A Hessian colonel, recognizing Sir William's new aide, spurred towards Vane. "My joy for you!"

"And mine for you, sir." Vane leaned over and shook the colonel's hand. The first Redcoats and Hessians, victorious, were tearing at rebel coats and pouches, seeking coins or rum, food or keepsakes. Vane watched them, then saw the enemy officers, faces drawn, walk with their swords ready to be surrendered. Vane took pleasure in the sight, but knew, perhaps better than any man, just how close this day had been. Had it not been for Washington's blunders it could well have been the Redcoats who now offered their reversed blades to the victors.

That horrid thought made Vane twist his mare away from the surrendering enemy officers. He rode through the sullen and defeated ranks and saw, far to the north, other British battalions marching in pursuit of the enemy. He put his spurs back, revelling in the sudden freedom of clean air that did not stink of smoke or blood. His mare's hooves drummed the earth. To his left, pale in the mist that still clung in patches to the wet soil, a house burned.

The fields were littered with the sad droppings of battle. Muskets lay in the grass. Bodies lay in clumps, sometimes alone. They looked oddly small. Most, Vane noted dispassionately, had curled fists. A wounded man clutching a seeping hole in his belly staggered southwards. A horse, one leg broken, tried to struggle from a ditch, then screamed as a woman, come to plunder the field, slashed its neck. The horse quivered, thrashed, died, and the woman, helped by two small children, lost no time in unbuckling its expensive saddle. Other women, camp followers who scented plunder, were coming with drawn knives to deal with the dying and the dead. The children acted as scouts for the women, seeking out the men who were too badly hurt to resist the knives and mauling hands. British and rebels alike were killed and plundered. Screams sounded. It was the noise of a field after victory.

A spurt of musketry splintered the clearing mist and Vane saw rebels running from the British advance. Green-uniformed horsemen were far to the east; American Loyalists on the Old York Road who would head those fleeing rebels off and savage them with sabre cuts. A cheer sounded, drawing Vane's attention north again, where a group of British prisoners, released by the day's fortunes, welcomed their liberators.

And Vane saw his stallion.

He saw the black horse with its white socks being ridden by a white-shirted man who jumped a rail fence then leaped from the saddle. He fell down and clutched the body of a dead man. Another man, a Redcoat, took the horse's reins.

Christopher Vane stared, scarcely believing his good fortune. He shouted, but was too far away to be heard. He would have to pay a reward to whoever had found the stallion, but better that than lose the horse itself. He kicked back with his heels and the mare, winded and tired by her day's exertions, went into a reluctant trot.

Then Vane saw the white-shirted man stand, turn, and hit the Redcoat. Vane shouted helplessly. The Redcoat stumbled and the other man was climbing into the saddle and galloping northwards.

The exhausted mare could never catch the black stallion. Vane shouted uselessly, then saw deliverance. From the wooded valley at the far side of the road, pursuing the rebel guards who had tried to escape, burst the green uniforms of the Loyalist hussars. Sabres, bright against the thinning mist, slashed down. A man, screaming, twisted with blood splashing. Rebels tried to surrender, but there was no war so bitter as that between fellow countrymen, and the American hussars gave no quarter. Six of the Loyalists, sabres reddened, had jumped the fence into the road to complete the encirclement of their victims and, in doing so, had headed off the stallion.

The boy who rode the black horse turned away from the horsemen as though he would set the stallion to jump the fence into the field. He rode, Vane noted, beautifully, but the stallion stumbled at the verge and gave time for Vane, who had mercilessly raked his mare's flanks with his spurs, to leap the low rail, turn, and, as calmly as if he met a friend in some English lane, lean over and take the black horse's bridle.

The stallion, recognizing its stable companion, whinnied and ducked its head. The horses nuzzled each other and Vane found himself staring into the wide, battle-maddened eyes of a young, good-looking boy. "Good afternoon," Vane said. "At least I think it's afternoon. Some bastard stole my watch, or perhaps I lost it. Are you English?"

"Sir?" Sam was shaking like a leaf in storm. "Yes, sir."

Vane leaned over and fondled the stallion's ears. "My horse. I do thank you. I suppose you'll want the reward?"

"Your horse?"

Vane could see that the boy's wits were gone to the wind, as if he had stood too close to a cannon's muzzle when it fired. "I couldn't afford him," Vane said conversationally, "but I thought he might win a race or two for me." He sensed that this boy was ready to snap. "I shouldn't really keep him with a mare, but it seemed a pity to geld him. Don't you agree?"

The boy turned and stared at a dead man who lay in the mud. In the field the last rebels died beneath the hussars' blades. A horseman laughed.

"He's called Hector," Vane said. "Not a very good name, but the man who sold it to me had no imagination, none. What's your name?"

"Me?" Sam seemed unaware that his mount had been captured. "Sam, sir. Sam Gilpin."

"Gilpin? A very English name." And a very English face, too, Vane thought. Not the usual surly, squat and toothless horror, but a fine-looking Saxon boy. The very face of England, Vane considered, and he wondered why such a boy would join the army. "You must ride well, Private Gilpin. Hector's a lively beast, isn't he?"

"Yes, sir." Sam was staring at Nate. Sam's eyes were puffy and the musket stains on his face streaked with tears.

"Gilpin! Off that bloody horse!" Sergeant Scammell, who had run after Sam, took his hat off to Vane, his only acknowledgement of the officer's presence. "You bastard! Off!"

"You'd better do what he says," Vane said in a kindly sort of way.

"Sir?" Sam frowned at the staff officer, then twisted to look at Scammell. "You killed him! You murdered him!"

"And you hit me, you bastard, and you're going to have a skinning for that, Sam Gilpin!" Scammell's face was bruised.

"He was my brother!" Sam's scream was filled with all his hopelessness and grief.

Scammell seized Sam's leg, twisted and pulled, and the boy tumbled from the saddle. "Bastard!" Scammell kicked Sam as Captain Vane, still scarcely believing his good luck in retrieving the stallion, pulled the horse away from the two men and led it towards a group of mounted officers.

Lieutenant-Colonel Elliott, introduced to Vane, offered a flask of rum and congratulations. News was exchanged, and relieved laughter sounded loud on the muddy road. A Highland regiment, plaids swinging, marched north in the pasture. From the village to the west, guns pursued the fleeing Americans with roundshot.

"You look as if you were in the thick of it, Vane?" Elliott said.

Vane glanced at the dried blood on his breeches. The morning's events seemed a very long way away. "It was my servant, sir. Fellow had the ill manners to die all over me."

"Could he cook?"

"Not well."

"Then you won't regret him. Always have a servant who can cook." Lieutenant-Colonel Elliott stared north. "My God, but the Yankee-doodles broke sudden!"

"Didn't they." A scream came from the roadside and Vane turned to see an American prisoner being forced to his feet. The prisoner was a wounded cripple who could not stand, so a lieutenant ordered a stretcher to be made from two captured rebel muskets and two jackets.

Then a shout made Vane look to where the fair-haired boy who had been riding the stallion was backed against the fence by the furious sergeant. Vane frowned. "That lad there, Sam Gilpin. Is he any good?"

Elliott clearly thought it odd to be asked such a question, but Vane was an aide to Sir William, and to be humoured. "He works miracles with horses. Christ knows why he didn't join the cavalry."

"Or why he joined the army at all," Vane said. "He seems to be in bad odour with his sergeant?"

Elliott smiled. "Scammell's not a man to cross, Vane."

Sergeant Scammell was spitting words into Sam Gilpin's face. "You hit me, Sam Gilpin! You hit me! I'm going to have you on a triangle and I'm going to have you flogged till your ribs are polished!"

Sam stared back, murder in his face. "You shot him!"

"He was running! And you didn't stop him! I'll have you flogged for that too, you bastard!" Scammell struck Sam's face once, twice, a third time. "You bastard!"

"Enough!" The voice came from behind Scammell. It was a sharp, authoritative voice that made the sergeant turn and look up to see the strange officer who had stopped Sam's panicked flight.

"Sir?" Scammell stood to attention.

Christopher Vane was not certain why, a moment before, he had asked Elliott's permission to intervene. Perhaps it was because he had seen Sam Gilpin's skill with the stallion, or perhaps it was the euphoria of victory. Whatever, Vane now held Sam's fate in his hand. "Were you running, Gilpin?"

"The bastard was running, sir," Scammell said confidingly.

"I didn't ask you, Sergeant, did I?"

"No, sir." All Sergeant Scammell's scorn for officers was invested in the two words.

"Well?" Vane looked back to Sam.

"He killed my brother, sir."

"I didn't ask you that!" Vane made his voice sharp. "Were you running?"

"No, sir!" In truth Sam did not know what he had been doing. He had just been filled with a hopeless rage.

"He's bloody lying, sir!" Sergeant Scammell had been hit by Sam Gilpin and Sergeant Scammell was not a man to let such an insult pass. He feared that this officer's intervention might interfere with natural justice, and felt he had to make his own position very clear. "He's a bloody liar, sir, and he's going to the triangle."

Vane had heard Sergeant Scammell's scorn earlier and could not resist swatting the man down. "You can't flog my servant. At least not without my permission, Sergeant."

"Your servant, sir?" Sergeant Scammell put as much outrage as he dared into his voice.

Vane chose to take the question as an honourable salutation. "Thank you, Sergeant." He looked at Sam. "Can you cook, Sam Gilpin?"

Sam stared uncomprehendingly at the blood-spattered officer.

"Can you cook?" Vane asked again.

"Cook sir? No, sir."

"But you can learn? And you can ride. Take it." He threw the stallion's reins to Sam. "And follow me."

Sam did not move, only stared.

"Well?" Vane was relishing the role of God. Just as Sir William had plucked him from the humdrum duties of a regimental officer, so Vane would now use his staff officer's patronage to rescue this private. "You'd rather be flogged?" Vane asked.

Sam suddenly broke free of the Sergeant and, hurrying lest this quixotic officer change his mind, went and scooped up his red coat that had fallen from Jonathon's body, then put a foot into the stallion's stirrup and swung himself into the saddle. Clutching the jacket, he looked towards the corpse of his brother and checked when he saw that two soldiers were stripping Nate naked ready for the common burial pit. All soldiers were stripped thus, but it was hard to watch. Sam would have liked to say a prayer, or even to have dug a separate grave, but there was no time, for his new master was impatient. "Come on," Captain Vane said, "I'm devilish hungry."

Sergeant Scammell could do nothing, the British had a victory, and Sam had been saved. He rode across a field of blood between the skeins of acrid smoke. Mister Washington had sought the battle, Sir William had won it, Sam was a twin no more, and everything, by the touch of fire and steel, was changed.

PART TWO

SIXTEEN

Mrs Elizabeth Loring, glorious Lizzie Loring, stood beside Sir William Howe and smiled in gracious welcome at her lover's guests.

Sir William himself was resplendent in a coat of brightest red that was festooned with loops and chains and lace of gold. A white silk stock, fashionably plumped about a golden pin, bulged between his collar turnbacks that were edged with golden braid. A gilt and enamel star blazed from a slanting blue sash that lay on his comfortable belly. Wigged, fashionably red-heeled, and happy, Sir William stood beside his paramour and was the proudest man in Philadelphia.

A minuet filled the room with sweetness. The musicians wore powdered wigs that tightly framed their sweat-sheened, absorbed faces. Their white uniforms were gaudy with scarlet turnbacks, crimson facings, and gilded epaulettes which caught the light of the tall candles that illuminated the music stands.

Mrs Loring, gracious Mrs Loring, wore a polonaise of blue watered silk, its skirt slashed and kirtled over a petticoat of ivory brocade. The blue silk gown was embroidered with lilac roses and cut very low. Beneath her breasts hung strings of pearls, hugging their silk-clad lower contours, while on their upper slopes, bravely bared and softly powdered, lay two small black beauty patches of heart-shaped velvet. Her golden hair was piled in a baroque confection of curls and swags that sparkled with pearl tears hanging on silver hooks from bows of crimson silk. The elaborate coiffure, which, like the dress, was so much more fashionable than any other in the room, soared to its peak a full fifteen inches above the top of her head.

Champagne, which, because the rebel forts still barred the Lower Delaware, had been fetched overland from the victualling ships in Chesapeake Bay, was poured into fine crystal glasses that tinkled a ragged rhythm beneath the sweeter sound of violins, bass viols, and flutes. Perhaps two hundred guests were present, perhaps more, but such was the prodigality of the Commander-in-Chief's invitation list that no one could be certain. They were there to celebrate the restoration of the monarchy to America's largest city. A great fire, banked within the marble fireplace, warmed the room so well that the glazed garden doors had been flung open and some of the guests had drifted on to the lantern-lit terrace. A chandelier, hung with crystal drops and blazing with three score of white expensive candles, shivered in the night breeze coming from the windows.

"Mr and Mrs Abel Becket!" A uniformed major-domo, magnificent by the double doors which led into the hall, announced the newcomers in a sonorous voice.

"Upon my word, it's Mr Becket! My pleasure, sir, my extreme pleasure!" And Sir William, who had never met the man before, did exude much pleasure at the meeting, treating Abel Becket as though he was an old, much missed, and valued friend. "And your dear wife. What signal honour your attendance does me, ma'am." Sir William bowed low over Hannah Becket's pudgy gloved hand. "You will permit me to name Mrs Elizabeth Loring to you?"

Lizzie offered her lace-gloved fingers to Mr Becket who seemed transfixed by the generous bosoms that lay just beneath his gaze. His face, unable to hide the disgust he felt, twitched away, but he could not ignore the mistress of the man upon whose efforts depended the restoration of the city's trade. He touched cold fingers to the lace gloves. "Mrs Loring."

"You must call me Elizabeth."

"Indeed, ma'am." Abel Becket had never seen as much of his wife's breasts as Mrs Loring saw fit to present to the world.

"Loyalist merchant," Ambrose Serle, Sir William's private secretary, whispered into his master's ear during this ill-matched exchange, "of importance."

"You must tell me," Sir William was amused by the shocked reaction of his guests to Lizzie's splendours, "how we can best serve your trade, Mr Becket? You merchants are our strength in the colonies, and we must not ignore you!"

"You can take the forts, Sir William." Abel Becket decided that bluntness was the best policy. "The river will freeze, sir, freeze! And if we don't have a chance to float our cargoes out we'll be ruined, and if the city isn't victualled you'll be ruined with us."

"I shall take the forts," Sir William said. "Indeed, that is my chief object in these coming weeks."

"Weeks!" Abel Becket, fearing that his purchase of black walnut might prove the ruin of his fortune, could not contain his indignation.

"Slow and steady, Mr Becket!" Sir William beamed happily. "Now, let me worry about the fortresses while you partake of some champagne. A scarce beverage, but one I'm partial to, and Mrs Loring can vouch that it travelled remarkably well!"

Abel Becket turned away from the shocking orbs, and wondered how any man, least of all a Commander-in-Chief and Peace Commissioner, could bring his mistress to meet respectable people. If this was how things were arranged in London then it might be better . . . But that line of thought was too dangerous, too rebellious, and he sheered away from it as he took his wife across the crowded room to the safer haven of the Revd MacTeague's company.

"What a dull man!" Lizzie said to Sir William. She had bright large eyes that now left Abel Becket's retreating back and fixed themselves on a red-coated officer whose sword slings were of new silver chain, and who wore bright new aiguillettes to denote his status as an aide-de-camp. "Is that your new boy?"

"Indeed it is. Captain Vane!"

Vane crossed to Sir William, was introduced to Mrs Loring, and bowed low before her beauty. "Ma'am."

Lizzie left her gloved fingers in Vane's hand. "Sir William tells me you showed exemplary bravery at Germantown, Captain?"

"He's very kind, ma'am." Vane, hearing the praise that was balm to his ears, could not hide his pleasure.

"Too kind, some say," Lizzie smiled, "especially to Americans."

Vane knew he was being tested, but quite to what purpose he was not sure. He smiled. "I can see why, ma'am."

Sir William was delighted with Vane's compliment, but Sir William was delighted with everything about this splendid evening. He gestured at the lavish room. "Isn't this magnificent, Kit? Quite the equal of anything in London!" The intricately plastered drawing-room, if not perhaps quite deserving of Sir William's exaggerated praise, was nevertheless ornately impressive. Mirrors fixed within elegant stucco panels multiplied the blazing spermaceti candles in shimmers of fractured light. The house, commandeered as Sir William's Philadelphia headquarters, was the most lavish of the great mercantile mansions in the city.

"You must enjoy yourself, Kit!" Sir William thus affably dismissed his newest aide and, as the musicians struck up the popular tune of 'Youth's the Season', he rocked up and down on his high red heels. At this moment Sir William was replete with a warm and generous happiness. Hamlet, his dog, was still lost, but that was the only cloud to mar Sir William's contentment, and he yet dared to hope that the silver tag attached to the dog's collar might effect Hamlet's safe return. All else was blissful. He had won a victory, Philadelphia was safe, his own wife was in England, and Lizzie's husband was in New York.

Sir William's nocturnal comforts were thus assured, but the aides still sought their own similar consolations. Christopher Vane exchanged impressions with John Andre who, like himself, had been scouting the feminine charms of the crowded rooms. Vane gestured towards a girl in a green dress that was swollen at her hips by old-fashioned panniers. "She has a charming smile, don't you think?"

Andre flinched dramatically. "Her teeth are atrocious, and she has breath like a cesspit. I made her laugh a moment ago and fell instantly out of love with her. How about the one in blue stripes?"

Christopher Vane shuddered. "If Helen launched a thousand ships, John, then I don't suppose that girl would cause a toy boat to be floated."

"You are difficult to please." Andre pointed towards the door. "How about the girl in the cream cotton? Didn't I see you clumsily trying to seduce her?"

Vane smiled. "I was beating her off, my friend. Do you like the creature? Her name's Peggy Shippen. I might award her two or three small rowboats."

"You're devilish unfair, Kit." The girl had golden hair, fresh skin, and blue eyes. "I think I would award her a flotilla." John Andre straightened his jacket. "You will excuse me?"

Miss Shippen was too fleshy for Vane's taste. He smiled. "I shall wish you joy of the battle, John, and a speedy surrender of the foe."

Vane, alone once more, wandered the sumptuous rooms, smiling at merchants' wives and picking at the great plates of oysters that were arrayed for the guests' delectation. He eyed the girls, but saw none that stirred him to the effort of flirtation. Lord

Robert Massedene was dancing with a tall red-haired girl whom Vane might have thought attractive if she had not already been enfolded in Massedene's arms.

"What do they call you, Captain Vane? Christopher, Kit, or Kitten?"

Vane turned and was surprised to see Lizzie Loring smiling at him. He bowed. "Never the latter, ma'am."

"I imagine not. Kit, then?"

"Indeed."

"And I'm Lizzie." She put an arm into Vane's and led him across the room to a table heaped with food. "Billy has been cornered by tradesmen, who bore me." She took an oyster and slid it into her mouth. "The best in all the world," she sighed.

"Ma'am?"

"The oysters, Kit! You surely admit that America has the finest oysters?"

Vane, who was frequently irritated by the colonists' habit of claiming all things American to be finer, larger, or more beautiful than anything in existence elsewhere, could not bring himself to contradict this dazzling American beauty who had such influence over Sir William. "They're very fine, ma'am."

"Fine?" Lizzie repeated his mild praise indignantly. "Our oysters, Kit, are culled from the beds of heaven, nurtured on the milk of angels, and are fit only for the gods to eat." She laughed, slipped her arm into Vane's again, and led him on to the terrace where a few late fireflies glittered prettily in the dark shrubbery which hid the slave quarters and the stables. "No girl, Captain?"

"I'm the duty aide tonight."

"How seriously you do take your duty," Lizzie said with an airy scorn, yet, by her intimate closeness to Vane, she made him feel the pleasure of other men's jealousy.

Lizzie danced two small steps in time to the music, then scooped a glass of the champagne from a passing orderly. "Do you think this is the beginning of peace, Captain?"

"Do you, ma'am?" Vane was guarded.

"Billy does. And he plans to stay in the colonies once the treaty's signed."

"Have the rebels accepted talks?"

"They will," Lizzie smoothed out her lustrous skirts and perched delicately on a stone balustrade beneath the lanterns that fluttered thick with moths, "as long as we treat them with dignity.

Today, Captain, you refused to allow a delegation of women to see Sir William?"

Vane realized that this clever and pretty woman had accosted him with a purpose, and he felt a resentment that she could so interfere with his duties simply because she was a general's whore. "The General was busy," Vane said coldly. The delegation had come to plead for the Patriot civilians who, remaining in Philadelphia, had been illegally imprisoned by the Loyalists before the British arrived. Vane had received the unfortunate prisoners' wives, then shrugged away their petition. It was clear, however, that the women had found their champion in Sir William's mistress. "They're all going to be released tomorrow," Lizzie said.

"If Sir William decides . . ."

"He has."

Vane shrugged off the defeat. "Doubtless the jails will soon be full again."

Lizzie watched him as though she truly wished to understand what was in his mind. "I'm told, Captain, that you're one of those men who believe the rebels must be punished for their temerity in defying King George?"

Vane wanted to say that his views were none of Mrs Loring's business, but knew this woman's power precluded such a challenge. "If we concede to the rebels at the negotiating table, ma'am, then we encourage other men to follow their example. The whole Empire will then seethe with hooligans! No, ma'am, rebels must be punished as a lesson to others."

Lizzie Loring pretended to consider his words. "But then, having whipped the children, how do you rule a nursery that is disaffected by hatred for you?"

"Let them hate us."

"So long as they fear you?" Lizzie mocked him with laughter. "You have pride, Captain Vane! Is that because you're a merchant's son?"

Vane stared into Lizzie's eyes that reflected the lanterns like tiny bright sparks, and he wondered who had gossiped about him. Massedene? "No, ma'am."

"The English hold such a ridiculous animosity towards tradesmen, don't they? It must make you eager for acceptance." Lizzie seemed oblivious to the fact that she was clawing at Vane's most sensitive fears, or else she believed that her beauty gave her the right to speak as she wished. She smiled. "But I wanted to plead with you to support Sir William's ambitions, Captain. He wants to make peace without more killing, and I believe that wish deserves the support of his military family."

"Indeed, ma'am." Vane said it neutrally. He allowed that Lizzie Loring might wish to surround her lover with cosy agreement, but Vane was not going to change his mind just because she bared half her breasts and smiled sweetly. Yet, he knew it would be dangerous to make an enemy of this woman who had such influence over the Commander-in-Chief. "I can assure you, ma'am, that no aide is as assiduous as I in the discharge of duty. Will that satisfy you?"

But Lizzie Loring appeared not to be listening to him. Instead, and distracted by a stir at one of the glazed doors leading from the house, she looked to her right and Vane turned to see what had drawn her attention.

He looked and the world stood still.

A woman, tall, slender, and young, stood imperious and splendid in the doorway. She wore a simple dress of scarlet cotton, but on her straight body it seemed a gown of the highest fashion. Her hair was witch black and curled softly about a narrow fine face that was given striking character by a touch of anger.

A lieutenant whose task it was merely to usher guests about the mansion this evening appeared at the woman's side and, seeing Vane, led her across the terrace. "Sir? May I name Mrs Martha Crowl?" The lieutenant was nervous.

"Your servant, ma'am." Vane bowed to her.

"Captain Vane, ma'am," the lieutenant said. "Sir William's duty aide."

"You can call him Kit," Lizzie had clearly sensed Vane's hostility towards her, "and I'm Elizabeth Loring."

The two women stared at each other and a flicker of sympathy must have shown in each face, for Martha gave a quick, intimate smile that struck like a dart into Vane's soul. He wondered by what magic such women communicated.

"Mrs Crowl would urgently like to speak with the Commander-in-Chief," the lieutenant explained. "I told her that Sir William was . . ."

"Sir William would be delighted to meet you," Lizzie interrupted as she waved the lieutenant away. "To my certain knowledge he's been trapped with some tedious merchants for the last half hour. Shall we rescue him?"

Sir William was indeed trapped, and also standing too close to the antechamber's fire which he feared would be scorching his silk stockings. However, he dared not move for fear of causing offence to a delegation of Philadelphia's merchants who had cornered him. They bored him, but Sir William knew he must show polite interest in their problems. These, after all, were the solid men on whom the wealth of the colonies depended, and the men who were among the staunchest defenders of royal power. "I do assure you," Sir William said for the third or fourth time, "that the river forts will be taken. Upon my word, gentlemen, they will!"

"They must!" a furniture manufacturer said gloomily.

"And they will!" Sir William wished one of his aides would come to his rescue, but doubtless they were all busy with young ladies.

Abel Becket demanded to know by what date the river would be free for traffic. "I have cargoes ready for Britain! Sawn walnut, Sir William, which is already late for the market."

"I'm sure, I'm sure." Sir William, his backside roasting because of its proximity to the flames, wondered what perverse fate had driven him to the company of a timber merchant. "But the river will be open in good time."

"Before the ice comes, I hope," Becket went on. "Or the French?"

The last remark piqued Sir William, who offered one of his rare frowns. Such talk was defeatist. "The French, Mr Becket, do not want to be embroiled in the rebellion! Oh, I don't deny they would like to see Britain embarrassed, but at the price of republicanism? France is a monarchy!" Sir William said the last patronizingly, as though a provincial American trader might not be expected to know much of Europe's governance. "Besides," Sir William brightened, "the rebellion will soon be over. We have had the good fortune to smite Mister Washington another blow. I cannot see his men enduring a winter, upon my soul I can't! And very soon, gentlemen, we will hear of General Burgoyne's success. New England chopped away!"

"Praise God," said the Revd MacTeague, who was eavesdropping on the conversation.

"I believe peace is a genuine and imminent likelihood." Sir William ignored the fat minister who was pestering headquarters to be allowed to hold a solemn service of thanksgiving for the victory of Germantown. Sir William wanted nothing solemn, only joyful things like the tune of 'The World Turned Upside Down' which the musicians were now playing to a quick tempo. A flash of shining blue passed by one of the terrace doors, and, much to his relief, Sir William saw Lizzie discreetly beckon to him. "You must forgive me, gentlemen?" he hummed and hawed as though matters of great military moment demanded his immediate attention.

And in a way, they did, for Martha Crowl, taken to the empty library of the house, confronted Sir William with a bitter accusation of callousness. Had Sir William, she demanded, visited the hospitals where the rebel wounded had been placed?

Sir William, who admired ladies of spirit, even when they interrupted his carousing, confessed that he had not.

But Martha Crowl had troubled herself to visit the hospitals, and now she told Sir William of the horrors in the overcrowded wards, and of the untended agony that the wounded suffered. Lizzie Loring, sitting at the room's edge, listened with Captain Vane.

"And my own brother," Martha said, "is dying in one such hospital."

There was silence in the library, except for the tinkling music that echoed down the corridor outside.

"I am so very sorry," Sir William said at last. He frowned, seeking more adequate words, but found none. "I am so very sorry."

"I have tried to have him moved," Martha said, "as I tried, Sir William, to take comfort to all the wounded. Both requests were denied me. Your doctors will not tend the American wounded until your own men are treated, but nor will they allow our own doctors into the hospitals. It is not civilized, Sir William."

"No." Sir William was evidently upset by Martha's news and Vane noted how he instinctively looked towards Mrs Loring for support. Sir William was also clearly intrigued by Martha's use of the possessive 'our'. "Might I ask, forgive me, but are you of the rebel persuasion, Mrs Crowl?"

"I am a Patriot, sir, and proud of it."

"I am grateful for your honesty. Truly." Sir William paused again. "And do I presume, ma'am, that as you are here alone your husband is fighting for Mister Washington?"

"My husband is dead, sir, but doubtless had he lived he would have fought in General Washington's ranks."

Sir William heard the stress on the word 'general', and smiled. "We stubbornly refuse to recognize his rank, ma'am, for which you must forgive us." He twisted to look at Christopher Vane. "Are you the duty man, Kit?"

"I am, sir."

"Perhaps you'll notify the hospitals that any civilians wishing to tend the rebel wounded must be offered every facility?"

Vane nodded. "Of course, sir. I'll have the order drafted tonight."

Sir William turned back to Martha. "You say your brother is dying?"

"Unless his leg is removed, yes." Martha hesitated, but could not resist rubbing salt into Sir William's discomfort. "And I should not even have known, Sir William, had I not insisted on searching the hospitals." Martha, like other women in the city who sought news of their relatives, had gone to discover whether any of the prisoners had seen Jonathon in the battle, but, instead of news, she had found Jonathon himself. "I insisted on being given entrance," she said defiantly.

Sir William smiled. "I am glad you did, ma'am."

"But they would not permit me to remove Jonathon."

"It will be arranged immediately." He turned. "Kit?"

"At once, sir." Vane looked at Martha. "Where is your brother, Mrs Crowl?"

"In the State House, Captain."

"You wish him moved where?" Vane was pencilling notes in a small book.

"My house is the limestone building on the corner of Fourth and Market. Might I suggest you bring Jonathon through the backyard and down the steps to the kitchen? I shall have a surgeon waiting."

Vane gave a condescending smile at the implied suggestion that he should carry a wounded rebel through the streets. "My servant will bring him, ma'am. Your brother's name?"

"Jonathon Becket."

Sir William gave a surprised start. "Not Abel Becket's son?"

"His nephew, Sir William, though Mr Becket has disowned any of his family who are Patriots." Martha said it with a biting scorn, then softened her tone as she bowed her head towards the Commander-in-Chief. "I am grateful to you, Sir William."

The bow was returned. "I only regret the necessity that brought you to this house, ma'am."

"I am thankful I came." Martha seemed surprised at the ease of her victory, then became flustered when Vane offered her his arm.

"You said the matter was urgent, ma'am. Shall we therefore deal with it urgently?"

"Yes, Captain." Martha, suddenly obedient, took the proffered arm and left the room.

Sir William blew out a long, appreciative breath. "I hope Vane knows what a chance he has! A beauty if ever, besides yourself, I saw one."

"Let us hope she teaches him some sense."

"You don't like Kit?" Sir William sounded surprised.

"He's an ambitious man, and a proud one. That's dangerous, William."

"But I'm a general and he's a captain, so I think we can sleep easy in our bed. Shall we return to our guests?" Sir William smiled his benevolent smile that would embrace a wilderness. He dreamed of peace, and he dreamed of laughter gilding that peace with happiness, to which end, and as Captain Vane went with the widow, Sir William went back to the dance.

SEVENTEEN

"Sweet Jesus."

The duty officer at the State House was an elderly and morose lieutenant whose breath stank of rum. A disappointed man, denied the promotion he believed he deserved, the lieutenant now held Private Sam Gilpin's authorization close to the guttering flame of a candle stub. "Sir William Howe?" The Lieutenant's voice implied disbelief.

"He signed it, sir," Sam said helpfully. In truth Sir William's private secretary had forged the signature, but only because he did not wish to further spoil Sir William's evening of pleasure.

"There is such a thing as daylight, you know? God said 'Let there be bloody light', and there was, but no! Sir William has to send you in the middle of the bloody night, doesn't he?" The lieutenant gave the seal-embossed paper back to Sam, grudgingly acknowledging its authenticity. "You are here to find one bloody Yankee and take the bastard away, is that it?"

"Yes, sir."

"Good luck, son. They've been dropping off their perches like poxed sparrows, so the bugger's probably dead." The lieutenant yawned. "Take a bloody lantern, don't set the bloody place on fire, and don't wake the bleeders up. They're trouble enough as it is."

Sam, thus admitted to the State House, helped himself to a lantern that he lit from the guardroom's candle. Life as an officer's servant, he was finding, was full of surprises; whether serving two breakfasts to the Captain and whatever whore had been taken upstairs the night before, or running such strange errands as this which had started when the Captain had returned early from the General's reception, rousted a sleeping Sam from the kitchen floor, and demanded that Sam immediately discover a wounded rebel soldier in the State House.

Sam, blinking awake, had sat up. "Rebel, sir?"

"Twenty years old. Called Jonathon Becket. He must have been wounded very close to the place where you assaulted that sergeant." Captain Vane liked to remind Sam of that crime, thus ensuring Sam's wary gratitude. "Go and find him. Someone must have a list of their bloody names. Wake them up, stir them up, use Sir William's authorization, and hurry!"

"Jonathon Becket, sir? Like the Archbishop?"

"Are we here to discuss history's crimes? For God's sake, wake up, Sam!"

"But I know him, sir! I had to look after him! If it's the same fellow."

"God sent me a paragon!" Vane had whirled on Sam with a sudden upwelling of good temper. "When God made you, Samuel Gilpin, he excelled his normally botched work. Up, thou scum, find him. There is a woman at stake. Put wings on thy feet and a lit cartridge up thy arse. In brief, Sam, hurry!"

Thus Sam found himself in the State House. No register of the wounded had been made, so Sam would have to go through the makeshift wards one by one, but it was not an unwelcome task. In the last few days Sam had been plagued by his memories of the wounded American boy who had tried to help Nate run, and who, for his pains, had been savaged by Sergeant Scammell. Sam also felt guilty. If he had fetched the horse quicker, or if he had agreed to run with Nate, then his brother might not be dead and Jonathon, who in some curious way seemed now to be a link with Nate, might not be lying in this hospital.

If Jonathon Becket even lived, which, in the stench and filth of the State House, seemed unlikely. Sam started his search upstairs, edging his way through the wounded rebels who moaned, cursed, and wept. The building stank of festering flesh, rotting wounds, vomit, dung, and death. The real hospitals, such as they were, had been given to the British wounded, so these rebels, casualties of Germantown, were consigned to the State House where they waited for agonizing death. Some slept, some were already dead, while others blinked towards Sam's sudden lantern flame and, desperate for help, reached pathetic hands towards the small light. "Friend?" a voice issued from the shadows. "Friend?" The man who spoke lay wrapped in a verminous blanket. Sam, flinching from the reek around him, stooped with the lantern, but the speaker was not Jonathon. The man's hand wavered towards Sam's sleeve. "Water? Please?"

Sam offered his canteen which the man gripped with an almost demonic force, sucking at the wooden neck as if he had not drunk in a week. The whole room, waking slowly and seeing the kindness, began a horrid and beseeching moan for help.

"Did you have to? Was this really necessary?" A petulant voice sounded from the doorway, and Sam turned to see a red-coated corporal blinking away sleep and looking at him.

"Corporal?"

"They do disturb our rest." The corporal had an oddly educated voice. "Now, lads! Please! Time for sleep! So good for you! Sleep! Nature's soft nurse!"

But the rebels were woken now, raising their hands, weeping for the water or food that Sam could not offer. He snatched up the empty canteen, retrieved his lantern, and fled from the room.

"It really doesn't help to raise their hopes," the corporal said chidingly. "You might think you're doing them a kindness, but in the long run you're being excessively cruel! It's what I told the women who wanted to look after them. Why? I asked them, Why prolong the suffering? But women do like to interfere, don't you agree?"

Sam leaned on the wall by an open window. Clouds flew silver-black beside a clean-edged moon. He gasped in the fresh, cool air. A cockroach scuttled across the windowledge. Touching his jacket, he thought of his brother and, as ever, had to choke back angry tears at the memory. Sam tried to console himself that Nate's quick death was a better end for a soldier than this lingering and callous torture. "They only wanted water," he said.

"They get it once a day," the corporal replied sternly. "It's a bother fetching it as it is! We're undermanned! And it isn't our job to look after enemy wounded. I'm a flautist!"

Sam tried to scour the thick stink of death from his throat. "They're starving!"

"All Mister Washington's fault, I'm afraid." The corporal dismissed the problem with a curiously elegant wave of a thin hand. "The custom of war declares that he must provide for his own men taken prisoner, and if he cannot be bothered to arrange their rations, then we are not obliged to do it." He had said the words in a curious chanting voice, as though he spoke them by rote. "Not that I don't feel for them, you mustn't think that. I do, indeed I do! I read them psalms!"

"I expect they like that," Sam said bitterly.

"I wanted to be in the Church." The corporal, woken up now, seemed to decide that he might as well serve his period of duty. He buttoned his jacket and buckled his belt. "It was either the Church or the theatre, but I end up tootling for King George. Or rather, acting as nursemaid for uncouth colonials. Such a trial!" He looked Sam up and down and seemed pleased by what he saw. "Are you supposed to be here, or is this a social visit?"

"I'm looking for a lad who was wounded at Germantown."

"He's probably dead. They die constantly, you know. We have to take the bodies out. Filthy! Verminous! But it's a mercy for them, really. There's not much to enjoy in life, is there, if you're crippled?"

"This boy was crippled," Sam said. "He had a twisted leg and a clubfoot?"

"Ah!" the corporal said with sudden enthusiasm. "The good-looking boy with the black hair? He was alive yesterday, I think." He beckoned Sam to follow him and, at the foot of the stairs, put a warning hand on Sam's arm. "Do be careful how you tread here, it isn't the most salubrious place." He led Sam through a corridor which, being the guards' latrine, was fouled with excreta and urine. Two rats, disturbed by the lantern light, scampered into darkness as the corporal pushed open a tall door and ushered Sam into a handsomely panelled room. "These," the disappointed musician said in his delicate voice, "are the fortunate ones. They're not so badly wounded, you see." He raised Sam's arm so that the lantern revealed more of the high-ceilinged chamber. "This is the very room where the rebels signed their Declaration of Independence." The corporal laughed.

"Their what?" Sam had never heard of any declaration.

"Never mind." The corporal looked at the wounded, who, seeing the lantern's glow, had begun their horrid moaning for help. "Not that it's done them much good, has it? Your fellow was over there, beneath the window."

It was hard to see how these lesser wounded were more fortunate than their comrades, unless it was that they would take longer to die. The room smelt putrid. The stench was of feverish sweat, of the bloody flux, and of flesh rotting on the living bone. There was fever and cholera here. It was a charnel house.

But, beneath the window and with eyes as bright as coals, Sam saw the thin, handsome face of the boy he had knelt beside at Germantown, and he saw, too, that Jonathon was now ill far beyond the single wound that Sam had tended. the boy's eyes were bright with fever, the thin body shaking in delirium, and Sam felt a welling of guilt and pity as he stepped across the crammed bodies to kneel beside the quivering boy. "Jonathon?"

There was no answer. Sam saw a louse crawl beneath Jonathon's collar. The boy stank of his own dung and sweat and blood. "Jonathon?"

"You've found him, then?" the corporal asked.

"Yes." And as Sam spoke the word, so Jonathon's eyes seemed to be invested with intelligence. Slowly they focused on Sam's eyes, then a puzzled look spread over the American's face. After the puzzlement came a look of such relief that help had come, a look that spoke of such hell that had been endured in this place, that Sam knew he would cry for pity if he did not speak. "I'm getting you out, Johnny."

"You're taking him?" The corporal sounded shocked.

"Orders," Sam said, "from Sir William Howe." He had learned, in the last few days, just what power he could wield with those magic words.

"Who's a fortunate Yankee, then?" the corporal asked of no one in particular. "Can you manage? I can't help lift him, you know, not with my back."

"I can manage." Sam lifted Jonathon from the mire and, the filthy body light in his arms, carried him to the house in Market Street where, just as Captain Vane had foretold, a physician waited in the candlelit kitchen. With him was a tall, elegant lady and a black maid who cried in shock as Sam carried the awful burden through the door.

"Oh God!"

The physician echoed the maid's horror. "Oh God!"

Sam laid the body on the table, then, because he did not know what else to do, he returned to the back door, to be checked by the doctor's angry voice. "You did the damage! You can help repair it!"

"Me?"

"You're a Redcoat, aren't you? One of the fine men come to save us from ourselves?" The physician spat the words angrily. "Come here, man! Your damned Captain's too squeamish to help, so you can do something for a Patriot."

The physician was stripping the clothes from Jonathon, cutting through the rotting, fouled, pus-stiff layers of cloth with long shears. The tall handsome lady blanched, while the black maid helped with quick and efficient fingers. "Are they doing nothing for them in there?" the doctor asked angrily.

"No, sir." Sam's voice was full of misery.

"Barbarians. Scum. Filth." The doctor said it as he lifted the last layer of linen away. Sam stared with fascinated horror at the twisted and lumpen flesh that was Jonathon's right foot.

"Don't gape!" the physician snapped. "Oh, my God! It'll have to come off. Water, Jenny! Sheets. Oh, God."

The leg was bloated, rotten, stinking.

"Can you . . ." the tall lady began.

". . . I can, Martha, but you're going to have to offer me peace!" The physician was almost entirely bald, with a bad-tempered plump face. He opened a wooden carrying case lined with velvet which held, in specially shaped indentations, saws and knives and augers and forceps and wicked, small scalpels. He took out a bone saw, two knives and one of the scalpels. The teeth of the saw still held flecks of dried blood.

The physician stooped to Jonathon's shrivelled right thigh and sniffed at the rancid flesh. "There's no skin to stitch over the stump. Have you got tar?"

"No," Jenny said.

"Then red hot pokers! A red hot flat-iron. Anything! You!" – this was to Sam – "come here!"

Sam, obedient, went to the end of the kitchen table where the doctor was looping a great leather strap around table and patient.

"Pull it tight," the doctor said. "I don't want him to move." Another strap went round Jonathon's waist and two more about his healthy left leg. "Pokers, Martha! Pokers!"

Martha thrust three pokers into the fire while Jenny worked the leather bellows. The physician peeled off his jacket and pulled on a blood-stained apron. "It's going to hurt him."

"Will brandy help?" Martha asked.

"I doubt he can drink it," the physician said, "but it'll help me." He looked belligerently at Sam. "He's strapped down, but he's going to flap like a landed fish. You're to keep him still, you understand? And don't watch what I'm doing, just hold him tight!"

"Yes, sir."

"Martha! Get the brandy, and more light, more light!"

They waited. Jonathon moaned and turned his head from side

to side. Then Martha came back to the kitchen with a couple of tall, twisted silver candelabras. She also carried a black bottle of brandy which the physician snatched. "Now, go to your brother's head, Martha. Hold his face, give him reassurance. He probably won't hear you, in fact he'll probably die, but we can try to undo what our royal masters have done. Jenny! Keep that fire hot!"

"Yes, sir."

The physician had hooked a razor strop on to a meat hook and was now scraping a knife blade up and down the leather. "They will tell you," he said to the kitchen at large, "that it takes twenty minutes to slice off a leg. That is mephitic, rank nonsense. I have done it in ninety seconds, and will do so now. Anything longer is too great a shock to the constitution. It is not pleasant for anyone, least of all the poor bloody patient, but if you want to give him even a quarter chance of survival, you will help me by not screaming, fainting, or otherwise displaying feminine weaknesses. This also goes for our gallant British soldier. Hold tight and think of England, but do not let that thought make you vomit. Are the pokers red hot?"

"Yes, sir." Jenny, clearly nervous of the physician's bombast, said it meekly.

"God bless us all." The physician laid down the sharpened knife and poured himself a generous cupful of brandy. He drained it. "If God is gracious, he'll stay unconscious. Hold him."

Sam lay his arms over Jonathon's midriff. Martha put her long, white fingers against her brother's even paler cheeks, and the physician took the long, wicked-edged knife. "Courage, all!" the physician said grimly, then plunged down with the bright feather-edged blade.

Jonathon uttered a scream that might have been that of a soul entering eternal perdition. At the same moment his body went into a paroxysm of such vicious power that Sam had to fight it down with all his country-bred strength.

"Keep him still!" the physician shouted, drawing out the last word as if to drown the awful scream that was so despairing and agonizing. Sam forced the body down as the gleaming blade flensed round the thigh to spill a shock of pus and blood on to the floor.

The knife was discarded and the bone saw snatched up. The doctor grunted, the saw teeth skidded, caught, then began their rasping noise. Jonathon, thankfully, had fainted. Sam was looking away from the operation, staring at the dark-eyed lady whose eyes, all unknowing, stared into his. A tinge of burning came from the hurrying saw.

The physician gave one last grunting heave with the saw, then a second knife slashed at the remaining flesh. "Pokers! Quick, girl! Quick!"

Jenny handed the first poker to the physician, and Jonathon's body jerked again as the red hot iron cauterized the savaged flesh. "Next!" Another steaming hiss and again the stench of roasting meat curdled Sam's nostrils. "Next!" And Sam closed his eyes as if darkness could blot out the awful sound and smell.

"Ninety-eight seconds!" The physician was sweating. "Bandages!" The bandages had been soaked in lead acetate to fight infection. "You!" – this was again to Sam – "Take the leg out and bury it."

Sam picked up the grotesquely twisted leg by the ankle and took it into the yard. There was no light, no way of finding a spade, nor any means of knowing where in the small yard he should bury the sawn-off limb. He dropped it on a small patch of grass, then sat, miserable, against the wall.

A cry made him look up. A small child, nightrobed and frightened, had appeared in a doorway. She called for her mother, and Sam, fearful that the child would see the severed leg, ran to the door and gathered the small girl into his arms. "It's all right, it's all right."

"The door was closed." The child, woken by the awful scream, had tried to go down to the kitchen.

"It's all right," Sam said soothingly. Behind the child he could see into a room so lavish that it reminded him of the Squire's house back home. He explained, as gently as he could, that the awful noise had been the sound of someone who had been hurt, but was now being made better.

"Who?" The child, with the resilience of her age, was entirely reassured by Sam's words.

"Someone called Jonathon."

"Uncle Jonathon?"

Sam heard the horror in the child's voice, and hastened to allay it. "He's going to get better! I promise!" Sam suddenly remembered the kick of the musket, the blossom of smoke, the exultation of an enemy down, and he thought how it all came to this; a soldier's reward of blood and saws and screaming in the night.

Nate, perhaps, had been lucky, and suddenly Sam knew that his brother's death and Jonathon's survival were inextricably linked; he also knew that he must keep the promise he had just made to a child if his brother's soul was to find its paradise beyond the furthest stars. A rebel's life must be saved, and Sam had promised it. Sam, through Jonathon, would make amends.

EIGHTEEN

In the belief that unalloyed pleasures could end a rebellion and seduce the affections of soured colonists, Sir William, aided by Lizzie Loring, determined to make the life of Philadelphia's society into a dazzle of ostentatious enchantment. Party succeeded party, dinners melded into candlelit suppers, while musicians, instead of inspiring the red ranks into the smoke of battle, whirled dancers around the city's polished floors. Philadelphia would see, and the rest of America would understand, that the British tyrants of rebel propaganda were, in truth, the bringers of joy and the only true hope for wealth and peace in the colonies.

Yet the war could not be entirely forgotten in the first weeks of the British occupation of Philadelphia. There was still the tiresome nuisance of the rebel forts on the lower river, and the city must be ringed with guardposts to protect its revellers from rebel raids. However, within that protective ring Sir William would have laughter, and his aides, who so recently had ridden amidst shot and slaughter, were ordered to become the ringmasters of enjoyment.

Captain Vane embraced the order with alacrity, for Captain Vane was in love.

On the night when Jonathon's leg had been severed, Vane had waited for the widow's thanks which, when they came, were brief but gracious. In the days that followed Vane besieged the widow with flowers, gifts and flattery. He was in love, and he loved with all the passion of a young man who had been starved of feminine company, and who believed he had met, in one woman, the very pattern of his secret longings. He told Sam he was in love, for a man could not keep such secrets from his servant, and he shared the happy news with John Andre.

"You claim she's beautiful?" Andre teased Vane.

"As a dark angel."

"Her breath doesn't stink?"
"Like rose-petals crushed in dew."
"Then her teeth are surely rotten?"
"Pure as polished ivory."
"Is she poor?"
"Blessed with wealth, John, beyond a man's dreams."
Andre looked alarmed. "She must have one imperfection, Kit."
"There is a daughter," Vane allowed, "but a sweet child."
Andre laughed. "Then I wish you much joy, Kit. You deserve it. But she's a rebel, surely?"
"A woman's mind," Vane said dismissively, "can be changed. They're notorious for it."
"But rarely in the way we wish. They're also notorious for that." Andre smiled. "So when am I to meet this paragon? Or do you not dare expose her to my fascination?"
"I shall bring her to Billy's Bacchanalia."
"Then I shall try not to swoon at her appearance."
Billy's Bacchanalia, the nickname for an open-air rout, was ostensibly a welcome for autumn, but really just an excuse to revel in the Neck – a lovely place of mature trees between the converging rivers where lavish houses, built as summer retreats by wealthy Philadelphians, graced the banks. It was in the garden of one such house that Sir William ordered a late dinner served so that the guests could eat and drink in the fading evening's light. Musicians played within carefully fashioned bowers among the trees from which, like pale moons in the afternoon sun, Chinese lanterns waited for nightfall. Guests sported in the Schuylkill, using the duck-hunters' punts that were moored along the river's bank.

The day was cloudy, but dry, and in the afternoon a game of cricket was played between officers of the cavalry and officers of the infantry. Few spectators watched the game because of the greater pleasure of watching each other. Lizzie Loring, magnificent in a dress of white satin slashed over a scarlet petticoat, carried a furled parasol about which was woven garlands of flowers to match those which graced her hat. She strolled on Sir William's arm and to left and right officers and their ladies bowed and curtseyed in welcome.

Martha arrived in a polonaise of midnight blue and with her dark hair piled almost as high as Lizzie Loring's. The two women had become friendly since their first meeting and Lizzie now drew her lover to Martha's side. Sir William bowed. "Your brother, dear Mrs Crowl, how is he?"

"The physician wants to bleed him. Do you think that's a good idea, Sir William?"

"I'm no expert." Sir William smiled at Captain Vane who stood proudly beside the widow. "But there is a view in London which holds bleeding to be a bad idea. I can't say it ever hurt me, though."

"I think bleeding is an atrocious idea." Martha's mind, despite her question, was clearly decided. "The poor boy's lost enough blood as it is, so I shall tell the doctor to take his leeches away."

"But your brother is recovering?" Lizzie asked anxiously.

"He becomes no worse," Martha said. "But Captain Vane's servant is being very kind to him, and that seems to help."

"He's a good fellow, Sam," Vane said. "And a genius with sick horses, Sir William."

"Doubtless your brother will soon be trotting," Sir William said genially before inviting Vane and Martha to share his coach for a visit to the lower battery which guarded the confluence of the Delaware and the Schuylkill. Other guests had gathered there to be offered wine and oysters. However, it was not the refreshments which drew the small crowd to the river's edge, but rather the distant sight of white smoke puffing across the southern marshes. Each new puff, jetting on the horizon, was followed seconds later by the dull crump of a gun's firing.

The guests watched the war which, as autumn threatened rain and chill winds, had been reduced to a struggle of fire in water, of blood seeping into salt marsh, and of wounded men screaming like the lonely cries of the gulls that scavenged at the grey water's edge. The river forts must be taken and so Sir William had moved troops into the wide immensity of salt marsh south of the city where gun batteries, shored and sandbagged against the seeping water, punched dirty white puffs of powder smoke into the salt-tanged air. The river swirled and slid between the stiff-grassed islands, making for Delaware Bay where Lord Howe, brother to Sir William and Admiral of the North American Fleet, waited with the ships that should soon unite Philadelphia once more with the open sea.

The British controlled the Delaware's northern bank, where, on the marshes of Province Island and Carpenters Island the British engineers made great rafts of treetrunks on which their guns could fire south at Fort Mifflin which stood on the aptly named Mud Island in the very centre of the Delaware's wide stream. The great guns, slamming back under the powder's explosive charge, drove the rafts into the salted mud so that the vast weapons tilted and more planks, treetrunks, ropes, and earth had to be fetched to strengthen the shaking platforms. And always the American cannon, firing from behind the landward-facing wooden parapets of Fort Mifflin, took their toll of gunners and sappers.

Beyond Mud Island, beyond the river's treacherous shoals, and beyond Bush Island where the Americans had a barricaded battery, lay the nine-foot parapets of Fort Mercer on the New Jersey shore. Forts Mifflin and Mercer, strongholds in a slough of wetness, were under siege, not just by land, but by sea. British gunboats and frigates, grey sails shivering as their guns fired, added the weight of their shot to the bombardment. Sir William would have liked more naval boats in the wide river, but the Americans had sunk vast obstacles downstream and it was painfully slow work to warp even a single warship through the current-ridden gap. This was war at a creeping pace; no glory here of shining sabres at the gallop or of colours lifted to a rising sun, this was the dour work of engineers and gunners, of mathematicians and measurers who doled powder into the stubby barrels of mortars as though it was gold; one ounce too much and the shell would fly far beyond the target to splash harmlessly in the river's swirl.

Martha, watching the distant gunsmoke from the comfort of Sir William's open carriage, smiled at the Commander-in-Chief. "You'll have to explain what's happening, Sir William. It's an utter mystery otherwise."

"It's just slow and steady work, my dear. We shall reduce Fort Mifflin by gunfire, then we shall use its guns to fire on Fort Mercer."

"Which will surely take a long time?"

"I fear so, unless they surrender. I wish they would, for they've proved their bravery and can achieve nothing more."

Martha, knowing that Sir William was complimenting the rebel garrisons for her benefit, smiled an acknowledgement. "But surely they could yet bring ruin to the merchants of the city, Sir William?"

"So the merchants tell me." Sir William returned her smile. "But the river will be opened."

Yet, so long as the Delaware's seaway was closed, so would cargoes gather dust in half-empty warehouses, and so would a scarcity of food threaten the city. Some Loyalist merchants urged an escalade on Fort Mercer, pleading that, once captured by assault, the fort's guns could be used to grind Fort Mifflin into powder, and Martha asked Sir William why he rejected the advice. Sir William, flattered by Martha's interest, shook his head. "Such an operation would take just as long! I would have to move artillery over the river, dig batteries, and open saps. Scaling ladders would have to be made and a breach opened. No, slow and steady will do the job just as well!"

"And in the meanwhile," Martha insisted, "we shall all starve?"

"I will not allow you to starve, Mrs Crowl. No, I shall build a floating bridge across the Schuylkill" – Sir William waved towards the swiftly flowing river – "and we shall bring food from the Chesapeake Bay."

"It seems an extraordinary undertaking," Martha said archly, "just to win a victory over a few troublesome colonials!"

Sir William did not rise to the bait, but Lizzie Loring, who still harboured suspicions of Captain Vane's belligerence, could not resist giving the line a tug. "Do you agree, Captain Vane?"

Vane played for time, hoping Sir William would change the subject. "Agree, ma'am?"

"That the effort expended is out of all proportion to the possible reward?"

Vane, denied his hopes that Sir William would obviate the question, was forced to reply. "If we lose the thirteen colonies then we encourage insurrection elsewhere. There'll be republican rebellions in Canada, the West Indies, even Ireland. It's like a contagion that must be checked at its source."

"I had no idea we were so dangerous!" Martha said, which made Sir William smile. The party broke up as Sir William suggested he really should pay some small attention to the cricket before the setting sun ended play, and Martha declared that it was a game impossible to comprehend and she would walk back to where the dancing would take place.

"I fear" – Martha put her arm into Vane's – "that our politics will never agree, Kit."

"We can try." Vane was so pleased that she had given him her arm that his thoughts were upon anything but politics. He gestured with his free hand at a grassy walk which went off at a tangent from the main path, wending its way into the shadow of trees that promised the chance of intimacy. "Shall we take that path?"

Martha, who knew well what he wanted, had no intention of granting it. Her friendship with Vane was useful, for he offered her protection against the venom of the Loyalists who resented her continued presence in the city. Martha was mindful, too, that an aide-de-camp to the Commander-in-Chief was a man who could well let slip details of British intentions that she could pass on to the rebels. However, she had no desire to pay for those details with intimacy though, for the moment, nor would she discourage Captain Vane from his infatuation. She ignored his invitation to take the shadowed path, declaring that she was impatient to meet his friends who waited where the musicians tuned their instruments for the dancing. Vane hid his disappointment, but consoled himself that the widow seemed content in his company. He was proud of her beauty as he introduced Martha to John Andre who, just as proudly, named Miss Peggy Shippen, whereupon Miss Shippen declared how much Philadelphia had improved during the three weeks that the city had been occupied by the British.

"Improved?" Martha asked.

"It's so much more amusing." Peggy looked around the lawn which was bright with uniforms and silk dresses. "So much more civilized."

"Civilized?" Martha pounced. "Are you saying we lack civility, Miss Shippen?"

"How can America lack anything," Andre deflected the argument, "when it has you, Mrs Crowl?"

Martha laughed. "America lacks nothing, Captain Andre, that it needs for independency."

"We're to be serious!" Andre lamented.

"You mustn't argue with Mrs Crowl about America," Vane said, "for she has the colonists' belief that America contains all that is choicest in the world."

"True," Martha said. "As any American can tell you, our architecture is the finest, our food is the best, and our scenery unsurpassed. No horses are as swift as ours, nor will you find servants so honest, nor divines so tediously devout. You're not going to argue with such modesty, are you, Captain Andre?"

Andre, who had enjoyed Martha's exaggeration, bowed surrender to her. "But is there nothing you lack?"

"An aristocracy," Vane intervened.

"Ah!" Martha smiled at him. "And what kind of lack is that?"

"The aristocracy," Vane said carefully, "is the fount of taste. Taste comes from pleasure, not money."

"Pleasure usually costs money," Martha said tartly. "But let us accept the distinction. So what results from money that is not governed by taste?"

"Money without taste, my dear Martha, leads only to a blowsy and vulgar display."

Peggy Shippen agreed, but Martha pretended to think about his words, then frowned. "I'm not sure I entirely understand you."

"Take this house." Vane waved towards the summer house about which the party spread across the shadowed lawns. "I don't deny its splendour, and certainly not the expense, but the gilding! It's laid on like plaster so the eye has nowhere to rest. A single detail, given prominence, would be far more expressive."

"And an aristocracy," Martha asked in a dangerous tone, "has natural taste?"

"Good taste or bad?" The voice came from behind Martha, and she turned to see a short, round-faced man. First he smiled at her, then he looked towards Vane for an introduction.

Vane was grudging, but obliged. "Mrs Martha Crowl, allow me to name Lord Robert Massedene."

"Your charmed servant, ma'am. I assumed Kit had an eye for beauty, but I never before realized how laudable was his admiration for the nobility."

Martha smiled. "Do you have natural taste, my lord?"

"I have none at all. The aristocracy, ma'am, founded their dynasties by being better thieves than anyone else. Whatever glittered, they took, and the true aristocracy has never lost that healthy vulgarity."

"Gilded thieves?" Martha asked with amusement.

"Who would now steal this land from you. I do hope you will resist us."

Martha was clearly charmed by his lordship. "You don't want to win, my lord?"

"Win what?" Massedene feigned alarm. "America, my dear Mrs Crowl, is a wilderness with an unendurable climate. It is too hot in summer, too cold in winter, and fit only for insects, snakes, and raving Baptists. God only knows why we fight for it."

"For their own good, of course," Vane, piqued by Massedene's nonsensical intervention, said it too sharply. "And because the majority of the colonists wish our rule to continue."

"I don't!" Martha said, then, seeing Vane's jealousy, she assuaged it by laying a hand on his arm as she looked back to Lord Robert. "What I don't understand, my lord, is why, if you dislike America so much, you are here at all?"

"Money, dear lady. I need the salary. We younger sons daren't lower ourselves to trade, so we must try to win renown by the sword. An entirely ridiculous fate, but we cannot all show good sense."

Vane, knowing that the reference to trade was aimed at himself, heard a minuet strike up and, careless that he might be showing rudeness to Massedene, turned Martha towards the music. "May I?"

"Why not?" Martha turned to smile a farewell to his lordship, then followed Vane towards the dance. "You don't like Lord Robert Massedene, do you?"

"I would deny any feelings towards him."

Martha showed her disbelief with a smile. "You positively bristled, Kit. Were you jealous?"

"You provoke such emotions in me."

Vane, his happiness restored by her smile, took Martha into his arms to join the dancers who scattered themselves in pretty array across the lawn, while the music drowned the distant gunfire which marked the flat land where men died. The sun emerged from a bank of clouds to swell red and splendid, and to pale the small lanterns hung among the leaves which were turning into the extraordinary and vivid colours of an American autumn.

Sir William Howe, returning from the cricket in his carriage driven by his trusted manservant Tom Evans, checked its progress to watch the dancers. "It's how I imagined it would be," he said to Lizzie.

Lizzie grimaced. "They say, my dear, that if you don't take the forts swiftly there will be hunger. And hungry people do not make good company."

"True," and Sir William's smile widened, for Sir William practised a deception on the rebels. He spoke openly in society about his slow but steady plans to take the forts, while in secret he prepared a daring stroke which, he believed, could free the city and bring peace in its wake.

For in three days' time Sir William proposed to do precisely what the city's merchants urged on him. In three days' time Fort Mercer would be assaulted from the land. Three thousand Hessian troops would cross the Delaware by night. Because their preparations for the crossing could not be concealed, the story had been spread that they went to scour central New Jersey for food and forage. In truth they would turn south and, by dawn, be ready to rush an unprepared Fort Mercer. It was a bold plan, and if the rebels should get wind of it, it would fail.

Thus, only a handful of men were privy to the secret. The Hessian commander General Donop knew, and was unhappy that, in the desperate need to keep the secret hidden, he could not make scaling ladders to assail Fort Mercer's nine-foot walls. Lord Cornwallis and his closest aides had been told, for Cornwallis was second-in-command and it would have been discourteous to deceive him. General Howe's own aides knew, for they must write the orders that would be distributed at the very final moment. Admiral Howe knew, for the handful of boats he could warp past the obstructions would distract Fort Mercer's defenders with broadside fire as the land assault went in, but beyond those men, all of whom Sir William trusted absolutely, no other officers had been informed.

But now, as they watched the dancers shimmer on the wide lawn, Sir William told Lizzie Loring. He told her because he knew how much she yearned for the fighting to end, and he told her because even a Commander-in-Chief could not resist boasting to his lover of the clever deception he had devised. "If I build a floating bridge, you see, everyone will know that the siege will take a long time, so, even though the siege will be over in three days, I must still boast of my plans for the bridge." Sir William chuckled happily. "You understand?"

"Perfectly, my dear." Lizzie linked her arm into her lover's arm and leaned snugly against his stout body. "So you're attacking in three days?"

"In three days, though naturally I trust you to honour the confidentiality."

"Of course, though I shall be hard pressed not to boast of your cleverness."

Sir William enjoyed the praise. The enemy, he declared, would be lulled to sleep, then hit with savage force and, he fervently believed, once the forts had fallen there would be peace.

"Truly?" Lizzie asked it eagerly.

"Truly." Sir William rapped the carriage door as a signal for

Tom Evans to drive on. "The river will be opened to the sea, my love, and wealth will flood in. The Loyalists will want their share, they'll come to us, and the rebellion will wither away." Sir William had come to these middle colonies because he had been told just how many Loyalists waited for a flag about which to rally. The fall of the forts and the coming of wealth would be their signal, and even the stubborn Mister Washington, who still lurked somewhere to the city's west and north, would surely see the futility of continued rebellion. Peace would come with the ships. Peace and plenty, and all depended on the swift fall of two stubborn forts.

So a secret must be kept if an assault was to open the river to wealth and peace. Sir William, watching the happy scene, dreamed of ending this war, and of the rewards peace might bring. He imagined himself as the most high, puissant, and most noble William, Duke of Philadelphia and Earl of Pennsylvania, Viscount Brandywine of Chesapeake and Baron Howe of Germantown, Knight Companion of the Most Noble Order of the Garter, and a member of His Majesty's Honourable Privy Council. No more money worries then! "What a prospect!" he spoke aloud.

Sir William's sudden exclamation was not at his hoped-for elevation to the highest ranks of the nobility, but because, as the carriage turned about a stand of trees, Sir William saw the sudden and glorious sight of the city illuminated by a wash of evening sunlight that, spearing across the world's rim, spread beneath the dull clouds so that the buildings seemed to glow with a golden and charming light beneath a darker sky. "The New Jerusalem," Sir William said.

"Complete with pharisees?" Lizzie asked.

But nothing could spoil Sir William's mood. He was experiencing a sudden upwelling of pure joy that he translated as a spiritual portent of victory. He stared at the city of brotherly love, and knew that, when the seaway was opened and the trade began to thrive, he could make a glowing, just, and happy peace in this well-named city. "I do believe that when the rebellion is ended, I shall live here." He paused, smiled at Lizzie, and, ignoring the existence of his own wife and of Lizzie's husband, amended the happy hope. "*We* shall live here, my love."

And, in such happy expectations, Sir William took his paramour to the sunset's party where lovers danced.

NINETEEN

"Eggs?" suggested the commissary sergeant.

"Just two for myself," Sam said. "Captain Vane doesn't like eggs any more."

"Your Jack-pudding's bleedin' fussy, isn't he? Gone off eggs? You'll want eggs, Tom?"

Tom Evans, Sir William's principal servant, confirmed that he would take eggs for his master, as well as buckwheat, cucumbers, oysters, clams, nutmeg, pulses, and mutton. "He fancies a roasted saddle. He'll need two for tonight."

"Lucky Billy, lucky Lizzie." The sergeant pushed open a door to reveal a dozen bedraggled sheep penned in a small yard. "You want to kill a couple for me, Sam?"

Sam drew his bayonet and obliged, then received one leg of mutton for his own master. Food shortages might threaten if the forts were not taken, yet this warehouse was a cornucopia; there were barrels of salted pork and beef, casks of limes, hogsheads of spirits, and tierces of rice. There were molasses, cone sugar in bright purple wrappings, currants, and cases of gin. There were baskets of salt, boxes of cheese, and firkins of butter; all of it guarded by a commissary that was swiftly becoming one of the richest trading houses in the city. Gold changed hands here for food, and Captain Vane daily expected Sam to find delicacies that were bought with the goods Vane appropriated from the house where, with two other officers, he lodged and which, with its rapidly depleting belongings, was the property of an absent Patriot. "It isn't stealing, Sam," Vane had said, "but punishing a notorious rebel."

"How do you know he's notorious, sir?"

"You've never heard of Benjamin Franklin?"

"No, sir." Sam had looked at the portrait of the house's owner which hung above the mantel. "Funny-looking bugger, sir."

"That funny-looking bugger, Samuel, is trying to get the French to join the war against us. I hope a Parisian whore gives him a very virulent dose of the pox. Now take that clock and don't accept anything less than three pounds for it."

Sam wiped the blood off his bayonet, then took the clock out of his haversack and offered it to the commissary sergeant, who shook the gilded and marble-mounted timepiece to ensure that its works did not rattle about in the case. "Two pound?"

"He wanted four, Sarge."

"He's pissing into the wind then, isn't he? Four pounds for that rubbish?"

"It's an eight-day clock, sarge! Very valuable!"

"Two pound."

"Two ten?"

"Two five."

"Done."

Sam took the coins, less the price of the lamb, eggs, and two bottles of claret. "Any Keyser's Pills, Sergeant?"

"Won't be any till the fleet gets through, Sam."

"Liquorice?"

The sergeant sucked a dubious breath. "Bloody scarce, Sam! It'll cost you five shilling!"

"Ah! Come on!"

"Five or nothing!"

Sam hesitated, then decided to tell Captain Vane that the clock had only fetched two pounds. Vane would be unhappy, but, as the clock was stolen anyway, the captain could not make too much of a fuss. "Bleeding robbery," Sam grumbled as he walked away from the warehouse with Tom Evans. "Five bloody bob for a scrap of root?"

Tom Evans never paid a penny, for it was rumoured that the crammed warehouse only existed because of Sir William's interest in the profits. Tom Evans, out of loyalty to his master, would never confirm the rumour. Indeed, as befitted the privileged intimate of a commander-in-chief, Evans rarely spoke to any of the other officers' servants. However, he had a soft spot for Sam Gilpin, who was always respectful and helpful. "You know how to cook a leg of lamb, Sam?"

"Put it on the spit, light the fire, and keep turning."

Evans flinched at such philistinism and gave Sam careful instructions on how to roast the leg, and how to prepare an oil and vinegar dressing to accompany it. "Eating it today, is he?"

Sam shook his head. "He's with Billy tonight. He wants this for tomorrow."

"Getting ready for the battle, then." Evans kicked at a dog which had smelt the meat in his sack.

"Battle?" Sam asked.

"Gawd, you must be bleeding simple, Sam Gilpin! They're attacking the bloody forts in two days. Hessians are crossing the river and your fellow's going with the grenadiers to the island!" Tom laughed. "You'll have to keep your head down, Sam!"

The news did not entirely surprise Sam, who had noted how Captain Vane had been more than usually secretive in the last few days. Vane would lock himself in the parlour of the lodgings and there write for hours, always taking care that Sam should not see the resultant paperwork. "How did you find out, Mr Evans?"

"Everyone knows!" Evans, eager to drive home his seniority in the strict hierarchy of military servants, took pleasure in displaying his knowledge which he had garnered while driving Sir William's carriage the previous evening. For Evans to have admitted that he only knew by eavesdropping would be to demean himself, so instead he used the news to demonstrate Sam's lowly status. "Everyone knows!" he said scornfully. "Everyone who's anyone, that is."

"I expect they forgot to tell me," Sam said lightly.

Evans laughed. "You'd better watch out, Sam! Your fellow's the kind that loves a scrap. His last man got chopped, didn't he?"

"He's fair enough," Sam rather liked working for Captain Vane. It was not an onerous job. The other officers' servants in the lodgings divided the work with Sam and, for the most part, he found himself looking after all the horses. He cooked occasionally, though not nearly as well as Captain Andre's man, who was a fastidious and fussy preparer of meals. Otherwise Sam's duties were cleaning Vane's uniforms which, because the Captain was in love, had to be done with meticulous care.

Indeed, it seemed to Sam that both he and Vane spent more time in Mrs Crowl's house than in their own lodgings. The Captain, naturally, went through the front door to pursue his siege of the widow, while Sam went in by the servants' backyard to fulfil the promise he had made on a battlefield. Sam took Jonathon food from the commissary warehouse, and medicines that Sam made himself.

The medicines were essential, for Jonathon was slow to mend. The ague which visited Philadelphia every spring and autumn threatened Jonathon's recovery and, to stave it off, Sam boiled willow bark in water, then fed it to the wounded boy. Mrs Crowl was amused by Sam's remedies, but not so trusting in them that she had not asked for the liquorice and Keyser's Pills which Sam had promised to deliver that evening.

Sam announced himself in Martha's kitchen with a mock fanfare. "Two tails of mutton, one box of candles, and the liquorice I promised." Sam flinched from the kitchen's steaming heat. "What on earth are you doing, Jenny?"

Jenny, aided by two kitchen maids, was heating water over the fire then pouring the boiling cauldrons into a vast, zinc-lined tub that stood on the kitchen flagstones. "I thought you were never coming!" Jenny ignored Sam's questions. "Look at the state of you!"

"I slaughtered a couple of sheep." Sam kept his best uniform for when he must attend the Captain, at other times wearing his old battle-stained red coat and grey breeches. "Tails?"

"On the table," the black woman said cheerfully. "And wipe your feet before you come in here, Sam Gilpin."

Sam looked at his boots. "They ain't bad, Jenny!"

"They're filthy!" Jenny poured a last great cauldron into the steaming tub, then shooed the two maids out of the room. "Your boots are like the rest of you," she said scornfully to Sam, "filthy!"

"Filthy, foul, stinking, disgusting, disgraceful, rank, nasty!" Mrs Crowl had come into the kitchen. "You hear me, Sam Gilpin? Nasty, horrid, awful, British. You. You're filthy!"

Sam, hurt by the insults, peered down at his red coat. "It ain't bad! A bit bloody, that's all."

"Not your coat, you idiot, you! Get your clothes off."

"What?"

Martha smiled at him. "You're going to have a bath, Samuel."

"No, ma'am! Please. Ma'am!" Sam was backing around the kitchen, at last understanding the purpose of the steaming tub. "No!"

Martha locked the back door. "I like you, Sam, God help me and you might be a British soldier, but you're actually, somehow, quite likeable, but if you're visiting this house I want you clean. And I want you to go on visiting! It's good for Jonathon, but you stink!"

"No worse than anyone else!"

Martha held out a wooden rolling-pin. "Hit the British bastard, Jenny!"

"No!" Sam decided to make a stand against the two women. "I ain't having a bath! I brought you the liquorice!"

"Sam, dear Sam" – Martha was trying hard not to laugh – "when did you last bathe?"

"Ain't never bathed. Not in hot water!"

"Good God! You mean that's a lifetime of muck on you?"

"I wash!" Sam said indignantly.

"You stand in the rain sometimes?" Martha enquired sweetly. "Look at your hair, Sam! It has things crawling under that muck! And you smell."

Sam stubbornly shook his head. "It's bad for you, isn't it?"

Martha smiled. "Educate me, Sam?"

"Bathing." Sam gestured towards the waiting tub. "Gives you the fever. Everyone knows that. It can kill me!"

"Then I'll slaughter a Redcoat for America and throw you in!" Martha advanced menacingly on the cornered Sam, who, close to panic, held up warding hands.

"Now, ma'am, please!"

"I bathe, Sam," Martha said confidingly, "once a week. All over, isn't that right, Jenny?" The black maid was too amused to speak. "And Jenny bathes, Sam," Martha said invitingly. "You can't smell us a mile off, can you? Pigs don't flee from us in horror, strong men don't faint, horses don't bolt. Even Captain Vane bathes! But you! You're foul! Now get your clothes off!"

Sam drew himself up to his considerable height and assumed the proper dignity of a captain's servant. "I am not, ma'am, going to undress in . . ."

"You pompous ass!" Martha said. "Jenny! Throw a bucket of water over him."

"No! Please, no!" Sam watched Jenny pick up a bucket. "All right. But I'll do it on my own!"

Martha nodded. "A proper reticence. Think of yourself as a horse, Sam. Give yourself a good hard scrub with a brush first. Then the soap. It's rather expensive soap, Sam, but you may use as much as is necessary. And don't forget your hair. Untangle that silly thing at the back and put it all under water! I want you clean, Sam."

"Yes, ma'am."

"We shall leave you in modest peace," Martha said, "and if you run away, you'll never be allowed back. No more of Jenny's ale, no more sitting by the fire while every other Redcoat catches fever in the swamps."

"Yes, ma'am, very good, ma'am."

Sam waited for the women to leave, briefly considered an ignoble flight up the kitchen steps to the backyard, then, weighing that salvation against the threatened withdrawal of Mrs Crowl's comforts, resigned himself to the dreadful ordeal. He listened at the kitchen door, then, having satisfied himself that no one lurked in ambush, he slowly undressed before putting a tentative foot in the water.

It was hot. He had never put a foot into hot water before and instinctively he pulled back.

"We're coming in!" Martha's voice called gaily from beyond the door.

"No!" But the door opened, and Sam's only escape was to plunge into the scalding tub. He bellowed in shock. Water splashed over the sides as Martha and Jenny, looking grimly businesslike, marched into the kitchen.

"Wash him, Jenny!"

"No!" Sam clutched his drawn-up knees, but Jenny simply reached into the tub, seized an ankle, and upturned Sam so that his head went underwater and he was forced to flounder back to safety.

"Nothing to be ashamed of," Martha said, then burst into laughter at the sight of Sam's outraged face. Jenny, also laughing, began scrubbing Sam's back. "Good God!" Martha said, "he's white!" Which only caused more merriment as Sam's misery plunged to a new low because Martha, shuddering with pretended horror, had picked up his clothes and dumped them into a bucket of cold water. She picked up his coat last. "Red coats," she said disdainfully, "are worn only by dancing-masters and ill-bred Carolinians."

"We taught your George Washington to dance, didn't we?" Sam said belligerently, then was forced to seize the stiff brush from Jenny before she plunged it embarrassingly deep. At least the soap and grime in the water were saving his modesty now. "It ain't fair," he said.

"Maltreated Sam." Martha smiled. "Nice Sam. What on earth are you doing in the army, Sam?"

"Fighting you lot."

Martha laughed. "Do you like it?"

Sam considered his answer. He had liked it well enough before Nate had died, and he supposed, now that the pain of his brother's death was receding, that he was liking it still. Better to be Captain Vane's servant than Sergeant Scammell's target. A week before, exercising the young stallion, Sam had met his old company returning from duty on the marshes. Maggie, they said, had fled into the wild unknown, and Scammell blamed Sam for it. Sam had avoided the Sergeant, but he knew that one day a confrontation must be endured.

"Well?" Martha insisted. "Do you like it?"

"Ain't bad," Sam said, but without much conviction. "As long as you don't get shot."

"You can't always order that happy event, can you? Jonathon couldn't."

"He was daft as lights!" Sam said. "Why did he go off and fight? He's rich. He could have had everything! So he scarpers off to get a bullet in his leg!"

"You think it's more important to be rich than honourable?" Martha asked.

"That, ma'am, is a question that only a rich person would ask."

"Very good, Sam." Martha unwrapped the precious liquorice root and dropped it into a pot. Suffused with hot water it was a valuable specific against the fever. "Were there any Keyser's Pills?"

"No, ma'am. I was lucky to get the liquorice."

"Damn you British," Martha said mildly. "Jonathon will be dead before you get supplies into Philadelphia!"

"No, he won't." Sam surrendered the brush back to an impatient Jenny. "They're going to take the forts the day after tomorrow, so the river will be open before the week's end. I'll get you Keyser's Pills by next week, I promise."

Martha stared at him, but Sam was oblivious of her sudden alertness. He was beginning to detect an odd pleasure in this equally odd situation. He reclined in the high-backed tub while Jenny scrubbed between his toes.

"The day after tomorrow?" Martha asked innocently.

"Hessians are crossing the river and the grenadiers are attacking the one on the island. The Captain's going, so I suppose I'll have to keep him alive."

Martha stared at Sam. "How do you know this, Sam?"

"Everyone knows!" Sam repeated Tom Evans' scornful answer, which, in all innocence, Sam believed.

"Do they indeed?" Martha walked behind Sam to start untangling the flour-matted queue of his hair. Oddly Sam found her touch far more embarrassing than Jenny's more intimate ministrations, and was glad when, with a shudder, Martha finally extricated the greasy leather pad about which the queue was bound. "But who told you, Sam?"

"Billy's servant." Sam had picked the nickname up from his master.

"So it's only gossip?"

"No!" Sam said indignantly. "The Captain's been scribbling for days now. Orders, I suppose. And all behind a locked door!"

"He never said anything to me," Martha said ruefully. "Nor did Sir William . . ." Her voice tailed away as she perceived, with an absolute conviction in the accuracy of her perception, how a great deception was being practised on the city.

Suspecting from Martha's silence that perhaps, contrary to Tom Evans' assertion, not everyone knew, Sam turned in alarm.

Martha saw his concern and divined it accurately. "Don't worry, Sam. I won't tell the Captain you said anything."

"You won't, ma'am?"

"Not a word. God bless you, Samuel Gilpin." And, to Sam's astonishment, the Widow Crowl stooped and gave him a swift kiss on a newly cleaned forehead. He blushed, but Martha nodded to Jenny who, grinning, yanked Sam's feet upwards. At the same moment Martha thrust down on his scalp so that his head was forced under water. He bellowed, got a mouthful of soapy filth, then came up streaming and protesting. Jenny attacked his hair with a brush to drag out the thick detritus of powder, candle grease, sweat, and grime.

"You're a royalist?" Martha, abandoning the mystery of Captain Vane's secretive behaviour, nodded towards Sam's upper left arm on which, in bold colours, the royal coat-of-arms was tattooed.

"Of course I am!" Sam said.

"Why?"

And Sam tried, between having his face splashed with water, to describe the safety of England's countryside, the cosiness of a place where each man had his liberty within a framework of due order.

Sam worked for the Squire, who deferred to an earl in the next parish, who had the ear of a duke, who would sometimes walk arm-in-arm with the King at Windsor. "We had a fellow condemned to hang," Sam spoke of a man in his village who had been convicted of horse-stealing, "but the King pardoned him. The Squire and Rector wrote a letter, and the King let him live!"

"Good old George," Martha said gently. "But Sam Gilpin could never be squire, could he? Or earl? Or duke?"

"They said I'd be head coachman if I hadn't taken the shilling."

"Oh!" Martha pretended to be hugely impressed. "Whereas here, Sam Gilpin, there'll be a market for a man who knows horses and coaches and harness. There's money to be made, Sam!" She smiled. "Golden hair, who would have believed it?" Martha crossed the room and fetched a huge cotton sheet. She ordered Sam's clothes to be thoroughly scrubbed and for Sam himself to stop being idiotic, to stand up, and to wrap himself in the sheet. "You haven't got anything Jenny and I haven't seen before. There's clothes on the dresser, Sam. They belonged to my late lamented husband, so they'll be a loose fit, but you can wear them till your uniform's dry."

"Yes, ma'am."

"And you'll take the liquorice up to Jonathon?"

"Yes, ma'am."

"And Lydia wants one of your dreadful bedtime stories if you can bear her company."

"It'll be a pleasure, ma'am."

"I'd be grateful." Martha paused at the door. "I'd do it myself, but I have to write a letter. Is Captain Vane calling tonight?"

"Dunno, ma'am. He's with Billy."

"I have a free night?" Martha said it mockingly, then left, and Sam waited till Jenny's back was turned before he scrambled out of the tub and seized the cotton sheet. He went into the scullery to dress and came out grumbling. "I feel like a plucked chicken."

"No one ever died by being clean, Sam." Jenny, mistress in her own kitchen, elbowed him out of the way. "And you're a good-looking boy, you don't want to waste it! Look at you in those clothes! You look like a King!"

Sam grinned sheepishly. It had been over three years since he had worn civilian clothes, but now he was in shirt, breeches, and stockings that had once belonged to a lawyer. The clean material on a clean skin felt strange, but not unwelcome. His hair was shining, and Jenny made him turn round so she could tie it with a black bow like any gentleman might wear. "You look good enough to cook!" Jenny offered happily. "Now go and see Master Jonathon!"

Jonathon, lying in the wide bed, did not even recognize Sam at first, but smiled as soon as he heard the voice. "What have they done to you?"

"Primped me up like a filly going to market, haven't they? How are you?"

Jonathon was pale, thin, and a sheen of sweat covered his face. The room stank because the cauterized stump still suppurated. "I can feel my missing foot. It hurts."

"I'm sorry."

"It wasn't much of a foot, was it?"

"I've seen better," Sam said, then, walking round the bottom of the bed, suddenly stopped. He stared at himself in a tall looking-glass that was built into the door of a linen press. "Bloody hell fire."

Jonathon grimaced with amusement. "Sam, Sam, gentleman."

Sam was staring at a tall, well-built man with golden hair and a strong, cheerful face. He turned to admire his profile, then laughed at his vanity. "If my mother could see me now!"

"She'll see you one day."

"Maybe." Sam suddenly thought of his poor mother's grief when, in a few weeks' time, she would learn of a son dead. He plucked at the white shirt. "Not like a red coat, eh?"

"It's better."

Sam abandoned his own reflection. "You need cleaning?"

Jonathon shook his head. "Jenny did it earlier. Tell me what's happening?"

So Sam sat by the bed and retailed the news of the city. How a cavalry colonel had been thrown out of a house, stark-naked, and been pursued by an irate husband. He talked of the patrols that tried to keep the thieves and drunks off the streets at night. He tried to describe the previous night's dancing under the trees at the Neck where, to his chagrin, Sam had been conscripted as a steward. "I hate doing that. All fancied up just to pour wine for a load of drunks."

"You'd rather be fighting?"

"That's proper soldiering, isn't it?"

"It seems odd, somehow, you being the enemy."

Sam shrugged. "I'm not, am I? Not till you're back and fighting." That was Sam's promise, the dream that he offered Jonathon.

It was a dream Jonathon liked, but he was losing faith rapidly. "I'm still a prisoner. They'll never let me out of the city, will they?" He stopped, turning his head on the pillow towards the sound of voices on the stairs, and Sam, hearing Martha's voice, wondered what new indignity was to be heaped upon him.

No indignity. Instead, following Martha into the bedroom, came a smiling golden-haired girl who held up a round cardboard box. "Keyser's Pills! Grandfather found them."

"Caroline!" Jonathon reached both hands towards her and Sam watched as the girl bent to kiss the wounded boy.

And Sam, still watching, understood why Nate had been willing to risk all for a girl.

This girl was far more beautiful than Maggie. This was a wild-looking golden girl with blue eyes and a firm set to her face that spoke of strength and determination, but who at the moment showed only joy for being with Jonathon. "We found the pills in Grandmother's bible-box," Caroline said.

"Your pills and Sam's liquorice." Jonathon's excitement had put a wash of colour into his cheeks. "That's Sam."

"Don't be fooled by his clothes," Martha said drily. "He's really a tyrannical monster come to enslave us. This is Miss Caroline Fisher, Sam." Martha paused. "She's going to marry Jonathon."

"I had heard." Sam grinned at Jonathon who had spoken so often of this girl.

Caroline smiled at Sam. "You're the one who's been so kind to Jonathon. Thank you."

"I haven't done much." Sam was bashful. "I keep saying he'll be dancing in a month. Right down Market Street and back, ain't that so, Jonathon?"

"I never could dance," Jonathon said.

"You just hop to the music," Sam said, "and I'll carve you a wooden peg."

"Pegleg!" Caroline laughed.

"There was a fellow in our village with a wooden leg," Sam said. "He used to dance up a storm!"

"Never!" Caroline said.

"We sawed an inch off his peg once," Sam grinned. "He

thought he was drunk. Went lurching up the street like a cart with a broken axle!" He laughed, suddenly at his ease. "Had my ears boxed for that."

"Deservedly," Martha said.

"He didn't mind! Thought it was a rare jest! He was the fellow who soaped the belltower steps so the sexton slipped off in a wedding. Came down like a flour sack in a tower-mill!" Sam was suddenly aware of hogging the conversation and, embarrassed, he stopped. He looked at Martha. "Sorry, ma'am."

"It's a pleasure to hear you, Sam." Martha was watching Sam and Caroline, and had seen how the girl smiled at Sam's tale, and how Sam blushed for Caroline, and Martha, feeling suddenly so much older and wiser than her twenty-six years, thought what mischief might be brewed here. A clean Sam, she thought, looked remarkably handsome in his borrowed clothes. "Perhaps you'll go and frighten Lydia with a bedtime story, Sam?"

"Yes, ma'am." Sam smiled a nervous farewell at Caroline, then, obedient, he left the room.

"But don't leave the house." Martha had followed him on to the landing. She hesitated, then smiled. "Caroline shouldn't walk the streets alone. You can see her to the quayside?"

Martha half expected Caroline, who prized her independence, to protest, but no word came from the bedroom. "I'll be glad to, ma'am," Sam said.

So, two hours later, but now in a damp uniform and with his hair once more flour-whitened and once more tight about its leather pad, Sam walked beside Jonathon's girl. Sam carried a bundle for Caroline; a gift of candles from Martha to Caroline's grandparents. A light rain fell, but Sam did not notice. He wanted to watch Caroline as though, in the intermittent pools of lantern light, he could fix the lineaments of her looks into his memory for ever.

They talked of Jonathon. "He'll never fight again, will he?" Caroline said.

"Not with a pegleg," Sam said. "But there's more to fighting than pulling triggers. There's more paperwork than you'd dream of! And he's a scholar, isn't he?"

"Yes." Caroline sounded wistful.

"Our lot are always scribbling," Sam said scornfully. "You can't put a shoe on a horse without a barrowload of paper. Waste of time."

Caroline walked in silence for a few paces. "Will Jonathon get better?"

"He'll get better." Sam said it with a grim determination.

Caroline smiled at Sam. "He's lucky to have you."

Sam shrugged. "He was good to my brother, you see. I owe him for that."

"Jonathon said your brother died."

"Yes." And oddly it was not hard to talk of Nate now, not with this girl. Sam found himself telling Caroline about Nate and Maggie, and how they had planned to run and find their perfect paradise together, and how the dream had ended with a bullet in his brother's back.

"What happened to the girl?" Caroline asked.

"I heard she ran off. Best thing, really."

Caroline walked in silence for a few yards. The lights of a gin shop glinted in her hair and made shadows on her cheeks and beneath her lips. "Poor Nate," she said suddenly.

"He was a fool." Sam smiled sadly. "He only became a soldier because of the red coat, and because of the money they never gave us. But he shouldn't have joined the army! Nate hated fighting. He used to run away from single-stick!"

"Single-stick?" Caroline asked.

"They're like wooden swords," Sam explained, "but heavier. It's a game we play in England. You fight with them, see, and the first to draw an inch of blood from the other fellow's skull wins."

They had entered a dark narrow alley which led towards the lights on the city wharves. Caroline's teeth showed white as she smiled at Sam. "I somehow think you were good at single-stick?"

"I loved it." They left the alley, coming on to the wide flame-lit quays. Sentry posts, each with its own blazing fire, were set all along the wharves, part of the great ring which the British had set about Philadelphia.

Caroline led Sam north towards one of the artillery batteries where the gunners, recognizing her, shouted a friendly greeting. "Got yourself a boyfriend, girl?"

"I'm sorry," Sam said on their behalf.

"They don't worry me." Caroline went down dark steps and untied a boat.

"You sail that yourself?" Sam asked with some astonishment.

"All by my small self." She smiled up from the dark well of the dock. Behind her, reflecting the small moonlight, the water rippled silver and black. She held out her hands for the bundle of candles. "You and I, Sam? We'll get Jonathon better?"

Sam handed her the package, and felt the warmth of the implied complicity. "We will." He watched as she pulled a single dark sail up the mast. "How do you know where you're going?"

"There's a light over there. It's home."

"Get there safely, miss."

Caroline smiled her thanks, then thrust a single scull over the shallop's transom. Sam, stepping back, saw a white rectangle on the bottom step. He ran down, picked it up, and felt the blob of wax that sealed a letter. "Did you drop this?"

Caroline was already fending the boat away from the quay. Her face, as she looked back, showed sudden alarm. "It fell out of the bundle," she said.

"Here!" Sam stretched so far across the widening gap that he almost fell into the water. Caroline reached towards him and steadied him with her hand. Their fingers clutched for safety and Martha's letter nearly slipped into the river. Sam lurched upright, safely handed the letter to Caroline, then apologized for his clumsiness.

"Thank you, Sam." Caroline's eyes seemed bright in the dock's watery gloom.

"Good-night, miss." Sam was remembering her touch, the warm strong touch of a girl.

"Good-night, Sam!" Caroline, with an easy skill, was twisting the single stern scull to drive the boat out of the wharf's shelter and into the wind. She waved when the boat heeled, then sat to the tiller.

Sam did not move. He watched the dark shadow all across the river, watched till the boat was nothing but a blur against the black shadows of the far bank. He felt something he could not describe, but knew it to be a part of happiness. Then he remembered that Jonathon was to marry Caroline and he flinched from what he had been thinking. Sam climbed the steps and walked into a dark city, but, whether he wished it or not, his head was filled and startled with the surprise of golden hair, the memory of fingers strong on his, and of laughter so easily shared. And Sam's world, for the best of all good reasons, but without good hope, suddenly seemed brighter.

TWENTY

On the morning of the attack on the rebel forts, Sir William Howe awoke with a wondrous sense of well-being, quite belying his forty-eight years and also in defiance of the port and fried oysters which, taken at a late supper, he had been sure he would wake to regret. On the contrary, however, he felt almost young again.

Abandoning Lizzie amongst a warm tangle of blankets, he went to his dressing-room where Thomas Evans shaved him and remarked that it was a fine day. It was indeed, Sir William replied as he inhaled the mingled scents of shaving soap and brewing coffee. A street huckster, up betimes, was crying his wares below, reminding Sir William of the noisy and cheerful chaos of London's streets.

Which thought only provoked a pleasant melancholy of happy London memories. The river stairs on a spring day when the Thames danced with sunlight. The Rotunda at Ranelagh Gardens. The Drury Lane Theatre where David Garrick was King, or the Little Theatre in the Haymarket where Samuel Foote would warn the women in the audience to loosen their stays lest their laughter provoke rupture. Sir William dreamed of Almacks on a winter night, of watching the whores in Covent Garden and guessing which would die of the pox and which marry into the gentry. And the coffee houses! Why, there were more coffee houses in the Strand alone than in all Pennsylvania!

"You're looking pensive, sir." Lord Robert Massedene, the day's duty aide, fetched in the morning business as Sir William was being arrayed in stockings, breeches, shirt, stock, waistcoat, coat, wig, shoes, and sword.

"I was remembering Somerset Coffee House, Robert. You recall that extraordinary plump waiter who's so very disobliging?"

"Slaughter's Coffee House," Robert Massedene said teasingly, "the Turk's Head? The Piazza?"

"Clifton's Chop House, eh?"

"Dolly's Steak House," Massedene riposted.

"Where the whores drink porter for breakfast!" The conversation only increased Sir William's happy disposition. "And we must make do with the London Coffee House on Market Street!"

"Where last night, sir, there was a rumour that General Burgoyne had surrendered."

But Sir William's good humour could not be dented. "Rumour, Robert! There's always rumour! How many times have we been told of Mister Washington's death, eh? Of quinsy, ague, flux, colic, even of battle!"

"That, sir" – Robert Massedene laid the papers on Sir William's table – "would be a death I would deeply regret."

Sir William, closing his eyes as Evans perfected the powdering of the wig, laughed. "You think they'd replace him with someone better?"

"Could they find worse?"

"I doubt it, Robert. He even makes me feel like an adequate general." Sir William smiled to show that his modesty should not be taken too seriously, then went to the table where a pot of coffee, sliced ham, bread and butter waited. He glanced at the waiting reports. "Do I have to read them, Robert, or will you just tell me the news?"

"Donop marched on time, sir. Your brother's ships are coming up river. The sun has duly risen. God, the preachers assure us, is in His heaven."

"For which, amen." Sir William spread butter on bread and cocked a professional ear to the gentle thumps that shook the casements. "No great increase in cannon fire, Robert. You think Donop's late?"

"We shall know soon enough, sir," Massedene said comfortingly. "Captain Vane will be first with the news, I'm sure."

"How he does yearn for the smell of powder!" Sir William had been amused by Captain Vane's earnest request that he be allowed to accompany the grenadiers in their assault on Fort Mifflin. "Is he so tired of life?"

"He is avid for reputation, sir. And victory."

"And for the Widow, I think." Sir William chuckled.

"Doubtless, sir. May I tempt you to some salted shad?"

"You may not." Sir William shuddered at the thought, then considered the notion of Vane and Mrs Crowl. "It would be a very good match for him. She's wealthy."

"And beautiful." Massedene spoke drily.

The thought of Vane's marriage had sparked Sir William's enthusiasm. "I do hope it works for them, 'pon my soul, I do! It's what the city needs, Robert! A romance in a city at war! A love story to unite us! My dear Robert, don't you agree?"

"I'm forced to wonder whether the Widow would agree, sir."

"Why ever not? Vane's a decent enough fellow. His people aren't from the top shelf, perhaps, but they're not negligible. She could do a lot worse!"

"She could do a lot better, sir."

Sir William stared at his aide, then, understanding, he gave a slow smile. "You're jealous, Robert! The Widow has conquered you as well!"

Massedene denied it, though without conviction. "It's Vane I find hard to stomach, sir. He has a tradesman's view of life. There's profit or loss, and nothing in between. I try to be civil to him, though."

"I'm sure you do," Sir William said quickly.

"And I don't deny his bravery, sir, and I trust he brings us news of victory today."

"Oh, indeed!" Sir William, reminded of the day's real business, carried a cup of coffee to the window as though he hoped to see victory across the intervening rooftops. He wondered if the tempo of the gunfire had increased, then allowed himself a silent wish for the safety of his aide, Christopher Vane.

Who, crouching beneath a dike to stay out of a chill wind, waited for the attack to start. Vane had been waiting since the first grey wolfish light before dawn, he had waited as the handful of frigates and gunboats, their topsails washed pink by the rising sun, had laboriously threaded their way past the sunken obstacles of the river bed and crept upstream, and still he waited. "Donop's late!"

"Sir?" Sam shivered as he huddled at the dike's base, armed with musket and bayonet.

Vane did not repeat the words. He was wondering why he had volunteered for this mission, and decided that, in truth, he could not bear to think of a great venture put at risk because it lacked his efforts. That, Vane decided, was a monstrous conceit, but it was still true. Ever since Sir William had plucked him from the shadows Vane had felt marked for greatness, and he knew that this period of youth was the mere apprenticeship to fame. He risked that greatness, of course, by offering himself to this fight, but he did not believe fate had death by battle marked against his name. "Are you frightened, Sam?"

"No, sir."

Vane turned. "Truly?"

"No more than another man, sir."

Vane smiled. "I've seen you frightened, Sam. I've seen you scared half to death! It was that sergeant. The one who was hitting you when I so kindly rescued you."

Sam thought about it. "Anyone'd be scared of Scammy, sir. Right bastard, he is."

"Describe his bastardy, Samuel. Amuse me." Vane, bored, wanted to pass the time, and so it was that Sam found himself describing Sergeant Scammell. He astonished himself by hearing a grudging admiration in his own voice as he depicted Scammell's bravery, but there was no admiration when he spoke of the night when Scammell had been on picquet duty before the battle.

"He killed that lad, sir!"

"Truly?" Vane was intrigued by the story.

"But don't do nothing, sir!" Sam was alarmed. "I shouldn't have told you!"

"I would not take from the army a man who sounds so valuable," Vane said. "We need ruthless men, Sam, if we're to put this rebellion down." Vane stood and stared across the river, wondering why Donop still did not attack. "Why did you bathe the other day, Sam?"

"Bathe, sir?"

Vane looked down on his servant. "I did notice, Sam! One day you're encrusted with filth, and the next you're suddenly smelling like a whore's parlour! Have you found a girl?"

"No, sir."

"I think you have. Who is this doxie?"

"Only a girl, sir," Sam said lamely.

"What kind of girl? A kitchenmaid?"

"Yes, sir." Sam seized on the invention, then, thinking he should say something more to embroider it, spoke the truth. "She's lovely, sir."

"I'm sure she is." Vane wondered just what kind of passion it was that private soldiers felt. Something squalid, no doubt, a mere passage of flesh that could not be compared with the sacramental ecstasy Vane felt for Martha Crowl. The thought of Martha, and of taking his victorious sword in a lover's tribute to her house, made Vane smile. Tonight, he thought, when this business was gloriously concluded, he would gently take the Widow past the constraints of friendship into the more exciting passions of love, and that thought was as exciting as the anticipation of the action that had yet, inexplicably, to start around the beleaguered forts.

Clouds raced their shadows over the long waters and hid the sun. A heron stalked the river shoals while Captain Vane impatiently strolled up and down the line of the dike. At any moment he expected to hear the thump of the light galloper guns that had accompanied Donop's Hessians, but, as the morning ached slowly, coldly, onwards, no firing came across the still grey sheets of water. Two frigates and three gunboats, with leadsman chanting the fathoms, inched upstream. By noon the clouds threatened rain, but a wind had risen to ruffle the water and heel the warships over. A rebel galley, nosing from one of the intricate creeks of the New Jersey shore, tried a shot at a frigate with its bow gun and was answered by a rolling, thunderous broadside that made a vast cloud of dirty smoke in the river's centre. The galley, unharmed, sheered gracefully away.

"This is insanity!" Captain Vane's temper, despite his happy anticipations of the night, was frayed by waiting. At dinner, taken at half-past one with the officers of the grenadier companies that would take the surrender of Fort Mifflin, he even thought of returning to the city to see whether Sir William, for some strange reason, had called off the Hessian attack, but curiosity held him to the marsh dike beyond which, heavy on the river bank, longboats waited to ferry the grenadiers to the shoals off Mud Island. The grenadiers were the shock troops of a battalion, and six battalions had contributed companies towards the capture of the island fort. The men, bored by waiting, slept beneath the dike or sharpened already-sharpened bayonets. Vane, fretting, snapped open the lid of his new watch that had once hung from a chain on Benjamin Franklin's belly. "It was supposed to be a surprise attack!"

"It could still succeed." A moustached major sliced a rancid slice from a joint of salt pork.

"They should have attacked at dawn."

The major put the pork in his mouth and chewed it slowly. "This is the army. When does anything happen on time?"

* * *

Sir William Howe, still in Philadelphia where he had been persuaded he must stay lest his absence alerted the enemy to some extraordinary effort, also fretted because of the advancing hours. "Is the man lost? Gone back to Germany? Damn it!"

Lord Cornwallis, a dour, efficient man who dined this afternoon with Howe, said nothing, but by his silence suggested that he, given the authority, might have arranged things better. Cornwallis wanted to return to London and Sir William felt a pang of jealousy. Why should Cornwallis go home? And what mischief would he concoct in the drawing-rooms and ante-chambers where the government's real business was conducted?

Lord Robert Massedene carved the brawn and waited for the guns to fire in the rhythm of battle. "Perhaps, sir," he ventured, "Fort Mercer surrendered without a fight?"

"Ha!" Cornwallis erupted.

"My lord?" Sir William challenged his second-in-command.

Cornwallis stared aggressively at Sir William. Finally, and with great deliberation, he merely said, "Your cook overcooks brawn."

"I have half a mind," Sir William ignored the horrid man, "to see the cockfighting this afternoon. Isn't there a pit on Front Street?"

"In Moore's Alley, sir, just by Carr's Store." Lord Robert offered the gravy boat. "And with some extraordinary fine birds, they say."

But there was to be no cockfight, for, at three o'clock, when dinner was still taking its stately course, a shout of the guards and a rattle of hooves proclaimed the coming of, if not news, at least excitement. Sir William, betraying the nervousness that he was trying so hard to disguise, threw down his napkin and, trailing half-fed officers, went to the courtyard where a blindfolded man sat on a horse. The stranger was escorted by two dragoons and, miracle of miracles, had Sir William's missing dog, Hamlet, on a long leash tied to one of his stirrups.

"Hamlet!"

The dog, yapping and frantic, tried to escape the leash. Sir William ran forward to help, then snapped at one of the dragoons, "Release him, release him!"

"The rebel, sir?"

Sir William, a frantic dog now in his arms, noticed for the first time that the blindfolded man was, indeed, a rebel. The man had come, a lieutenant of dragoons said, under a flag of truce, and had been blindfolded so he could not carry back details of the defences that barred the northern approaches to the city.

The man, released from his blindness, bowed to Sir William. "My name is Colonel Mitchell."

"Sir William Howe," Howe introduced himself.

Mitchell smiled. "Your dog, I guess? We found him with our army, sir, but his collar betrayed his true allegiance."

"And you brought him back! Upon my honour, sir, I'm grateful! Most grateful!"

"He comes, sir, with General Washington's compliments, and upon General Washington's particular orders."

"That's kind of . . ." Sir William paused, not wanting to dignify the rebel commander with due rank, but gratitude made him gracious ". . . General Washington, and you will inform him, sir, that I am in his debt. You have not, I trust, been badly treated?"

"Indeed not, sir."

"And you will dine with us? We have brawn, a fine claret little bruised by shipping, and, I think, a pumpkin pie!"

Mitchell smiled at the General's eagerness, but shook his head. "If it doesn't offend you, sir, I must leave."

"There is no thanks I can render?" Sir William, truly delighted by Washington's gesture, stroked the small dog which, happily, seemed none the worse for its adventure. "No gift I can return, Colonel?"

Mitchell gave a crooked smile. "General Washington, sir, asks nothing of you in the belief that he can take whatever he wants."

"Very good! Very good! Bravely said, sir!" Howe beamed at his officers, expecting to see them share his jollity, but, except for Massedene, they seemed unamused. Howe, though, was enjoying this wry confrontation. "You will give the General," the word came more easily the second time, "my respects, sir, also my best wishes to his wife and my regrets that we should find ourselves as enemies."

"At least," Mitchell seemed somewhat bemused by this affable reception, "we no longer need count General Burgoyne amongst our foes."

"The rumour has reached you, has it?" Howe's delight at being reunited with his dog could not be spoilt by such tittle-tattle. "I just hope Gentleman Johnny never finds the rascal who spreads such scandal about him!"

"More than a rumour, sir. He surrendered at Saratoga."

"Splendid! Splendid!" Sir William was all happiness. "My thanks, sir, my sincerest thanks! I regret the need to blindfold you again, but you will understand?"

The rebel colonel left, and Sir William went back to dinner where, with indulgent joy, he fed brawn to his prodigal pet. He fussed and combed the dog, only ceasing when, from the south and west, the guns at last rose to a thunder of death to tell the city that a battle was waged where the water mingled with mud about two forts.

And where, scrambling over a dike, Christopher Vane went forward with the grenadiers who were to take possession of a beaten fort.

The battle had flared suddenly. One moment the warships had coasted out of range, the next a crash of gunfire beyond Fort Mercer informed the waiting troops that at last, at long last, the Hessians were attacking.

Ships went about, sails flapped like monstrous wings and were sheeted home, then broadsides thundered from the chequered sides. On the marshes every gun in every British battery opened fire. The grenadiers' officers, bawling orders, chivvied their men over the mud and into the waiting boats that were manned by seamen from the fleet. The heron, legs trailing, disdainfully flew between the spreading smoke that wavered in thin skeins above the river, then was fed with more smoke that gushed from jets of flame as great guns hammered back on trails or carriages. Mortars, squatting evil on their beds, arched shells over the shallow water. The shells, their burning fuses leaving pencil traces in the sky, exploded in stabs of flame within the courtyard of Fort Mifflin.

Sam, scrambling with the cheering grenadiers, followed Vane down to the mud and into the left flank boat. He could see smoke beyond the far fort now, a sign that the Hessians were attacking in New Jersey, but he was far more worried about the closer Fort Mifflin which was now ringed by British guns. "They're not firing back, sir," he said hopefully.

"Perhaps they're holding their fire for us, Sam," Vane teased his servant cheerfully. Or perhaps the fort had been so battered by gunfire that its men just waited for a chance to surrender. "But we're sitting at the spikes, Sam, sitting at the spikes!" Vane's mood soared at the prospect of action.

"Spikes, sir?"

"Front seat at the theatre, Sam, where the spikes stop the audience mauling the actresses. But we'll give our Yankees a mauling, eh?"

"Put your backs into it. Row!" The bo'sun on Sam's boat seemed to think it was a race with the other eleven launches that, oars rising and dipping, crept across the shoal water. Gulls, startled by the cannon fire, wheeled overhead.

A different note intruded on the gunfire; a deeper sound betraying a larger gun, and Sam saw a spreading cloud of smoke come from the ramparts of Fort Mifflin. A frigate, sailing slowly past the water ramparts, seemed to shiver as the enemy ball struck home.

"That fort ain't a dead 'un!" a lieutenant called from the bow.

"Will be soon!" Vane's exhilaration was blissful. The waiting was over, and he would charge with these splendid men into the churned wreckage of the gun-hammered fort. Now, on the verge of action, an unbidden daydream entertained him. Martha had somehow reached the fort and was in deadly danger, from which he, Captain Vane, would rescue her. She would be tearful with gratitude and would melt with the affection that he so desperately wanted from her.

"*Augusta*'s gone aground!" The bo'sun suddenly shattered Vane's dream. The seaman was pointing at the frigate which had taken the enemy's opening shot.

"No!" Vane said, but, despite his denial, the *Augusta* was lowering boats that would attempt to tow the frigate off the shoal. "Not that it matters," Vane muttered to himself.

"It doesn't?" Sam, crouching by his master, wanted reassurance.

"She can still fire, can't she?" Vane flinched from an oarsplash. "And the Yankees aren't putting up much of a display."

The words were no sooner said than the complete line of the water-facing ramparts of Fort Mifflin erupted in flame-jetted smoke as the American batteries poured their fire at the stranded frigate. The guns' thunder filled the air, and the river became a loud and murderous duel between the fort and the grounded *Augusta*. The second frigate, bow guns cracking sharp, sailed to the rescue.

"I thought we was occupying a beaten fort!" Sam protested.

"The more enemy," Vane said loudly, "the more glory!"

Sam's boat grounded on a mud shoal and a sergeant's sharp voice ordered the men over the side. "Get your feet wet, you bastards!"

"Skirmish order!" a major in the next boat shouted. The other launches ran their keels on to the mud and the bright red coats of the grenadiers spilt into the shallow water. "Forward!"

"Into the breach, Sam." Vane lifted his face to the smell of the powder smoke and the rumbling of the heavy cannon balls in their flight. "On, you noble English!" he laughed, and drew his sabre.

It seemed madness to Sam. They were a half-mile from the fort, and most of that half-mile was a glutinous stretch of water-logged mud into which men sank up to their knees. There were small rippling creeks, the ribs of an abandoned boat, and always the sticky, clinging, sucking mud across which a chain of men were approaching the smoke-wreathed fort. The other battles, across and on the river, seemed extraneous, something happening in another place and nothing to do with Sam.

The grenadiers, at last reaching the more solid ground of Mud Island, crouched at a bank of sand. They were waiting now, Vane explained, for Fort Mercer to be captured and for its guns to be turned on Mifflin. The rebels in the latter fort, who had watched the grenadiers struggle over the mud, were beginning a desultory musket fire. The balls cracked and hissed overhead, but the distance was too great for the fire to be effective. However, the distance was not so great that the rebels' insults, shouted from behind their parapets, could not be heard.

"Ignore them!" A major strolled behind the crouching men. "We'll make them eat their words soon enough! We'll go for the abatis, lads! You'll take casualties, but that's what you joined for! A soldier's heaven is carpeted with whores, so don't be feared! Take your blades to the bastards and give them hell!"

They waited. The artillery duel filled the sky with a great rumbling as if massive casks were being rolled on boards overhead. Sam, watching the fort over the dune's crest, saw wooden palings flung about like firewood. Mortar shells, blasting scarlet, churned flame and smoke within the courtyard. Above the fort, somehow unscathed, the rebel flag still snapped in the smoke-thick wind.

As did the flag above Fort Mercer. That fort's guns, far from having been captured by the Hessians, were firing at the grounded frigate. A second naval boat, much smaller and further down river, was also aground and also under cannonade.

"She's on fire, sir!" Sam was staring at the *Augusta*.

Captain Vane was still keyed to the coming battle, but he turned to watch the *Augusta* just as a lance blade of fire, pure as a lightning's stab, drove up from amidships and went on, spearing up, higher than the highest topmast.

For a second it seemed that every gun on the river stopped firing as, around the watery arena, men stared at the stricken boat. The lance of fire twisted, faded, then, just as it seemed the boat was safe, the whole frigate blasted itself apart in a great gouting flame-filled explosion. A mast, launched like an arrow, cartwheeled in the air, then shattered into its constituent spars. Deck planking was scattered to the clouds. A sail, burning and twisting like a giant bat from hell, flapped grotesquely across the sky. A whole ship, all its great solid mass and grace, was turned into a maelstrom of dark stinking smoke and death. Debris, spat from the boiling fire-lit cloud, splashed into the water.

For a few numbing seconds it was oddly silent.

Then the shock of the explosion came with a deafening noise that, like an earthquake, seemed to shake the ground. A wave, cresting on the shoals, was driven towards the island. More explosions, punching the onlooking soldiers' ears, swept over the marshes as powder barrels in the ship's ready magazines exploded.

Ash, driven by the flames and carried by the wind, sifted like black snow on the waters. Great ribs stood clear in the fire that raged in the opened hull. The water, flooding back from the explosion's thrust, caused smoke, black as the clouds of hell, to boil up over the broken waves.

"Oh, Jesus Christ." Vane stared open-mouthed.

The second grounded boat was also aflame, the fire flickering in the delicate spider web of masts and spars. Boats rowed its crew away from their doomed vessel.

Then, from the rebel fort, came a cheer; a triumphant, jeering, and derisive cheer. One man stood on the nearest bastion and cupped his hands towards the grenadiers. "You bastards! Do you like the American welcome?"

"Fuck him!" Vane, his mood plunging to despair, seized Sam's musket, cocked and aimed it, then fired at the taunting rebel.

"Missed!" The man laughed, jumped down, and a small cannon, loaded with canister and held back for the grenadiers' attack, opened fire. The balls, whistling and snapping, flayed overhead.

"Back!" The grenadier major, knowing that everything had gone wrong this day, shouted at his men. "Back!"

Captain Vane wanted to go on; he wanted to charge the impudent fort. Madness and revenge made him incoherent. He wanted to go forward, but he was given no choice. "Back!" The grenadier major shouted the order again, and back Vane went. He stumbled over the clinging, dreadful mud, retreating with the infantry who were pursued by the American's taunting, killing cannonade. Sam helped one grenadier who had been pierced in the leg with canister. Another man was face down in the mire, sinking, drowning, except that he was already dead with a ball in his spine. Canister balls flicked and gouged the slick mud, and every step of the grenadiers' retreat was marked by more shouted insults.

They floundered to the boats. Two men were dead, three injured. The second grounded warship, a sloop set afire by its own crew lest the enemy refloat her, exploded, but in the day's misery it went unnoticed. The smoke of two broken ships drifted over the river, and at dusk the boats still burned to cast a lurid, rippling light across the shoals.

And over Fort Mercer, as over Fort Mifflin, the rebels' striped flag still flew.

"Sir William will take it hard!" Vane himself seemed close to tears as, with Sam beside him, he rode from the Schuylkill's middle ferry to the city. "It went wrong, Sam, dreadful wrong! I hate to bear the news!"

But Vane did not need to bear the news, for Sir William had already heard, and Sir William, in despair, sat by a fire with a sleeping Hamlet at his feet. He tried to smile as Vane, muddy and exhausted, came into the room, but he could only manage a grimace. "I know what happened, Christopher."

"I'm sorry, sir."

Sir William shook his head. "It doesn't matter."

"The forts will fall, sir." Vane found himself offering consolation. He noticed Hamlet, but this was no time to make a comment, for he had never seen Sir William so downcast.

"Oh, the forts will fall!" Sir William said. "But for what, Kit? We can't win here! We can't take every town and every village and every bridge and every damned farmhouse! And if we did, how would we govern them? They've tasted victory. They'll never let go now, never!"

"Victory, sir? It was only a repulsed attack! We'll attack again."

"No." Sir William slowly lifted a single sheet of paper as though it weighed a ton. "Brought by a cutter from New York, then overland."

Christopher Vane, his shadow cast long by the flickering candles, crossed the room and took the paper. He read it once, then again, then closed his eyes. "Oh, God." The shame of it was too much, pricking his eyelids with tears. He heard the Widow's laughter in his head. Defeat.

"Saratoga," Sir William said the name bitterly, "wherever in God's holy bloody hell Saratoga may be."

Vane opened his eyes, expecting to see the whole world changed, but Sir William still sat in the leather chair before the fire and a cold wind still plucked at the window panes to bring, from the street, a man's voice in drunken song. Vane looked back at the despatch. "The whole army? Surrendered?"

"To rebels." Sir William, in a fit of anger, scared his dog by snatching the paper back. He threw it on to the fire. "I prayed it wasn't true. I prayed!" Sir William paused, looking suddenly much older than his forty-eight years. "I've done my best, Kit. I've been reluctant to fight, but I've won every battle I was forced to fight. I've restrained the hotheads in the hope that we can persuade the rebels to talk. I've tried to protect their women and their houses. I've offered them amnesty, redress of their grievances, peace! They talk of tyranny, and I have practised decency! Christian, gentlemanly, English decency!" He shuddered suddenly. "Perhaps I should give them what they want. Fire and sword and hate without end!"

Sir William was preaching Vane's gospel, but Vane could not take advantage of it. He felt too sorry for this kind and broken man. "But you won't, sir."

"No. And now the French will come in. It's all they needed. Saratoga!" Sir William closed his eyes. "A hundred thousand men. A hundred thousand men! That's what I needed, and they give me thirty to hold everything between the Floridas and Canada. Thirty thousand men, less the six thousand at Saratoga. Jesus!" He thumped the chair's arm, making the dog whimper. "If I walk on water and turn the loaves and fishes into a feast, will that be sufficient for London?"

But Vane could offer no answer. God had doffed his red coat, and an army's hopes were ashes in a cold wind, drifting to an empty sea.

TWENTY-ONE

Captain Vane walked cold streets. He could no more believe what was reported from Saratoga than he could believe what he had seen with his own eyes on the marshes. He went to change out of his muddy uniform before seeking the Widow's solace, hoping that her allegiance to friendship would let her give sympathy, even love, in this sad night. Vane wondered how many men had died; men whose names would be posted in church porches throughout Britain and Ireland to say that sons and husbands had been killed to keep the plague of republicanism out of America.

Vane turned into the alley which led to his lodgings and had to step aside as a drunken John Andre, reeking of rum, staggered towards the street. "Kit?"

"It's me, John. Are you all right?"

Andre seemed to consider the question. "I'm drunk, but I'm going to Mrs Taylor's. Best thing to do, Kit, after a defeat. Get drunk and get rogered. Would you care to come?"

"I've given up whores, John."

"Good God Almighty." Andre stared in disbelief at Vane, then turned and shouted at the torchlit street. "He's in love! He's in love!"

"John!" Vane protested.

"It doesn't matter, Kit. I'm just drunk. Can you believe the news from Sara . . . Sara . . . wherever it is?"

"No."

"Nor I." Andre found a flask of rum in his tail pocket. "Perhaps it isn't true. Why don't you marry the Widow?"

"I'd like to."

"I was going to marry once, did I tell you?"

"Many times, John."

Andre leaned on the alley wall and drank from the flask that he then companionably offered to Vane. "Her name, if you can credit it, was Honora Sneyd." Andre seemed to be laughing, but Vane suddenly saw that his friend was shaking with drunken tears. "Sneyd!" Andre said. "She had a consumptive's beauty, Kit. Why do we love the helpless? We should look for strapping girls with thighs like grenadiers, but we always fall for the fragile, God damn us. She threw me over, so God damn her as well. God damn all women. Till the next."

"Go to bed," Vane said.

"Not to my own," Andre said with drunken dignity, "not tonight. Tonight, as Miss Shippen shows a modesty I despise, I am for Mrs Taylor's and you are not." He sucked at the flask, which now proved empty, so he threw it into the street where it clattered on the flagstones. "Have you asked for the Widow's hand yet?"

"Not yet."

"Faint heart never won fair trollop. And if you don't, Kit, others will. Do not say I did not warn you!" Andre, with a great effort, pushed himself from the wall and staggered into the torchlight.

Vane ran after him. "What do you mean?"

Andre, his shoulder seized, turned. "I mean, my dear friend, that we can be made more miserable than worms by women. Yours, my dear Kit, is giving a reception tonight. Were you invited?"

"A reception?"

"Music, wine, jollity. Your friend and mine Lord Robert Massedene told me."

"Jesus Christ!" Vane twisted away and ran, his feet given speed by the jealousy which, like a flood of bile, poisoned him. He turned on to Market Street, scattering a patrol from his path, and ran towards Martha's house.

Where he found the windows blazing with candlelight, and music spilling into the street to enrage a group of Loyalists who were only prevented from taking revenge for this unseemly celebration by the presence of four armed Redcoats who, with stoic faces, guarded the house front.

Vane climbed the steps and shoved open the unlocked front door. Laughter sounded from the upstairs parlour. Vane pushed open the door in time to hear a toast being announced. "To Saratoga!"

"To Saratoga!" Perhaps a dozen of the city's most strident Patriots were in the room which was lit by a shoal of tall white candles. Every guest drank, except for Robert Massedene who, with quiet amusement, watched the proceedings. Three musicians, two violinists and a flautist sat in the window bay. In front of them, proposing the toast, Martha was dressed in a flamboyant dress of scarlet silk that was looped with ribbons to match those in her hair. "Captain Vane! You still have the mud of the marshes on you!"

"Where I watched men die today, ma'am." The presence of Massedene had enraged Vane almost as much as this flaunting of a rebel victory.

"Were they Redcoats who died?" an elderly man, a respected doctor in the city, enquired of Vane.

"What if they were?" Vane turned savagely on the doctor.

"I am here because of a British defeat," the doctor said with cold dignity, "so why should I cease my celebration because of your news?"

"God damn you!"

"Enough!" Lord Robert Massedene crossed the room. His voice, when he reached Vane, was low and peaceable. "It really might be better if you left, Kit."

Vane knew that his anger trembled on the edge of a duel, and he knew, too, how Sir William's rare but formidable anger was provoked by duels, so, mastering the rage, he looked at Martha. "Do you wish me to leave, ma'am?"

"I think you should have a glass of wine, Kit." She smiled at him and, with her natural and quiet grace, took Vane's arm and led him into the small breakfast room which lay behind the parlour. She closed the door behind them. "I would have invited you, but I only heard about Saratoga this afternoon."

The word was like a knife in Vane's pride. "You'd invite me to celebrate that?"

"Why ever not?" Martha seemed amused. "I attend all the celebrations of British prowess, Kit. Would you deny me this one chance of enjoying a Patriot victory?"

Vane turned away to stare through the window at the lights of the city. "You could hardly expect me to take pleasure in such a thing, but it seems Lord Robert has a more pliant allegiance."

"I think not. He informed me of the surrender with great regret, but he was also kind enough to offer his protection to me tonight. You were not available, otherwise, naturally, I should have asked you first. Would you have been as kind as he?"

Vane turned from the window and, as if with a great effort, said what was dearest to his heart. "I would be kind to you." He paused, hoping she would reply, and he saw how, in the small candlelight, the shadows made her face mysterious and enchanting so that the thought of losing her was unbearable. "I would be most kind to you, dear Martha."

Martha smiled her gratitude. "I too hope we shall be friends, but it should be on the understanding that my opinions will not change, any more, I suspect, that yours will."

Vane thought of all the men to whom he had declared his passionate love of this woman, and he thought of the disgrace if he were to lose his status as her particular companion. "I would be more than friends. You know that."

Martha paused, then nodded. "I had suspected it, Captain Vane."

"And?" Vane, his anger of a moment before quite forgotten, spoke the word with a great yearning.

It was Martha's turn to go to the window and stare into the night. Her face was reflected in the darkened pane as she spoke. "I never wanted the British to come to Philadelphia, Kit, and I wept on the day you arrived. I should perhaps have fled, but I wasn't brave enough. I couldn't bear to think of Lydia and myself being harried pell-mell across Pennsylvania, always wondering if Redcoats would appear in the next uncomfortable little town. So I stayed." She turned to him. "And I hope, indeed I know, that one day you will leave. Till then I will not willingly make an enemy of a particular man, but nor can I make anything more than a friend of any man who wishes to see my nation defeated."

Vane had listened with growing despair and now seized on just one sentence. "We won't leave. Redcoats will grow old and die in Philadelphia, but we won't leave!"

Martha shook her head in gentle contradiction. "You gave up Boston to take Philadelphia. What will you give up to take Charleston? Or to defend the West Indies if the French come into the war? And they will! Today's news will bring them over the Atlantic because they want the sugar islands! One island is worth the trade of two of these colonies, and London would rather surrender Philadelphia a dozen times than yield Antigua. So you're already defeated, Kit, you've lost! Don't you understand that?"

Vane shook his head wearily. "We haven't lost. We won't lose!" It was a stubborn declaration of faith, something to cling to as he heard the greater hopes of love sliding away.

"You've lost." Martha was implacable. "And if you don't accept it, the loss will be worse. Sir William knows! He wants peace, and what do you gain by persevering with war?"

"We shall win," Vane said obstinately. "We lose now because we're led by men who wish to be kind to the rebels, but that will change! We'll bring real soldiers here!"

"Like you?"

Vane straightened. "Like me, ma'am. And we'll win!"

Martha shook her head sadly. "Dear Kit! You merely want to kill rebels now to salve your pride."

"That isn't true!"

"Of course it's true!" This time it was Martha who showed a pang of anger. "You despise us, Kit, and you can't bear to be beaten by people you despise!"

"I do not despise you."

Martha made an impatient gesture. "You think our taste is blowsy and vulgar. You said so yourself. We lack an aristocracy. You mock our merchants for their opulence. You patronize us, Kit!"

Vane flinched under her lash. "I never patronize you."

"You patronize my people, my city! Do you wonder that so many Americans hate the tyranny of Britain? How would you feel if strangers came by boat to flaunt their so-called superiority in the streets of London?"

"There's no tyranny here."

Martha sighed as though she were explaining something very simple to a person of slow or obstinate understanding. "It's the tyranny of ignorance, Kit, and of stupidity, and of unthinking arrogance!"

"I would think, madam" – Vane was stung into an equivalent scorn – "that colonists dependent on our benevolent protection from the depradations of savages and Frenchmen are not best qualified to be judges of tyranny, stupidity, or arrogance."

"There! You see? You patronize me!" Martha's voice was loud enough to still the hum of conversation in the next room which, almost at once, started again.

Vane seemed to quiver with anger. However, when he spoke it was not anger that he expressed, but a terrible and wounded plea. For Vane to lose this woman would be to suffer a public rejection and so, in desperation, he checked the rage and sought her pity instead. "I can't patronize you. I love you!"

Martha heard the agony, and knew what a hollow hurt soul lurked in this man. He thought the world despised him for his birth, and he sought solace in the trappings of success. Vane, Martha knew, would always want a gaudier uniform than the next man, and a more beautiful woman than his rival. She made her voice as gentle as the music that started to play in the next room. "You do me honour, Kit, but I cannot return your love. However, I will be a friend, as long as you understand that we simply do not need you any more. Not for protection, nor even, though you would scarce believe it, as arbiters of our infant taste."

But Vane, stung by her rejection, did not hear the kindness in her voice. "You were quick enough to seek our help when your brother needed rescue! How American that is! To declare your self-sufficiency, then whine for help whenever a painted savage shows his face among the trees!"

"That's stupidity, Kit, and you know it!" Martha's voice was sharp. "I asked for help because it was in the British power to give it. It was the British who put Jonathon into that hospital!"

"And who released him! And what gratitude did we have?"

"Dear God!" Martha closed her eyes in exasperation. When she opened them there was nothing but scorn in their dark gaze. "What pathetic hopes, Captain Vane, you did have of that night."

Vane saw that all his hopes had been doomed, that even before this night they had been doomed, and that all Martha had ever wanted was a red-coated sleeve to ward off the enmity within a Loyalist city. He saw too that she pitied him, and that realization sparked the anger he had tried to conceal. "Damn you, madam."

Martha stepped back and opened the door which led to the servants' back staircase. "It seems we are not to be friends, captain. Good-night. Please don't call again."

"God damn you!" Vane snatched up his cocked hat and slammed his way down the stairs and into the street. He barged through the small crowd outside and thought he heard a peal of mocking laughter come from the house behind.

A cold night wind came from the dark river. Somewhere a dog barked and a child cried. Clouds, edged with silver, sailed before the moon. Sentries' boots echoed from Chestnut Street and the glare of their torches flickered long shadows from the pavements' stanchions. Vane walked slowly, blindly, not knowing where he walked, nor caring. He had been rejected. He had been scorned and spurned and pitied, and the desire for revenge was pure and fierce.

A whore lurched out of a shop doorway. "Colonel? Colonel?" They called every officer colonel. "Lonely?"

"Get out of my way!" Vane's rage exploded. He backhanded the woman, hurling her on to the wooden shutters of the store. Christopher Vane, come to Philadelphia, had met defeat and a woman's laughter seemed to echo in the night behind him. There would be no peace with such people till victory had forced its price from their defiance. Captain Christopher Vane, in this inchoate war that spluttered along a coastline, had found his enemy and she had slashed his pride, for which offence, Vane swore, he would one day see her grovel as he, this night, had pleaded for her kindness, and been rejected.

TWENTY-TWO

The Revd MacTeague, knowing that all Loyalist hopes had been dealt a savage blow by the extraordinary events in the northern wilderness, chose Ecclesiastes 7, verse 6 as his text for the next Sunday. "For as the crackling of thorns under a pot, so is the laughter of the fool: this also is vanity." The unseemly joy, he preached, with which a few in the community had greeted the sad happenings at Saratoga, was of no more account than a burning thornbush. Their vanity would be punished and their cackling joy turned into lamentation. But it was a sermon of small comfort to Loyalists whose belief in the invincibility of the king's army had been so broken.

Hunger added its misery to Loyalist defeat. The cargo ships, still barred from the city by the rebel forts, languished in the Delaware Bay while the convoys of army wagons, dragged from the Chesapeake Bay across roads that had been turned into morasses of mud by the autumn rains, could not bring a tenth of the food the city needed. Indeed the wagons' priority was powder and shot for the siege guns, not food for hungry bellies, and so the city's larders emptied and prices doubled. Some produce arrived from the countryside, but many farmers were scared of the rebel patrols that willingly enforced George Washington's decreed punishment of two hundred and fifty lashes for any man or woman caught trading with the enemy. Such farmers, unwilling to sell their food for the paper money of the rebels, hid their harvests until the red-coated forage parties arrived with British gold.

The Revd MacTeague, invited to dine with Abel Becket some two weeks after the dreadful news of Saratoga, picked moodily at the salt pork. "I cannot conceive how these disasters could have happened, truly I cannot."

"The Calvinists," Becket said darkly, "intimate divine intervention."

"Watermelons were the cause of Saratoga!" Hannah Becket declared.

"Watermelons, ma'am?" The Revd MacTeague was accustomed to Mrs Becket's frequent references to food, but he failed to make any cogent connection between the disaster at Saratoga and watermelons.

"It is an incontrovertible fact, Mr MacTeague, that watermelons provoke the fever. The most eminent physicians will assure you of it! It is my belief that the rebels arranged for General Burgoyne's men to partake of watermelons!"

The minister sensibly chose not to argue with such wisdom. "It sounds most plausible, ma'am."

"Not that a watermelon could be had here," Hannah Becket, an ample woman, was now well launched on her favourite topic, "even if a body had a taste for one! What are we to do for food? Salt tongue at three shillings a pound! Buckwheat almost gone! Cod, none! Are we to live on mere aspirations?"

"The forts will be taken," her husband said.

"So you say, and so we pray, but molasses? None. Cheese? Mere shreds! A shilling a tierce for dried peas, cone sugar quite gone! Calves' feet? A very delicacy these days, and I am partial to a jelly."

"I saw some very fine cucumbers, ma'am," MacTeague suggested diffidently.

"Cucumbers! Cucumbers! Do the British expect us to starve on salad greens?"

"The forts," Abel Becket's voice demanded his wife's silence, "will fall!" If the forts could not be taken by sudden escalade, they must be starved and cannonaded into submission. For submit they must, or else a score of Philadelphia merchants, among them Becket himself, would be ruined. That prospect, which had been made more gloomy by the disaster at Saratoga, made Abel Becket a poor after-dinner companion to the Revd MacTeague when the two men retired to Becket's study.

MacTeague sipped his tea. "Your nephew's health is much improved."

Abel Becket jabbed at the fire which, made of green wood, burned badly. "His future is his own now. He spurned me."

"Lesserby disagrees."

The mention of his lawyer's name made Becket wary. "I cannot see why he should involve you . . ."

"I am your pastor, as I was your brother's, and as I am Jonathon's. I visit Jonathon. At first I despaired of him, but he is improved."

Abel Becket was not concerned with Jonathon's health. "What did Lesserby want?"

The priest smiled with a false innocence. "Lesserby told me of your discussions with him, and I am now cast in the role of a humble messenger and charged to tell you that, under the terms of your dear brother's will, there is no legal certainty that Jonathon can be denied his portion of your business." MacTeague sipped tea again. "He will be twenty-one in April, I believe?"

"In April." Becket scowled towards the fire's weak flames.

"And he will certainly live till April," MacTeague said.

"One prays so," Becket said automatically.

"Indeed, indeed." The soft pummelling from the distant gunfire of the continuing siege on the marshes sounded beyond the window, then there was silence again.

Abel Becket had presumed Jonathon's death. Now he heard of his nephew's survival and he understood precisely what that news implied. He turned to the priest. "Jonathon will be in his sister's power."

"Indubitably." MacTeague nodded. In April Becket would be forced to pay one quarter of his profits to the junior partner – if profits there were, which all now depended on the men who struggled in the miasmic waters of the river flats. "And the money," MacTeague said meaningfully, "will doubtless be put to work against our interests? You heard of your niece's indiscretions two weeks ago?"

"Indiscretions!" Becket exploded with anger. "A flaunting, MacTeague! Wantonness!" Martha's celebration, which seemed, by Lord Robert Massedene's presence, to have the tacit blessing of Sir William, had caused deep offence amongst Philadelphia's Tories. "She'll not take Jonathon's profits if I can help it!" Becket said.

"Lesserby says you cannot help it."

"But Jonathon's a rebel!"

The priest shrugged. "Mrs Crowl also has a lawyer. Your action will be contested. It will take money, much money, and Lesserby is not sanguine, not sanguine at all."

"It will take money right enough," Abel Becket said gloomily. Philadelphia lawyers were a match for the devil himself, and twice as expensive.

"Unless . . ." MacTeague said teasingly.

Becket glanced sharply at the plump, shrewd priest. "Unless?"

MacTeague carefully placed his teacup on the hearth, stood, and walked to the window. "Medical opinion is divided on the efficacy of bleeding, Becket. Some new opinion preaches against it, though I profoundly disagree with that notion. Your niece, however, shares that modern opinion. She denies Jonathon the benefits of scarification and, though he is much mended, he is not yet fully recovered. Could that be because he lacks proper medical attention? I ask myself that question, indeed I do." He turned. "Allow me, very humbly, to remind you that you are Jonathon's legal guardian until April. If it is your opinion that he will only live if he is bled, then bled he must be." The priest shrugged. "Though I doubt whether the procedure can be peacefully done in Mrs Crowl's household?"

Becket understood instantly. "I should bring him here?"

"Should a boy not convalesce in the happy surroundings of his own home? And if Jonathon were here, Becket, he could not sign away his interest in the business to his elder sister, could he?" MacTeague went back to his chair and carefully lifted the dish of tea on to his lap. "There is, however, one obstacle. The boy may be beyond the reach of our law. He is, officially, a prisoner of the British and they have signed him over to Mrs Crowl's household. They could insist he stays there."

"But she's a rebel!"

"A popular one!" MacTeague shook his head sadly. "Our city is now ruled by men who value entertainment and frippery above sobriety. In that society Mrs Crowl is an ornament. That creature of Sir William's has become an intimate of Mrs Crowl's!" For a fleeting and disloyal second MacTeague was tempted by the thought that Saratoga might be a divine judgement on British immorality. He thrust the thought away. "But I have a suggestion for you."

"Please," Becket invited.

"I am thinking of the proposed bridge at Middle Ferry. You are selling them the materials?"

"Not unless they increase the price they've offered." Becket was scornful of the proposed floating bridge which, after the failure of the assault on Fort Mercer, would have to be built on the Schuylkill's bank. The bridge would undoubtedly quicken the trickle of wagon-borne supplies, but it would shift no heavy cargoes of black walnut.

"The British are suddenly impatient." MacTeague closed his eyes and steepled his fingers before his face. "They need nails, tar, cables, timber, and all before the river freezes. A gift, Mr Becket, will make them look very gently upon the giver." The priest's eyes opened to stare at Becket.

"A gift?"

"You must think on the matter. I believe the officer at Sir William's headquarters who is most inimical to Mrs Crowl is a Captain Christopher Vane." MacTeague chuckled.

"Vane?" Becket asked.

MacTeague, who made it his business to listen to the city's gossip, relished this titbit. "It seems he was unfortunate enough to declare an attachment to your niece and received short shrift for his pains! He was sent packing!" MacTeague was clearly amused. "He is not pleased, Mr Becket, not pleased at all, but those wounded by Cupid's arrow rarely are. Mrs Crowl's new beau is a lord, no less, but I think Captain Vane will be a match for him. And I am sure that, in return for a gift of some worn-out timber and frayed rope, Captain Vane would be happy to arrange for a prisoner to come to your loyal house?" MacTeague looked at the clock on the mantel and pretended surprise. "So late already! Mrs MacTeague will be making my tea. You must forgive me. Such a good dinner!"

MacTeague proved to be a happily accurate judge of the purchasing power of nails, elm, tar, and cables, and so, at dawn two mornings later, Ezra Woollard went with two men to the back door of Martha's house, while Abel Becket, with four others, went to the front. The men were all workers made idle by the emptiness of the wharves and were eager to earn the coins which Abel Becket had promised them. It was a cold morning. Wisps of mist drifted above the stumps of the poplar and buttonwood trees which had once lined the streets, but which had long since been cut down for fuel.

Becket hammered on the street door. Jenny, the black maid, answered it and was pushed aside by the surge of big men. Jenny screamed. One of the menservants ran up from the basement, a pistol in his hand, to find himself staring down the brass-rimmed muzzle of Abel Becket's horse pistol. "Lift that gun," Becket said, "and I'll kill you. You know who I am?"

"Yes, Mr Becket."

"Open the back door."

The servant turned as Ezra Woollard's hammering echoed through the kitchens, then whirled back again as Jenny screamed at him to keep the door shut. Abel Becket slapped her. Jenny screamed at the servant again. "You keep it shut! Keep it shut!"

"I told you to be quiet!" Becket slapped her again, breaking her lip, then one of the big loyal stevedores took Jenny in his hands and pushed her face against the wall. The manservant, appalled by the blood and the promise of more, fled to open the kitchen door.

"What in God's name are you doing?" Martha, dressed in a silk robe and with her hair in a mob cap, appeared at the stair's head. Lydia, dressed in a flannel nightgown, clung to her mother's skirts.

"I've come for my nephew." Abel Becket faced his niece from the foot of the stairs.

"Don't be ridiculous. He isn't well enough to move. Nor does he wish to move."

There was another rush of feet as Ezra Woollard's men jostled up the stairs from the kitchens. The hall was suddenly filled with big men, but their courage faltered in the face of Martha's defiance.

Her voice was cold and scornful. "Let Jenny go. Do you hear me, you oaf! Let her go or I'll have you in the courts! This is my house, you are not invited, and you will all leave."

For a second her voice checked them. The man holding Jenny relaxed his grip and the maid twisted away, only to be stopped by Abel Becket's arm. "Hold her!" He pushed Jenny back, then climbed the stairs towards his niece. "If you stop me taking Jonathon to where he can receive proper medical care, then I will have you in the courts! He is my ward, made so by an order of the judiciary. So stand aside."

Martha did not move. "He is receiving proper care, uncle, and you are making yourself ridiculous. Go away. And take your oafs with you."

Abel Becket stopped two steps beneath her. "The doctors advise he should be bled. Stand aside."

Martha did not move and her voice, though not loud, reached every man in the hallway. "If you bleed him, you will kill him."

"Stand aside."

"You need so many men to deal with one woman?" Martha's scorn was magnificent. "You can go to hell, Abel Becket."

Becket climbed the last two steps and Martha pushed him back.

He gripped her arm to save his balance and, for a second or two, uncle and niece grappled grotesquely at the stair's head. Lydia, scared of what was happening, screamed, then Ezra Woollard shouted at the hired men to help. Their feet pounded on the stairs, and Martha was thrust aside by the rush. Abel Becket, scenting victory, pushed her backwards. Martha fell, dragging her sobbing child down with her. The wharfmen were opening her doors, searching, but Abel Becket, who knew the house well, shouted at them to climb the upper flight of stairs.

Jenny, released when the men made their whooping charge up the stairway, had fled from the front door. Martha, regaining her feet on the middle landing, clutched Lydia to her breast, then twisted away as her uncle shouted from the top floor that Jonathon had been found.

Martha pushed Lydia into the parlour and tried to climb the upper stairs, but Woollard stopped her. "He has the right, Mrs Crowl."

"What would you know of rectitude, Woollard? Out of my way!"

"Keep her out of here!" Becket shouted, then Martha heard above Lydia's terrified weeping her brother whimper with pain as the bedclothes were snatched away from him.

"Jonathon!" Martha shouted her brother's name, then tried to push past Ezra Woollard, but the big man easily stopped her. Martha clawed at him, trying to scratch at his eyes, but the foreman laughed, gripped her shoulders in his big hands, and pressed her back against the landing wall. Lydia, peering from the parlour door and seeing her mother so treated, ran and pounded puny fists against Woollard's thigh. He slapped the child to send her reeling down the landing in pain and tears.

Jonathon screamed with pain as he was lifted by one of the stevedores. "Let him alone!" Martha shouted, but her brother's limp, blanket-covered body was carried on to the top landing where his one foot was jarred against the newel post to cause another horrid and gasping cry of anguish.

"Look at him!" Becket shouted down at Martha. "You're a witch! He needs bleeding, woman, bleeding!"

Martha tried to free herself to comfort Lydia, but Woollard, his breath stinking in her face, held her fast. His hands pressing on her shoulders made her gown gape at the neck and Woollard grinned down at her. "A half-naked witch, aren't you?" The closest stevedores laughed. Martha was weeping, trying to wrench her shoulders free, but Woollard leaned his considerable weight upon her.

Then new voices sounded in the hall downstairs and Ezra Woollard twisted his face away from Martha to see a red-coated officer come running up the stairs. Jenny, keeping her wits about her, had summoned one of the British patrols that were charged with keeping the peace on Philadelphia's streets.

A very nervous and young lieutenant appeared at the stairhead. He flinched from the child's screaming, then frowned to see Martha in such obvious disarray and under such duress, but he was clearly too young and too confused to know what he should do.

Martha wrenched uselessly against the hands that held her. "These men have broken into my house," Martha shouted at the lieutenant. "They're kidnapping my brother, and you will stop them!"

"She's mad," Woollard said confidingly. "Brain sick."

"I think you should let her go, sir," the lieutenant said with an uncertain and ineffective authority.

Woollard shook his head. "It's nothing to do with you. Leave us alone."

A red-coated sergeant, burlier even than Woollard, and with a scarred face, edged past his lieutenant. "The officer," the sergeant said wearily, "said to let the lady go. So let her go!" The sergeant's authority was old, practised, and reinforced with a musket. "You heard me!"

Woollard, as though stung, released Martha who clutched her robe tight and ran to scoop up the sobbing, terrified six-year-old. She clutched Lydia to her body, but stared at the officer. "They're kidnapping my brother!"

"Get out of the way!" Above them, Abel Becket pushed through the stevedores, making a path for the man who carried Jonathon. He checked when he saw the scarlet uniform. "Who are you?"

"Lieutenant Jarvis, sir. Of the seventh."

Becket looked scornfully at the sergeant's musket, then at Jarvis's men who, with bayonets fixed on their firelocks, peered hopefully up the stairwell. The merchant took a paper from his pocket which he held towards the nervous Jarvis. "This is a warrant, Lieutenant, duly signed at your headquarters, giving Jonathon Becket into my care."

"No!" Martha tried to snatch the paper, provoking another wail from her daughter, but Becket pushed Martha aside and thrust the warrant into the lieutenant's hands.

Jarvis read it. His sympathies, like those of his men, were entirely with Martha, for she was a woman, and beautiful, but the paper bore a seal he recognized. He read it again and sought some escape from its implacable wording. "The lad's in pain, sir?"

"He's in pain, Lieutenant, because he is not receiving proper treatment in this house."

"You're a liar!" Martha screamed at her uncle, and Lydia echoed the scream with a pathetic and frightened howl.

"But still, sir" – Jarvis hesitated to abandon the women's cause – "it might be better to give him a few more days? Let him recover? Doesn't do to shift the wounded about, sir, not if it can be helped."

"It might be better," a new and languid voice spoke from the hallway, "if you were to obey your Commander-in-Chief's warrant, Lieutenant?"

The voice was mocking, casual, and triumphant. Captain Christopher Vane, whose immaculate uniform betrayed that he had been warned and ready that a disturbance might occur at this hour, climbed the stairs. He took off his cocked hat. "Good morning, Mrs Crowl. Can't you keep that wretched child quiet?"

Martha snatched the warrant from Jarvis's hand. " 'Signed on behalf of the Commander-in-Chief by Captain Vane.' " She read the words scornfully. "What were you paid, Captain?"

"You're being offensive, ma'am. Your brother requires skilled medical attention which he will now receive. You men! Make way!" This was to Jarvis's soldiers in the hall. "Mr Becket!" Vane pretended to notice Becket for the first time. "Good morning, sir!"

Jarvis, outranked, could only watch as the moaning and pale Jonathon was carried down to the hall. The stevedores, grinning because of their victory over a notable rebel, followed. A table had been broken in the hallway and two of the delicate banister supports, made from turned mahogany, had been snapped. Christopher Vane, the last man to go downstairs, flicked at the freshly broken wood. "This is not chargeable to the army's account. You resisted a lawful order, ma'am."

Martha was still hugging Lydia close. "I would not take your money if you offered it on bended knee. You've killed that boy!"

Captain Vane, victorious, stood in the patch of morning

sunlight that came through the open street door. His smile was mocking, almost pitying, but Martha heard the pathetic echo of his former pleading voice in its new and arrogant tone. "I can always arrange for your brother to be fetched back here, ma'am."

Martha, at the head of the stairs, shuddered. "Were my uncle's thirty silver shillings not enough for you, Captain?"

Vane pushed the broken table aside with his foot. "I had another price in mind, ma'am."

"Get out!"

Jonathon was gone now, and Martha was helpless to stop it. The stevedores, in triumphant procession, bore her brother down Market Street while Jarvis's men, defeated by Vane, tried to disperse a small crowd that had been attracted by the fracas. Vane lingered, relishing his triumph. Jenny, her lip bleeding, edged past the British officer and climbed to take Lydia into her comforting arms. "Get out," Martha said again to Vane.

But Vane wanted to enjoy the full measure of this victory. "Perhaps this will teach you, ma'am, not to celebrate at inappropriate times?"

"I'll celebrate your defeat, Captain. Now leave this house!"

Vane smiled. "I was thinking of quartering myself here, ma'am. You have an empty room now, do you not? Don't you think we could be happy here?"

"In a house where you once grovelled for my affections?" Martha laughed at him. "If you dare come to this house again, Captain Vane, I will burn it down around you. Now leave!" Vane still showed no signs of obeying her, so Martha plucked a vase from a table on the landing and hurled it down the stairs.

Vane stepped nonchalantly aside, watched the vase shatter into fragments, then went to the door. A Patriot had been humbled, and Captain Vane had gained a small, but not yet full, measure of his revenge.

TWENTY-THREE

Captain Vane went to the small stables where Sam spent most of his time and told Sam that he was never again, ever, to visit Mrs Crowl's house.

Sam, astonished by the abrupt order, said nothing. He could see from his master's face that there was nothing to be said.

The next day, perhaps because Captain Vane needed his servant's loyalty at a time when he felt the rest of the city was mocking his failure, Vane offered a lame explanation to Sam. "The physicians insisted that Jonathon was to be moved, Sam, and the lawyers! It's no good fighting lawyers."

"Yes, sir."

Sam's dutiful but unenthusiastic response irritated Vane. "For God's sake, Sam! If you're going to sulk I'll damn well replace you! You want to go back to that sergeant?"

Sam, who was pounding ginger roots in a mortar as medicine for a sick horse, offered a defence of the Widow. "It was just that Mrs Crowl was kind to me, sir."

Vane heard the hurt in Sam's voice and, because Vane liked Sam's efficiency, offered further explanation. "Mrs Crowl is a rebel, Sam, and rebels have a way of being kind to your face and treacherous behind your back. I don't expect you to understand it, but I do expect you to trust me. It's for the best, Sam."

"Of course, sir." Sam knew as well as Vane why Jonathon had been moved; not because of doctors and lawyers, but because the Widow had thrown Captain Vane out of her house. It was a lovers' tiff, and Sam had no intention of letting such a thing prevent his visits to the Widow's house. He pretended to obey Vane's order, but Sam's freedom as an officer's servant gave him ample opportunity to visit the warm kitchen where Jenny ever offered a teasing welcome and where, more importantly, Sam could pretend that his meetings with Caroline were accidental.

The kitchen's warmth became welcome as the days became colder. Winter's promise was in the great skeins of geese, their wings filling the air with a feathered beat that stretched across the autumn sky. Each day the flocks winged southwards and, at dusk, they dropped in unnumbered thousands to the marshes where the rebel forts still defied all Sir William's efforts.

Since the repulse of the attacks, the river fighting had become grimmer. A floating bridge, made with Becket's timber, was thrown across the Schuylkill at Middle Ferry, and wagons carried new supplies, new ammunition, and new men down to the marshes. Heavy guns, slung off warships, were taken to the siege. Floating batteries were made, then so loaded with cannon that they sank and had to be raised and strengthened before they could be towed to the shoals from which they would open their devastating fire upon Fort Mifflin. New mortars were bedded on the dikes to arc shells into the defences.

The marsh reeked of powder smoke. Men died in waist-deep water. More guns were fetched, then yet more guns had to be dragged through the ever colder October days. No one in the city could remember an October so cold, nor a year when the leaves glowed so prettily.

The fever became worse. In the city soldiers shivered in damp huts and their dead bodies were buried in a common grave with their enemies who perished in the inadequate hospitals. Food grew scarcer. Some country folk, willing to risk General Washington's two hundred and fifty lashes, brought corn and hogs through the defence lines. But there was never enough food. Firewood was scarce. Plunderers, in search of furniture to burn, broke into empty houses, and musket shots cracked in the city streets as the provosts tried to stop the thieves. And each succeeding day brought colder winds and smaller fires. Sir William's lavish revels might distract the city's wealthy, but the mass of people, like the common soldiers, suffered.

The month's ending was marked by gales that shrieked over the marshes and tore shingles from roofs in the city. The last bright leaves of autumn were whirled into the mud. On 25 October, the seventeenth anniversary of King George III's accession, a solemn service of thanksgiving for the monarch's long reign was held, but the Revd MacTeague's voice was drowned by the howling of eldritch winds about St Paul's. The river was whipped to whitecaps. The pontoon bridge across the Schuylkill broke and its vast boats drifted downstream amidst the shattered planking, while, on the marshes, the wind drove salt water over the gun-weakened dikes to drown the batteries and turn the powder barrels into casks of grey and freezing sludge.

November brought calm, but with the calm came frosts that made the brittle grass of the wetlands into an expanse of shining, white spikes. Men shivered and watched the cat ice creep across puddles, and wondered if the river was swirling more slowly, ready to lock the city up in ice and bring starvation to a garrison. The merchants, cursing the few men who stubbornly held two shattered fortresses, regretted the monies spent on cargoes for England and wondered whence would come the credit to see them through a winter.

Sam prospered in the suffering city. His skill with horses saw to that, for it was a rare day on which some sick animal was not brought to Sam's stable. Even one of Sir William Howe's horses, a bay stallion which had the colic and of which Sir William had entirely despaired, was brought to Sam and cured. For other horses he cut corns from tender hooves that he afterwards treated with butter of antimony. He boiled linseed into a jelly for sick beasts, and even remade saddles for officers who galled their horses' backs. Captain Vane watched him reset a saddle tree one afternoon. "What do you do with all the money, Sam?"

The money was all in a leather bag hidden beneath a loose stone of the kitchen floor, but Sam was too fly to admit its existence. "I don't get no money, sir. Miserable skinflints, you officers."

Vane laughed. As the gossip about Vane and Martha died, then was forgotten, so the old ease between master and servant had returned, for it was hard for two men to live in such close conjunction without affability, particularly for Captain Vane, who now used Sam for a duty which far exceeded the usual demands of an officer on his man. That extra duty which made Sam so intimate with Captain Vane's secrets was, Sam noted, a direct consequence of the Widow's rejection of Vane. For, as the nights grew colder, Vane would send Sam to the city's most fashionable brothel on William's Alley with orders to bring back a girl. "You know the sort I like, Sam. No insipid blondes."

On one such night, when the stars were a cold brightness above the dark streets, Sam was sent on his usual errand. He carried a torch, for Sir William had ordered that any man found after dark without a torch was to be deemed a plunderer and, if such a man would not halt on demand, he was to be shot.

It was freezing, but Sam had a hooded watchcoat and thick gloves. He knocked on the door of the discreetly shuttered house, and shivered as the maid let him into the elegantly furnished hallway. "Cold as bloody Muscovy out there." Sam rolled the torch on the outer steps to extinguish the flames.

"Who is it?" a voice spoke from the parlour.

"Captain Vane's man," the maid replied, and the parlour door immediately opened.

A short, cheerful and motherly woman stood there, her ringed hands raised in benediction. "Sam! How very chilled you look. Come inside, child. Thank you, Marie!" Mrs Taylor, like Tom Evans, had developed an affection for the ever willing and helpful Sam who had dosed and steamed the strangles out of one of her carriage horses. "How is the Captain?" she now asked.

"He's bad-tempered, ma'am. He hates the cold."

"This isn't cold, boy, this is merely brisk! It will get colder, you mark my words." Mrs Taylor poured Sam some tea from the pot which stood on the fire's trivet. "But I trust the Captain keeps his bed chamber warm? I cannot risk my girls catching the cold."

"It's warm enough, ma'am." Sam smiled his thanks as Mrs Taylor invited him to sit down. "He'd like Belinda, if that's possible?"

"Dear me, no! Belinda is spoken for. Belinda is at General Grey's." Mrs Taylor happily boasted of the high company her girls kept, and Sam encouraged the indiscretions, for all such scraps of gossip were eagerly snapped up by his customers at the stables. "I shall ruminate." Mrs Taylor picked up her black-bound ledger, found the day's page, then looked up as a peal of laughter sounded from an upstairs room. "Lord Robert Massedene," she explained. "Such an amusing young man."

"And a gentleman," Sam said warmly. His regard for Lord Robert Massedene stemmed from the days after Jonathon had been snatched from Mrs Crowl's house and Sam had heard, through the gossip of the servants in Sir William's house, how his lordship had striven to have the wounded boy returned to his sister. It had been to no avail. Sir William's need for a floating bridge was more pressing than Jonathon's happiness. Besides, Sir William had been assured that Jonathon would receive the best medical attention in the city and neither Lord Robert Massedene's nor Lizzie Loring's entreaties could persuade Sir William to offend a prominent Loyalist merchant at the expense of a notorious Patriot widow.

So Jonathon had been abandoned to his uncle's care, and Sam could no longer visit him. "I tried to see him," Sam told Mrs Taylor, who provided a sympathetic ear to his misery, "but they told me to go away."

"He's a hard man, Abel Becket," Mrs Taylor said. "The milk of human kindness has curdled in him. It's the war, you know. It changes people, Sam, but it is undoubtedly good for business."

"Mr Becket wouldn't even let Caroline see Jonathon!" Sam sounded outraged.

"Well, he wouldn't, dear, would he?" Mrs Taylor said reasonably. "I mean, she's an intriguing creature, but hardly a fit bride for a Becket! He's an educated young man."

"She can read." Sam was defensive.

"I can read, dear, but I doubt that makes me suitable either!" Mrs Taylor sighed. "Not that there'll be any marriage, Sam, with anyone! I hear the young man's dying."

"Dying?" Sam had heard of Jonathon's decline, told it by Jenny who had heard it from one of Hannah Becket's kitchen maids, but this was the first time Sam had heard how serious Jonathon's new illness was.

"It isn't the leg, dear," Mrs Taylor said, "but the quinsy."

Sam stared at the kindly woman. "You're sure?"

Mrs Taylor gave a coquettish shrug. "I shouldn't say, really, but I know you're a discreet young man. His priest visits us, dear. Not for that, of course! But to offer spiritual comfort to the girls. He likes to talk."

"The quinsy?"

"So he says."

"I can cure that!" Sam said robustly.

"If you're allowed to try," Mrs Taylor said dubiously before looking down at the pages of her book again. "I've got a new girl with, well, darkish hair? Sacharissa?"

"That ain't her name!" Sam was amused by the wondrous names Mrs Taylor invented for her employees.

"It is the name of a poetic heroine. I am astonished to find you so ignorant, Sam Gilpin. Sacharissa's foible is that she is unwilling to leave the house, but the exercise will be good for her, and I can assure her that she'll be safe with you?"

"She'll be safe," Sam said.

"And she can't lie idle here, can she? Very well, Samuel. What has Captain Vane sent tonight?"

"This, ma'am." From the watchcoat's deep pocket Sam drew out a tube of morocco leather from which Mrs Taylor extracted an ivory-barrelled spyglass edged with brass filigree work.

"Very nice," she said.

"He thinks it's worth three nights, ma'am."

"I think it is, yes." Mrs Taylor wrote the details in her ledger. "Is it another of Mr Franklin's possessions?"

"Yes, ma'am."

"I shall keep it for him." Mrs Taylor was collecting the more valuable possessions of the Patriots which she declared she would one day return to them. She stood. "I shall fetch Sacharissa for you."

Sam also stood, and sought, against hope, one last reassurance. "How bad is Jonathon, ma'am?"

"Very." Mrs Taylor shrugged. "The doctors bleed him four times a day. They say it's the only cure for quinsy, but . . ." She shrugged and left the sentence unfinished. "Help yourself to the tea while I prepare Sacharissa for her outing."

Sam waited. A bell-mouthed blunderbuss with which Mrs Taylor protected her girls from unwanted callers lay on the mantel beneath a neatly worked sampler that Sam laboriously deciphered. It read "Peace be to this house", while beneath the text, and beneath a carefully worked alphabet, the sampler was signed in neat scarlet stitches: "Margaret Taylor, Aged Seven, 1733".

"You'll be quite safe, girl, don't be fretful," Mrs Taylor's voice sounded in the doorway. Sam turned, and found himself staring into the brown eyes, not of Sacharissa, but of Maggie.

"Good God!" Sam said.

"Sacharissa, dear," Mrs Taylor said.

"Sam?" Maggie said.

Sam stared in pure astonishment at her. "Maggie?"

"Oh, dear," Mrs Taylor said. "Such an ugly name, and I should know."

"I thought you'd gone!" Sam said. "They said you'd run away!"

There was an instant fear in Maggie's eyes. "Is Scammy with you?"

"No. I ain't seen him in weeks! I'm not with him any more, you see."

"I told you" – Mrs Taylor ushered Maggie into the room – "that you're going to entertain Captain Vane. A most genteel young gentleman."

"Where's Nate?" Maggie seemed oblivious of her employer. She was dressed in a fine woollen cloak and wore her hair piled high on her head. She was clean, pretty, and oddly changed. Her teeth had been cleaned, her face painted, and Sam thought she would not be out of place at any of the fashionable receptions which he was sometimes forced to attend as an orderly.

"Nate?" Maggie insisted, then, as if sensing the news from Sam's face, she crumpled on to the sofa and began to cry.

"The brickdust!" Mrs Taylor yelped in alarm and plucked a handkerchief from her sleeve. She dabbed at the girl's eyes. The shortages in the city had driven most women to the use of powdered brick instead of rouge, but before Mrs Taylor could prevent them tears had streaked the carefully applied dust.

"What happened?" Maggie wailed.

"Didn't you know?" Sam asked.

"I thought he'd been caught trying to desert," Maggie said, "that he wasn't coming . . ." her voice died away.

Sam knew no gentle way to break the news. He felt helpless, he wanted to stay silent, but Maggie's ruined face stared beseechingly at him and so, with a shrug, he told her. "Scammy shot him in the back." Sam felt tears at his own eyes. "He's dead, love."

Mrs Taylor patted Maggie's shoulder. "Get it all out, dear, before you go to work."

"I can't go!" Maggie sobbed.

"You can't starve! Of course you go to work!"

"But he might see me!"

Mrs Taylor sighed. "Do you know this sergeant, Sam?"

"I know him, ma'am. But she'll be all right." From the watchcoat's second pocket Sam drew out a small pistol. "See, Maggie?"

"Sacharissa!" Mrs Taylor insisted.

"But Scammy knows I'm here!" Maggie cried.

"He doesn't, dear." Mrs Taylor shrugged at Sam, then persuaded and bullied the girl into gloves, hat and shawl. "Do your face when you get there, dear. You'll be safe!"

Sam, the torch relit from one of the brothel's candles, took the girl's shivering arm and helped her into the alley. She made Sam tell her more about Nate's death.

"What happened to you?" Sam asked when he had finished the grisly story. "I heard you'd run off."

"I didn't get far," Maggie's voice was utterly miserable. "I'm no good for anything but this, Sam."

"That ain't true." They walked in silence past the Friends' Meeting House where shapelessly dressed figures filed into the night.

"I waited for Nate," Maggie said forlornly. "Two days, I did. Then I walked up by the river. A dog chased me."

"Poor Maggie."

"I got to Frankfort, but it wasn't any good. I had to leave, Sam. You can't make money as a maid." She sniffed. "Mrs Taylor's nice."

"I like her," Sam said warmly.

"But Scammy knows I'm here!" Maggie's terror was palpable.

"He wouldn't recognize you!" Sam said. "You look wonderful, Maggie! You look like a real lady!"

Sam's reassurance was wasted. "The Colonel came, he recognized me!"

"Elliott won't tell Scammy." Sam was not at all certain that he told the truth. "Anyway, Scammy's forgotten you by now!"

"He doesn't forget. And he likes the money, Sam! It was a guinea a night sometimes! But I get three now!" Maggie said with an obvious pride.

"That's good, isn't it?"

"I'm saving up, see?" There was pathetic vivacity in her voice now. "Can't run on your own, Sam, you have to have money. I might get a ship!"

"Back to Connecticut?"

"London!" It seemed Maggie had a new dream now; no longer the promised fifty acres with its three hogs, but the brighter dream of a bigger city. "Or perhaps I'll meet an officer, Sam, someone who likes me? But not if Scammy finds me."

"He won't," Sam said. They were walking in the centre of Fourth Street, where the night's cold had frozen the muddy ruts into hard, awkward ridges, but it was safer to stay in the street centre than to risk the pavements which were so close to the dark alley entrances and to the deep, shadowed doorways of the stores. The flames of Sam's torch lit the spreading rime of frost on the hard mud.

Maggie shivered. "What's this captain like?"

"He's all right." Sam thought about Vane as he helped Maggie over the frosted mud. "He can be funny at times, but I ignore that. You just do as he says and don't argue."

Maggie looked at him, her eyes made bright by the tears which glistened in the torchlight. "Is he. . . ?"

She hesitated, but Sam knew what she was asking. "He ain't rough, dear, I promise."

She smiled up at Sam. "You got a girl?"

Sam paused for a second, thinking of Caroline's bright hair, then shook his head. "No."

Maggie held his arm close. "If you want, you know? I mean you was nice enough, really."

Sam laughed. "I was horrid to you, Maggie."

"You don't know what horrid is, Sam." She stopped suddenly, scared by an infantry patrol that walked along Arch Street in search of men breaking the curfew.

Sam felt Maggie shiver. "It's all right," Sam said. "Just walk with me."

The patrol paced across their front. The men, like Sam, were in hooded watchcoats that made them look like ghostly monks. The last man in the patrol stopped to look at Maggie as Sam hurried her past. The man went on watching until Sam plucked her into the shadows of Cherry Alley.

"He recognized me!" Maggie said.

"He just fancied you!" Sam pushed open the back door of Vane's lodgings and helped Maggie off with her cloak. "It's upstairs, love."

"It always is." She dabbed hopelessly at her face.

When the couple had been served with wine and pickled oysters, Sam went back to the kitchen where wax, tallow and lamp black boiled in a pot to make boot blacking. Sam watched the viscous bubbles burst and wished that Maggie had not returned. He suddenly perceived the war as a maelstrom that sucked innocent people into their own destruction; it had killed Nate, reduced Maggie to a pathetic Sacharissa, and now threatened Jonathon with the hard, racking death of quinsy.

But that, at least, was something Sam could try to cure. Not with bleeding, but by an older way, and Sam would have to find the ingredients to make that ancient magic work. He would start tomorrow, and pray the doctors did not kill Jonathon first.

A sound in the alley made him go to the door. He stared into the darkness, telling himself a cat had jumped on to the waterbutt's uneven lid, but, unsettled by Maggie's terror, Sam felt a shiver of apprehension. Was Scammell prowling the darkness, looking for his woman? Sam closed the door. There was so much unfinished business. Jonathon, Scammell, Maggie, even Caroline? But Caroline, he told himself, was not his business. She was Jonathon's, and Jonathon must be saved.

To which end Sam spent the next week searching for the ingredients he needed for a miracle and, as he did, so the fighting on the river came to its inevitable end. More of the obstacles that had prevented Lord Howe's ships from sailing up the river in force were dragged away, and the battle fleet, its heaped sails towering above the wetlands, made a stately progress towards the stubborn forts. The *Fury* and *Roebuck*, *Somerset* and *Liverpool*, *Pearl*, *Isis* and *Vigilant* opened their gunports and fired across the stark blackened ribs of the *Augusta*. The big ships' bluff sides were like chequered cliffs in a mist of gunsmoke that, minute after minute, was pierced by jets of flame hurling iron at the two forts. Gulls screamed. The answering fire from the American forts died slowly.

It could not last. Fort Mifflin was the first to fall, not to assault, but to the hopelessness of men caught in a meat grinder. One by one their guns were blasted from carriages, their wounded froze and died in bloody puddles, their walls were scorched and breached, and still the mortar shells churned carnage into horror and the solid shot drove splinters that gutted men alive. One dark cold night, the island garrison slipped across the river in boats, and dawn came up to see the fort ablaze, but with its flag still flying over the flames.

Five days later, and a full month after the first unsuccessful assault, Fort Mercer gave up the fight. The garrison took to the last galleys and gunboats and, in a freezing dawn, tried to run the wide river's gauntlet past the city. From the Pest House Quay to the guns at the end of Vine Street, the British batteries of Philadelphia opened fire. Rebel boats were shattered into shards of wood, oars tumbled, and men fell into the cold river to be picked up by smaller, following craft that were rowed through the spouts of water hurled up by cannon fire. Only the small boats came through; the larger ones all sank in the slow-turning flood.

A dozen prisoners, unable to swim to their comrades' boats, were taken from the river and marched, teeth-chattering with cold, to the 1st Grenadiers' headquarters behind the Pest House Battery.

There Major Zeigler, Sir William's Hessian interpreter, spoke with the captured rebels. He wanted to know the fate of the Hessian General Donop who had been wounded and captured during the failed assault on Fort Mercer.

After the interrogation, Zeigler sought out Sir William. General Donop, the Hessian reported, had died three days after his capture. "A bad death, Sir William, painful."

"I'm sorry, Otto."

The Hessian shrugged. "War is cruel, *ja*? To us and the rebellers. But they were warned we were going to attack."

Sir William, standing by a window of his headquarters, turned to stare at his interpreter. "They were warned?"

Zeigler found a small notebook and leafed through the pages. "*Ja*. A rebeller lieutenant told me so. He was boasting, of course, but he says the fort heard of the attack the previous day. They were able to man a deserted bastion which killed a lot of our men." Zeigler closed the notebook. "That's bad, sir."

"Yes." Sir William frowned. Only a handful of his men had been privy to the secret attack, but Sir William, with a sinking feeling, remembered he had also told Mrs Loring, and, his face grimacing with the realization of his fault, he looked back to the window. "It won't happen again, Otto."

"You knew about it, sir?" Zeigler was puzzled by his master's calm reaction to the news of treachery.

"Otto, look!" Sir William, abandoning the grim news of betrayal, suddenly pointed through the window to where, above the roofs of the city and hazed by the smoke of the fires which cooked Philadelphia's meagre suppers, the first tall masts of approaching warships could be seen. The merchant ships followed, and thus Philadelphia was saved, the seaway was open, and the merchants' fortunes would be rescued.

And Sam, with Caroline's help, planned a miracle.

TWENTY-FOUR

The cup was just over five inches high and carved from a dark, tough-grained wood which had been lovingly polished to a glowing sheen. "It's ivy root," Sam explained. "I dug it up from behind the State House."

Martha turned the cup in her hands. It must, she thought, have taken hours of obsessive work to make such an object; the bowl had thin shining walls that swelled from a narrow stem standing on an elegant base. "Did you turn it on a lathe, Sam?"

"I did it with a knife, but Miss Caroline polished it."

Sam's words somehow suggested that, if the cup held any merit, it was solely due to Caroline's work. Sam smiled at Caroline as he spoke, and she smiled back.

Martha saw the exchange between them, and saw too how the effort to save Jonathon's life had brought Sam and Caroline into this willing and close complicity, so close that Martha did not have the heart to tell these two young people that she had already despaired of Jonathon's life. "It's beautiful," she said as she put the cup down.

"It'll do," Sam said modestly. He sat at Mrs Crowl's kitchen table with Caroline opposite him and cups of tea between them. Rain slashed and seethed on the cellar steps behind. Jenny and the kitchenmaids were pickling oysters in the big larder, filling the basement with the smell of nutmeg and vinegar.

The kitchens were now the warmest rooms in most of the city's houses, for the shortage of fuel meant that fires must be rationed, and kitchens, where fire could cook as well as warm, were the only rooms where fuel was not stinted. Food and goods had come with the merchantmen that followed Admiral Howe's warships, but the city was expected to provide its own firewood and so the pretty woods of the Neck were shrinking beneath the soldiers' axes.

Just as Martha's hopes for her brother shrank – and Sam's reliance on an old magic did not enhance those hopes. She could sense all Sam and Caroline's belief pathetically expressed in that glowing and beautiful cup, but Martha also read more, much more. Sam's English country magic demanded an unused cup made of ivy wood, but Martha knew the cup did not have to be this well made. Any crudely hacked-out receptacle would have satisfied the magical formula, but Sam and Caroline, working together, would not be content with anything but the very best. The cup, Martha thought, was a reflection of what they meant to each other, but were too stubborn to admit. She thrust the thought away. "So we have the cup," Martha said, "and now just need to fill it?"

"There's a fellow called Cathcart," Sam said, "Lord Cathcart?"

"17th Dragoons," Martha nodded. "I've met him."

"He has a mare in foal. Right upset he is, what with the winter and all that. I reckon she's near term. It could even be tonight!"

"And she'll suffice?"

"She'll suffice," Sam tried out the word. "As long as I get to her first. I'm spending my nights there, but if the Captain wants me home, then . . ." He shrugged.

"Let's hope he doesn't." Martha listened to the rain. It had fallen ever since the forts had been taken; a storm that was flooding cellars and turning the streets into quagmires. No house could be kept clean in this weather. Visitors came with mud splashed to their hips. Mud was in the carpets, on the stairs, and grimed into clothes; mud that would stay until the spring cleaning.

"And if it is tonight, I still think I should . . ." Sam, stubbornly reverting to a well-worn argument, was cut off by Caroline.

"I'm doing it," she insisted, then, to stop Sam making any protest, she looked at Martha and recited her well-rehearsed lines. "I go down the alley behind the college and it's the fourth gate on the left. I climb the wall . . ."

". . . which has broken glass on the top," Sam interrupted.

"I'm not feared of glass," Caroline said. "I go over the right side of the wall by the stables so I don't wake the slaves. I follow the passage at the back of the stables and there's a window above the smokehouse roof. That leads to the servants' stairs. Up one floor, through the door on to the landing, and Jonathon's room is straight in front of me."

"And there's a dog in the yard," Sam said in tones that suggested Caroline could not deal with a hostile dog.

"I'm going into the house, Sam!" Caroline stared defiantly at the Redcoat. "What would Jonathon think if I didn't try?"

The magic required a cup, a potion, and that either Sam or Caroline should insinuate their way into Abel Becket's house. This could not be done openly, for Abel Becket had refused Sam entry, just as he barred from his house anyone who might encourage his nephew's patriotism. So the house would have to be broken into, and Caroline was insistent that she should take that larger risk. Sam would gather the elixir, but Caroline would deliver it.

"I should come with you, then," Sam said.

"And who looks after the front of the house?" Caroline demanded.

"I can do that, then come round the back!"

"I'll be long gone by then," Caroline said scornfully. "But you wait for me there in case I have trouble getting out."

Sam, knowing this argument was lost, nodded reluctantly. "I suppose that's the best way."

Martha smiled at their agreement. "The most convenient night is a Thursday because Mr Becket's always at a lodge meeting."

Sam shrugged. "It depends on the mare, ma'am. We might have to go any time."

Martha looked at the girl. "Don't get caught by Mr Becket."

"Thump the bugger," Sam said, then immediately blushed for using the word. "Forgive me, ma'am."

"I wouldn't mind thumping him," Martha said, "or your precious Captain."

"He's all right," Sam said defensively. He felt trapped by the antipathy between Martha and Captain Vane, for, though he liked Martha, Vane had never been unkind to him, and Sam was mindful that Vane had extricated him from disaster, and had subsequently given Sam the privileged and profitable life of an officer's servant. That life might end if Vane knew Sam visited this house, but Sam reckoned that what the Captain did not know the Captain could not fret over.

And nothing would prevent Sam from visiting this house, for it was here, in the smoky kitchen, that he shared a happy intimacy with Caroline. Sam told himself that they only shared an obsession with curing Jonathon, an obsession that had produced the cup. He dared not hope for more.

The clock in the hall struck four and Sam grimaced. "I have to go, ma'am. He wants me macaronied."

"Macaronied?" Martha asked.

"All prinked up, ma'am. I have to serve a supper party."

"Poor Sam." Martha waited till he had plunged into the seething rain, then turned to watch Caroline wrap the precious cup in a scrap of sacking. "Are you sure it wouldn't be better if Sam went into my uncle's house?"

Caroline shook her head. "If I get caught, the worst they'll do is throw me out, but they could arrest Sam as a thief! Besides, Jonathon will want me to come."

"I suppose he will, yes." Martha, as the winter drew on and as the Patriots clung together for support in an occupied city, had found herself drawing closer to Caroline. She admired the girl's spirit, used her to carry messages across the water, but still feared for a marriage which Jonathon's illness might, of itself, make redundant. Martha now edged her way towards the touchy subject. "You like Sam, don't you?"

"I like Sam." Caroline, still staring at the table, sounded almost defiant.

"More than you like Jonathon?" Martha was immediately penitent. "I'm sorry. That was unfair."

Caroline looked up. "I promised Jonathon, didn't I?"

"Yes. But sometimes promises are traps we set for ourselves."

"Only if you break them," Caroline said with a stubborn defensiveness.

Martha paused again. "Do you love Jonathon?"

"I love him." It was said flatly. The truth was that Caroline, quite irrationally, blamed herself that a cripple had gone to war, and the guilt had provoked in Caroline a mixture of pity and affection which, if not love, had provided a convincing substitute to the wounded Jonathon.

Martha's silence was an expression of her scepticism. The wind and rain beat at the house in a crescendo of fury that made her instinctively glance towards the stairs as if listening for her child's voice. "Maybe," Martha broke the silence, "it's best not to marry for love. I didn't, and was perfectly happy. We exchanged vows, then I made his house the most elegant in the city and he made me wealthy. He'd have preferred a son to a daughter, but that could have been remedied in time." Martha grimaced at her memories, then leaned closer to the dull glow of the fire.

Caroline had listened to Martha's words and half understood their message. "So Jonathon and I can be happy?"

"Jonathon will be happy," Martha spoke wryly. "He's passionate, and as long as he thinks you love him then he'll be grateful."

"I do love him," Caroline insisted.

"But the maggot in the apple," Martha went on as though the younger girl had not spoken, "is when the regrets begin to gnaw at you. It's when you see the man you might have married, and know you're bound to the one you shouldn't. There were times . . ." Martha paused, thinking that she was about to reveal too much, then shrugged. "There were times when I even wanted him to die. Then he did, and I felt dreadful. Dreadful."

Caroline said nothing.

Martha wiped at a smear of spilt tea. "What will you do if Sam stays in America? He might, you know. Will you shut your front door to him? Will you persuade Jonathon never to see Sam again? Because if you don't, my dear, then it's Sam you'll dream of in the long nights."

Caroline would not face the question. "Sam's a Redcoat," she said flatly, "and he's proud of it. He'll go back where he belongs one day."

"The curious thing about America," Martha said in an apparent change of subject, "is that anyone can belong to it. And I like Sam, so I might very well try and persuade him to stay in America."

"He won't," Caroline said.

"Meaning you'd rest easier at night if he didn't?" Martha probed.

But Caroline did not rise to the question. Instead, she twisted in her chair to listen to the rain's pounding. "Might I sleep here tonight?"

"Gladly."

Caroline slept in the borning room next to the kitchen, but Sam did not sleep at all. He had macaronied himself and at three in the morning he helped a drunken but happy Captain Vane to bed. Then, to the curses of the other servants who were trying to sleep in the kitchen, Sam changed into his old uniform, pulled on his watchcoat, and went out into the night.

The rain spat now, driven by a swirling, howling wind that gusted about the street corners and flattened the flames of Sam's torch. A cedar shingle, blown from a roof, rattled against a shutter and Sam, startled by the sudden noise, turned. He was haunted by the suspicion that he was being watched, by the apprehension of shadows moving just beyond the corner of his vision. He told himself it was nonsense, that Maggie had put an unreasonable fear of Sergeant Scammell in his head, but still he waited cautiously for a sign of his enemy. There was none; only the wind-torn and rain-fretted shadows.

He went on, turning into an alley, then pushing through a gate to see a slit of lantern light above a stable door. Instantly Sam feared he was too late, but Lord Cathcart's groom, waiting beside the mare's stall, shook his head. "You almost missed it, Sam."

Sam latched the door. "Is it coming?"

"Any time. Poor little bugger." The groom shivered. "It's too cold a night to be born."

Sam ducked under the chain. The mare was trembling with fright, but Sam gentled her. The wind howled at the roof. The other horses, made nervous by the mare and the weather, stirred uneasily in their stalls.

The foal came a half-hour later, slithering in blood to the straw, then struggling to stand on its skinny legs. Sam crouched under the mare's belly where he held a wooden canteen to the swollen dugs. The mare snapped once, but Sam soothed her, then used his fingers to draw the mother's first milk into the canteen. When the small barrel was full, he put the half-cleaned foal to suckle.

Sam paid the groom some of the coins he had earned from doctoring officers' horses, then carried the canteen into the grey wet dawn. He had carved the cup, and now he had the beestings; the first milk of a mother which, served in a virgin cup of ivy, would raise the very dead from their graves. No medicine was stronger, and no medicine had ever been prepared with so much love. Now all that was needed was for the magic to be smuggled to Jonathon in the big, servant-guarded house; into which, this coming night, with Sam's help and some small luck, Caroline must go.

TWENTY-FIVE

"The playhouse merely needs a lick of paint," Captain John Andre said happily, "and we shall have a season of unalloyed and wicked delight. We shall give the city's ministers apoplexy, so only good can come from it. Perhaps you'll be one of the players, Kit?"

"I'm no actor, John." Vane had to raise his voice to be heard over the hubble of conversation and music. The fall of the forts and the arrival of the battle fleet were deemed sufficient cause for celebration, and so Sir William's spacious house was again filled with officers and their ladies. The darker, white-faced blue uniforms of the navy mixed with the gaudier army coats. Saratoga was being forgotten, or at least drowned with wine, beneath the crystal-splintered light of the chandeliers that alleviated a rainy dusk beyond the windows.

"We shall begin the wickedness in the New Year." Andre bowed to a passing lady, then looked back to Vane. "The problem, as ever, is women. I can find gentlemen players, but not enough women. You think Mrs Taylor's girls would oblige?"

"They aren't at their best in costume," Vane said drily. "Nor, I imagine, is she." He gestured towards Lizzie Loring who, resplendent in green silk, held court in the room's centre. But for once Lizzie was not the centre of attraction, for, standing close beside her was an extraordinarily uniformed man of immense height. "Who in God's name is he?" Vane asked in wonderment.

"General Charles Lee, but always known as Charlie." Andre clearly relished the man. "I'll introduce you."

"But what on earth is that uniform he's wearing?"

Mrs Elizabeth Loring was asking the same question of General Charles Lee, whose tall and painfully thin body was clad in an outrageous harlequinade of yellow coat fringed with white silk burdened by high, glittering epaulettes. A red sash, carrying an enamelled badge of a black eagle, crossed a pale blue waistcoat. A scarlet velvet stock was pinned about his throat, his breeches were of white satin, and his knee-high boots were topped with bands of scarlet leather. Over one shoulder, its sleeves hanging loose, was a fur-edged pelisse of cloth of gold. His sabre scabbard's fittings were of silver. "It is," General Lee said haughtily, "the uniform of the Polish cavalry. It was made for me by a ship's tailor. Isn't it positively delicious?"

"You were never in the Polish army!" Lizzie said.

"If you were not so beautiful, and I not so desperately in love with you, I would strike you for doubting my veracity. I was, ma'am, a Polish soldier! Three years in the saddle, smiting the heathen Turk. Hello, John!" The erstwhile Polish warrior smiled at Andre, whom, before Sir William's expedition to Philadelphia had sailed south, Lee had known well. "You're still alive? No rebel has cleansed the world by killing you?"

"I'm alive, Charlie, and delighted to see you. May I name Kit Vane to you? He's a new aide of Billy's."

"Another son of Albion for the slaughter?" Lee nodded a cheerful greeting to Vane who, having returned it, offered a bow to Lizzie Loring.

But Lizzie, who had taken Martha Crowl's side in the battle over Jonathon's fate, pointedly ignored Vane's greeting, turning instead to General Lee. "Did you resign from the Polish army too, Charlie?"

"I resign from every army, but only after I have assured its victory." The English-born Lee had served with the Poles, the British, and was now a general in the rebel army. He had made his name in America by saving Charleston from the British, had afterwards been raised to second-in-command to George Washington himself, then, during a retreat across New Jersey, he had lingered too long with a tavern whore and thus been captured by the pursuing British cavalry. Lee delighted to confirm the story. "It's rumoured that His Excellency, jealous of my triumph at Charleston, arranged for the trull to be there, but I doubt it. The poor man doesn't really believe such ladies exist."

"His Excellency?" Christopher Vane asked.

"General Washington demands to be treated with the most absurd dignity. How the dull man would hate this uniform!" Lee gave an odd, high-pitched giggle, then gazed happily about the busy room. "And how lucky you all are."

"Lucky?" Lizzie asked.

"That I am here to brighten your gloom." Though in truth Lee was fortunate to be in Philadelphia himself for, when first captured, it had been suggested that, as a former British officer, Lee should be executed for treason, and it was only his assertion that he had formally resigned his British commission, together with his undoubted popularity with Sir William, that had saved his life. Now Lee was a most favoured prisoner. A rumour, one of the many that accreted around his thin figure, said Lee had suggested the assault on Philadelphia as a means of ending the war.

But it was a war that Sir William no longer wanted any part of. Sir William wanted to go home; to which end he had written his resignation that would be offered to the government in London. Sir William had not lost a battle, but he was a beaten man.

As his party gathered in the lavish rooms downstairs, the Commander-in-Chief stood in the library, alone except for his brother, and stared through the persistent rain at the thin inadequate spire that carried the State House's weathercock, and he thought how, given time, he would have liked to pull the spire down and put up a proper cupola. "And the clock," he said aloud.

"Clock, Willie?" Admiral the Lord Howe looked up from reading his brother's letter of resignation.

"At the side of the State House. Perhaps you haven't seen it? A quite ridiculous brick tallboy! I think a cupola with a four-sided timepiece would be better. A blue dial with golden hands would look good." Sir William shrugged. "If they don't relieve me, Richard, perhaps I'll build it. It would be pleasing to leave Philadelphia better than we found it."

"Indeed." Lord Howe shared his brother's predilection for the Americans; a liking which had been cemented when the people of Massachusetts, following the death of the eldest Howe brother in the French and Indian wars, had subscribed a memorial that now stood in Westminster Abbey. Lord Howe, older and stouter than Sir William, dropped the letter. What in the younger brother's face was coarse, in his lordship was subtly changed into a heavy and statesmanlike cast. "How many people know about this, Willie?"

"You, me, my secretary who made the fair copy, Lizzie, of course, but no one else."

"I wish you'd reconsider."

Sir William, crushed by Saratoga and worn down by the long siege of the forts, turned from the window and poured out words of exculpation. London would not listen to him, London believed the vast majority of the colonists were loyal, and perhaps they were, but not so loyal that they would take up arms. The war could be won, Sir William said, but not by the small forces now scattered between Halifax and the Floridas. "I'd need a hundred thousand men here, Richard. And for what? So the colonists can rebel again in ten years' time?" It was hardly a new lament. Gage, the first general to fight against the rebels in this war, had said the business could not be done. The commander of Britain's army had warned against conquering a wilderness. Others, like the Earl of Effingham, the Viscount Pitt and Admiral Keppel, had resigned their commissions rather than fight against their own kind in a land so vast that it defied the mapmakers. Near half of Parliament opposed the war, and Sir William, a member of that Parliament, wanted to go home and add his voice to the war's opponents.

"If London accepts your resignation," Lord Howe said dubiously.

"If they don't, then they must let me negotiate!" Sir William had turned back to watch the clouds darken above the sheeting rain.

"If negotiations can keep the French out," Lord Howe said slowly, "then maybe London will agree?"

"We must offer the rebels everything they want, everything! No revenue duties, no taxes, no more placemen from London, and all they need yield in return is their independence." Sir William turned again to his brother. "If the King can be persuaded that republicanism is defeated, he might not notice that the rebels have won everything else."

"But what if they think they can win their independence?" Lord Howe crossed to his brother's side and cast a sailor's professional eye, first at the State House weathervane, then at the clouds. "The bloody French are itching to join the dance."

"Bugger the French," Sir William said. "And God knows what Mister Washington will make of them! If he thinks us tyrannical, wait till he's under King Louis's tender care! Or does he think the bloody Frogs will help the rebellion out of the goodness of their treacherous hearts?"

Lord Howe shook his head. "I hear the French have been offered their old lands in Canada. And all our sugar islands."

Sir William, despite his gloom, had to laugh at the rebels' presumption. "They received a bloody nose when they tried to take Canada for themselves, so I suppose they might as well invite the French to take it!"

"It isn't Canada." Lord Howe hunched his broad shoulders beneath epaulettes that no amount of cleaning could quite rid of the tarnish of salt. "If the bloody Frogs do come in, Willie, I'll need men to garrison the islands."

"Men!" Sir William crossed to the table and unstoppered a decanter. "And where do they come from? Do I give up Philadelphia to garrison the sugar islands? Doesn't London know what's happening here?"

Lord Howe, taking a glass of wine, ventured to remind his brother that London would rather lose the wealthiest American colony than forgo the greater profits of a sugar island. "Damn the Yankee colonies, Willie, but keep the sugar. Or keep both?"

"Both?"

"Stop the damned Frogs from intervening."

"Oh, indeed, yes. Indeed." Sir William knew what was coming.

"By destroying that bloody man Washington."

"The winter will do that for us." Sir William glanced at the window which was now darkened by nightfall. "They say the birds started south early, Richard, which evidently means a harsh winter."

"The rebels will endure winter if they know the French are coming. They'll hold on!" The Admiral's voice became insistent. "But if the French hear that Mister Washington has dangled on a rope's end, they'll think twice, Willie! They won't want to put their troops into a shambles. They're hesitant already, because they're scared of getting their usual whipping. They're worried Saratoga might be a false signal. If you can crush Washington before the snow comes the French may sheathe their swords."

Sir William stooped to his dog that slept by the fire. "I'm not sure it was a false signal. Oh" – he hurried to prevent his elder brother interrupting – "Johnny wasn't outfought!" Sir William had now received reliable reports of Saratoga. Burgoyne, harassed and skirmish-ridden, had been stranded in a hostile wilderness where he could not be supplied. Hunger and thirst had been the allies of the rebel soldiers who had defeated Burgoyne, and the first of those spectres had already haunted Sir William in Philadelphia. "I should have marched to meet him, shouldn't I?" Sir William's confession of fault, spoken mildly, seemed to be addressed to his dog, though the Admiral chose to reply.

"You weren't to know that, Willie. Not then."

But Sir William could not be so easily consoled. He was thinking of all the shattered dreams. If the British went to Philadelphia, the American Tories had said, the middle colonies would rise for their King and the rebels would be beaten by their own compatriots. It had not happened. Instead, Sir William held the city and the rebels ruled the countryside almost to the very ends of Philadelphia's pavements. There was no peace, no dukedom, no New Jerusalem. Sir William looked up at his brother. "You know Washington sent Hamlet back to me?"

"He did what?" There were times when the Admiral found his younger brother hard to understand.

Sir William flinched with a pain in his back as he straightened up. "Under a flag of truce. I thought that was a remarkably decent thing to do."

"Thank him before you kill him. And do it before the spring, Willie. The French won't make a move till the weather improves."

Sir William nodded heavily, as though the effort of launching another attack on the rebels was, however necessary, too onerous to contemplate with any pleasure. He folded his resignation letter and hid it in a drawer, then gestured towards the library doors. "I suppose we should go down? Your admirers wait to applaud you."

And applause did greet the Admiral who had brought supplies into the city. The clapping rippled across the ballroom, was reinforced by huzzahs, then with loud shouts of bravo as the brothers, uniformed arm in uniformed arm, came down the wide stairs.

As the applause died away, Christopher Vane was astonished to find the rebel General Lee at his elbow. Lee bent towards Vane. "You will forgive me, Captain? I know we've scarcely been introduced, but I wondered if I might beg a favour of you?"

"Of course, sir."

Lee plucked at the lace cuffs which protruded from his yellow sleeves. "John told me to talk to you." He lowered his voice to a confiding whisper. "When this folderol's over, would you be so kind as to name me at a decent house? John said you knew one. There's nothing on board ship, you see, unless you fancy midshipmen, which I don't."

Vane smiled. "I have a house. Mrs Taylor's."

Lee's eyes flicked from side to side as though he feared eavesdroppers. "Clean?"

"Very."

"Red girls?" Lee asked anxiously.

"Red, sir?"

"I was married to a Princess of the Seneca Indians once. Well, sort of married, just as she was a sort of Princess. Got a taste for them, you see." Lee said the last apologetically.

Vane, despite Lee's rebel allegiance, was amused by the man. "I haven't seen a red girl, but she's got whites, cuffies, octoroons, mulattos, even a Chinese?"

Lee smiled wolfishly. "You'll do the kindness of naming me?"

"With great pleasure, sir."

"I mean it's no good asking Lizzie for a rogering. She's too damn loyal to Billy." Lee suddenly stretched to his full height and stared towards the entrance hall. "Oh, my sainted arse. Who is that?"

Vane looked. The Widow Crowl, on Lord Robert Massedene's arm, had come to the celebration. Vane said nothing. He had hoped that Martha's defeat over Jonathon would end her defiance, but instead, and bolstered by the new friendships of Lord Robert Massedene and Lizzie Loring, the Widow still flaunted her patriotism in the face of her enemies.

"Well?" Lee asked.

"She's one of your rebels, sir."

Lee heard the distaste in Vane's voice and put it down to jealousy. "Robert has seduced her?"

Vane had to fight to keep anger from his voice. "He protects her, sir, or else the Loyalists would whip her from the city."

Lee stared unashamedly at Martha who, as ever, looked superb. She wore one of the slashed skirt polonaises that Lizzie Loring had made fashionable in Philadelphia, and her hair, though not so highly piled as Lizzie's, was magnificently sculpted and hung with jewelled ribbons. "That's a woman to make the winter amusing," Lee said reverently.

Martha looked towards the exotic Polish uniform and Vane turned away, but fractionally too late, for the Widow had seen him and, without a qualm, now strode across the wide room towards him. Guests turned to watch, for everyone in Philadelphia society and every officer in the garrison knew what bad blood existed between the two.

General Lee preened himself for the introduction, but Martha ignored the tall man. "Captain Vane?"

"Ma'am." Vane bowed, wishing his heart would calm. He needed wit now, not hostility, and he feared that the right riposte would only come to his lips after the Widow had turned away.

"You have heard about my brother?" Martha asked loudly enough for every interested listener to hear.

"I heard, ma'am, that his leg is wonderfully improved and I rejoice for it."

"Your rejoicing, Captain, like your celebration of victory this evening, is premature." Martha's gaze was bitter. "He has the quinsy and the fever. I hope you are proud of your work?"

"I will pray for him," Vane said scornfully.

"Save your prayers for yourself, murderer." The room had gone as silent as if an angel had passed over Vane's grave. Even Sir William and Lord Howe watched the Widow now. "If my brother dies, you will need all your prayers for you will have none of my mercy." Martha paused, then, with magnificent scorn and in a voice loud enough to reach the deepest recesses of the great room, she fired her parting and lacerating shot: "Kitten." She turned away and the room suddenly filled with the babble of conversation as people pretended that no embarrassment had been observed.

"Oh dear me," Lee said. "Dear, dear me!" He stepped away from Vane as if fearing that he might catch a contagion.

Vane turned on Lee. "You wish to leave now, sir?"

"Now?" Lee had not proposed leaving the reception for some hours.

"Now, sir." Vane's anger was made worse by impotence. He had clashed with the Widow, he had hurt her by removing Jonathon, but she had used her connections to come back and thus humiliate him in society. "I'm going now, sir."

Lee looked around the room, then shrugged. "Either that or a midshipman, I suppose. Very well, Captain. To the fray!"

They went into the night, where, in a cold wind, Captain Vane dreamed of revenge's solace.

TWENTY-SIX

Caroline waited in the shadows of an alleyway behind Abel Becket's substantial house and, through chattering teeth, counted aloud to three hundred.

An infantry patrol, miserable in the cold rain, slouched past the alley's far end and Caroline shrank back under an archway that led into the college grounds. "Two hundred and three," she whispered, "two hundred and four."

The sound of music came thin above the hissing rain from the British Commander-in-Chief's headquarters which were only a short distance away. Caroline could not remember a time when so much music had been played in the city: there were military bands on the Centre Commons, orchestras in the big houses, and sailors singing in the grogshops. "Two hundred and ten, two hundred and eleven, two hundred and twelve."

The city was drenched with music, drunkenness, and gambling. The preachers of Philadelphia spat vitriolic sermons against the prevalence of gambling amongst the garrison officers, but the diatribes only encouraged more gambling. Two guards' officers had opened a book in the London Coffee House on the length of the various sermons. The longest so far had been a four-and-a-half-hour peroration by a splenetic Presbyterian who, as he finished, had been mockingly applauded by a group of winning officers in the gallery. Sir William had thereafter forbidden such provocations, though he would not ban the craze for gambling. Caroline's grandfather, reading his morning scripture across the river, had said that gambling was the devil's work. Caroline now wondered what Caleb Fisher would make of his granddaughter's nocturnal prowling. "Two hundred and sixty, two hundred and sixty one."

A late carriage splashed past the alley, its lanterns showing mud-spattered horses and dripping trace chains. Caroline recognized the Galloways' equipage. Many of the city's merchants would no longer attend Sir William's hedonistic receptions which offended Philadelphia's sturdy and protestant soul. Caroline merely despised such frivolities which only made her more grimly determined that the British should be defeated. Martha Crowl attended the parties, of course, but to Caroline the Widow was an exotic creature who went her own way in life. "Two hundred and ninety-nine," she counted, "three hundred." Caroline readied herself, hoping that Sam had counted at the same speed as herself.

Sam was in another alley; one that debouched into Market Street almost directly opposite the front of Abel Becket's big house. It was almost ten o'clock, yet the street was far from dark. Sam, for once, carried no lit torch as a protection, but the pitch-soaked links bracketed outside the city's main guardhouse flickered shadows on the rain-battered street. The deepest shadows were thrown by the bright lanterns which hung outside Sir William Howe's house, and before which the rain slanted in heavy silver streaks. It was like the days before the flood itself; rain and more rain, rain that drummed on the roofs of the carriages that waited to take Sir William's guests home, rain that sluiced down gutters, that flooded the streets, and soaked Sam to the marrow of his bones.

He counted to three hundred, took a deep breath, and stepped out of the alley.

Sam's first stone smashed a pane of glass in a window of Abel Becket's parlour. The thrown missile thumped against the closed shutter inside the window thereby provoking a woman's scream. The second stone clattered uselessly on the limestone wall between the windows, the third shattered the fanlight above the front door, while the fourth struck the door just as it was snatched open by a servant.

Sam ducked back into the alley. The footsteps of a patrol drawn by the sound of breaking glass slopped through muck and mud as their torchflames made grotesque dancing shadows in the street. But Sam, having drawn Abel Becket's household away from the rear of the big home, had fled in the darkness to wait for Caroline.

Sam's evening had begun at Martha's house where he had given Caroline the beestings, then taken her to the alley behind Abel Becket's stable yard. Sam had thought to bring an old horse blanket which, before he went to break windows, he had folded, then thrown across the shards of glass that were cemented into the wall's top. Now, hearing the crash of breaking windows, Caroline jumped to hook an arm over the thickly folded wool. A spike of broken glass spiked through layers of cloth and tore her flesh. She hissed with the pain, but tried to ignore it as she scrabbled her boots for purchase on the wet bricks. Her hand found a grip and she pulled herself safely up. She wore a heavy haversack at her belt that made the climb awkward. Blood trickled warm on her forearm.

She perched for an uncertain moment, then jumped down into the space behind the stables. Dogs, disturbed by the breaking glass, were barking in every yard on the street, and the bitch chained outside Abel Becket's feedstore snarled at the black shadow that suddenly materialized in its territory. Caroline fumbled in the haversack then threw the beast the quarter leg of mutton that Sam had stolen for just this purpose. The dog smelt the meat, snapped at it, and Caroline fondled the bitch and waited until it licked her hand in a sign of acceptance. Abel Becket's carriage horses stamped behind their bolted doors.

Caroline paused for a moment, letting her eyes adjust to the darkness in the yard, then, swathed and shawled in disguising black, she ran to the smokehouse and pulled herself on to its sloping tiled roof. Her boots slipped once, but the thick metal chimney gave her a purchase as she explored the sash window that opened from the servants' stairway.

The window was locked as Martha had warned it would be. Caroline slipped her knife's blade between the two sashes and tugged at the metal latch. It seemed much harder than the window in Martha's house on which Caroline had practised, and the rain made her knife handle slippery. For a second Caroline felt despair, then the latch reluctantly yielded to the blade's pressure. The sash weights thumped and echoed as she pushed the window up. A canvas curtain inside billowed fierce from the wet wind, then subsided as Caroline, safe inside, pulled the window shut. She stood still, the knife in her hand, and listened.

Voices, alarmed and drawn by the broken window glass, shouted from the front of the house, and a clatter of pans sounded from the kitchen at the foot of the stairwell, but there was no sound close to Caroline. The blood had reached her wrist. She wiped it on her thick skirt and, in the darkness, climbed the uncarpeted steps.

A pale chink of light betrayed the landing door. Caroline fumbled for the lever, pressed it, and flinched as the hinges squealed. But no one saw her and no alarm was raised as she sidled into the corridor. She could hear a man's voice downstairs explaining that drunks must have been responsible for the broken windows and that if Mr Becket cared to submit a bill to the duty officer at the city guardhouse then such a bill would be received most sympathetically.

Caroline, dripping water and blood on to the deep carpet, crossed the corridor and opened Jonathon's door. She almost recoiled from the fetid smell of sickness. As she stepped into the room, Caroline knew she smelt imminent death.

The last time she had seen Jonathon the boy had been mending fast. The pain from his stump had gone, he had been putting on weight, and colour had come back to his cheeks. Now Jonathon looked weaker than a new-born kitten. He shivered as he slept, sweated as he shivered, and his skin was a sickly yellow-white in the light of the single shielded candle that burned on a dresser beside the bed.

"Jonathon? Jonathon?" Caroline whispered the name as she unslung the rain-soaked haversack and put it on the bed. "Jonathon?" She could see scars of clotted blood on Jonathon's arm; square after square of scabs that made a strangely regular pattern. She put her hand on Jonathon's forehead and was astonished by the heat she felt. "Jonathon?"

Jonathon's eyes flickered open, closed, then opened again. He stared at her, and it seemed to Caroline that he did not recognize her.

"Jonathon?" She smiled at him, feeling such a welling of pity that tears started at her eyes. "It's Caroline."

"Dreaming." Jonathon's voice, thanks to the quinsy, was like a rasp on stone.

"You're not dreaming, Jonathon. I'm here!" And now Caroline was crying because the look on his face was so relieved and so astonished and so pleased that she felt as if her heart was being torn in two. She held him, and her cheek felt the fierce, fever-burning heat of his face. He was saying her name over and over again, sobbing it in disbelief and joy.

Caroline gently pulled herself away. "You have to sit up."

Jonathon frowned. "I can't."

"Of course you can." She put her arm under Jonathon and lifted him, noting how little he weighed. "What are they doing to you?"

"That thing." Jonathon, in a gesture so feeble that it could not have stirred a butterfly's wing, indicated some strange device that stood beside a bible on a chest beneath the window. Caroline ignored the odd implement for the moment, propping Jonathon on the bolster and pillows instead. She saw how the bedsheets and blankets were stained from the daily blood-letting and she felt a surge of fury that he should have been reduced to this pathetic weakness by the doctors. Yet not so weak that he could not suddenly laugh. "You came!"

"Of course I came. I tried before, but your uncle's servants wouldn't let me in." Caroline was talking just above a whisper as she unbuckled the knapsack and took out the wrapped cup and the canteen.

"I . . ." but whatever Jonathon wanted to say was drowned by an awful, racking cough. He fought for breath afterwards, his thin chest heaving beneath the red flannel that had been wrapped round his ribs. "I'm dying."

"You're not dying," Caroline said stoutly. "You're going back to the army!" She was pouring the first of the beestings into the cup.

"And you?" Jonathon asked.

Caroline knew what he wanted. "I'll come with you. But only if you drink this!"

Jonathon rolled his head away from the beestings to stare at the shutters. The light of the watch torches flared there, and men's voices were loud on the pavement beneath. "What's happening?"

"Sam broke some windows so I could get into the house. Head up, now!"

Jonathon obeyed. Caroline very carefully supported the back of his head and held the cup to his lips. His black hair was soaked with sweat. "Drink it all now." It was like tending a child.

Jonathon, trusting her, drained the cup. It took a long time, for his throat was swollen with disease. He grimaced at the last drop, then watched as Caroline poured more of the creamy yellow liquid into the cup. "What is it?"

"Sam's magic," Caroline said. "Mare's beestings. More now!" She held the cup to Jonathon's lips again, then wiped the trickles from the heated skin. "Last bit!" She poured the dregs from the canteen into the cup and made Jonathon finish them. "That wasn't bad, was it?"

Jonathon, exhausted by the tiny effort of drinking the beestings, shivered as Caroline helped him down into the bed again. He held her hand, gripping it as though he would never let go. "What day is it?"

"I don't know. Wednesday? You don't want to worry about days, Jonathon. Just about getting better." She leaned over to the chest and, with her free hand, picked up the odd metal device. "What is it?"

"A scarificator."

"Scarificator?"

"A bleeding machine." Jonathon looked with hatred at the device which, to Caroline, resembled an oversize nutmeg grater. It was a steel box, three inches square, with a handle protruding from one face while the opposite face was pierced with holes like a colander. There was a trigger on the handle, just behind a small lever which Caroline, taking her right hand from Jonathon's fevered grip and, exactly as if she were cocking a musket, pulled back.

"Hold it away from your other hand." Jonathon's voice was weak, but his breathing was easier.

Caroline obeyed and, with some trepidation, pulled the trigger. The implement jumped like a snapping mousetrap in her hand as a dozen symmetrically arranged blades, each wickedly sharp and shaped like a gouge, sprang through the holes. Each small blade was stained with dark clotted blood and Caroline understood now the regular patterns of scars on Jonathon's arm. The machine was a device for bleeding patients, drawing the blood in one quick and multiple sting of pain. "They're barbarians," Caroline said.

"It's the very latest thing from London."

"They're not using it on you again." Caroline pushed the scarificator into the pocket of her skirt.

"They'll be angry if it's lost," Jonathon said.

"You think they'll blame you? You have to defy them!"

"I don't feel very defiant now." He lay exhausted, his hand seeking hers again. His voice, when he spoke, was almost drowned by the harsh tattoo of rain on the windows. "Do you think I'll ever leave?"

"You'll leave," Caroline said, and she began to tell him of the preparations she had made. She had cooked some portable soup – a broth dried to solidity that could be soaked back into soup in hot water and which kept for ever. Sam would help them find horses so that she and Jonathon could ride north to join Washington's army. She made her words sound hopeful, trying to offer Jonathon a cause to make true.

"I can't ride," Jonathon said.

"You can! We can't get the boat past the rapids until the river settles down in spring, so we'll have to ride if you want to go soon. Anyway, there was a rector in a village near Sam who only had one leg. Sam said he rode sidesaddle. That's what you'll do!"

"My uncle won't let me go."

"He won't know, will he? If I can get in here, then I can get you out. And you'll get better, Jonathon. Sam says everyone gets better after beestings."

"How is Sam?"

"He wishes he could see you."

Caroline stayed with Jonathon till he slept. Once there were footsteps close outside the door, but no one came in. Caroline, stroking Jonathon's forehead and trying to put some of her own strength into this boy to whom she had promised her life, waited till the clock in the hall struck the half-past eleven. Then, very gently, she kissed his hot forehead. He murmured in his sleep, but did not wake. She left him the carved ivy cup as a reminder of the stolen visit.

Candlelight flickered from the open stairwell at the end of the corridor as Caroline slipped across, then she was on the dark servants' stairs. She went down to the window, eased it up, and climbed into the seething rain that drummed on tiles and shingles and flagged yards.

The bitch recognized Caroline and licked her hand. Caroline, fearing the wall's broken glass, went to the wide carriage entry and unbolted the small door that was let into one of the big, spiked gates. She pulled it open and stepped into the utter darkness of the shadowed alley.

"Caroline!" The voice was Sam's, and it was a strangled and desperate voice. "Run! Run!"

Then the shadows took form, moved, and the threat of the darkness overwhelmed her.

TWENTY-SEVEN

Having thrown the stones, Sam had dodged down the alley, turned left towards Fourth Street, and there had slid into the shadow of the entrance to a bookseller's shop. Across the street, and illuminated by torches that hissed in the rain, the provosts had found an unlicensed grogshop. Barrels and bottles were being tossed on to the pavement, and disconsolate soldiers and sailors were being marched south towards the Pest House Quay where they would be locked into waterlogged cells for the night. Sam, if he was discovered on the streets without a torch, would receive the same treatment.

In an upper room above a furnituremaker's further down Fourth Street a group of officers were making music. Some played flutes and violins, the rest sang, and Sam listened to the delicate music as the fighting and shouting from the grogshop died away. An unshuttered window in the musicians' room cast a dim wash of candlelight on to the rain falling in a silvery spray on the pavement. A legless civilian swung past the bookseller's doorway on muscular arms, then splashed grotesquely through the roadway's thick mud. Two women, sheltering like Sam in another shop doorway, laughed briefly. The provosts, hearing them, went to do business with bottles of confiscated rum as payment.

Sam waited a half-hour. Then, when the street was empty of provosts or patrols, he slipped into the rain and ran north. He crossed Market, sprinting through the mud for fear of the sentries outside the guardhouse, then slipped into the alley that ran behind the college. He could just see the dim shape of the horse blanket on the wall's glass-trapped coping to tell him that Caroline was still inside the Becket house. No noise of protest came from the house so, shivering in the cold rain, he backed into the arched gate of the college to wait for Caroline.

The movement was sudden beside him, flickering in the shadowed shelter of the gateway, and Sam, expecting a blow, twisted hard away, bounced off the gatepost, and came back fighting.

A musket butt slammed into his belly, and a second man, coming from another entranceway, jabbed another reversed musket into Sam's head, knocking his hat off.

Sam slipped, fell, and a boot thudded into his thigh. He pushed up, hands reaching into the darkness, and again a musket butt swung at him. This time the dark night exploded scarlet and white as a musket thumped his skull. He could hear his assailants breathing and grunting, then a heavy man dropped on him. A knee was pushed into Sam's belly and a bayonet was sudden and cold at his throat.

"One word, Sam, and you're fucking dead."

Sam kept silent. His head was spinning, and his eyes playing tricks with light in the blackness. The pain in his skull was dreadful, but he was not so dazed that he did not recognize Sergeant Michael Scammell's voice. "Who's the whore, Sam?"

"Whore?"

The bayonet shifted at Sam's throat, breaking the skin. Scammell chuckled. "You came here an hour ago with a whore. You left, she went over the wall, and now you're waiting for her. Robbing the gentry, are you?"

"She lives here."

"Don't fuck with me, Sam!" Scammell hissed the words. Whoever helped the Sergeant crouched by Sam's side, the musket raised ready to crack down on Sam's skull if he should try and heave Scammell off his belly. Sam's head was in the mud, held there by the bayonet. "I don't care about your whore," Scammell said. "Only about mine. And you was seen in the street with Maggie a couple of weeks back. I've been keeping an eye on you ever since, Sam." Scammell chuckled. "She works for a Mrs Taylor, doesn't she?"

"Dunno, Sarge."

"You know, Sam! And I know. Elliott was there, wasn't he? Three guineas he paid! Three guineas! I want that money, Sam, and you're going to get it for me, because she's mine, boy." Scammell's voice hissed above Sam in the darkness. "She's mine! She was nothing when I met her, nothing. A bull whore that I made into a guinea girl. You understand me, boy? She's mine."

And if Scammell found Maggie again, Sam thought, then her price would soon drop back to the five shillings. Sam's head, though still hurting like the devil, was clearing. He could see the dark shapes of the two men above him, but Sam took a shred of hope because his right boot had found a purchase on a sprung plank of the door beside him. He braced himself, ready to heave, but knowing he must bide his time until the right opportunity came. Even then, he thought, he was unlikely to escape both men. He wondered who Scammell's helper was, then knew he had to somehow keep Scammell talking until some chance, however slim, occurred. "Maggie doesn't want you, Sarge."

"I don't care what Maggie wants," Scammell said. "It's what I want, innit? She's mine, boy, mine!"

"If you know where she is," Sam tried feebly, "then why don't you get her?"

"'Cos the old cow who runs her won't let anyone in, will she? Officers' territory, that, too good for a bleeding sergeant, but your Jack-pudding sends you to fetch his doxies, don't he? So the old cow'll let you in, Sam, and you're going to bring Maggie here."

Sam said nothing. Scammell laughed. "This is what you're going to do for me, Sam Gilpin. You're going to Mrs Taylor's and you tell her that your Jack-pudding wants Maggie now. Then you bring her to me instead of him. You understand?"

"She mayn't want to come, Sarge." Sam shifted slowly. In one of the deep watchcoat pockets he had the small pistol that he usually carried about the city. He inched his right hand towards the pocket, but Scammell's knee obstructed him and any untoward movement might alert the Sergeant to the weapon's existence.

"She'll come," Scammell said, "'cos you'll make her come, boy. Who's your whore, Sam?"

"She ain't a whore."

Scammell chuckled. "They're all whores, Sam, every last damned one of them. Watched you, I did. Saw you with her! Pretty thing, isn't she? Maybe I'll take her instead of Maggie."

Sam heaved and Scammell, ready for it, slapped a handful of gritty mud into Sam's face. The filth slopped into Sam's mouth and Scammell, as he forced the foul mixture into Sam's face, chuckled again. "That'll keep you quiet, Sam."

Sam choked, gagged, and spat, but the bayonet twisted, pressed, threatened, and he lay still, listening.

Rain slapped and pounded in the alley. It gushed and ran from the gutters of the college and swirled in the open drains. Sam, moving his hand as slowly as a stalking cat, tried to reach the small pistol, but Scammell, sensing the movement, twisted the blade and again Sam went very still.

Sam heard the window go up. He braced himself, but Scammell's fingers groped for his eyes and pressed beneath the sockets in a threat to jab down and Sam knew he was beaten. He lay still. The window thumped down. A dog whined and its chain rattled on cobbles.

He could just see the silhouette of the wall's top where the blanket lay folded, and he watched it, fearing to see Caroline's shadow, but wondering if her coming would distract Scammell for a second. Then bolts on the gate squealed and grated.

"George!" Scammell hissed the word, and Sam instantly knew who the other man was.

George Cullen, who boasted of having killed three women before running to join the army as an escape from the justices. Cullen, who delighted in pain and who always volunteered to wield the red-hot iron with which men who stole from their comrades were branded. Cullen, who loved every flogging and who crouched in the bivouacs like a mad dog with a lolling mouth and wild eyes. Cullen.

The gate opened. Sam spat the mud from his mouth, twisted his head away from the pressing fingers, and heaved with his right leg. "Caroline! Run, run!"

The bayonet sliced up Sam's jawbone as Scammell was jerked forward. Caroline screamed, then the scream was abruptly cut off as Cullen draped her with a greatcoat and forced her down into the alley's mud.

Sam was thrusting up to throw Scammell over. He clawed with his left hand for the sergeant's face, but his right was plunging into the pocket and scrabbling for the pistol. The sergeant chopped down with his left fist, then laid the seventeen-inch blade across Sam's throat. "If you don't stay still, fucker, I'll take your whore now, in front of you! Is that what you want?"

Sam went still, but the pistol was in his hand now. The weapon was tangled in the cloth, but, very slowly, Sam eased the flint back as he tried to twist the short barrel towards Scammell.

Caroline was squirming and kicking, but Cullen slapped her twice through the thick wool of the sopping coat, then contemptuously picked her up and slammed her against the brick wall. She gasped with the sudden pain, then gave up the struggle.

"Right, Sam!" Scammell, victorious, chuckled. "She's your whore, right?"

"No."

"I watched you, boy! Mooning after her. She's pretty, too. I know officers who'd pay a pretty price for a little girlie like her. You like her, George?"

Cullen laughed. His right hand, pressing through the greatcoat, was pinning Caroline's throat against the wall. With his left he lifted her skirts.

"Very nice," Scammell said. "Very nice. So listen, Sam. You go for Maggie, and you bring her back to me. If you don't, Sam, then you won't see this doxie again. I'll have her, and George will have her, and I'll sell her to every poxed Jack-pudding in the battalion. You want that, Sam? You want the officers riding her?"

Caroline suddenly twisted because Cullen's hand was groping around her waist. Cullen grunted as he slapped her head against the wall, then pushed his left hand back beneath the coat. "Little bitch was going for this." He pulled out her knife and tossed it on to the ground.

"You've got an hour, Sam," Scammell said.

"Maggie might be working!"

"Then you'll have to find her, won't you?" Scammell eased the bayonet away from Sam's throat. "Are you going to do it?"

Sam pulled the trigger.

He did not dare leave Caroline with these men, even for a minute, let alone an hour. He had to fight now, and he prayed that the clinging cloth of the pocket would not trap the flint's fall, and he prayed that the rain had not soaked through the coat to turn the powder in the pistol's pan to grey sludge.

The pistol fired.

The report was muffled by the cloth and by the seething rain.

Flint sparked on steel, the fire travelled to the charge, and the bullet was driven up through the layers of thick wool and felt to be deflected by a metal button. The small lead ball seared across Scammell's inner thigh like a red-hot whip lashed on to the tender flesh, and the Sergeant jerked back. Sam heaved up, pushing Scammell upwards and away, and tore the pistol free of his smouldering pocket. The bayonet slashed at him, missed, and Sam hit Scammell in the face with the pistol, hit again, and suddenly was free. He threw himself to his left and scrabbled for one of the two muskets.

Scammell, the pain and blood spreading from his thigh, clawed at Sam's legs, but Sam kicked him, found a musket, and hauled himself to his feet.

"One fucking move and she's dead!" Cullen had his own bayonet at Caroline's neck. Caroline, hearing the fight, had tried to break free, but had only succeeded in shedding the coat which had muffled and blinded her. In the tiny light that seeped from the streets her golden hair, from which her shawl had been torn, seemed very bright.

Cullen had pinned Caroline to the wall with his left knee that he had raised to thrust into her belly. Scammell climbed to his feet, bayonet in his hand. "If you want her back, Sam, you fetch Maggie."

Cullen grinned because he had saved Scammell's careful plan, then suddenly yelped as a pain stabbed through his leg and clawed down his flesh. Caroline, in the flurry and noise of her bid to escape, had cocked the scarificator. Now she thrust it against Cullen's thigh and pulled the trigger. She dragged the blades down, gouging blood-seeping grooves of torn flesh that made Cullen instinctively snatch at the pain's source. As the bayonet left her throat, Caroline twisted away. "Run, Sam!"

Sam hammered the musket's butt at Cullen's head as Caroline tore herself free, then Sam abandoned the weapon and ran with her. He took her hand and pulled her along. He turned left at the alley's end, away from the guardhouse, and they sprinted up Fourth Street. A dog barked. A patrolman, seeing the dark running figures, shouted.

Sam twisted at the corner of Arch Street. Scammell and Cullen were on the pavement, both men limping, but the sight of the patrol drove them back into a doorway.

"Come on!" Caroline tugged his hand. She has seen another patrol in Arch Street and she dragged Sam further up Fourth, then twisted into Race Street past the gloomy German Reformed Church. Caroline was laughing. The rain was on her face, the wind in her cheeks, and the Redcoats were chasing her.

"Here!" Sam had seen a half-open gate and he tugged her towards it. They lost their footing, skidded in the mud, then fell through the gate into a pitch-black alley that was covered with a pitched timber roof. Sam pushed the gate shut and crouched, listening, but could only hear the pounding of blood in his ears and the sound of breath in his throat.

Then a voice, speaking close behind, made Sam gasp and turn. "Who are you?" It was a man's voice that came gently from the alley's thick darkness.

Sam bunched himself to fight this new threat, but Caroline hushed him. "We're running from the lobsters," she said.

"I know all about running away," said the strange man. He sounded elderly. "I'm just locking up, children. You will find the gate easy to climb when the soldiers are gone. God bless you." The man shuffled past them, the gate closed, and Sam heard a key grate in a padlock. The footsteps of the closer of the two patrols were loud beyond the arch, and Sam heard the old man bid the soldiers a courteous good evening. No, he had not been troubled by any hooligans.

"Where are we?" Sam whispered to Caroline.

"It's the city synagogue," she whispered back.

"The what?"

"Never mind!" She took her hand from Sam's and laid a finger on his lips. The rain drummed on the boards above them and dripped through the gaps in the crude roof to splash on the flagged alleyway.

Sam sat with his back against the synagogue wall. Caroline sat beside him. She was shivering so he took off his heavy watchcoat and draped it about her shoulders so that, encircled by the coat and his arm, she had to lean against Sam and he could smell her wet hair and feel the warmth of her face close to his cheek. He put his other arm around her and she buried her face in the cloth of his red uniform. It all seemed so natural. Sam hugged her tight and close, warming her, holding her, while beyond the alley's gate the footsteps faded away.

"We shouldn't," Caroline murmured into his coat.

"No" – though Sam did not move.

Caroline pulled away, forcing Sam to release one of his arms. She had been laughing as she ran from the Redcoats, but now she sniffed as though close to tears. "Jonathon's terrible, Sam. They're murdering him!" She suddenly threw the scarificator, which she had clung to throughout their escape, across the small alley.

"He'll get better." Sam spoke with an absolute confidence. "I've never known beestings to fail."

Caroline seemed not to hear. "I told him he'd go back to the army, but he never will, Sam. Never! I'm telling lies to make him better."

"That's a good thing to tell a lie for," Sam said staunchly, "and he's got you to live for, hasn't he? Better than beestings, that is!" His right arm was still about her shoulders, yet Sam knew Caroline could never be his for they had both made their promises to Jonathon, and promises could not be broken. "He'll get better," Sam said, "'cause I've said he'll get better."

Caroline smiled at the obstinacy in his voice. "Do you ever give up, Sam?"

"Never." There was a glimmer of light from carriage lamps as a coach splashed past the synagogue. Sam waited until the sound had faded. "If you give up, the Green Man will get you."

"The Green Man?"

"A sprite, a Jack-in-the-woods." Sam's voice was soft in the darkness. "He has a devil's soul and a green skin. He lives in the woods, see, and he eats you if you get frightened. You can hear him sometimes. He has feet like great tree boles moving in the leaves, and a voice like a gale."

Caroline listened to the conviction in his voice and supposed that the Green Man was the terror which English country mothers used to get their children to sleep. "The Green Man lives in England?"

"I never heard of him here," Sam said, "only in England. My grandad saw him once up in the top woods. A girt thing he was." Sam's voice took on the burr of his native village as if, for a moment, he thought he was back there. "A great thing shifting among the dark trees, but if you don't fear it, it won't trouble you."

Caroline was silent for a while. She seemed content to leave Sam's right arm about her shoulder and even eager for the security of his closeness, for slowly, almost tiredly, she leaned against him once more. "Do you miss England, Sam?"

He smiled. "Not now."

"No?" She sounded disbelieving and Sam, although he knew he should not, answered Caroline by gathering her into his arms again and Caroline, though she knew she should not, let herself be drawn into their safe encircling embrace again.

"I promised Jonathon," Caroline's voice was very small, "that you'd help find us horses when we go."

"I'll do that."

"Perhaps the river would be better, though." She sniffed.

"Boat would probably be a good idea," Sam said.

"But we'd have to wait till spring." Caroline said it softly.

"There are rapids between here and Trenton." She paused, then shrugged in Sam's arms. "He shouldn't go back to the army, not with one leg, but he insists. Maybe he'll change his mind."

"Maybe," Sam said.

"Martha says he should study law. She says it doesn't matter if a lawyer's only got one leg."

"Won't stop him counting the money, will it?"

Caroline stirred and her face looked palely up at Sam. "But lawyers live in the city, don't they?"

"Some live in the country," Sam said.

"Not Jonathon. Whatever he does, he'll be the best, and the best lawyers aren't in the country."

Sam supposed she was right. "I couldn't live in the city," he said. "I'm glad to have seen one, but I couldn't live in it. Like being in prison!"

"Yes."

There was silence again between them. Caroline still shivered and Sam held her very close and gently stroked her hair, but with a touch so light that Caroline could almost persuade herself that it was unintentional. She rested her head on his shoulder again as the rain crashed on the flimsy shelter above and rippled down the wall opposite.

"Will you stay a soldier, Sam?"

"I don't have a lot of choice, do I?"

"But with those two men?" Caroline shuddered.

"They ain't all like that. I had a decent officer, Captain Kelly, but he got killed. He was a nice fellow. Most of them are decent sorts of fellows. Weavers."

"Weavers?"

"No work back home, you see, so they join the army." Sam grinned. "We have enough weavers to put a blanket over Philadelphia."

She pulled away from him again, but not so far that he must let go of her. "But do you really want to stay a soldier, Sam?"

The new urgency in her voice made Sam hesitate. "Not like I used to, perhaps."

"What do you want?"

Sam hesitated again. What he wanted was what he had now – this girl in his arms – but that was something that could not be said because of a boy who lay in sweating sickness. Sam shrugged. "I want to be left alone, I suppose."

Caroline frowned. "You don't want liberty?"

Sam smiled. "It's just a word, isn't it? Means nothing."

"People fight for it."

"Liberty's a pot of ale, your own hearth, and a full barn."

"Is that what you want, Sam?" Again she was insistent.

This time Sam looked at her. "A piece of land wouldn't be a bad thing, and a few mares to breed from." He paused for a regretful second. "I sometimes dream about that."

"You can have it here, Sam!"

"Three hogs and fifty acres?"

Caroline frowned, not understanding. "Fifty acres?"

"That's what the rebels offer us, but they don't give it you. Leastways, I hear they don't."

"But suppose they did?"

"I can find a rough old bit of land in England, if that's what I want. But it isn't." Caroline kept silent, not because she did not want Sam to continue, but because she wanted him to say what it was that he desired, and she wanted him to say it without invitation. She wanted that gift on this cold night, and Sam, pensive beside her, offered it. "What I want I can't have."

Caroline's voice was very quiet. "So you do give up sometimes? The Green Man will get you, Sam, and gobble you up."

"Will he?"

They had come too close to the forbidden subject and, in her unhappiness, Caroline shrugged. "I don't know, Sam, I really don't know."

And Sam, because he could not help it and because he wanted to, kissed her.

He only had to lean forward a few inches. He did it slowly, letting her withdraw if she wished, but she stayed still and he kissed her wet cheek, then put an arm around her shoulders and drew her face to his as though he would warm her and comfort her and hold her against the dark for ever. Caroline sighed and stayed. The dirt on Sam's face was harsh on her skin, but she felt comforted.

Sam could smell her hair. He could feel a pulse in her neck throb beneath the fingers of his right hand.

He held her close, but had nothing to say, for he knew, and she knew, that there was nothing to say. Instead, they must keep their promises to Jonathon, and the kiss was just a moment stolen from what might have been, but which could never be, and so they clung to each other and the rain beat like a fury across the sleeping city, and seethed on the black river, and drenched the far dark woods where, except for the rebels, no Green Man stalked.

TWENTY-EIGHT

The dead season came.

Winds brought sleet from an aching sky above a frozen land. The river was grey as Welsh slate, promising ice in the long dark silences of the American winter. Philadelphia's straight streets, bereft of their trees, were bleached to a stark paleness in which the red-coated soldiers, shrunken by the wind, moved slow and shivering. The wind cut at faces, made skin raw, and chilled fingers blue.

The last merchantmen had sailed to England. There was still trade between the city and New York, and southwards to the Caribbean, but winter threatened to end all navigation between Philadelphia and the sea. The smaller streams froze, the river's edge seemed daily more sluggish, while the grasses on the empty marshlands were frosted into stiff white spikes. Lord Howe took the fleet north to the deeper, safer anchorage of Rhode Island, leaving only a handful of small warships to fend off the rebel gunboats that still sometimes snapped at the shrunken seagoing trade.

The city's mood grew bleaker with the cold. The merchants must wait for their cargoes, sent to London, to yield profits for the next year. Some of the merchants were already ruined, their cargoes wrecked on the rebel obstacles that were yet to be entirely cleared from the river bed. Some Whig citizens, despairing of Philadelphia's future, put their goods to auction and left the city before the snow and ice turned discomfort into misery.

Most of Sir William's men were still bivouacked outside the city limits, crowded into huts that disfigured the land around the Centre Commons, but the quartermasters were already searching the streets for empty houses and shops that would serve as winter quarters. The citizens feared for the time when the great mass of Hessians and Redcoats, along with their women, would flood into the city proper. Food was already scarce, and fuel for fires scarcer. It had not been like this, people said, when the rebels had ruled Philadelphia.

Yet the greatest outcry against Sir William's rule came when he ordered the sequestration of a dozen of the city's churches. All but one were dissenting churches, and the order brought a delegation of ministers, deacons and laymen to the army's headquarters. There were Lutherans, Methodists, Presbyterians, Seceders, Baptists, a gloomy minister of the German Reformed Church who spoke no English, two Anglicans, and three Quakers who, though their meeting house was not threatened, came to protest against the tide of ungodliness that now flooded Philadelphia.

Sir William offered tea, small talk, then gently told the city's righteous that their churches were to be turned into stables.

"Stabling?" A Presbyterian, famed for his anti-British sentiments, stared with outrage at Sir William. "Horses in God's houses? You can use empty warehouses for stabling!"

Sir William, who was attended by Christopher Vane, sighed patiently. "Horses need stalls. They can't just roam around, they're not sheep! Your church has box pews, I believe? Box pews make splendid horse stalls. And horses need large doors. No, I fear it has to be the churches!" Sir William smiled affably at his audience who, dressed sober as crows, stared back with undisguised hostility.

Abel Becket, who had come with the Revd MacTeague because St Paul's was the one Anglican church marked for desecration, pointed out that the South Street Playhouse had long been disused for the drama thanks to the pressure of godly men in the city and was now empty. It had been used as a hospital for wounded officers who had either recovered or been buried, and surely, Becket pleaded, such a building could be used for stabling. "It would spare one house of God, Sir William."

"It might," Sir William allowed, "but you would be even more unhappy, gentlemen, if I were to stage plays in one of your churches."

"Plays?" The Presbyterian sniffed the sulphurous presence of the devil in his city.

"But of course! The winter is the time for diversions." Sir William smiled. "And I was ever taught, gentlemen, that though prayers can be well said without a church, the drama cannot be decently spoken without a stage."

After the meeting, which went about as miserably as he had expected, the Commander-in-Chief politely showed his guests to the outer hallway. Christopher Vane fell into step with Abel Becket. "May I ask how your nephew does, sir?"

Becket, disgruntled by the meeting, seemed in a churlish mood, but his news was surprisingly good. It seemed that Jonathon was mending with remarkable speed.

"Remarkable indeed!" MacTeague had overheard the answer, and now turned to Vane. "It demonstrates the healing effects of a loving home and much prayer. Jonathon now takes solid food and even essays exercises on his flute."

"I'm so very pleased," Vane said. "It proves how right we were to move him." Jonathon's recovery had become the touchstone of victory between Vane and the Widow. "I trust," Vane said to the Revd MacTeague, "that you will mark the young man's deliverance with prayer on Sunday?"

"In a stable?" MacTeague asked, then, because he had been promised a generous rent for the sequestration of his church, he nodded. "Such prayers will be offered. You may be sure that Jonathon's happy redemption will be proclaimed."

Vane saw that Sir William had been cornered by a Presbyterian and a Baptist who were rudely demanding to know if an adequate food supply could be ensured for the next three months. Vane turned to Becket. "And your nephew is seeing the error of his former ways, sir?"

"He will, he will!" Becket said forcefully. "He can expect no part of his patrimony if he does not take the oath of loyalty, Captain."

"If there's any help I can give?" Vane suggested, then turned because the Baptist minister, whose voice was as harsh as a corncrake, was berating the Commander-in-Chief. "You're imprisoned in the city," the Baptist said, "you're cornered by Patriots, Sir William, and we'll starve unless you go!"

"We're hardly imprisoned." Sir William was determined to keep his temper.

"I call it imprisoned!" the Baptist said. "And unless you take more care of the Lord's commandments, Sir William, then His wrath will smite you!"

Sir William, in an attempt to rid himself of his unwanted guests, opened the front door himself. A small snow was falling, though not settling.

The Revd MacTeague, eager to be seen as a more civilized man than his Baptist colleague, chuckled. "I pray that you smite Mister Washington, Sir William."

"In this weather?"

The Baptist gave a harsh laugh. "It does not seem to deter Mister Washington?"

Sir William had to fight back an irritated retort. He had lived long enough in America to know how blunt the colonists could be, even when talking to their betters, and he knew the priests expressed a concern that worried every Loyalist in the city. The rebel army, forsaking its winter quarters and reinforced with men come from their triumph at Saratoga, had marched close to the city, perhaps hoping to tempt Sir William into battle, or perhaps making a show of defiance to prove that the British were imprisoned within their own lines. Abel Becket expressed a wish that the rebel defiance be punished, but Sir William offered him no hope. "It's December, Mr Becket. Winter is not, nor ever has been, the fighting season."

Sir William finally closed the door on the delegation, then groaned with an exaggerated despair. "American preachers almost persuade me that this is a barbaric country. Ignorance allied to passion, Kit, is a dangerous conjunction. Perhaps we should win this war just to save America from its preachers?" Sir William chuckled to show that he did not want the words taken seriously, then reported in the city and hurled vengefully back from the rabid pulpits.

Vane crossed to warm himself at the hallway's fire. "Let's just hope they believe you, sir."

For Sir William was again attempting to deceive the gossips and spies within the city. Winter might not be the fighting season, but late on the very next night, 4 December, beneath a starlit darkness in which the moon was suspended like a sliver of hard white metal, the army marched. The battalions followed the frost-hardened road through the Northern Liberties, passing the defensive redoubts where torches, lighting the guardposts, revealed pinched and cold faces. The soldiers carried four days' food on their backs and a battle's-worth of cartridges in their cartouches.

The guns crunched the frosted earth under iron-rimmed wheels while the cavalry sought more level ground at the road's edges. Company after company, squadron after squadron, battery after battery, all marched north from Philadelphia in a freezing night beneath stars that were a million diamond points in blackness.

Sir William, cloaked and scarfed and gloved against the bitter cold, rode behind the leading brigade. He dreamed of surprising the enemy, a dream that his second-in-command, Lord Cornwallis, rudely dispelled. "You ordered the city's bakers to make forty thousand loaves of ration bread! You think Washington hasn't heard of that ten times over? Twenty times? The damn city's thick with spies!"

Sir William ascribed Lord Cornwallis's choleric tone to the aggravations of the freezing night. He found his second-in-command a difficult man to endure. Undoubtedly Cornwallis was energetic and able, but Sir William sometimes felt that his lordship's very existence was an implicit criticism of himself.

"If you hung a few of the malcontents," Cornwallis went on, "it might discourage the rest. Nothing like a few bodies on a gibbet to remind people of their loyalty."

"A victory would be a more salutary lesson," Sir William said mildly. As ever when action was imminent, he became optimistic. The war might have broken Sir William's dreams and even driven him to offer his resignation, but he had never been defeated on a battlefield. And he saw the wisdom of his brother's advice. If George Washington could be broken on the icy wheel of a surprise attack, then the French would shrink from joining a lost cause and the rebellion's leaders would seek for the peace that Sir William so earnestly desired and in search of which Sir William marched north at dead of night, hoping to fall like a thunderbolt in the winter's dawn. Perhaps this time his victory would be complete and the French would be so dazzled by the thunderbolt's flames that they would keep their troops safe home in France.

Except that, at three in the morning, when the leading battalions reached a small ridge, they saw a band of light stretching across their front. Camp fires blazed in darkness, a thick row of fires, mile upon mile of flames, and yet more fires flared bright as signal guns warned the rebel army of the British approach.

"Ready and waiting," Cornwallis said with the satisfaction of a man whose doom-laden prophecy had been proved right.

"And doubtless fearful of us," Sir William said mildly.

"So attack, sir! Attack!"

But the thunderbolt hesitated. Sir William knew what chaos could come in night fighting, nor did he wish to thrust his brave men down the moon- and frost-whitened roads until he could see just what reception the enemy might have prepared for them. "We shall wait for dawn."

"March up the road now," Cornwallis urged, "and take them with the bayonet!"

"At dawn."

But at dawn Sir William saw that the Americans, clearly warned, had built earthern fortifications on their ridge and barred the roads with sharp-staked abatis.

"We can break through!" Cornwallis urged.

"I've no doubt we can," Sir William said, "but at what price? There'll be no replacements for our casualties, none! Every man who dies here is a gift to the enemy. We shall let Mister Washington attack us."

But Mister Washington, mindful of his defeats at Sir William's hands, would not leave his fortifications. For two days the two sides waited. Plumes of smoke smeared the sky behind the British lines as forage parties, coming across small farms, looted and burned. The frost limned the trees a delicate and brilliant white until a cold rain, starting on the second day, drenched the ice from stark black December branches.

On the third day new supplies came from the city and Sir William cautiously probed to his right. "I can't batter through without grievous losses," he told his aides, "so we shall manoeuvre him into disaster."

Hopes rose that afternoon. General Washington, seeing British cavalry isolated on the Bethlehem Road, ordered the Pennsylvania militia to attack.

But the cavalry was not isolated. Two battalions of Redcoats guarded the flank and for ten minutes the two bodies of infantry exchanged musket fire, then the British fixed their bayonets. They advanced in a silent and menacing close order, and the rebel militia retreated. A few American muskets banged smoke over the hard earth, a few red-coated men dropped from the ranks, but still the long blades came forward. The militia was not trained to face such attacks and their fear of the blades turned retreat into flight.

But the British did not follow and there was silence again on a battlefield. Crows pecked at the dead who had been stripped of their uniforms. Sir William still probed cautiously to the east, but he neither found a route about the enemy's flank, nor could he tempt the rebels out of their positions into the open ground where superior British training might decimate the enemy.

"We shall go back to the city," Sir William announced after a third day's fruitless manoeuvring.

"We'll do what, sir?" Christopher Vane, the aide in attendance, sounded horrified.

"It's too cold to stay any longer." Sir William shivered on his horse, staring into the bleak landscape.

"We should attack!" Vane, caution scattered by the cold and by the frustration of these havering days, heard himself lecturing his Commander-in-Chief. "If he lives through this winter, sir, he'll raise rebel hopes. We have to end him now!"

"Be careful, Vane!" Sir William, astonished at Vane's temerity, offered the caution.

But Vane's tongue could not be curbed. At last, at long last, the British army had marched to crush the rebels, and now, after days of half-hearted manoeuvring, Sir William would merely march back again. "It will take a thousand deaths, sir!" Vane urged, "but a thousand pages in the history books will tell how you ended a rebellion! If we just slink back we'll be the laughing stock of every damned Patriot in the city! Attack, sir! He's far more frightened of us than . . ." Vane stopped, suddenly knowing he had gone much too far. He shivered, then offered Sir William a self-deprecatory smile. "I apologize, sir. My old loquacity, I fear."

But Sir William, staring at his aide in the cold dusk of a winter's day, would not be mollified. His voice was like ice. "I am not frightened, Captain Vane, and if you have a mind to keep my affection I would be grateful if you would refrain from offering me jejune lectures on the conduct of military operations!" Sir William shuddered, as though he was boiling up for an even more savage outburst, but he managed to control his temper. "Good day, sir!" Sir William twisted his horse away from Vane and for once Vane's apologies, spoken with his rueful charm, had not worked. He felt the chill of estrangement, but also a surge of resentment that Sir William's pusillanimity would let George Washington live to fight another year.

Sir William marched back to Philadelphia and ordered the troops to move into their winter quarters. The old huts by the Centre Commons, deemed too frail for winter's cruel cold, were torn down and their timbers were either chopped for firewood or made into the bunks which were crammed into every abandoned house. Philadelphia's population rose sharply. Not only was the army in residence, but refugees from the ravaged hinterland came in search of shelter and food. There was scarce enough of either.

Only the wealthy did not suffer privation. The shops, replenished by the ships which had sailed upriver after the capture of the forts, offered luxuries to the affluent. Fine spermaceti candles could be had at five shillings a box. Superb false teeth, made with teeth drawn from the corpses of Brandywine and Germantown, were obtainable for eight guineas a set, while watch-chains, court plasters, hair powder, wigs, silk stockings, and pomatum were all plentiful. Wine, brandy, gin, arrack and rum were ever available, yet supplies of cheese, flour, meal, rice and meat were already as scarce as in the weeks before the river forts fell. Prices rose, beggars multiplied, and the lowering, darkening sky threatened the snow that would make the misery worse.

It was the dead season; a time when the weak things of the earth died, but Jonathon mended.

Martha heard of her brother's recovery from servants' gossip and from the Revd MacTeague. She passed the good news on to Caroline, though Caroline already knew because one of the kitchenmaids in Abel Becket's house now smuggled letters between Caroline and Jonathon.

"It was Sam's beestings," Caroline said.

"I rather think it was." Martha heard the pride in the young girl's voice. "So! Jonathon will be on a wooden leg by spring." She said it cheerfully to see how Caroline responded.

The response was not enthusiastic. Instead, Caroline punched at the small logs in the kitchen grate with a poker. "Spring." She said the word flatly.

"When the promises come home to roost?"

Caroline smiled a rueful acknowledgement. "He wants to go to Trenton. He says he'll clerk for the army. He knows he can't fight."

"And you'll go with him?"

Caroline nodded. "I promised."

"And your grandparents?"

Caroline stared at the flames. "They've always known I'd have to go one day. Most girls are married at fifteen, aren't they?" She looked at Martha almost defiantly as she posed the question. "If not earlier!"

"I suppose they are, yes."

"And I can make him very happy."

"Yes, you can." Martha stood and walked to the small window that looked up into her courtyard. Sleet tapped on the pane. "How's Sam? I haven't seen him for many a long day."

"Sam's busy. He's doctoring horses and saving money."

Martha heard the warmth in Caroline's voice that had been absent a moment before. Martha turned. "Do you see Sam often?"

"Sometimes." Caroline was evasive.

Martha went back to the fire and stretched out thin hands to the flames. "Would you like some advice?" She did not wait for an answer, but offered the advice anyway. "It might be best if you stayed on the other side of the river. If I see Sam I'll tell him you can't come to the city till the danger of ice is past."

Caroline did not reply, but just stared into the small flames.

"Or I could say you were frightened of those men who attacked you?" Martha suggested. "But whatever I say, my dear, it will save you a deal of confusion."

Caroline frowned. "I'm not confused." She stopped, remembering the night in the alley beside the synagogue. She shook her head. "Sam's a Redcoat."

Martha heard the echoes of troubled loyalties. "Sam's a Redcoat of whom you're very fond, and I can't say I blame you. But you've a promise to keep."

"Yes, I do."

"So stay on the other side of the river." Martha's voice was firm now. "You don't scratch at a half-healed wound. Let it alone."

Caroline looked at the older woman. "And your messages?"

Martha shrugged. "There's only gossip in them now. There'll be no fighting till spring, but if I've something of importance to send, I'll have a servant deliver it to you."

Caroline looked into the fire again. "I'll tell Sam I can't come to the city till the ice melts. It wouldn't be fair for anyone else to tell him."

"He's a Redcoat," Martha said lightly, "so he must be accustomed to bad news."

Caroline did not smile. "And I can't see Jonathon anyway" – her voice was wistful – "so it's all for the best."

"Yes. It is."

Caroline left, and that night the first heavy snow came. It snowed all night and all the next day. Heavy, soft, thick flakes of snow whirled around rooflines and heaped in alleyways to cover the ordure in courtyards. It drifted to smooth the frost-rutted roadways with a glinting, brilliant coating. The rooms of the city, lit by reflected light from the snow, seemed brighter and, for a few days at least, spirits rose. In the twelve days of Christmas there were snowball fights on the Centre Commons, while high-prowed, horse-drawn sleighs, jingling with belled harnesses and slick on their steel-lined runners, appeared in the streets. There were sledge races on the Neck, and an ice feast in one of the abandoned summer houses on the Schuylkill's bank. By New Year the river was hard frozen so skates could hiss and scrape on the gleaming ice.

And each day Sam watched for the ice's melting, but instead it seemed to thicken. January turned to February in the hardest winter of living memory. The snow turned to mucky slush, then was freshened by new falls. The food supplies shrank and men died of scurvy. Their teeth fell out, they shivered, they curled against bare walls and simply died. Only the rats seemed fat. Two rats, gutted and skinned, made a decent stew. "It's rabbit, sir," Sam would tell Captain Vane, and the Captain did not press to discover how his servant found rabbit meat in Philadelphia's winter. Forage parties still trudged out into the blizzards to search the nearer farms for hidden supplies, and sometimes, in the short cold days, musket fire echoed over the pitiless land to tell of a brutal skirmish between Redcoats and rebels.

Such rebels were on patrol, for General Washington had pulled the Continental Army back to winter quarters at a place called Valley Forge. Lizzie Loring thought it sounded like a very cosy place.

"Cosy?" Sir William asked her.

"All those blacksmiths' fires in a valley? I imagine they're very snug."

"I seem to recall we burned down the forges last summer, and their deserters tell us it's the most hideous place."

Lizzie stood at the bedroom window. Icicles hung from the eaves beneath a grey sky in which the sun, low over the State House roof, was paled to a sickly yellow disc. "Is that what you'll say when you desert us?" She turned. "Will you say how hideous America is?"

Sir William was touched by her unhappiness, but could offer small consolation. "Perhaps they won't accept my resignation?"

"But if they do?"

"You can come to England?"

"I can't imagine Lady Howe appreciating such a thing. Nor can you."

"No." Sir William, wearing a skullcap and heavy robe, stroked his sleeping dog which lay curled at his feet by the fire. "But if there's peace, my dear, I'll stay."

"Will there be peace?"

Sir William looked hopelessly at his lover. "If the French don't come, yes."

"And if the French do come?"

Sir William thought about his answer as he stirred the negus which warmed on a trivet by the flames. "It will be a different war, my love. A war about sugar and islands and fleets. Maybe the Spanish will join the French? It will be an old-fashioned European war, and all because of threepence on tea." He said the last words bitterly.

"And you'll leave" – Lizzie, in her own misery, took no notice of Sir William's – "and you'll tell England that America was never worth fighting for, and that it's a hideous place with dull people and ranting preachers and a foul climate."

"No," Sir William said, "I won't." He stood, crossed to her, and gathered her into his arms. "I shall say it was the place where I knew the greatest happiness of my life. Then lost it."

It was winter, and the land was palled with white, waiting for spring.

PART THREE

TWENTY-NINE

The building was cavernous, dark, and echoing. It reeked of paint, but on this night in early April 1778 that thick stench was mingled with the odours of powder and perfume.

Silks and calico rustled in the darkness. A woman giggled and was immediately hushed.

Only four lights, each an oil lamp placed within a reflecting hood, burned in the building's gaping interior. The small flames cast a flickering and yellowish glow on to a painted scene that depicted green hills, deep woods, and a steam flowing towards a stone-built village with a spired church. The painting hung like a vast curtain across the stage of Philadelphia's theatre, reviving sweet memories of the English countryside for the officers who stood in the pit's darkness.

Somewhere deep in the theatre a hidden drum began a slow and menacing beat.

A trumpet, much closer at hand but still hidden, seared an abrupt fanfare that made the crowd shiver with a delicious alarm. More than two hundred people were standing in the darkness to watch the lit stage. Lovers' hands, vouchsafed the secrecy of the darkened pit, linked fingers.

The fanfare ceased. The drummer gave a final flourish. Then there was silence except for the rattle of rain on a high window.

A pause, just long enough for the spectators' apprehension to increase, then a disembodied voice sounded from the apparently empty stage.

> Once more ambitious of theatric glory,
> Howe's strolling player appears before ye!

On the word "appears", the four lights at the front of the stage were abruptly doused and other lamps, placed behind the painted scene, were unhooded. The English landscape had been painted on a scrim, a great sheet of gauze, and the effect of obliterating the darkness behind the scrim and the light before it, was to make the gauze and its rural scene vanish. It was a cunning theatrical trick that never failed to raise applause, as it did this night. In an eyeblink the hills disappeared to be replaced by a black-cloaked man whose face was hidden by a deathly white papier-mâché mask.

The man put his right foot forward, placed his clenched right fist against his left breast, and, as the now transparent scrim was reeled invisibly upwards, his fine declamatory voice again echoed in the theatre's pit.

O'er hills and dales and bogs, thro' wind and weather,
And many a hair-breadth 'scape I've scrambled hither,
For we true vagrants of the Thespian race
While summer lasts ne'er know a settled place.

The hidden drum began to beat, softly at first, but rising, and the caped man mimed panic.

Now beats each Yankee bosom at our drum,
Hark! Hark! Alarm! Howe's strollers come!

On the last word he snatched the papier-mâché mask from his face and hurled it into the wings. There was more applause, even louder than before, as the popular Captain John Andre thus revealed himself and bowed to his audience. At the same instant two doors, one on either side of the stage's small apron, were thrown back and lines of uniformed men marched in carrying tall candelabras, brilliant with flame, to light the theatre's interior.

Andre again held up a hand for silence. He smiled. "My lords, ladies, gallants, friends! The Society of Gentlemen of the Army and Navy, which I have the humble honour to represent this night, welcomes you to the playhouse!"

More applause. The candelabras were being placed on linen-covered tables that were heaped with food and wine.

"A playhouse where we, this winter, have been delighted to offer you the rarest gems of the dramatic art! *The Constant Couple*!" There were mocking cheers at the mention of the play's title, cheers that Andre checked with an upraised hand. "*The Wonder! A Woman Keeps a Secret*!"

There were more cheers and laughter, which again Andre checked with a raised hand. He walked to the front of the stage while musicians came from the wings to set up their chairs and stands behind him. Tonight, instead of drama, the theatre would hold a subscription ball for the widows and orphans of those who had lost their lives in the King's service. The benches of the pit had been pushed under the gallery to make way for dancing, while, in the antechamber, two Hessian officers had established a faro bank for the gamblers who could not endure an evening's entertainment without their gaming. It was a night for revelry, and Captain Andre thanked all who had paid to attend, raised laughter by imitating the preachers who claimed the theatre had corrupted Philadelphia's youth, and enjoined each guest to an evening of celebration.

Applause followed his speech. "He did that remarkably well!" Sir William Howe clapped enthusiastically. "He wrote the poem, y'know? John's a talented fellow."

"Indeed." Charles Lee smiled at Lizzie Loring. "I'm astonished you have never graced John's stage, Mrs Loring?"

"Lord, no, Charlie! I ain't a player!"

Sir William spied Martha on Lord Robert Massedene's arm and waved to attract her attention. "Amongst my other sins, dear Mrs Crowl, do you see me as a corrupter of American youth?"

"Dear Sir William." Martha, splendid in vivid blue silk and with her piled hair looped in ribbons of the same colour, gave the Commander-in-Chief her hand to be kissed. "Whom have you corrupted?" she asked.

"The clergy say everyone."

"They should be grateful for the business, should they not? Clergy need sinners like pork butchers need hogs. Dear Lizzie." Martha exchanged kisses with Lizzie, then looked back to Sir William. "If you really wish to avoid the corruption of our youth, why don't you send Charlie back to General Washington's army?"

"It will be done within the fortnight." Sir William smiled at the rebel General. "I shall miss you, Charlie, 'pon my word, I shall."

"I shall miss you, Sir William. I fear I return to a dull existence. Our Congress is proposing a ban on horseracing, gaming, cockfighting, plays, or expensive diversions." Lee shook his head sadly. "I sometimes wonder why I fight for the rebellion at all."

"Why do you?" Sir William was genuinely curious.

The tall Lee, who still sported his gaudy Polish uniform, shrugged. "To get my name in the history books, I suppose."

"You think history will remember such a little war?"

"One dares hope?"

The musicians, their music arranged, watched their leader's violin bow beat once, twice, then sing on its strings. It was the same small orchestra that had played all winter long at the city's revels whether in military headquarters or in the houses of the richer Loyalist merchants who cared for such entertainments. They played for the same guests who had made the same endless round of parties; entertainments to make people forget their hunger and cold.

The city had not starved, though it had been close. The forage parties had fought vicious battles in the hinterland, suffering ambush and loss, but always bringing some food back. The farmers, ordered not to sell their food to the British, nevertheless hid it from the rebels in the hope of gaining British gold and so, with such precious hoards brought back by foragers, the city had survived.

As the dancing began, Martha took Charles Lee aside. "I particularly wanted a word with you, Charlie."

Lee had become friendly with Martha through the winter, drawn by her beauty as much as by a shared allegiance. Now he looked back towards Lord Robert Massedene. "Robert won't be jealous?"

"Robert and I are amiable friends," Martha said firmly, "and nothing more. He is a dear man, but I didn't stay in the city to be suborned by an enemy."

"So there's hope for a friend?" Lee asked mischievously. "I'd like to take a beautiful wife back to Valley Forge and watch General Washington pretend not to notice."

"It won't be me, dear Charlie, but you really are returning to General Washington?"

"Did you ever doubt it?" Lee teased Martha, knowing full well that some of the Patriots believed him to be altogether too friendly with his British captors. "I'm to be exchanged for General Prescott, taken at Saratoga of blessed memory, but whether His Excellency truly wishes for my return, I cannot tell."

"Why ever should he not?"

"Plump George dislikes me intensely, but he dislikes any man who has had success against the British. I doomed myself in his affections by winning at Charleston, and I wager you that Gates and Arnold earned His Excellency's displeasure at Saratoga."

Martha took a glass of wine from a table. "You're saying General Washington's jealous?"

"I'm saying he has the spite of a woman, and her appetite for flattery."

Martha listened to the splenetic words impassively. She had seen the same jealousies within the British command, between Sir William and the recently departed Lord Cornwallis, and she supposed it was impossible for ambitious men in authority to live in amity. "General Washington must have some merits, Charlie."

Lee shrugged. "He's brave as a lion and stubborn as an ox, though, God knows, a man who's defeated so often needs to be."

"All he needs do," Martha said wistfully, "is survive till the French come. If they come."

"If." Lee said the word darkly. The rumours had been strong all winter, but the French still hesitated, weighing what losses they might suffer around the globe if they came to the rebellion's aid. Another rumour, just as keenly discussed about the city, was that Sir William had offered his resignation and would be replaced. Lee, taxed on the rumour by Martha, shrugged. "I imagine Lizzie would tell you, would she not? Poor Billy. He never made up his mind whether he was fighting us or stroking us." Lee watched Sir William fondly. "He'd really like to make peace, but I fear that won't happen."

"We must encourage his hope," Martha said tartly. "If Billy is persuaded that peace is attainable, he'll be reluctant to wage war, will he not?"

Lee looked at her thoughtfully. "That is a quite dishonest notion, dear Mrs Crowl. I like it."

Martha, pleased with the compliment, smiled. "If Billy does go, who'll replace him?"

Lee spread his hands in a gesture of ignorance. "Henry Clinton, perhaps?"

Martha had never met the American-born General Clinton who now commanded Britain's New York garrison. "Is he able?"

"As able as Billy, if that means anything, and, like Billy, he was always an opponent of the war. But command changes some generals; the prospect of victory overcomes the scruples of morality, and I fancy Sir Henry might be more avid for military victory than Billy."

"But he is able?" Martha insisted.

"He isn't negligible," Lee allowed, "so we'll have to find a general who can win battles if we're to defeat him."

Martha watched the dancers dip and swirl before the stage. "You, Charlie?"

"My humble wish is merely to serve the sacred cause of liberty." Which humbug only served to tell Martha that the rebel command was, indeed, Lee's ambition. Lee smiled maliciously. "Though I hear our new golden hope is an unfledged French aristocrat? Have you heard of him? Lafayette? The shifts we are forced to, dear Mrs Crowl. Youths scarce out of their cradles become generals on His Excellency's whim. Never mind!" Lee gave an exaggerated sigh. "Perhaps the infant Lafayette can teach George to dance? The French make good dancing masters." He offered his arm. "Shall we?"

Martha stepped back from the offered arm. "But I haven't asked my favour of you, Charlie."

"My dear Martha, I have waited all winter."

Martha dutifully smiled at the dutiful flirtation. She saw Christopher Vane thread his way through the gaudy crowd and, lest she caught his eye, she turned into the shadows beneath the pillared gallery. "It's a favour for my brother."

"I forgot! How is he?"

"Wonderfully recovered. They've fitted him with a wooden leg, and soon he'll be unleashed on to the city's streets. Or so I'm told." She paused, letting a naval officer edge past them. The fleet had returned when the ice melted in March, bringing powder, shot and rations for the coming campaign. Martha looked at Lee again. "Jonathon wants to rejoin the Continental Army."

Lee frowned. "With one leg?"

"He never had two anyway, but he can clerk, can't he?"

"I suppose so." A sudden whoop made them both turn to see Christopher Vane leading a Scottish reel. Sir William applauded his aide. There had been a coolness between the two men earlier in the winter, following the fruitless sally to Germantown, but Sir William was not a man to harbour grudges and Kit Vane, to Martha's regret, was again in Sir William's favour. The commander-in-chief laughed delightedly as some paroled rebel officers, free to live within the city, joined the dance. Above them, at the edge of the stage, a bonneted Highland officer danced alone above crossed swords.

"The British at play," Martha said icily.

"They play a damn sight better than George," Lee said testily.

Martha, not wanting to provoke another burst of jealousy,

went back to the subject of her brother. "As you're returning, Charlie, I wondered if you'd be kind enough to offer Jonathon your assistance?"

"Gladly. Of course! Unless things are a lot better, which I doubt, the Commissary Office will be glad of a clever man."

"And his wife."

"Wife?"

"Jonathon plans to marry."

Lee noted the unenthusiastic tone of Martha's voice. "You don't approve?"

"I like her extremely."

"But?" the rebel General probed.

Martha veered away from the subject. "Jonathon can't leave till the end of April. He has to stay and sign papers, or else lose his inheritance. Will you be gone by then?"

"I fear so. Did you want him to travel with me?"

"He couldn't. Officially he's a prisoner. I'll have to smuggle him out of the city."

Lee laughed. "You're rather good at smuggling things out of the city, aren't you?"

Martha smiled. "I really don't know what you're talking about."

"Nor do I," Lee said happily, "but naturally I will do all I can to help your brother. It will be an honour. He and his bride will want lodgings, and he needs a post. Shall I write and tell you what I can arrange?"

"That would be kind."

"How do I communicate with you?"

"Care of the Fisher house at Cooper's Point."

"Your favour is so easily granted." Lee bowed. "Now you can return it by dancing with me and thus giving the gossips a chance to decry our characters."

Lee offered Martha his arm, and they joined a quadrille that had been made gaudy by the discovery of some costumes which had been shared among the dancers. Lizzie Loring was in a cape of gauze that glittered with spangles. Sir William, presented with a massively plumed hat, swept it off in gallant obeisance to the applauding revellers whose laughter filled the candlelit arena.

Christopher Vane, handing off one partner to link arms with another, saw that he must inevitably be drawn to offer a hand to Martha so, with an elegant sidestep, he left the dance. He stepped under the gallery, took a glass of wine, and saw Major Otto Zeigler, Sir William's Hessian interpreter, standing gloomy and alone in the shadows.

"I'm drunk," Zeigler said in bald reply to Vane's greeting.

"And why not, Otto?" Vane watched Peggy Shippen, draped in a robe of royal purple, staring enraptured into Captain Andre's face.

"We should be fighting, not dancing," the Hessian grumbled.

"Indeed."

"You English don't know how to fight a war. You can dance, *ja*, but you don't fight. You are betrayed and you do nothing! Nothing!"

"We . . ." Vane turned, but Zeigler had abruptly gone into the antechamber where, with a marvellous dexterity, the Hessian officers ran their fast and profitable faro bank. Zeigler sat, took out a handful of coins, and joined the game.

Christopher Vane, the dancing suddenly forgotten, went into the antechamber and stood behind the interpreter. He watched for a while as Zeigler, drunk beyond caring, lost money fast. Faro was not a game of finesse but merely of luck, in which the players guessed the order in which the cards would be revealed. Zeigler consistently backed the Pharaoh itself, the King of Hearts on which any wager was doubled.

Vane leaned down beside Zeigler. "What do you mean, Otto, betrayed?"

Zeigler searched his pockets for more coins and found two guineas. "My last funds," he said. "If I lose these I shall blow my goddamned bloody brains out." A score of officers had similarly killed themselves because of the winter's gambling debts.

"What do you mean," Vane asked again, "betrayed?"

"Who damn cares?" Zeigler havered his last two guineas between the Pharaoh and the Three of Diamonds, then, with the air of a doomed man, plumped for the lesser card.

"Tell me, Otto!"

"I might kill myself and you pester me! Pester!"

Christopher Vane, smiling, took the two guineas from the Three of Diamonds and put them on the Pharaoh. "I'm feeling lucky tonight, Otto."

"For Christ's . . ." Zeigler's hand shot out to move his money back to the safer card, but Vane gripped the Hessian's wrist and held it firm until the bank began revealing their deck. Vane estimated there were sixty or seventy guineas depending on this hand, but only Zeigler's money was wagered on the Pharaoh.

"You can be a bastard, Vane." Zeigler, his wrist released, watched the cards turn. "It's my last money. If I lose that I have nothing. Only a bullet."

"I told you, I'm feeling lucky. I pay your losses, you keep your winnings."

The sixth card of the bank's deck was the King of Hearts. Money was scooped from around the table, doubled from the bank's hoard, and the whole golden pile pushed towards the drunken Hessian. "Sweet Jesus." Zeigler stared at his fortune.

Vane scooped all of the winnings into his handkerchief. "Now come and talk to me."

"That's my money!"

"You can have it when you've talked to me."

Zeigler grumbled, but obeyed. He fetched himself a bottle of claret and staggered to a small table where Vane waited for him. "Donop," Zeigler explained when Vane repeated his question, "was betrayed."

Vane had to think for a moment before he remembered that Donop was the Hessian general who had led the attack on Fort Mercer in the autumn. The General had been wounded in the carnage of the failed assault, captured, and had died three days later.

"They knew we were coming." Zeigler poured himself a glass of wine. "You do not have a glass. You need a glass. Gentlemen do not drink from the bottle in front of ladies." He turned and peered at the women who sat round the faro table. "Even whores."

"Why do you think Donop was betrayed?"

"You do not have a glass!" Zeigler said in drunken indignation.

Vane patiently fetched himself a glass, poured himself wine, and sat again. "Why?"

"Because I was told it, that is why! You have my money!"

"I shall give it you. Who told you?"

Zeigler belched. "My God. We shall bet one guinea a bottle, Kit? We shall then drink the bottles, *ja*? The first to fall on the floor loses." He laughed, pleased with the idea. "You agree?"

"Who told you, Otto?"

Zeigler frowned in the effort of memory. "I once drank seventeen bottles against a Russian. No one outdrinks a German, Kit, you know that? He was a big fellow, too! I shall fetch the bottles." He made the declaration with great decisiveness, but was too weary to rise from his chair. Instead, he finished his glass of wine, poured another, then shook his head. "They shouldn't have beat us. We were betrayed, Kit, betrayed!"

"Who told you?"

"The rebeller prisoners!" Zeigler said indignantly, as if he had already explained the whole matter. "The ones who fell in the river. I talked to them to find out about Donop. One of them told me." He paused, and Vane prayed that the moment of lucidity would continue. Zeigler belched again. He was sweating and short of breath. He must have been drinking, Vane decided, since midday.

"What did the prisoner say?"

"It was a long time ago," Zeigler said wearily.

"I know it was a long time ago, but what did he say, Otto?"

"He said they knew!" Again Zeigler was indignant. "The rebellers were told! They were ready! They were waiting!" He shouted the words, attracting glances from the faro players.

"Fort Mercer was warned?"

"*Ja*! Here." Zeigler feverishly searched his pockets to produce a small notebook that he slapped as proof on to the table. He searched the pages. "A Lieutenant Lynch told me, there! You see? I make a note of it."

The note was in scribbled German and meant nothing to Vane. "What did he say?"

"He said they were warned! I want my money."

"How could they have been warned. No one knew."

Zeigler helped himself to Vane's glass. "No one keeps secrets, Kit. They all have whores, don't they?" He picked up the pack of cards that waited for the dollar whist which would start later in the evening. "Blab, blab in bed, my friend. Blab, blab. No secrets!" He spilt the cards across the floor in disgust. "And four hundred of my countrymen are dead in a ditch!"

"And Lynch didn't tell you who brought the letter?"

"No. He was boasting at first, but then he became, how do you say, like the grave."

"Silent," Vane said. It made sense, too. Vane had seen newly captured prisoners brimming with defiance, not ready to accept that they had been defeated, and Vane had listened to them taunt and boast to their captors. Doubtless this Lieutenant Lynch, dragged from the cold river, had wanted to flaunt a victory in the face of his captors and had thus allowed himself the indiscretion.

"You are not drinking," Zeigler accused Vane.

"I am drinking." Vane felt the horror of Zeigler's revelations. Only a handful of officers, those closest to Sir William, had known of the attack on the forts. One of those officers had, at best, been indiscreet or, at worst, was a traitor. Vane remembered, too, how Sir William's December march north had been betrayed, else why had Washington been fortified and ready? He frowned. "Why didn't you tell anyone earlier, Otto?"

"I did! I told Billy, didn't I? But Billy doesn't care." The German began to laugh, then solemnly declaimed a mocking verse that had swept the city:

Sir William, he, snug as a flea,
Lies all this time a'snoring,
Nor dreaming of harm, as he lies warm,
In bed with Mrs Loring.

Vane, in his growing impatience with Sir William's inactivity, had assiduously spread the scurrilous verse himself, but nevertheless smiled polite appreciation as though he now heard it for the first time. "Billy must have done something, Otto?"

"He said I should forget it. Forget it! Four hundred men dead! And I must forget it!"

Vane looked sideways through the arch. Sir William was dancing with Martha Crowl, and the sight put a spasm of hatred through Vane's jealous soul. Forget treachery? That was typical of Sir William who believed that a soft answer would turn away wrath. The rebel army had been at Valley Forge all winter, scarce three days' march away, yet Sir William had done nothing. Vane, seeing victory frittered away by inactivity, had broadcast the mocking verse to try and shame his master into action. Instead, Sir William danced with Martha Crowl, who was allowed to flaunt her patriotism in the highest circles of the British command.

Zeigler gave a sour laugh. "The English aren't serious about war, Kit. I like Billy, truly, but you cannot be nice to the enemy." He suddenly became angry. "Nice! Nice! Nice! You must hit them and cut them and make them frightened. We shouldn't be dancing here, we should be slaughtering Yankees!"

"We can't if we're betrayed."

"Then hang the betrayers." Zeigler put the bottle to his lips and finished the wine. "Where's my money?"

"Here." Vane pushed the handkerchief across the table, but

palmed some of the coins into his own hand. "Is Lieutenant Lynch still alive?"

"Who cares?" Zeigler hiccupped, then rested his head on the golden pile of guineas. "I shall sleep."

Christopher Vane took the small notebook and tore out the page with the prisoner's name. He pushed the folded paper into a pocket. The war was not lost yet. The French still havered, and there was yet a chance that the enemy could be brought to battle in the early spring. Crush Washington and the French would flinch from another beating, but not if the British were betrayed. And Vane, watching the Widow glitter in the candlelight, was determined that, this time, there would be no betrayal to cheat the royal army of its victory.

THIRTY

White clouds sailed across a blue sky. There was warmth at last in the sunlight. The nights were still cold and the wind could yet cut like a blade, but the land had lost its deadness and a sparkle touched the waters. Spring was bringing its green to a seaboard, and Philadelphia prepared for a new season of war.

Gunners practised their aim by firing at casks floated down the Delaware, the infantry ran with full packs to harden muscles grown lazy in winter, and cavalry sabres spewed sparks from grindstones as edges were honed for the killing.

Horses as well as men had to be hardened and Sam exercised his charges into battle strength. He took them to the Neck and pounded them across softening ground to put muscle beneath their pelts. Back in the Lutheran church that had been their winter stable he would bang their coats with bundled straw, then brush them till they gleamed. He trained Captain Vane's young stallion to war; firing muskets close to its ears, shouting at the beast, trying to scare it, yet always reassuring the horse that, whatever danger seemed to threaten, it could live and survive. Sam taught the stallion to rear and lash out with its hooves so that infantrymen, trying to attack its rider, would flinch away. Each morning the training went on, and each morning Sam would lead his string of horses past Jonathon's house and once, soon after the river ice melted, Sam had seen Jonathon through a downstairs window. He waved, but Jonathon did not see him.

A month later, on the morning after the theatre's subscription ball, Sam was rasping down the hoof walls of the black stallion. A breeze fretted at the broken windows which let out the fumes from a brazier which stood in the chancel of the church. Sam, whistling tunelessly as he worked, was alone. He had stripped off his red coat and donned a farrier's apron. Sparrows which had taken up residence in the church during the harsh winter flew down to peck at oat husks.

He heard the church's main door open and, assuming it was another groom, called out a cheerfully rude reminder not to leave the bloody door open.

"You're just another arrogant Englishman," said a voice, "ordering us humble colonials about."

Sam dropped the file, let go of the stallion's fetlock, and stared down the aisle. "Jonathon!" He kicked the stool over and ran down the church. "Just look at you! Pegleg!"

"Hello, Sam." Jonathon smiled with shy pleasure at the reunion.

Sam had no shyness. He threw his arms around Jonathon who had stumped in on his one good leg and on one leather-tipped wooden peg. Two crutches gave him stability. "I told you!" Sam said triumphantly. "I said you'd be walking!"

"It's my first proper walk," Jonathon explained. "They fitted it two weeks ago, and I've been hopping round the house ever since." He leaned against one of the empty stalls to take the weight off his stump that had been rubbed raw by the friction of the leather cup strapped to his thigh. "It's better than the old leg but it's awful sore."

"It will be." Sam saw there was a new hardness in Jonathon's face; lines put there by pain. "It takes time to settle a wooden leg, you know."

Jonathon still smiled. "I have to thank you, don't I? It was the beestings."

Sam shrugged the thanks away. "Caroline did most of that."

"She says it was you." Jonathon looked up the aisle towards the vestry door. "She said she'd meet me here."

Sam felt an immediate quickening of his pulse, but knew he must hide the sudden excitement. "Here?" He asked the confirmation casually, as though he did not care one way or the other.

"There is a guard on me," Jonathon spoke mockingly, but through the still open door Sam could see a servant leaning against the outer porch. Jonathon pushed the door closed with his crutch. "My uncle still thinks I'll run away, so I'm only allowed outdoors with a groom to keep me loyal. He's had enough of horses, though, so he won't come in."

"Then how does Caroline. . . ?"

"We write to each other." Jonathon's face was still thin from the illness, but there was colour in his cheeks and a brightness in his eyes. He grinned, evidently pleased with his cleverness. "One of the kitchenmaids smuggles letters to Martha's house, and Martha sends them to Caroline."

"I haven't seen Caroline, oh," Sam shrugged, "for months!"

"She says she was frightened by those two men. Remember? I have to thank you for that, too."

"She was wonderful!" Sam said warmly, then remembered how he had held Caroline in the wet night after their escape, and the remembrance of that intimacy, which seemed so long ago, made him silent.

Jonathon looked up the aisle again, evidently impatient. "She said she'd come in the back way."

"She always used to," Sam said, "before . . ." Again his words tailed off. "You must have missed her?"

"More than the leg." Jonathon laughed grimly, then heaved himself on to the crutches and began pegging and lurching towards the chancel.

Sam walked beside him. He saw the stallion's ears prick back and he knew someone had made a sound in the vestry. Sam told himself that his winter dreams about Caroline had been just that: dreams. Absence made the heart grow fonder and also made the absent one seem even more desirable, and so Sam tried to convince himself that when Caroline walked through the low arched door he would see a commonplace girl and he would have no cause to feel the jealousy of which he was so ashamed.

Then the door opened, and she stood there.

Jonathon hurried forward, clumsy on his crutches, and for a moment Caroline looked past Jonathon and stared at Sam.

And Sam, who had been so impatient for the ice's melting, suddenly felt tongue-tied. "Hello, miss."

"Hello, Sam." Caroline said, then she walked towards Jonathon, and Sam turned away as the two embraced at the foot of the chancel's steps. He stroked the stallion and tried not to listen to the joy of the reunion behind him.

But Jonathon would not let Sam be excluded from that joy. He bombarded Sam with questions. Wasn't Caroline looking well, wasn't this the happiest day, and wasn't it wonderful to be together again?

If Sam was to answer, then Sam was forced to look at Caroline, and he saw that nothing had changed. Nothing. He blushed. "It's been a long time, miss."

"Nearly four months, Sam."

Caroline was not commonplace, she could not be dismissed from Sam's dreams, and he saw how his vision of her, which he had conjured in the long snow-silenced nights, had been so wooden and wrong. He had not remembered the life in her face, or the defiance and wildness and humour of those blue eyes and strong jaw. "I've been busy," Caroline explained lamely. "It's calving time."

"It would be, yes."

"But Jonathon wanted to meet me." Caroline seemed to need to explain their sudden presence. "I said we should meet here."

"I'm glad."

Caroline took her hand from Jonathon and walked to the nearest box-pew where she fondled Lord Robert Massedene's grey gelding. "We need your help, Sam." Her voice was strangely flat, almost unfriendly.

"Anything."

She turned to him. "We're going soon."

"In three weeks." Jonathon bubbled with eagerness. Plainly they had planned this escape in their secret correspondence, but now Sam must be told.

"You're going north?" Sam had waited so long to see Caroline, and now she was going. He could hardly bear to look at her.

"By boat to Trenton," Jonathon said. "I can't do any fighting, Sam, but I can clerk."

"For the rebels?"

"Yes." Jonathon gave a small, embarrassed laugh. "Of course."

Sam forced a smile. "Perhaps I'll have to shoot at you again?"

"Maybe."

"The difficulty," Caroline interrupted in a flatly determined voice, almost as though their friendly trivia annoyed her, "is getting Jonathon out of the city. He's still a prisoner, so he can't get a pass."

"I suppose not," Sam said. Sir William, in the last few weeks, had instituted a system of passes for anyone wanting to travel beyond the ring of British guardposts. It was intended to deter paroled rebel officers who, even though they had each put up a one-hundred-pound bond to seal their promise not to attempt an escape, still tried to rejoin Washington's army.

"But the sentries know you, Sam." Caroline turned to face Sam and her look was almost defiant. It was as though she expected Sam to resist her demands. "If you were helping a drunken officer into a boat, no one would take any notice, would they?"

"No."

"So we need a uniform."

Sam wiped his hands on his leather apron. "What time of day were you thinking of going?"

"At night." Jonathon glanced towards the main door of the church, obviously afraid that his uncle's groom would overhear this conspiratorial plotting.

"Better be a naval uniform then," Sam said. "They're the only officers on the river at night. Going back to their ships, you see . . ." His voice petered out.

"Can you get me one?" Jonathon asked.

Sam nodded. "And the pegleg won't matter so much. There's a couple of navy fellows on stumps."

Jonathon smiled. "I knew you'd help, Sam."

"Daft as lights, I am," Sam smiled back.

Jonathon glanced towards the main door again, then looked sheepishly at Sam. "Do you mind if we go in the vestry?"

"It's a tack room now," Sam said.

Caroline had gone back to Jonathon's side. "Thank you, Sam."

Sam heard the farewell in her voice. "It was good seeing you again, Miss Caroline." The formality seemed strange, but to use any other form of address would have been to hint at their former brief intimacy that Caroline, by her attitude, was at pains to deny.

"You could take the uniform to Mrs Crowl?" Caroline asked in her distant voice that hurt Sam.

"I can."

"I'll try and come again, Sam." Jonathon held out his hand. Sam took it and felt the strength of the grip. Jonathon, using his hands to replace his missing leg, had put on muscle.

"I'll get the uniform," Sam promised, then watched as Caroline helped Jonathon into the vestry. The door closed behind them.

Sam stood for a moment, then went back to the stallion. He rubbed its nose. "You shouldn't have dreams, eh? Daft things, dreams. Only let you down." He sat, lifted the hoof, and worked on the horny hoof walls till the stallion's frog stood proud to give the horse a grip. Sam had waited for so long, and let his hopes soar to such dizzy, silly heights, and now he had been flattened. He closed his eyes suddenly, as though he was afraid of tears.

Sam's eyes were still closed as the vestry door opened behind him. He listened to the footsteps on the chancel's flagstones. He dared not look in case he was disappointed.

"Hello, Sam."

He opened his eyes to find he was not disappointed.

Caroline stared at him, then gave a small, embarrassed shrug as though the explanation she was about to give was not really necessary, but perhaps dutiful. "He went out the back way. He daren't stay away too long in case they get suspicious."

Sam tacked the horseshoe on to the hoof. Later he would take the stallion to a forge and secure the shoe properly, but the job would suffice for the moment. "He daren't be seen with you?" Sam spoke without looking up from his work.

"He's frightened of his uncle. Frightened he might not get his inheritance." Caroline sat on the pulpit steps. "He'll be better when we reach Trenton."

"Where you'll marry him?" Sam, as he watched how the stallion stood on the filed hoof, had tried to make his voice careless, but he heard the edge of bitterness in his words.

"I promised." Caroline spoke guardedly.

Sam patted the stallion's withers. "That's better, boy, isn't it? You won't be slipping and sliding now."

The stallion whinnied in answer. Caroline was silent. The sound of wagon wheels and of a whip cracking came from Race Street. "How are you, Sam?" Caroline broke the silence.

"Glad that the spring's come. Everyone is. Winter chafes the nerves, doesn't it?"

"Yes."

"And hard winters you have here. But the fighting time's come, hasn't it, boy?" He addressed the question to the stallion which, in affection, nudged its muzzle against Sam's cheek.

Caroline stood again, then climbed the chancel steps. The sunlight, coming through the broken window above her, glinted on her hair. "What's going to happen to you, Sam?"

"To me?" Sam laughed as though the answer did not matter, though in truth he had given the question much thought through the winter months. "I shall be all right."

"Tell me."

Sam hesitated for a second, then shrugged. "I cured the General's horse of the colic and his man reckons Billy might give me a job in his stables."

"Is that good?" Caroline's voice was bleak.

"It could get me out of the army."

"I thought you enlisted for life?"

Sam smiled. "You do, but if they like you they fiddle the papers, see? If the general wants me in his own stables at home then he'll fetch me out. When the fighting's over, of course."

"Is that what you want?"

Sam led the stallion towards its pew. "It's better than carrying a musket."

Caroline nodded. For a few seconds she said nothing, then her voice was oddly quiet, almost inaudible. "I've been hoping that you'd come with us, Sam."

At first Sam thought he had misheard, then, turning to look at her, he saw from her face that he had not. "To Trenton?"

"That's where we're going."

For a moment Sam did not know what to say. He shrugged, half-laughed, then shook his head. "You want me to fight my own side?"

"There's plenty of Redcoats who've changed sides, Sam."

"Aye. My brother wanted to, and look where he is now. I've watched them, miss, with blood dripping down their legs from the whips."

"You're frightened?" Caroline spoke with a hint of scorn.

"No, miss, I'm not frightened." Sam led the stallion into its stall. He did not tie the head rope, but just latched the low door shut. "But I'm a bit like Jonathon, you see. Only one thing will make me run, and it isn't the liberty you go on about."

Caroline said nothing. She held her hands towards the charcoal in the brazier.

Sam knew the moment had come to say the words he had rehearsed through the long weeks, but now that they should be said, he found the saying too hard and chose a circumlocution instead. "I kept waiting for the ice to melt."

Caroline stared into the flames. It was as if she had not heard his words, but finally, and as softly as before, she answered him with an evasion to match Sam's own. "We made Jonathon better, Sam."

"We did."

"And we knew what that meant."

"Aye, we did."

Caroline still watched the tiny flicker of flames about the glowing charcoal. "I wasn't asking you to come for me, Sam."

"What for, then? Fifty acres of land and three hogs?" Sam's voice was scornful.

The scorn prompted Caroline to look at Sam again, and to put an urgent pleading into her voice. "It's a whole new country, Sam. A whole future, something for ever! Something good and shining. Not like the Old World, Sam. Can't you see that? We're going to make a new beginning, Sam, and it won't be rotten and corrupt. It will be clean!" All her passion and all her hopes seethed in her voice. "God's country, Sam. A good country. You could be happy, Sam, you could – "

Caroline stopped speaking because the main church door had banged open and a red-coated officer, sword at his waist, came into the church. His loud and strident voice echoed down the aisle. "Sam! Sam! Sam!" Captain Christopher Vane strode between the horse-occupied pews. "Sam, you varlet! Have you finished? I have need of . . ." Vane's voice tailed away as he caught sight of Caroline. He stopped abruptly, stared, then swept off his hat to offer a low, sweeping bow. "Dear lady. I don't believe we've met?"

Caroline said nothing. Vane, who was clearly in one of his more cheerful moods, straightened up. "Aren't you going to introduce me, Sam?"

Sam's embarrassment was excruciating, but he managed to stumble out an introduction. "Miss Caroline, sir. Captain Vane, miss."

"Miss Caroline!" Vane said the name as though it belonged to an angel. He stared shamelessly at her, struck by her quick and lively beauty. This might be a peasant girl, but she could make the heart race in springtime, and Vane, astonished by her, felt the jealous impulse that must have spurred ashlar lances to break against dragons' hides. This girl, he thought, was too good for a mere groom! "Are you Sam's mysterious kitchenmaid?"

Caroline was quick. She nodded. "Yes, sir."

"My dear Sam, no wonder you keep her a secret!"

"I shouldn't be here, sir." Caroline edged towards the vestry door.

"Please! Miss Caroline!" Vane was at his most charming. "I wouldn't want to drive you from Sam's side."

"No, sir. I have to be going." She nodded at Sam and almost ran out through the tack room.

Vane waited till the outer door banged shut. "My God, Sam! She might be golden-haired, but she's quite lovely."

"She's nice, sir."

"Nice?" Vane whirled on his servant. "Good God, boy! Men have killed for less! Is this where you meet her? No wonder you spend so long in the stables, Sam. So would I! If you ever tire of her?" Vane saw the flicker of irritation on Sam's face, and quickly shook his head. "Forget I said it, Sam. I had no right. I apologize." Vane smiled. "But really you're foolish, Sam."

"Foolish, sir?"

"A soldier should never become attached to a pretty girl. Always choose an ugly one. The essential pleasure is no different, and they're much easier to leave behind. They're also damned grateful." Vane laughed, then fondled the stallion's nose. "How is he?"

"Footing properly now, sir."

"Truly?"

Sam smiled. "Stand away from him, sir." He waited till Vane, with a puzzled expression, had obeyed, then gave a short sharp whistle. The stallion whinnied, gathered itself, and jumped clean over the low door of the pew. It trotted obediently to Sam and lowered its head for his affection.

Vane laughed. "Teaching him tricks?"

"He's a good one, sir. The best." Sam led the stallion back into the stall and tied the head rope. "He's fine now, sir. Did you want to take him out?"

"No, no. I'm just passing the time of day, Sam." Vane looked around the church's bare interior, almost as if this were the first time he had seen it. "It's a dull church, isn't it?"

"Yes, sir." Sam wondered why the Captain was making such inconsequential conversation.

"Dull, dull, dull." Vane turned to look at the nave. "A church needs mystery, Sam. It needs the dark space behind the altar. It's like a country. It needs a touch of ghosts and vengeance, of kings and nobility, of history that reeks of the inexplicable, but not here! Oh, no! Here they will have sweet reason and I pray to their profitable God that they stay a dull and boring people, for if they encounter a mystery there will be nothing in their creed to explain it. What was the name of that sergeant who so scared the tripe out of you?"

The last question was asked so suddenly, and came so abruptly in the middle of one of Vane's eloquent diatribes, that Sam could not gather his wits. "Sir?"

"The one who was married to what's her name? Sacharissa?"

Sam sounded horrified. "Scammell, sir?"

"That's it! Thank you, Sam." The Captain turned to leave.

"Sir!"

Vane turned back. "Sam?"

Sam was alarmed. Since the night when Scammell had tried to hold Caroline against Maggie's return, Sam had neither seen nor heard of Sergeant Michael Scammell, and he would have liked that happy ignorance to continue. "You're not going to report him, are you, sir?"

"Report him?" Vane was all innocence.

"'Cause of what I told you? About the boy at Germantown, sir? The one he killed?"

"It was murder, Sam!" Vane teased Sam with a mocking tone. "Do you think he shouldn't be punished?"

"He should be hung, sir, but if he knows I told you then he'll kick the liver out of me."

Vane laughed. "I'm not going to report him, Samuel, so calm your troubled self. My reasons are altogether more whimsical. I am informed that the beautiful Sacharissa has formed an attachment, Sam. She is enraptured, and the officer concerned does not wish for any trouble from her husband. You follow me now?"

"They were never church married, sir."

"Nevertheless I have promised to square the man, so don't worry, Samuel. I am not about to invite the wrath of Sergeant Scammell on your head."

"He's a bastard, sir," Sam said warningly.

"Bastards will bring us victory. Those and good horses like you, my friend." Vane patted the stallion's neck. "Thank you, Sam."

Sam watched the Captain go and wondered why the skin of his spine was suddenly chill. He shivered, then, without really knowing why, drew his winter-blunted bayonet and, with his usual care and skill, sharpened it on a stone. Spring had come, and dark things stirred themselves for war.

THIRTY-ONE

Captain Christopher Vane met Sergeant Scammell outside a stone building which had windows disfigured by rusted iron bars. Vane, even though he had only glimpsed Scammell once, and that in the litter of a battlefield, recognized the Sergeant instantly. A tall man with knowing eyes whose good looks were too savage to be called handsome, Scammell gave the impression of being a man who could never be astonished by any of the world's callous ways. "You're Sergeant Scammell?" Vane asked, as if to belie the shock of recognition.

"Sir!" Scammell still bore the scar on his leg gouged by a bullet in a winter's night. He knew this officer was the master of the man who had inflicted that scar and, because of it, Scammell was wary.

"My name is Vane, Captain Vane."

"I remember you, sir." Scammell's eyes searched Vane's face, seeking for a weakness that could be exploited. "Orders, sir?"

"To do nothing, say nothing, unless I tell you." Vane turned and tugged on a bellpull to provoke a mournful clanging somewhere within the gloomy building.

Scammell watched the street, despising the civilians who hurried past in the small rain. Scammell had been told by a puzzled Lieutenant-Colonel Elliott that Captain Vane had requested his help, and Scammell knew that such a request, because it was a request and not an order, probably did not presage trouble for himself. But he was still curious and somewhat nervous. "Did Sam tell you about me, sir?"

"He told me you murdered a boy at Germantown." Vane said it harshly, and was rewarded by a flicker of fear on the tall Sergeant's face.

"I should have murdered more than one boy." Scammell spoke the challenge softly.

Vane ignored the words. He wondered whether he had given away an advantage by revealing so early his power over this intimidating man, yet the revelation should secure the Sergeant's loyalty. And Vane needed that loyalty. He was ashamed of the need, bitterly so, yet ambition and jealousy led Vane inexorably onwards. A war was being lost because of hesitation, and it was time for someone to become brutal. Vane rang the bell again and was immediately rewarded by the door's opening. A British sentry admitted the two men into a wide entrance hall that twitched with a gibbering, slobbering horde of maniacs who, as fast as their chains allowed, shuffled to investigate the newcomers. "Welcome to Parliament, sir," the sentry said confidingly to Vane.

"What's that?" Vane edged away from a half-naked, dribbling man who was trying to lick the rainwater from his topboots.

"That's what we calls 'em, sir. The lunatics." The guard booted a woman back against the wall. She pulled a heavy breast out of her rags and offered it to Captain Vane. Scammell, following the officer, laughed at the sight.

Vane waited as the sentry unlocked the iron grating which gave access to that part of the asylum which had been taken over as a prison for captured American officers. The New Jail on Walnut Street was full, but the asylum had cells, bars and locks as secure as any proper prison. It also stank like a prison. Vane's nose wrinkled with distaste as he followed the sentry through the cellblock reeking of excrement. There was no heating in this part of the asylum; a single lice-ridden blanket was provided for each prisoner and a thin, fetid layer of straw put into each cell. The prisoners, those who had survived the bitter winter, were in rags, and most of them huddled in fever-racking shivers in corners of their cells. Vane, whose arrival was expected, was shown into a large stone-walled room where a table and chair waited. A sour-faced lieutenant, one of the jail's duty officers, ordered the prisoner James Lynch to be fetched. "You'll want tea, sir?" he asked Vane.

"I'm not here to entertain him, Lieutenant," Vane said curtly. "Just leave us."

While he waited, Vane took papers, an inkwell, and quills from his sabretache and arranged them on the table. Sergeant Scammell, watching the officer, linked his fingers, reversed his hands, and pushed outwards till the knuckles cracked. The sound made Vane look up. Scammell smiled. Vane, sensing that this man saw into his soul, sat and pretended to be busy with his papers.

The door opened and a prisoner dressed in a thin ticken jacket over soiled calico breeches was thrust into the room. The man had a face paled by long imprisonment, and uncut hair that he had pathetically tried to tie into a semblance of respectability. He shivered from the cold. "You again." The rebel prisoner spoke scornfully.

Vane was still sorting through the papers on the table and did not bother to look up. "Indeed it is. Good morning, Lieutenant."

Lieutenant Lynch turned and inspected the Sergeant who waited behind him. Scammell's face made the rebel officer shiver, then turn back to Vane. "I want parole!"

"So you said at our last meeting." That meeting had been four days before, in the early morning after the subscription ball, and the outcome had driven Captain Vane to seek Sergeant Scammell's help. He still hoped that help would not be required.

Lynch still insisted. "I have a right to parole! I'm an officer!"

Vane looked up at him. Lynch's face was pockmarked, scarred, and gaunt. The winter's hunger and disease had nearly broken him, yet there was still a feverish defiance in the haggard face. Vane shrugged. "You may have parole, Lieutenant, on the payment of one hundred pounds."

Lynch, who could not even imagine amassing such a fortune, spat his protest towards the elegant Captain Vane. "It's our right! It don't take money!"

Vane smiled. "You forfeited your right, Lieutenant, by your dishonourable behaviour. If American officers could keep solemn oaths, then no bond would be required."

"I don't need lessons in honour from the English!" Lynch still had a trace of an Irish accent, and all the defiance of that race.

"It's evident you do." Vane sounded amused. The oath of parole would release a captive rebel officer to live freely within the city, but the oath also bound such a man, on his solemn honour, not to attempt to rejoin Washington's army. Too many American officers, despising the oath as an anachronistic foible, and seeing within it their chance to escape, had made the promise, then run. George Washington, in his correspondence with Sir William, had deplored their behaviour, but not returned such men to captivity. The correspondence was entirely consumed with matters concerning the comforts of prisoners, and both sides, with equal cynicism, assured the other that their prisoners received only the finest attention. Vane smiled at Lynch. "You have a hundred pounds, Lieutenant?"

"You know I don't."

"Then you must stay as His Majesty's guest." Vane opened his inkwell and dipped a quill in the liquid as if to demonstrate that the pleasantries were now over and the proper business of this meeting could begin. "Your name is Lieutenant James Lynch, and you were an officer in the garrison at Fort Mercer. Is that correct?"

"And why aren't you feeding us? We get slops, you bastard! It ain't food!"

Sergeant Scammell shifted against the wall, as if eager to teach this rebel a lesson in manners. Vane ignored the Sergeant. "Your Mister Washington is required to provide your rations, not us. Would you kindly answer my question, Lieutenant?"

"You know damn well who I am. How many times do you need to ask me, Englishman?"

"As often as is necessary," Vane said mildly. He wrote Lynch's name on a clean sheet of paper. "You recall the Hessian attack on Fort Mercer?"

"I remember killing a score of you bastards."

"Who brought you warning of that attack?"

"No one."

So far the questioning had followed the course of Vane's first interrogation of Lynch: virulent protests at the conditions inside the jail interspersed with blank denials. Vane let excess ink run from the quill's tip, then laid the feather down beside the paper. "You told Major Zeigler that you were warned. I wish to know who brought that message."

"There was no message."

Vane stood, walked to the small barred window, and stared into a courtyard where tiny shoots of new grass showed green beneath a dead, black tree. "There was a bastion at Fort Mercer which your garrison abandoned. On the night before the attack it was re-occupied. You would not do such an arbitrary thing, Lieutenant, unless you had been given warning of an imminent attack." Vane turned, his boots scraping on the stone. "I know you were warned. You boasted of receiving the message when you were first captured. I have a record of your words."

"I lied. We weren't warned. We beat you square, Englishman, and we'll beat you square out of this whole country!"

Vane sighed and walked back to the table. He wanted the name of the messenger, for the messenger could lead him to the next link in this chain of betrayal. He searched the papers on the table and brought out a sheet that bore a red-wax seal. "This, lieutenant, is a warrant which grants me the authority to deliver you to our guardpost on the Wissahickon Road. There you will be provided with clothes, a horse, and money. You may then go free to wherever you wish within the colonies." He put the paper on the table where Lynch could read the words. "All you need to do is tell me who warned you of the attack on Fort Mercer."

Lynch stared at the paper, then looked up at Vane. "Piss on you, mister."

Vane walked close to the rebel. "What elegant officers Mister Washington is reduced to employing. No wonder your men run like rabbits in battle." Vane stared at Lynch as though daring the man to attack him. Lynch seemed to be tempted, but controlled himself. Vane sighed. "Sergeant Scammell!"

"Sir?"

"You heard my questions?"

"Distinctly, sir!"

"You might be more efficacious than myself at eliciting the answers?"

Scammell understood the intent, if not the exact meaning of the words. "I might, sir. But I want a word first."

Vane turned, astonished at the Sergeant's defiance, yet helpless in the face of it. The orders he gave were illegal, and well Scammell knew it, so Vane could do nothing but nod and gesture to the door. "Outside."

They were gone five minutes, leaving Lynch to contemplate his fate. They were five minutes in which Captain Vane made a pact with the devil, and Sergeant Scammell discovered the desperation for victory that burned inside the Captain.

At the end of that five minutes, the cell door re-opened and Sergeant Scammell ducked under the lintel. He came in alone, locked the door, then stared into Lynch's face. "You have one minute, fuckpig, to tell me everything."

"I am an officer and you call me – "

Scammell did not bother to wait the minute, but started his work.

Christopher Vane walked away from the sound. He wanted clean air, unsullied by excrement and horror. He kicked the lunatics aside and went into the street where, leaning on the asylum's outer wall, he filled his lungs with the damp chill of the April air.

What he did was wrong, and he knew it. It was dishonourable, and that galled him, yet from the dishonour, and from the devil's pact he had made with a sergeant, could come one of the keys to victory. There was a traitor, and the traitor was close to Sir William, and there could be no victory unless the traitor was stopped. And victory, Vane persuaded himself, justified any act, for victory would discourage France and crush an insolent rebellion. This spring, despite Sir William's vacillations that sprang from his hopes of peace, the army would have to make one great effort to trap and destroy the rebel army, but that effort would be in vain if it was betrayed. And so Vane vindicated what happened now within the bare, cold room, yet, even as he thus persuaded himself, the sudden fear of discovery griped at his belly.

A jingle of harness made him turn. Coming down the street and drawn by two spirited greys was a high-sprung phaeton with yellow wheels and a scarlet body. On the driver's box, the reins held with an aplomb more usual in a coachman, sat Sir William Howe. Behind him sat Lizzie Loring.

Christopher Vane, not wanting to be seen, twisted away. He was hiding from his own kind, like a criminal, and he had an urge to plunge back into the madhouse to end the savagery that could destroy him.

Instead, safe again inside the asylum, he listened to the horrid sounds which slowly, slowly faded. It took twenty minutes, but at the end of that time Sergeant Scammell came out of the cell with the answers that Captain Vane had sought. "It was a bugger called Davie Logan, sir." Scammell's hands were bloodied. "He's a ferryman, sir, somewhere up the river. He has one eye and a broken nose."

Vane stared at the big Sergeant. "He's not from the city?"

"Up river, sir. A few miles."

"Jesus." Vane said it softly. He had expected the name of someone within Philadelphia. He had hoped for the name of Martha Crowl, but now he was given a name that meant nothing, and a name which belonged to a man who lived out of Vane's reach. He swore softly. "Are you sure?"

"I'm sure." Scammell's voice was grim.

"How's the prisoner?" Vane's question was perfunctory.

"Dying, sir."

Vane's gaze snapped up. "Dying?"

Scammell, who had the measure of this officer now, gave a scornful grin. "And what the hell else did you want? How were you going to explain one beaten Yankee?"

"I ordered you to frighten him!"

"I did." The words were implacable.

"Christ!" Vane moved to the cell door, looked inside, and almost retched again. He had to steady himself on the door's jamb. "Oh my God."

"I'll say he attacked you, sir." Sergeant Scammell was quite unmoved by the bloody and twitching thing on the floor. "We had to kill him, see? He went berserk, he did."

Vane could not speak. He had intended Lynch to be scared, he had wanted the prisoner to confess the name, but he had never dreamed of savagery such as this. He forced back the retching, then thought that, just as surely as Sergeant Scammell, he could hang for this. He doubled over, gagging.

Scammell stepped past him and drew his bayonet from its scabbard. He stooped, and Captain Vane turned quickly away from the sight. Lynch's breathing, which had been hoarse and whimpering, suddenly stopped.

Scammell stood up. "There won't be no trouble, sir."

"Jesus." Vane was having to snatch for breath.

"He attacked you, fought like a bloody lunatic, and I had to kill him." Scammell wiped the blood from the bayonet and left the cell. He was in command now.

Vane nodded weakly. "Yes, Sergeant."

"He ain't the first prisoner to go to hell, sir."

Vane needed the reassurance desperately. "I'm sure."

"And Maggie, sir?" Scammell, taller than Vane, looked confidingly down on the officer. "I'll come tonight?"

The Sergeant's confiding and conspiratorial tone clawed at Vane's self-esteem. He straightened up, determined to regain mastery of this horrific relationship. "You'll get your woman back, Sergeant, when I discover whether you've earned her."

Scammell's eyes seemed to flare with a defiant rage, then the ingrained respect owed to an officer took over. "Earned her, sir?" The Sergeant glanced into the cell. "You wouldn't say that was proof . . ."

"When I discover whether the man told you the truth."

"He told the truth." Scammell was stubborn.

"I'll have to find that out for myself, won't I?" Vane heard the whipcrack of authority coming back into his voice. "In the meantime, Sergeant, you'll tell no one."

"I ain't a choirboy like your Sam, am I?" Scammell's tone was scathing.

"No, you're not." Vane walked away from the cell, going to tell the lies that would explain murder, but also taking the name of Davie Logan that was the next stepping stone on this bloody path. Logan. Vane wondered how in hell's name he was to find the distant Logan, yet discover the ferryman he must, for, just as Lynch had led to Logan, so Logan would lead to the next traitor, then the next, until the traitor in the city was at Vane's mercy and could never again betray the King's cause. In which cause Captain Vane had stepped on the path of horror, but he had done it willingly, for it could lead to victory.

THIRTY-TWO

General Charles Lee, no longer arrayed as a Polish cavalry general but in the duller uniform of the Continental Army, took his leave of Philadelphia in late April. A travelling coach had been provided for his comfort, and its rack was heaped with gifts from British officers. There were cases of wine packed in sawdust, two hams, a cask of pickled oysters, and a fine pair of riding boots made by Sir William's London bootmakers. "They'll help you run away all the faster, Charlie."

"I shall miss you, sir, indeed I shall." Lee embraced Sir William, then kissed Mrs Loring. "Dear Lizzie, I cannot persuade you to accompany me?"

"We'll take you prisoner again soon enough, Charlie."

"You make promises so easily." Lee again clutched Sir William to him. The sorrow of parting was genuine.

"Inform General Washington of my peace proposals!" Sir William admonished.

"I shall, sir! I shall encourage him!" Lee swung himself into the saddle of Sir William's own horse. Lee would ride the first dozen miles on the borrowed mare, and only then would he use the travelling coach which, despite the day's heat, had leather curtains drawn tight behind its windows.

A half-dozen staff officers, Christopher Vane, John Andre and Lord Robert Massedene among them, would ride the first leg of the journey with the exchanged rebel General. On the previous night a mixed force of British infantry and Loyalist cavalry had marched to attack a rebel encampment at an upcountry tavern called the Crooked Billet, and the staff officers, released for the day, would accompany Lee that far then come back with the returning troops. Six servants, including Private Sam Gilpin, carried food and wine for a farewell luncheon in the open air.

"Who are you hiding in the coach, Charlie?" Sir William's question was jocular.

"A dozen of your deserters, sir."

Sir William laughed. "God bless you, Charlie."

"And you, sir." The two men shook hands, then the coachman cracked his whip and the horses clattered out of the yard on to Market Street. Lee and the British officers rode ahead, while the servants stayed behind the lurching coach.

Lee's entourage made a happy cavalcade. The officers displayed their horsemanship in the city's streets, then galloped for sheer joy through the Northern Liberties. For once the countryside to the north was known to be free of rebel patrols, and the red-coated young men could ride with abandon.

It was the year's first such day of careless freedom. All spring the rebel patrols had ambushed and galled the forage parties that still sought hoarded food from the northern farms. As the weather warmed, and as the land became easier for horsemen, so the rebel activity had increased. Bitter skirmishes left Redcoats dead in scrub and farmland. In the forests between the small fields the Americans were at home, and red-coated companies, trained to the close-order drill of the open battlefield, lumbered clumsy and vulnerable. The rebels, becoming accustomed to victory, jeered at their floundering enemy.

But victory had made them overconfident. On the day before Lee left to rejoin Washington's army, the rebel patrols came together to make a force of over fifteen hundred men. They had planned to sweep the country close to the city's defence line and to attack the wood-cutting parties that daily dragged cooking fuel back to the beleaguered city.

But a Loyalist farmer had brought news of the gathering to the city, and the British, vouchsafed their enemy's whereabouts, had marched to make the night attack. "It looks," Lord Robert Massedene spurred to ride alongside Vane and pointed towards a smear of smoke that rose above the spring-brightened horizon, "as if we've been successful."

"We'd know by now if they'd failed," Vane said curtly. He still disliked Massedene, and that dislike was still fed by the jealousy which the Widow had provoked the previous autumn, but, working so closely together in Sir William's entourage, the two officers could not ignore each other. Vane treated his lordship with a wary politeness, while Massedene, to Vane's secret displeasure, constantly behaved as though the two had never been estranged. Massedene thus irritated Vane now. "You seemed recovered this morning, Vane?"

"Recovered?"

"We all thought you were feverish these last few days. Billy was quite worried!"

Vane instantly remembered the twitching and bloody thing in the asylum cell. The guilt, like a slithering beast coiled in his belly, stirred cold and he rowelled his horse ahead so that Massedene should not see his face. "It was a touch of cold, my lord, nothing more."

"Billy thought you were fretting for action."

"Aren't we all?" Vane called back. There was a hint of petulance in his voice, a petulance shared by many of Sir William's army. Spring had come, yet still Sir William did not march to strike at the rebel's army. The troops still lingered in their winter quarters, wondering if the rumours about the French and about Sir William's resignation and about the peace negotiations were true. Some officers, resentful of their sheathed swords, grumbled that Sir William loved America more than Britain. Others, like Vane, urged him to march. But Sir William preached patience. "We'll be offering peace terms soon, and very generous ones! Let us not provoke their hatred when we seek their affection."

Yet a Loyalist farmer, watching the gathering of the rebel forces at the Crooked Billet Tavern, had forced Sir William's hand. Such a flaunting of American power, so close to the city, could not be ignored, and thus, at midday, ahead of the lurching and creaking coach, the staff officers came across the scene of the previous night's carnage.

Six Redcoats had been wounded in the night, but over a hundred rebels lay dead. Charles Lee, sitting on Sir William's mare, looked with horror at the bodies. "What happened?"

"They ran." A major in the green uniform of the Queen's Rangers, the Loyalist cavalry that fought such a bitter war against their fellow colonists, gave a harsh laugh. "Sentries fast asleep again, just like Paoli's Tavern."

Christopher Vane walked his horse among the bodies. The rebel camp fires still smoked. A canvas sack of cornmeal lay beside one fire, and next to it was a pair of boots too shabby to be taken as plunder. The boots' owner, in his holed stockings, lay killed by a sabre slash five yards away. His clothes had been ripped apart as

Redcoats sought the coins that men sometimes hid in the seams of jackets or breeches. A British tin canteen, punctured with a bayonet so that the sharp edges would make a rasp for grinding corn, hung about his bloodied neck.

"Who were they?" Lee asked.

"Lacey's men," the Rangers' major seemed happy to boast to the rebel general.

"We were betrayed," Lee said bitterly.

"A payment for all the times we've been betrayed," the major said harshly.

Lee turned his borrowed horse away. The Crooked Billet Tavern still burned and a roof beam, collapsing in a spew of sparks, made the mare shy sidewards. A barn, which had been used as a straw store behind the tavern, was a smoking ruin. Among the embers, and half hidden by the smoke, Lee could see curled and blackened corpses. There was a smell of roast flesh in the air.

"Patriots?" Lee asked.

The major nodded. "Set fire to the straw with their musket wadding." He laughed, as though he thought the rebels' fate was a just one.

Lee spurred away from the horrid sight. Vane stayed. He was fascinated by the burnt bodies. They were blackened and shrivelled by the flames, only recognizable as humans by the shrunken shapes. He turned round as hoofbeats sounded behind him and saw Sam Gilpin, drawn by an equal curiosity, coming to look at the corpses. "That will teach you, Sam, not to fire a musket in a straw barn."

"They didn't, sir." Vane raised an eyebrow, and Sam, staring with horror at the blackened men, explained, "They was pushed back in, sir, after the fire started."

Vane gave an abrupt laugh. "Don't be absurd, Sam."

"That's what they say, sir." Sam nodded towards a dozen green-uniformed troopers who lolled beyond the burning tavern. "Boasting of it, they are."

"Pushed in?"

"They'll deny it, sir. But the major helped." Sam nodded towards the Rangers' officer who led Charles Lee on a triumphant tour of the massacre.

Vane heard the ring of truth in Sam's words. Troopers would callously boast of such a thing to a private like Sam, but the horror would be formally and strenuously denied by the officers. "Did they say why they did it?"

"One of the buggers fired from behind, sir."

"They deserved it, then. It will teach them not to be treacherous."

Sam flinched from Vane's callousness. "You sound like Sergeant Scammell, sir."

Sam, still intrigued by Vane's questioning in the stables, had mentioned the Sergeant's name deliberately, but, even so, he was astonished by the effect of his words. Vane turned the stallion towards Sam and the muscles of his neck distended like taut cords. "How dare you, Gilpin? You insolent bloody bastard!"

"Sir, I – "

"And shut your godamned face when I'm talking! My God, but you get above yourself! You think because you're my servant that you're above discipline? I can have you flogged, Private Gilpin, till blood pours over your boot tops, and don't forget it!"

Lee and Andre, attracted by the anger, had turned to listen. Sam said nothing. He had seen how febrile and excitable Captain Vane had been ever since the day when he had met Caroline in the church, but he had not seen anything like this sudden and vicious temper. "You make me sick!" Vane shouted. "You're a bumpkin! An impudent ignoramus, and I'm sick of you! Now get out of my sight!"

"I'm sorry . . ."

"Bugger off!"

Sam turned his mare. John Andre, troubled by the outburst, spurred his horse toward Vane, but Vane kicked his heels back and went past his friend. He sought the major instead. "You must tell your men to keep their mouths shut, Major."

The Ranger glanced towards Lee, but the rebel General was out of earshot. "Why?"

"You know why." The anger was still in Vane's voice.

The major, who had been a Pennsylvanian farmer before he took up the sabre, resented Vane's tone. "And who are you to give me orders, Captain?"

Vane took a deep breath to calm himself. "My name's Christopher Vane, sir. I'm from Sir William's staff."

"My name's Moir, Major William Moir."

Moir was a large man with a weathered face and hands which looked big enough to strangle an ox. Moir's eyes were never still, flickering disconcertingly about the scenery. It was a habit he had learned in the forests where, like all the Rangers, he fought a cat-

and-mouse game with the skilled American ambushers. There were lines creased about those watchful eyes.

Vane, not wanting to give offence to the American officer, smiled. "I don't care, Major, if you burn every damned rebel between here and the mountains. I'll help you push the bastards into the flames, but your men should keep their silence."

Moir nodded curtly. He glanced dispassionately towards the smoking barn where the corpses lay. "Fuckers shot at us from behind. We'd already taken the tavern, but they still fired."

"Then you did the right thing, but Sir William wouldn't like to hear of it."

Moir gave a grim small smile. "There are lots of things out here that Sir William wouldn't like. It ain't a very gentlemanly war, Captain."

"You can be assured that Sir William won't learn from me." Vane felt as if a burden was lifted from him. He was not the only man who saw the path of savagery as the one clear road that would lead to victory. Popular as Sir William was, his strategy was binding and pinching the fighting man like a tight riding boot. A rebellion was not defeated by pussyfooting about the rebels, but by blind savagery and overwhelming force. "And in return, major, you can help me."

Major Moir's eyes, for once, remained still as he looked suspiciously at the elegant Captain Vane. "A favour?"

"You know this area?"

"I grew up in it."

Vane felt the renewal of hope. He had taken a name from a bloody cell in an asylum, but no one in the city had recognized the name and Captain Vane had begun to feel despair. "I've been looking for a man called Davie Logan. He has one eye and a broken nose . . ."

"I know Davie," Moir interrupted. "He got the broken nose in a mill with a drunken preacher, and lost the eye when the preacher's wife attacked him with a firedog."

Vane, despite his excitement, was amused. "A preacher?"

"Just some poor Baptist howling with rum," Moir said dismissively. "Why are you looking for him?"

Vane did not answer the question. "I hear he's a ferryman?"

"Anyone with a boat on the river's a ferryman," Moir said, again dismissively. "Davie's more than that. He carries food down to the city."

"And carries messages back?" Vane suggested.

Again Moir's eyes settled on Vane. He thought for a few seconds, then nodded. "Like as not." His voice betrayed that he had never considered the possibility, but that now, on thinking of it, it seemed a most likely proposition. "My God, yes! He carries produce to the city, see, and why would the bastards let him do that unless he was doing something for them in return? Christ!" Moir smashed a big fist into an equally big hand, then looked worriedly at Vane. "Are you certain?"

"I know he warned Fort Mercer of our attack last autumn. A prisoner confessed as much."

Moir was unconvinced. "Those bastards will tell you anything for a loaf of bread."

Vane decided that he must offer something in exchange for Moir's knowledge. He twisted in his saddle and looked towards the smoking corpses. "Some things happen in the city, Major, that Sir William doesn't know about." The saddle creaked as Vane turned back. "The prisoner told me the truth. So how do I find Logan?"

"A hard bastard to catch. One flicker of trouble and he's on the water." Moir stared northwards. "And there's more than a few rebel households between us and him."

"But if he delivers food to the city, won't I find him there?"

"Big place," Moir commented bleakly. "And he may not sail all the way there. He could meet another boat halfway." He shrugged, and Vane felt his hopes, which had been raised so high, suddenly sag. Moir shook his head. "There's precious little produce to deliver at this time of year, Captain. Davie might not travel downriver for another two months."

Vane stared at the drifting smoke. "Could a patrol of Rangers find him?"

"Nothing would give me more pleasure," Moir's voice was grim. "But to travel that far we'd need Sir William's permission."

"I'll seek it."

"You won't get it." Moir gave a sour laugh. "The new policy seems to be bent on cuddling the bastards. We were only allowed to come here because the fools conveniently climbed on to the chopping block." Moir suddenly clicked his fingers. "There's one man who'll know who Davie Logan trades with. Ezra Woollard."

"Becket's foreman?"

"There's nothing that happens on the river that Ezra doesn't know." Moir's praise was grudging. "If any man knows Davie's movements, it's Woollard."

"My God, but you've been helpful." Vane had been at a dead end, until he met this big Pennsylvanian.

Moir nodded towards the barn. "And you'll say nothing . . ."

"My dear Major Moir, they set themselves alight with musket wadding." Vane, alerted by a warning look from Moir, turned to see Charles Lee approaching.

The rebel General held out his hand. "Will you forgive me, Captain Vane? I can't stomach a meal here."

"We shall miss you, sir." Vane, forcing his attention away from Moir's revelations and assuming again the polished elegance of a staff officer, walked his horse towards the carriage. "Perhaps we'll meet on the battlefield?"

"Not if Billy can make peace." Lee sounded wistful as he made a wide circuit about the horror in the barn. "Come and have dinner when we're all friends again, Vane. I'll be a great man in a new country. Maybe they'll name a city after me?"

John Andre had joined them. "I'll come to your city, Charlie. I'm sure it will be a roistering sort of place!"

Lee reined in his horse, struck by some awful thought. "My God! Do you think they'll name a city after plump George? What a dull place it will be!" He laughed, then slid off the borrowed horse's back. "God keep you, Captain Vane."

"He has so far, sir." Vane shook Lee's hand.

The other staff officers one by one embraced Lee or shook his hand. More gifts were pressed on the rebel General, good wishes showered on him, and ribald but friendly insults offered. The coachman, who would return to the city when his errand was over, stared stoically ahead into the sunlit landscape where burned bodies buzzed with flies.

"You can all dine with me when you're prisoners!" Lee bowed to the staff officers, then opened the carriage door. John Andre, riding close to the coach, thought he saw the figure of a shawled woman inside.

"Who is she, Charlie?"

"My plunder from Philadelphia." Lee quickly closed the door, but raised the curtain and lowered the window. He slapped the door panel twice. "Good luck, you bastards!"

"Good luck, Charlie!" The coach lurched forward and Andre

tried to catch a glimpse of the shawled figure, but the woman kept her face well hidden. The coach bumped off the verge on to the road and rattled northwards. When it was some twenty yards away, a rebel flag was suddenly unfurled from the window.

"The bastard!" Andre laughed at Lee's parting gesture.

Then, suddenly, the coach's other window dropped open and a girl leaned out. "Sam! Sam!"

Sam, laying out food in the pasture beyond the road, looked up at the waving girl.

"Goodbye, Sam!" It was Maggie, unshawled and hair free, happy beyond her dreams, and travelling to be introduced to General Washington as Mrs Lee. "Come and see us, Sam!"

Sam stared, then laughed. He waved and blew a kiss. Maggie had found her paradise beyond the hills and was riding there in a travelling coach.

Christopher Vane stared and was appalled.

"What is it, Kit?" Andre, seeing his friend's face, asked with real concern.

"Sacharissa." Vane said the name like a man in a trance.

Andre chuckled. "So it is! Lucky Charlie!"

"God damn him! I'd promised her to someone else!"

"There's plenty more where she came from," Lord Robert Massedene said drily.

But Vane was thinking of Sergeant Scammell, and of a devil's pact, and he wondered how he was to keep that bargain of horror now. But that problem could wait, for he was close to the next link in the chain of treachery that would lead him to the enemy in Sir William's camp. In a field where the roasted flesh had given him solace, Vane felt hope.

THIRTY-THREE

On the morning after his excursion to the Crooked Billet, Sam returned from exercising the horses to find Sergeant Scammell standing in the kitchen. "Miss Sam!" The Sergeant was cutting a piece of cheese from a wheel. "Am I making your nice kitchen dirty?"

"What the hell are you doing here?"

"That's not nice, Samuel. That's no way to greet an old friend, is it?" Scammell walked round the table, holding the cheese knife like a weapon. He pushed the blade into Sam's belly, but Sam neither moved, nor showed fear. Scammell laughed. "I ain't forgotten, boy. I owe you a fucking beating."

"Any time, Sergeant."

"No, boy. In my time." Scammell shoved the knife hard enough for its tip to tear Sam's old coat and prick the skin, then he pulled it free and tossed it on to the table. "I hear my whore went off with a Yankee Jack-pudding yesterday."

"She found herself a man, at last," Sam said.

Scammell did not rise to the insult. "More than she had with your brother! This your uniform?" Scammell fingered Sam's newer red coat that was hanging by the hearth. Sam had cleaned it and pressed it because he had to be an orderly at an elaborate dinner party that Sir William was giving today. All the staff officers' servants were required to be present. "No," Sam said, "it ain't mine."

"Then it doesn't matter if it gets dirty, does it?" Scammell picked up a blackball from the table.

"Don't do it," Sam said warningly.

Scammell turned, looked into Sam's eyes, and gently put the blackball back on to the table. "You're getting above yourself, Sam. I hear you upset your Jack-pudding yesterday. You do that once more and he'll send you back to me, won't he?"

Sam said nothing. Captain Vane, ever since his furious outburst the day before, had been curt with Sam, and Sam was fearing just such an outcome as Scammell described. Sam did not understand what had happened to the Captain, nor what connection Vane had with this half-mad, half-cunning sergeant.

Scammell laughed softly. "He's all right, your Jack-pudding. Ain't as soft as I thought. A few more like him, Sam, and we wouldn't be snivelling in fucking Philadelphia, would we? We'd be giving the rebels a kicking." Scammell peeled the rind off the cheese and dropped it on to the floor. "How's that little whore of yours? Ain't seen her around . . . and I've been watching."

"She isn't mine."

"Perhaps I'll find her," Scammell gave Sam a sideways look. "She'd earn me a pretty penny, wouldn't she? Perhaps your Jack-pudding will get her for me, Sam. He was going to give me Maggie back . . ."

"He wasn't," Sam said in derisive disbelief.

"Sir!" Scammell dropped the cheese and slammed to attention as Captain Vane pushed open the door from the hall.

Vane seemed embarrassed to see Sam. "You're back early."

"They didn't need much exercising after yesterday, sir."

Vane grunted. "I suppose not. Here." This last was to the Sergeant and accompanied a bag that clinked with coin.

"Sir! Thank you, sir!" Scammell was suddenly very correct.

"That will be all, Sergeant."

"Sir!" Scammell about-turned, his right boot slamming on the cheese rind, then he stalked past Sam and banged his way into the small backyard.

Sam felt the tension run out of him as the Sergeant left. Captain Vane, obviously discomfited because Scammell had been discovered in the house, fingered Sam's hanging jacket. "Did I hear him say that I was giving him his wife back?"

"Yes, sir." Sam's voice still held resentment for the clawing he had been given the day before.

Vane frowned at Sam's tone. "There are some things which are hard to understand in war, Sam. Cruel things."

It was evident that the Captain was using a soft tone as a reparation for the day before, but Sam was in no mood to accept the olive branch. "But Maggie was a nice girl, sir."

"Nice?" Vane turned fast. "Nice? You're nice, Sam, I can be extraordinarily nice when I want to be, perhaps even George

Washington can be nice. Billy's nice! What's that got to do with war?"

"Don't know, sir."

"War isn't nice!" Vane was irritable again. "War is bloody, Sam. It's the last refuge of the politician. It's what we do when nothing else works. I used to think it was beautiful! Banners and chivalry and horsemen in glory, but it isn't! It's blood and pain and burnt bodies. It isn't nice, Sam! It is not nice! But it is necessary, and this one's necessary if all those levelling bastards aren't going to inflict a republic on the colonies. And if we try to be nice they're going to succeed. Do you want to lose this war?"

Sam, hearing the extraordinary intensity in his master's voice, wondered again just why Sergeant Scammell had taken money from the Captain. "No, sir. I don't want to lose."

Vane's mood, so unpredictable and quick to change these days, suddenly softened again. "I'm sorry, Sam. I shouldn't have shouted at you yesterday." Vane had turned away so that he did not need to show his face while he made the embarrassing apology. He fingered the cleaned jacket again. "You have to be macaronied today?"

"Yes, sir." Sam's voice was warmer now.

"I suppose I'd better hoist on the flummery myself." Vane paused. "And Sam?"

"Sir?"

"I'm glad Sacha . . . Maggie went with Lee."

"Thank you, sir."

"Now bugger off, you rogue." It was obvious that Vane was relieved that the tension between them was over. "And don't spill any wine at dinner."

Sam grinned. "No, sir."

It was a lavish dinner, needing six long tables joined in a horseshoe shape to seat all the senior officers and their aides who were invited. Admiral Lord Howe had come to the city from his battle fleet anchored in Delaware Bay, bringing a score of naval officers with him. Sam, with the other pressed orderlies, poured wine and served cuts of beef and goose and lamb.

There was a reason for the dinner, but Sir William was loath to reveal it until the wine had softened his men's mood. Instead, he listened to the conversations about him and marvelled at the bellicosity of his command. Toasts were drunk to the skirmish at the Crooked Billet, and Sir William felt how these men fretted to be unchained. The prospect of the French entering the war did not deter them one jot. Most doubted the likelihood, while others positively welcomed the thought. "Let them come," a colonel growled. "It's what we English are good at, killing Frogs!"

A naval captain cheered the colonel's words and proposed that, should the French declare war, a great party should be held to celebrate the opportunity of slaughtering Britain's traditional enemies. "A party like there never was before in America!" The colonel raised his glass. "To the French, gentlemen, may they come to the killing!" There was enthusiastic applause. Admiral Lord Howe, who shared his younger brother's hopes of peace, did not join in.

Lord Robert Massedene shrugged at Sir William. "Would you host such a party, sir?"

"To celebrate the imminent downfall of the French? It's a happy thought, but I won't be here to do such a thing, Robert. My resignation is accepted and Sir Henry Clinton will replace me as soon as a boat can bring him from New York. Might I trouble you for the gravy?" The request for the gravy was spoken in the same careless voice with which Sir William had confirmed the rumour that he was indeed leaving.

The gravy remained unpassed.

There was a silence about Sir William, a silence which spread as the whisper went around the tables.

"Of course," Sir William pretended not to have noticed the shocked silence, "I shall stay on in America as a Peace Commissioner, but I think it would be monstrous unfair on Sir Henry were I to stay in Philadelphia. It will have to be New York, I fear. Never a town I liked particularly, but," he broke off, reflecting that after all the years, and all the fighting, and despite their victories, the British were still pinned to three tiny enclaves on the edge of a continent, "there's not really a great deal of choice, is there? Might I beg the gravy, Robert?"

"Gravy, sir." Lord Robert Massedene passed it.

A chorus of protests inundated Sir William. It was to make this announcement of his imminent departure that he had arranged the dinner party, and he was touched by the dismay it caused. Men who had been urging him to greater zeal now protested his departure. Sir William held up a hand to stop the noise, was disobeyed, and wiped tears from his eyes. "Until now people complained that all I did was lie a-snoring. Isn't that so, Kit?"

Vane reddened. He had not thought that the scurrilous verse, which he himself had spread so eagerly, could possibly have reached Sir William's ears.

Sir William saw the blush and laughed. "I thought it most amusing. We both did!"

For once Christopher Vane was flummoxed. "We shall miss you, sir. Both of you."

"Soon gone, soon forgotten," Sir William said, hoping it would not be true.

"But we shall not let you go, sir." Vane rapped the dinner table with a serving spoon, demanding silence from all the officers. "We shall not let Sir William go," he started again, "without a farewell party that will be remembered for ever in these colonies!"

The proposal was loudly cheered. Sir William shook his head modestly. "You would celebrate my leaving?"

"Your triumphs, sir," Vane said firmly.

Sir William laughed. "It will be a very small party, Kit. What will you serve? Humble pie?"

"No!" Vane's protest was loud enough to make Sam, busy at a side table, turn to face the guests. Vane, who had a favour to ask of Sir William, now launched himself on a well-rehearsed piece of flattery. "Since you came to America, sir, you have faced the enemy six times in open battle. Each meeting, sir, resulted in your victory. You have captured New York and Philadelphia. From Bunker Hill to Germantown you are unbeaten. I therefore propose a celebration to rival the triumphs of ancient Rome!"

"Seconded!" a naval captain shouted, and all the guests, this time including the Admiral, beat with cutlery on the table to support the brave words and to pleasurably embarrass Sir William.

"'Pon my word, Kit, you make it sound creditable!" Sir William's face was wistful.

Vane raised a hand to check the noise in the dining-room. "I speak, sir, for the motion."

"Stand up, Kit!" someone shouted, and the command was echoed until Vane pushed his chair back and quieted the room with a gesture.

"At Bunker Hill, sir, you took the field and kept it. At Brooklyn Heights, you tumbled the enemy into the flight of a disordered rabble. At White Plains, you hurled them from their fortifications. Three thousand enemy surrendered to you at Fort Washington. At

Brandywine, you turned them, panicked them, and defeated them. At Germantown, you repelled their sudden attacks and punished their temerity with defeat. You have taken their so-called capital. You have never been defeated." Again Vane checked applause. He stared about the room. "Does anyone oppose the motion?"

"No!" There was a roar of approbation. The kindly Sir William's caution was forgotten in the flood of affection that surrounded him.

"I think, sir," Vane bowed to Sir William, "that the motion is carried. We shall celebrate your great victories in a fitting style."

Sir William gave Vane a rueful, though grateful, smile. "Perhaps we can celebrate peace instead, Kit?"

"Victory is peace." Vane stated his creed, and again a cheer echoed about the great room.

At the dinner's end, while most of the guests lolled comfortably with port and brandy, Sir William took his customary walk in the garden. He liked to stroll alone, but this evening Vane begged for the privilege of accompanying his master.

"Gladly!" Sir William smiled, still evidently warmed by Vane's egregious flattery. "It was kind of them to applaud, my dear Kit, but hardly apposite?"

Vane smiled. "No, sir?"

"Three thousand enemies taken at Fort Washington don't balance six thousand men lost at Saratoga." Sir William walked in silence for a few paces, while his dog, for whose benefit this evening walk was taken, rooted about in the shrubbery. "Our only chance of success is if the rebels accept our peace terms."

"If you say so, sir." Vane, disagreeing, did not want to express his disagreement.

"And the French itch to join the dance." Sir William spoke sadly.

"The rebels, sir, might contemplate your peace terms if they suffered another defeat?"

Sir William laughed sourly. "I believe we had this same conversation six months ago? One more victory, and peace would follow, isn't that what we said? Well, we had our victory, but it didn't do us much good, so perhaps you're right. Perhaps I should let you hotheads take the reins for a while. Isn't that what you want, Kit? I know you want something, or was that very skilful flattery a simple expression of your goodwill?"

Christopher Vane forced a smile. "I thought I was being very subtle, sir."

"No." Sir William paced the lawn in silence for a few seconds, then looked sideways at his aide. "When I appointed you, Kit, last summer after you'd been so very brave, what did you hope would happen?"

"Happen, sir?"

"Your ambitions, what were they?"

Vane was embarrassed. "To please you, sir."

"Your work does. Very much. You're very efficient." Sir William smiled. "I'm sometimes tempted to think it's because of your training in a counting house, or is that unfair?"

Vane hated his family's background of trade to be mentioned, but he could not deny it. "Not unfair, sir, no."

"But in some ways I'm disappointed." Sir William offered Vane a kindly look, as if to suggest that this criticism was not to be taken too much to heart. "You see the war, Kit, as a personal crusade, and it isn't. We're just the instruments of policy, nothing more." The Commander-in-Chief stopped his pacing and turned to face Vane. "So you flatter me, hoping to soften me, and I fear it might be in aid of one of your personal vendettas. Who is it this time?"

Vane was horrified at the reprimand. For a second he was tempted to abandon his mission, but he had the scent of treachery in his nostrils and he was convinced that, by scotching whatever stank, he could tip the fragile balance of defeat and victory. "I don't know if it's a vendetta or not, sir. What I do know is that our attack on the river forts last autumn was betrayed. I also know who carried the warning to the forts."

It seemed he must have surprised Sir William, for the Commander-in-Chief appeared struck dumb. His only reaction was to flinch slightly, then rub his back that had been giving him trouble in the last few days.

"I'm talking about betrayal, sir." Vane's voice was insistent.

"I suppose you are, yes."

"The man who delivered the warning, sir, must have confederates within the city. I want your permission to find the man and question him."

"A man, you say?" Sir William's interest seemed polite, rather than urgent.

"Yes, sir."

Sir William arched his back and stared up at the topmost branches of an apple tree on which the blossoms were just showing as tightly budded curls. "How many thousands of souls live in Philadelphia? Thirty thousand? And another ten within a handful of miles? And perhaps a third of them are disposed towards the rebel cause. I can't see that finding one out of so many will help our efforts."

"Sir!" Vane spoke a shade too firmly, but he forced Sir William to look him in the eye. "Only a handful of men knew of your plans, sir. Only a handful! That isn't thousands!"

Sir William, forced to the point, started his slow pacing again. "And how did you discover this man's existence?"

"A rebel prisoner confessed, sir."

"Ah!" Sir William at last showed a flash of interest. "Whatever prompted such disloyalty in the man?"

"He wanted his freedom, sir."

"And you gave it to him?" Sir William sounded astonished at such evidence of venality.

"I said I would urge his case on you, sir, that is all."

"I certainly won't barter a man's freedom for dishonouring his allegiance! I will not! Besides, such a man will say anything to gain an advantage. Anything!"

"I believe this man, sir." Vane did, too, for Lieutenant James Lynch was buried in the plague pit to the west of the city. The prison authorities, with enough sins of their own to hide, had shown no scepticism at Vane's story. Lynch had attacked a British officer, and Lynch had died. The matter was closed.

Sir William seemed to accept Vane's forceful avowal of the prisoner's truthfulness. "So what did this disloyal prisoner confess to you?"

"He named the man who brought the warning to Fort Mercer, sir. A ferryman called Davie Logan. He lives up river, has one eye and a broken nose."

The final details came lamely off Vane's tongue, but they amused Sir William. "And what do you wish to do about this one-eyed and hobbling ferryman?"

"I've talked to the Rangers, sir, and they say we should be able to find Logan. They're enthusiastic, sir. I know that Logan himself isn't important, but we should know who gave him the information. If I can find that out, sir, we've found the person who betrayed all our plans this winter."

Sir William privately noted how the man who had evidently betrayed the attack on the forts was now held responsible for every setback of the winter, but he did not remark on such an expansion of Vane's argument. Instead, Sir William dug the point of his boot into the grass. "You talked to the Rangers?"

"Yes, sir."

"That was precipitate of you."

The words were said mildly, but Vane detected a further reproof in them. He had tried hard, with his earlier flattery, to restore his old and easy relationship with the Commander-in-Chief, and now he offered a plausible excuse for encouraging the Rangers to vengeance. "I only wanted their local knowledge, sir." Then, hearing the timidity in his own voice, Vane offered Sir William a rueful smile and took refuge in a frank admission of the truth. "That isn't true, sir. What I want to do, and what I need your permission to do, is ride north with the Rangers and find this man Logan. We can do it inside a day, sir, and the Rangers are confident of success."

Sir William, his hands clasped behind his back, walked a few paces in silence. "I fear you won't like this, Kit, but I must forbid you to pursue this matter."

"Forbid me?" Vane astonishment was clear.

Sir William offered an apologetic shrug. "You mustn't get excited about such things. The enemy have spies, yes. But so do we. How else could we have caught those poor fellows at the Crooked Billet?"

"But this treachery is close to you, sir. Too close for safety!"

Sir William's reply was checked by the opening of one of the doors leading on to the upper terrace. Lord Howe, resplendent in his admiral's braid, frowned at his younger brother. "Damnedest thing, Willie."

"Richard?"

"Boat cloak and hat. Both gone! Your fellow Evans swears he hung them in the hall. I came to see if you'd borrowed them?"

"Not me, I fear." Sir William spread his hands in a gesture of ignorance.

"Bloody thieves!" The Admiral growled his way back into the house.

Sir William, recovering the thread of the interrupted conversation, looked sadly at Vane. "Perhaps you do deserve an explanation, Kit."

"I'd be grateful, sir."

Sir William frowned to himself. "Otto Zeigler told me much the same news three or four months ago. He didn't know about this Logan fellow, but he knew enough to cause me some grief." Sir William shrugged. "I did nothing. I had particular reasons for doing nothing."

Vane, sensing that he was being taken into the General's deepest confidence, kept silent.

Sir William stared at the pale grass which had been bruised during the frost months. "As you say, only a handful of people knew of the attack; all of them officers I trust implicitly. But I did tell one other person."

"Ah." Vane felt the acute embarrassment of a young man who was being shown the weakness of an elder man.

"Indeed. Not that Lizzie's a traitor, that's nonsense! But she can be indiscreet, and she's become monstrous fond of Martha Crowl!" Sir William smiled ruefully. "I know you don't like the Widow, but I like her. Indeed I do."

"Love your enemies? Do good to those who hate you?"

"What I especially like about Mrs Crowl," Sir William said gleefully, "is that almost alone of my enemies she does not quote the Scriptures to me. But I have no doubt she would betray my plans to her friends."

"And you would leave her unpunished?" Vane said it a shade too forcefully.

"It was my fault, Kit. I betrayed my own confidence, and I cannot attach fault to an avowed rebel if she takes advantage of such foolishness." Sir William shrugged. "I daresay that if you found your one-eyed waterman and could persuade him to talk with you, he would lead you to Mrs Crowl, but I cannot see what purpose we will have served. She cannot betray us again, not unless I am indiscreet again. No, Kit, I must ask you to do nothing." He saw the disappointment on his aide's face. "Besides, I daren't upset an applecart while the peace negotiations are being proposed. And Mrs Crowl has been useful to me in those negotiations, indeed she has!"

"Useful?" Vane could not disguise his astonishment.

"It's most useful to have an enemy touchstone," Sir William said happily, "and now that Charlie's gone back to the rebels I really can't expect to find a better one than Mrs Crowl." Sir William chuckled. "And Charlie took his whore with him, I hear?"

"Yes, sir." Which had cost Vane five precious guineas.

"And he'll urge peace on General Washington." Sir William, now that the peace he wanted was so desperately needed, was happy to grant the enemy commander his proper rank. "Mrs Crowl is most sanguine about the chances of a treaty. Her views encourage me, indeed they do."

"She would encourage you, sir," Vane said bitterly. "As long as we believe there might be peace, we're hardly likely to make outright war."

Sir William offered a tolerant smile to his aide's scepticism. The smile, far from placating Vane, only goaded him into one of those indiscreet outbursts that he so often regretted. He was feeling sore at Sir William's refusal to let him hunt with the Rangers, and, even though he could still tap Ezra Woollard's knowledge, Vane had assumed that a swifter result could be obtained with the help of Major William Moir and his vengeful Loyalist horsemen. "I must assume, sir, that Sir Henry Clinton might feel differently about these traitors?"

Sir William's face showed instant anger. "Sir Henry has not succeeded me yet, nor will he until I see fit to relinquish this command. You will not correspond with Sir Henry on this matter, or any other!" Sir William was related to the King, albeit on the blanket's other side, and there were times when he was capable of a most royal and frigid hauteur. This was one of them. "Do not get above your station, Captain Vane! You are my aide because I appointed you, and I can just as easily return you to obscurity!"

Vane, knowing he had gone too far, blushed. "I apologize, sir."

But Sir William was not placated by contrition. "You will forget this matter! That is an order!"

Vane was horrified at the reprimand. This affable man, to protect his mistress and pursue his chimera of peace, was ordering Vane to ignore treachery. Vane pretended compliance. "Yes, sir. Of course."

"If you disobey me, Captain Vane, I shall return you to regimental duty. There will be no advancement for you, none!"

The chill was back now, a gulf fixed between men who had been so close when, in the hopeful days of last autumn, Sir William had believed that with the fall of Philadelphia peace and happiness would be restored to the colonies.

But peace had not come, and happiness now was burning rebel prisoners in a straw-filled barn, yet still Sir William pursued his dream of amity. However, Sir William's dreams were not Captain Vane's, and Vane would not be so easily cheated. Sir William had mentioned the Widow, and such a mention could only sharpen Vane's desire for revenge which, if it could not be expedited by a cavalry patrol on the river bank, might be found closer to home in the knowledge of a warehouse foreman. Sir William wanted peace, but Vane wanted victory, and he would have it.

THIRTY-FOUR

Abel Becket, dressed in his old-fashioned black Steinkirk stock above his usual sober suit, was unnaturally loquacious as he walked beside the limping Jonathon on the quayside beneath the dark loom of a moored merchant ship. "She carried finished goods to the planters on Antigua. Clocks, chronometers and navigational instruments from London. Enamelled watch-cases from Switzerland, French glass, and sword blades from Austria; luxuries, and all to Antigua! You mark that!"

"I haven't forgotten our business, sir." Jonathon stumped beside his uncle and looked up at the salt-streaked hull of the *Deirdre-Ann*, a merchantman that was now being loaded with a cargo from Becket's warehouse.

"We purchased those finished goods with specie lodged in London. They were delivered on our behalf to Antigua." Abel Becket repeated the island's name with a kind of wonder that such a small place could afford so many luxuries. "And the Antigua planters paid us with molasses, rum, indigo and unsawn mahogany."

"As they always do, sir."

Abel Becket pretended to ignore his nephew's sardonic tone. "And from here she'll carry the sawn mahogany, walnut, oak and linseed to Europe. Trade, Jonathon, trade! It's the lifeblood of this coast."

Jonathon steeled himself for the sermon which he knew was coming, for his uncle missed no opportunity these days to mock his nephew's rebellious allegiance. "Not liberty, Jonathon, but trade! Liberty's a shibboleth, a word mouthed by politicians to rouse the mob! And at the rebellion's end, my boy, the mob will still be a mob, the price of bread will have doubled, and only the lawyers will be rich. Liberty's a word to stamp on coins, but the coins are made by trade, Jonathon, trade!"

"So you're fond of telling me, sir." Jonathon was inured to the propaganda now. He was staring towards the merchant ships which waited in the river for their turn at the wharves, but he was not interested in those great movers of trade; instead, he searched for a glimpse of Caroline's shallop. However, the only moving vessel was a British sloop which, with topsails set, slipped its mooring to glide southwards on one of the neverending patrols to deter the rebel gunboats that still haunted the lower river.

"You can negotiate the gangplank?" Abel Becket asked Jonathon in a rare moment of solicitousness.

"I can, sir." Jonathon's stump was still an agony of soreness, but he was determined to overcome the pain. Each morning he smeared the leather cup of the wooden leg with butter to ease the friction, yet, within minutes, it was as if needles of fire stabbed at the raw flesh. He had insisted on discarding the crutches, using a stick instead.

The gangplank was steep but ridged with battens of timber and provided with a rope balustrade. Jonathon forced his way up, ignoring the torment in his stump and determined not to show any weakness in front of the British sailors who, under Ezra Woollard's wary gaze, lowered roped stacks of timber into the *Deirdre-Ann*'s holds. On either side of the gaping hatches were cannons, testimony to the dangers of American privateers. Roundshot was stacked on gratings about the mast steps.

Woollard offered his confiding grin to Jonathon. "You're as nimble as a squirrel, Master Jonathon."

Jonathon suppressed his instinctive dislike of his uncle's foreman who, in his days of greater prosperity, had offered marriage to Caroline. "I try, Mister Woollard."

"We'll soon have you swarming up the ratlines!" Woollard gave a knowing and mocking laugh, then turned to bellow an order at the men who hoisted the precious timber with ropes threaded through intricate blocks. There had been a time when such scenes had been Jonathon's bread and butter, when he would have supervised the lading himself to prevent the peculation of ship's captains and wharfmen, but now he did not care. He watched as burly men rolled hogsheads of dried beef up the aft gangplank and as great tuns of fresh water were lowered into the stern hold.

"I'm thinking of opening a proper chandlery," Abel Becket said. "There are captains who want nothing more than to linger in port and will claim a broken shoe-buckle as reason enough."

"Indeed, sir."

Becket smiled at his nephew. "And I thought perhaps you might care to organize such a chandlery for me? You could use the old rope store? It will only need a lick of limewash."

"I'd enjoy that, sir." Jonathon must needs pretend an enthusiasm for his return to work, but it was only a front for, in less than a week's time, he would be given the papers of his father's inheritance to sign, and on that day, if Sam had found the naval disguise, Jonathon intended to leave Philadelphia and forget all about trade and chandlery. He would travel north with Caroline, north to the rebel army, and only when the battles were done and the great issue decided would he retrieve what, if anything, was left of his property.

Yet, to admit such a plan to his uncle was to court disaster, for his uncle would permit no such thing. Thus, for just a few more days which he counted with the avidity of a prisoner expecting release, Jonathon must dissimulate, pretend a fascination with the purchase of hemp and tar and indigo and canvas and timber, when all he dreamed of, and all he wanted, were Caroline and victory.

Becket ducked under the break of the poop and, after a perfunctory knock, pushed open a high-silled and polished door. "Good afternoon, Captain."

"Mister Becket! A pleasure, sir!" A tall, grey-haired man with the wind-hardened face of a sailor marked his place in the bible he had been reading and held out a hand in greeting. "And this is your nephew?"

"Indeed it is." Abel Becket, at that moment, even seemed proud of Jonathon. "Captain Carroll, Jonathon, Master of the *Deirdre-Ann*."

"A fine ship, sir." Jonathon felt the words were expected of him.

"She is, too. Six years old this Whitsun and built of nothing but the finest English oak." Captain Oscar Carroll had a soft voice that contrasted strangely with his harsh face. He was also afflicted by a tic which drew down his left eye in disconcerting spasms that seemed like batteries of confiding winks. "Your uncle tells me you're a rarely promising trader, Master Jonathon?"

"It's kind of him to say so, sir."

"It's a fine life, that of a trader, but not as fine as a tar's life, eh?" Captain Carroll gestured round his cabin as proof of his assertion, and the cabin was indeed a comfortable and snug place.

It was panelled in a pale oak that bore paintings of sea monsters within each frame. The galleried windows looked on to the moored ships in the river and Jonathon, invited to sit down, stared longingly for a sight of the small, dark-canvassed shallop. His uncle talked of London with the English sea captain, speaking of merchants who had their offices in Fish Street Hill and Pudding Lane. The mood in London, Captain Carroll said, was one of irritation. The rebellion had disturbed trade. Some merchants complained of the army's failure to bring the rebels swiftly to heel, while others averred that the army should never have been sent in the first place. "There's sympathy in London for your rebels. They're costing us a rare sum of money and there's those who don't think the game's worth the candle!"

"The devil never lacked adherents," Becket said grimly. He paused as a steward brought in a can of hot sweet tea. "Have you been troubled by privateers?" Becket's question to the Captain was anxious.

Carroll shook his head. "I've seen none myself this year, but I hear they took a fine Bristol craft in the islands a month back." The Captain, his face quivering with the involuntary spasms, packed a small-bowled pipe which he lit from a shielded candle that evidently burned for just such a convenience. "But the northern route home is safe."

"And news of the French?"

"Watchful, watchful." Carroll, after the enigmatic reply, puffed a cloud of aromatic smoke that curled beneath the painted beams of his cabin. "They do say in London that Philadelphia might be abandoned, Mr Becket." It was evident that Carroll was floating a rumour to see how this prominent Loyalist merchant would react. "I've heard that if the French declare war we'll need men in the islands, and the good Lord alone knows where we find more men."

"Not from the Philadelphia garrison." Becket's tone defied contradiction.

"If you say so." Captain Carroll nevertheless sounded dubious.

Abel Becket, hearing the vacillation in the Englishman's tone, pressed his argument. "You agree the British are intent on holding the colonies? If so, how can they abandon the largest city in America? No, Captain, Philadelphia is safe."

"For your sake, I pray so. I helped carry the Loyalist folk out of Boston, and it was not a happy day, Mr Becket, not happy at all!"

"Philadelphia will not be abandoned." Becket used his most decisive tone.

"I'm glad of that." Carroll, abandoning the topic, turned to Jonathon who, thus far, had sat silent. The Captain's twitching face seemed to wink at Jonathon. "I hear you took that wound with the rebels, Mister Jonathon?"

"Yes, sir."

"Foolishness in youth leads to wisdom in age, does it not, Mister Becket?"

Abel Becket did not answer the complacent saw, looking at his nephew instead. "You have learned your lesson, have you not, Jonathon?"

"I've learned not to close with infantry armed with loaded muskets."

Jonathon's quip was rewarded with a smile from the ship's captain. "At least there'll be no infantry to trouble you in London, that's for certain."

The word hung in the cabin like the smoke from the Captain's pipe. "London?" Jonathon's voice was a croak.

"You'll forgive us, Captain Carroll?" Abel Becket demanded.

Carroll glanced from uncle to nephew, then nodded. "With pleasure, sir. With pleasure." Carroll slid down the bench and ducked out into the spring sunlight where the loading still continued.

The door latched shut. A rippling light was reflected on to the cabin ceiling from the waters at the ship's stern. The deck above was loud with men's feet and the creak of a windlass, but Jonathon, sensing disaster, was oblivious of everything except his uncle's narrow face. "London?"

"Did you imagine, for one instant, that I would permit you to take a proportion of my trade and hand it over, with its profits, to the rebellion?"

Jonathon was trembling. "London?" It seemed he was capable of saying nothing else.

"You are diseased, boy!" Abel Becket used his harshest voice. "Diseased with disaffection! Your sister carries the contagion, and that slut you write to . . . oh yes, sir, I know of your letters! You need quarantine and, by God, you will have it!"

"You can't . . ."

"I am your guardian. I do what is best for you." Uncle faced nephew over the cabin table. "Good God, boy, don't you know what a favour I offer you? London! The greatest city on earth! I never had such a chance, never!" Abel Becket produced a packet of papers from an inner pocket. "There is a draft of money, sufficient for a frugal life for a twelve-month. A letter of introduction to Mr John Martin of Angel Passage. You will reside with his family and work in his counting house!" Abel Becket suddenly offered his nephew a rare smile. "Mr Martin, a particular friend of mine, has a daughter. A not wholly ugly girl, I am told, and – "

"No!" Jonathon's protest was not just at the prospect of marrying a London girl, but at this whole fate which had been sprung on him with such abruptness.

"Take a care!"

"I will stay here – "

"You will do as you are ordered!" Abel Becket thumped the table, rattling the can of tea and jarring some chessmen that were arrayed on a board. "You have disobeyed me once, sir, and you will not do so again. And you have been punished! The Lord saw fit to take your leg, and if you tread the paths of disobedience again I doubt not that He will take your life! You will go to London, sir, and there, at the heart of the world's commerce, you will learn mastery of trade. There, sir, is your money, and there, sir, is your letter of introduction." The papers were pushed across the table. "Your dunnage was brought aboard an hour ago. I have enclosed a bible in your bag that you will read each day . . ."

Abel Becket's words had broken off because Jonathon, despite the pain in his raw stump, had abruptly flung himself along the polished bench towards the cabin door, but, before he even cleared the table's edge, the door swung open to reveal a tall red-coated British officer. Jonathon, utterly taken aback by the sight, froze.

Captain Christopher Vane seemed oblivious to the charged atmosphere in the cabin. He nodded a greeting to Abel Becket. "The paper you wanted, sir." He took a folded document from his pocket and held it towards the merchant. "The official pass, sir. I didn't submit it to Sir William himself, but I think you'll find it will pass scrutiny." Vane looked at Jonathon. "You must be Jonathon?" Jonathon said nothing, but Vane did not seem to mind. "You're a most fortunate young man."

"Fortunate?"

Vane gestured towards the paper that Abel Becket now perused. "You are freed, Mister Jonathon. You are no longer a prisoner of His Majesty's army, and are thereby empowered to pass beyond the city limits. I think you'll find everything is in order, sir." This last was to Abel Becket who, smiling, put the paper into his pocket.

"I thank you, Captain Vane."

Vane hesitated. "And Mr Woollard. . . ?"

"Is ordered to tell you whatever you wish to know." Becket waited till the Englishman had gone, then looked at his nephew. "Do you still wish to escape? You heard Captain Vane. You're a free man now. You may leave this cabin, but I doubt that either Captain Vane or Ezra Woollard will permit you to pass from the deck."

Jonathon stayed still. He knew he could do nothing at this moment.

Abel Becket, seeing his nephew's defiance broken, smiled. "Mr Martin will return you in one year, though if he judges you still to be of a traitorous sympathy he will, on my behalf, keep you in London." Becket leaned earnestly forward. "The Lord spared you for a purpose."

"I have no purpose in London." Jonathon's voice was miserable.

"Did you think I would let you marry that Fisher slut? Did you believe that all my work, all my profits, all my diligence, would go to her?"

"If I have to wait ten years, I will marry her."

Becket scorned the defiance with a sneer. "Other men would have disinherited you, or left you to rot in the prison you deserved, but I am showing you favour, sir, favour! London and learning and opportunity!" Becket eased his way from behind the table and stood. "You will thank me one day."

There were tears of rage in Jonathon's eyes as he stared at his uncle. "I will curse you."

"Your passage is paid. You have a gentleman's accommodation in the ship's stern. Pray use my London friends with politeness." Abel Becket picked up his hat. "You sail on the evening tide." He held out his hand. "Farewell."

Jonathon neither took the hand nor answered, but merely turned away. His uncle left.

Jonathon waited. About him, shivering to the small breeze's touch on furled sails and bare poles, the *Deirdre-Ann* creaked. The stern windows would not open, but even if they had, there was a red-coated sentry at the pier's end who would have raised the alarm. Jonathon was trapped.

The flooding tide raised the ship, bringing ever closer the moment when she would turn her blunt bows to the sea and take her cargo across the huge waters where Jonathon would be far from rebellion and far from his love. He searched the river for a shallop, but did not see it.

The gulls shrieked above hatches being battened down for sea. The wind freshened, and Jonathon waited for the night during which, he swore, he would escape this ship and the long fate of exile that his uncle had so cleverly arranged. He would not go to London, he would not be driven from his country; he would escape.

THIRTY-FIVE

Captain Christopher Vane, after delivering the pass that had been Abel Becket's price for the help Vane needed, was forced to wait until the foreman had finished a discussion with a tall grey-haired man whose face twitched in a series of uncontrollable tics. Woollard, conscious that the red-coated officer waited for him, drew out the discussion which ended when Woollard handed the grey-haired man a bag of money.

Vane, when Woollard at last was free, nodded at the foreman. "You remember me?"

"Indeed, sir." Woollard, picking up a knife and a tallystick, did not look at the Englishman, but instead watched the timber being swung aboard.

"Mr Becket suggested you would talk with me," Vane said.

"He said you needed help," Woollard said bluntly, then looked challengingly at the British officer. "And that you were paying for it by releasing young Jonathon?"

"True." Vane followed the foreman to the ship's starboard rail where, from between two salt-encrusted cannons, Woollard could watch the loading continue. "Do you disapprove?" Vane asked.

"Disapprove?" Woollard gave a humourless laugh. "If Master Jonathon's going to share this business, then the more he knows of trade the better. Though I doubt he still has either the leaning or the liking for it, but good luck rarely comes to the deserving, does it? What the hell's that?"

The last question had been directed at a naval longboat that was being rowed past the *Deirdre-Ann*'s counter. The boat, painted white, had been gilded about its gunwales, while a carved swan's head, unpainted as yet, reared above the bows.

"It's for the Meschianza," Vane offered in lame explanation. "There's going to be a parade of boats."

"The Meschianza?" Woollard had difficulty in pronouncing the odd word.

"A celebration for Sir William's departure."

"I wish you'd celebrate hanging George Washington." All Woollard's scorn for the frippery of the city's high social life was apparent. Like other Philadelphians, he could not understand why so much money and time were being expended on a lavish celebration while the rebel army was still uncrushed. Yet, however much Woollard might resent English airs and graces, he had the reputation of being a staunch Tory, and he had been ordered by Abel Becket to answer Vane's questions. "I know Davie Logan well enough," the foreman assured Vane. "We sold him his shallop four years back, and the devil's own job we had to get the money from him."

"Do you know where I'll find him?"

Woollard did not answer until he had cut another notch in his tallystick to record the safe lading of a timber stack, then, in a churlish voice, he said that Logan had a house up beyond Pennypack Creek.

"I know that." Vane was finding it hard to keep asperity from his voice. "But I want to know where he berths in the city."

Woollard's expression suggested that Captain Vane's ignorance was somehow pathetic. "Logan owes too much money in this city to risk berthing at a Philadelphia wharf. No, Captain, he's using a middleman."

It was the first relevant information that Vane had gleaned from this uncomfortable interview, yet, if it was progress, it was also dispiriting. Vane had come here believing that all he needed to do was find Logan, and that Logan would lead him to the Widow, and now he had discovered another link in the chain. He hid his disappointment. "A middleman?"

Woollard stared at Vane as though he were mad, then, with an insolent slowness, he turned towards the New Jersey shore and spat towards it. "Over there, Captain."

"Explain!" Vane put some of the snap of command into his voice.

Woollard, affronted by the tone, took his time, but he had been ordered to this task by his master so, with whatever bad grace he could muster, he explained how the farmers of Pennsylvania found it difficult to trade with the city because their roads into Philadelphia were heavily patrolled by rebel forces only too ready to use the whip. It was much easier, Woollard said, for the farmers in New Jersey because, not only were there fewer rebel patrols, but they merely had to ship their goods to the river bank opposite the city. That could not be construed as supplying the enemy, because, until a week before, the British had not occupied the New Jersey bank. Once at the New Jersey shore of the river, the produce was sold to local people who, in turn, sailed it across the Delaware to Philadelphia's market. "The middlemen," Woollard explained, "who make a profit out of our hunger."

"So Logan carries produce to Cooper's Point?"

"Near enough." Woollard sounded laconic as he cut another notch in his tallystick.

"To any particular person at Cooper's Point?"

The foreman paused. "I don't like Davie Logan," Woollard said eventually, "but he's a waterman on my river, and one good day, Captain, he'll be a customer of mine again, and I don't want folks saying that Ezra Woollard betrayed a riverman."

The words had been said as a challenge, and Vane felt a flare of temper that almost made him command the answers he wanted. He resisted the temptation, suspecting that such a command would only make this big man even more stubborn. Woollard might be loyal to his watermen, but Becket was certain he was also loyal to his King, and Vane must trust that the latter allegiance was stronger than the former. "I have reason to believe," Vane said carefully, "that Davie Logan is an enemy of the Crown."

"There are plenty of those enemies, Captain." Woollard's voice was neutral.

"I also believe," Vane hid his irritation, "that Logan delivers messages to Philadelphia on the rebels' behalf."

"Not Logan," Woollard said, "but his middleman."

Woollard's obtuseness was aggravating Vane, but he accepted the distinction. "If you say so."

And Woollard, for the first time since the conversation had begun, gave a small smile. He turned, leaning on the rail to stare north towards the great bend of the river. "You see that small pier up there? Not the ferry pier, but the smaller one this side of it?"

Vane could just see, at the far side of the glittering reach, a ramshackle timber jetty that prodded into the water from the New Jersey bank. A leaning branch marked a shoal just beyond the pier, and Vane pointed to it. "Where the perch is?"

"Aye." Woollard spat over the side. "And if you watch, Captain, you'll see a fair-haired slut sail a boat from that pier. A young girl. She's called Fisher."

"Fisher?"

"Caroline Fisher."

Vane wrote the name down. Sam's girl was called Caroline, he remembered, then Vane thrust that irrelevant thought out of his mind. "And this Fisher girl . . ."

"She's a rebel." Woollard seemed to grimace as he said it. "She's a flaunting, insolent, devil of a girl, Captain."

"And she lives at Cooper's Point?"

"A half-mile south, with her grandparents." Woollard, turning back to check on the cargo, glanced at Vane's notebook. "Caleb and Anna Fisher, they're farmers of a sort."

Vane wrote the names down. "Also rebels?"

Woollard shrugged. "Depends which way the wind blows, doesn't it? I always thought Caleb was a Tory, but he reared a rebel granddaughter."

"And Davie Logan trades with them?"

"They sell his produce. But I don't doubt they take a few shillings off the top of each barrel."

Vane closed the book and pushed it into the tail pocket of his uniform coat. "I would be most grateful, Mister Woollard, if you would keep the details of our conversation private."

Woollard offered Vane his second smile. "If my keeping quiet, Captain, leads to the punishment of that damned girl, then I'll keep silence till Doomsday."

Vane heard the echoes of an old lust. He smiled. "I assure you, Mister Woollard, that, if it is deserved, she will be punished."

Woollard nodded and cut another notch in the tally. "She hasn't been coming to the city much of late, but she's here today." He jerked his chin northwards. "You'll see her boat at Painter's Wharf. A new shallop, with a higher bow than most and a white sternpost."

"She brings the produce to market?" Vane guessed.

Woollard nodded. "And to some private houses."

Vane drew a bow at a venture. "Mrs Martha Crowl, perhaps?"

Woollard gave him a sharp glance. Vane's arrow, shot in the air, had fallen plumb on target. "Aye," Woollard spoke slowly, "she goes to the Widow's house. That's where she met the cripple and bewitched him. And it was the Widow who bought her the new shallop."

Vane knew now. Vane knew! The enemy lay revealed before him. He felt the soaring exultation of success, but hid it behind a calm, measured expression. "You've been very helpful. I thank you."

"If you need the slut whipped, ask me. But she's a slippery devil. If you cross the river, Captain, she'll like as not disappear in those woods." Woollard's earlier surliness had been replaced by a grim helpfulness. "You'll talk to her today, perhaps?"

"I doubt it." Vane was unprepared for any such confrontation, and did not want to alert the girl to his suspicions. "But if you see her come to the city in the next few days, you can let me know? A message at Sir William's headquarters will always reach me."

"I'll do that."

Vane smiled his thanks. "Do you have time to show me Painter's Wharf?"

Woollard shook his head. "I have to stay aboard, captain, till she casts off." He nodded meaningfully towards the cabin where Jonathon was immured, and Vane, understanding, walked down to the quay where the evening's shadows lengthened from bollards and cables.

He sauntered up the busy wharves. Sentries and gunners manning the centre battery saluted him and Vane casually touched his hand to a tip of his cocked hat. A drunken seaman reeled out of his way. A cauldron of caulking pitch boiled on one quay, shimmering the air above with its seething heat. Vane stepped over coiled ropes, fish traps and mooring rings. Great ships towered above him, their holds busy. A sailor threw slops from the side of a merchantman and a tumble of gulls shrieked down from the sky. The dockside whores watched Vane with bruised, dark eyes and ignored a preacher who, bible in hand and earnestness on his young face, tried to mend their ways. The smell of hemp came from a ropewalk where a gang of Negroes twisted a vast windlass to make a cable that could hold a fully laden ship against a tempest's destruction.

The northernmost quays were too small for the great ships, so it was there that the shallops and flatboats were crowded together in filthy docks. Baskets of fish were being hoisted from the boats to be spilt into barrels in cascades of silver. A woman offered Vane a sack of oysters. This was where the city's food came, but, except for the fish market, the warehouses were sadly empty. Philadelphia must wait until the turning year swelled the crops. Vane turned back to the oyster seller and paid her a shilling for the sack. "Which is Painter's Wharf, ma'am?"

"Second from the end."

Vane found the wharf and strolled to the dock's edge. A dozen shallops, their sails bent on to booms, jostled in the littered water beneath him. One had a limewashed sternpost and a high, flared bow. It was the boat the Widow had bought, and Vane knew he was seeing, in Caroline's neat shallop, a rebel weapon.

Vane abruptly turned away. At the very end of the wharves where a brick wall edged the northern shipyards, another British battery, protected by a crude parapet of undressed stone, faced the river. Vane walked to it. "Mind if I take the air, Sergeant?"

The sergeant in charge hid his chagrin at being disturbed by some strange officer. "Honoured, sir."

"I thought your men might like some oysters?"

"Thank you, sir."

Vane smiled at the gunners who, before he came, had been lolling beside their weapons with lit pipes. They had hastily extinguished the tobacco when his epaulettes appeared. "Carry on smoking, lads! I'm sure you know the dangers better than I do!"

The sergeant, grateful for such solicitousness, grinned. "Guns ain't loaded, sir."

"They're not?"

"Ain't seen a rebel in six months!"

An old battered spyglass, used for watching the fall of shot, lay on the firestep. Vane took it, slid the brass shutters from the outer lenses, and stared across the river. The small riverside hamlet of Camden slipped past the glass as he panned the instrument left. The land between Camden and Cooper's Point, Vane saw, was thickly wooded, but he could just see a handful of weather-boarded houses tucked into the trees. Further to the left, beyond the outfall of the Cooper River, he could see the timber palisade of the small British wood-cutting garrison. It had been placed there a week before, a tiny fortress that edged the vast woodlands which could provide timber for Philadelphia's cooking fires. There were few rebel patrols to disturb the felling parties. Vane, staring through the spyglass, could see Redcoats pulling buckets of water from the river.

Vane lowered the glass and settled comfortably into one of the gun embrasures. The peak of his cocked hat shadowed his face. The wind was chill, but he was sheltered in the embrasure and happy to wait till dusk if it was necessary. The river flowed beneath him, its sound oddly comforting.

The shallop with the white sternpost appeared a half-hour later. Vane, lulled to a semi-sleep, did not notice it, but the sergeant, made familiar because of Vane's friendly behaviour, drew the officer's attention to the boat. "That one's worth a look, sir."

"Sergeant?" Vane was startled awake.

"Not the boat, sir. The doxie. A proper darling, she is."

Vane pulled the glass open and trained it. For a second all he could see was the dark red blur of the loose-sheeted sail, then he focused the telescope properly and edged it sideways until he could see a girl twisting a single scull over the shallop's stern. She controlled the boat with a careless skill. Her back was turned to the battery and Vane had an impulse to shout a pleasantry that would make the girl turn round. He bit the words back. If this girl was one of the traitors who had drawn the Hessians to bloody ruin at Fort Mercer, then Vane would rather stay unremarked and unsuspected.

The freshening wind hit the sail as the shallop cleared the lee of the high wharves and Vane watched as the girl shipped the scull inboard and sat to the tiller.

She had to turn to sit, and the spyglass was suddenly filled with her face. Vane immediately recognized her, and hissed with astonishment.

"She is a little darling." The sergeant heard the indrawn breath and took it for admiration. "Keeps it to herself, though. Bleeding waste, if you ask me."

Caroline Fisher. Sam's Caroline. Vane stared. She seemed even prettier now than when he had met her in the church. He saw a girl with sun-bleached hair and bright eyes; a face to launch a thousand shallops on the waters of lust. A girl to love and leave, but now a girl who must be hunted and punished, and Vane felt a beat of excitement at that thought. And what, he wondered, was Sam doing with such a girl? She was not a kitchenmaid at all, but a rebel who took her unsuspected boat in and out of a British garrison.

The girl turned and stared straight into the lens. Vane almost turned the telescope away, then realized that the clumsy instrument hid his face to stop the girl from identifying him. He pretended to be nothing but an idle and salacious scrutineer and, recognizing it, the girl first laughed, then thumbed her nose at him.

"A spirited trollop," Vane said.

"But keeps it to herself, sir."

"As you said." As the girl turned away, Vane collapsed the glass and twisted out of the embrasure. "Do you ever search the shallops?"

"Wouldn't mind searching her, sir. No, not really. Once in a while we root about the bilges, but you never find nothing."

To the south, from the bigger wharves, the *Deirdre-Ann* warped herself into the river. Vane saw the topsails drop to the wind and heard their great thump as the seamen hauled on sheets. The first ripples of a long passage appeared at the merchantman's stern.

Vane glanced once more at Caroline's shallop, but it was far off now, tacking towards the ramshackle pier below Cooper's Point. Sam, Vane thought, Sam. Honest Sam, so upright and honest Sam, but treacherous as well? Vane's first instinct was to find Sam and to order the truth from him. Then a wiser thought came to Vane's head. This day's new knowledge was secret, and was best kept secret till it could be useful. Vane turned to look at the gunnery sergeant. "You'd recognize the girl again?"

"Gawd, yes, sir!"

"I might ask you to give her a message, Sergeant."

The sergeant, entirely but quite naturally misunderstanding Vane's intentions, grinned. "Of course, sir."

"Her name is Miss Fisher." Vane ignored the insinuation in the sergeant's expression. "Until I tell you, I don't want her troubled. And when you do give her the message, you don't mention me. Understand? You say it's from someone called Sam. Just Sam." Vane handed the telescope to the sergeant. "I may not ask you to do it for some days, Sergeant, but there'll be a guinea in it for you. What's your name?"

"Pollock, sir."

"Good-night, Sergeant Pollock."

"Good-night, sir."

Lynch had led to Logan, Vane thought, and Logan to

Caroline, and Caroline went straight to the Widow's house in a boat that the Widow had purchased. So now an insolent rejection could be balanced by revenge, and all Vane needed was the proof. And Sam, treacherous Sam, would provide the means. Vane went to that evening's pleasures a happy man.

THIRTY-SIX

Matthew, Mark, Luke and John,
The bed be blest that I lie on.
Four angels to my bed,
Four angels round my head,
One to watch and one to pray,
And two to bear my soul away.

Lydia Crowl paused. "God bless Mama, God bless Uncle Jonathon, God bless Caroline, God bless Jenny and all the servants, and please God send us the French army and liberty and kill all the lobsters. Amen."

"You're not supposed to say that," Martha observed mildly, "when Sam's here."

"Except Sam," Lydia quickly added to her prayer, then opened one very blue eye to peer past her clasped hands. "Hello, Sam."

"Hello."

"I'm going to bed." Lydia, with all the energy of a six-year-old, suddenly scrambled under the sheets from where she solemnly watched Sam. "Caroline was here."

"Was she now?"

"She told me about the Green Man. She said you knew all about him."

"I do." So Sam, urgently pressed, told of the great creaking and rustling monster that moved through the night woods in search of small American children. "He'll come and eat you," he said to the by now invisible Lydia.

"You'll frighten her," Martha said.

"Eat you all up, he will! But you can stop him!"

Two small eyes reappeared over the edge of the sheet. "How do I stop him, Sam?"

"By saying your prayers and being good."

"I am good, aren't I?"

"You're wonderful." Martha stooped and kissed her child. Curtains, soaked in vinegar and herbs to fight the stench in the city's streets, hung at the window. "Sleep well."

"I want a kiss. From Sam."

Sam, who had been sent upstairs by Jenny, obliged Lydia. Outside, after she had closed the door, Martha smiled. "All the girls like you, don't they, Sam?"

"I wouldn't know, ma'am."

Martha wrinkled her nose. "It's good to see you again, even if you do need a bath."

"Yes, ma'am." Sam grinned. "I've brought you the clothes for Jonathon."

"God alone knows why you help us, Sam, but I do thank you."

Martha led him down the back stairs to the kitchen where Jenny was admiring the naval officer's cloak and hat. The cocked hat was edged with gold braid and bore a gold-clasped black plume on its peak.

"Dear God!" Martha picked up the hat, then tried it on. "You stole Lord Howe's hat, Sam?"

"I expect he has another one," Sam said sheepishly.

Martha laughed. "Jonathon will look very fine in it, won't he?"

"He'll have to wear a sword underneath," Sam said, "to look right. And a white stock at his neck."

Martha put the hat on the table. "Will it be dangerous for you, Sam?"

"No!" Sam was derisive of the risks involved in getting Jonathon past the sentries at Painter's Wharf. "He just has to pretend to be drunk, doesn't he? Who'd think twice about a drunken officer in Philadelphia?"

Martha sighed. "I wish Jonathon wasn't going. The world's going mad, Sam. Mad!" Martha sat on the opposite side of the table. "Have you seen what they're doing at the Wharton mansion?"

"I was there this morning," Sam said. The Wharton mansion, Walnut Grove, lay in wide gardens to the south of the city. Lawns led from the spacious house to the river. The mansion's owner, a Patriot, had fled Philadelphia in the autumn, and now his home was to be the setting for the great Meschianza. Tables, rugs, porcelain, crystal, silverware, draperies, lanterns, chairs, tapestries, mirrors and chandeliers were being borrowed from the city's wealthy families to decorate the extravaganza. Fireworks were being concocted by naval armourers, while cooks already planned the exotic feast.

"Lord Robert Massedene wants me to attend," Martha said. "But I won't dress up for him. A Turkish slave girl, indeed! I've never heard such nonsense!"

Jenny laughed. "You'd look good, ma'am."

"I shall go in red and white stripes, with the word Saratoga embroidered on every seam." Martha seemed cheered by the happy thought.

"It'll be a good party," Sam said wistfully.

"Sir William always gives good parties," Martha said. "It's his one glowing and undoubted talent. I'm sorry he's leaving. My enemy is a kind man, as indeed are you, Sam."

"I like Billy." Sam avoided Martha's compliment.

"And the dregs will take over from him." Martha sounded bitter again. "Did you hear how they burned those prisoners at the Crooked Billet?" Sam did not reply, and Martha, sensing his evasion, rapped the table. "Well? Did you?"

"I was there, ma'am. Not at the fighting, but the next day."

"Is it true?"

Sam paused. "I don't know."

"Sam!"

Sam, pressed into a corner, shrugged. "The Rangers said they did, but I don't know."

"It's becoming vicious, Sam. They commit murder and say it's war. It'll be women and children next."

"No!" Sam was scornful.

Martha ignored his protest. "That's why I don't want Jonathon to go. There's no honour left, Sam. It's becoming horrid. But if he has to go, and I suppose he does, I'd rather you went with him."

"Me!" Sam sounded astonished.

Martha smiled her thanks for the inevitable cup of tea that Jenny placed on the table. "Don't sound so surprised," Martha said tartly. "I know Caroline asked you."

"She did, yes," Sam admitted, then shrugged. "But I said no."

"Another Englishman who doesn't want liberty?" As Martha spoke, she saw Sam's face darken in scorn. "And don't give me one of your sturdy English replies, Sam! There is such a thing as liberty!"

The intensity of her voice made Sam defensive. "I never said there wasn't."

"Then tell me what it is."

Sam shrugged. "It's what my brother dreamed of, isn't it? Always over the hill. Always another pasture away."

"You think the rebels are dying for nothing?"

"My brother Nate did! And I've seen your rebels, ma'am. I've even killed a few of them, if you'll pardon me for saying it. And they ain't no different to us! Just ordinary boys pushed into battle. Fighting for your liberty doesn't make them special! There ain't no special heaven for rebels, ma'am."

Martha leaned back. "Liberty isn't heaven, Sam, it isn't a blessed reward. People will still die in sorrow and poverty when they have liberty. It's simply, only, the freedom to choose your own life, and no one promises you success. I don't hate the English. Some of you are even likeable. But I hate having some fat arrogant man in London telling me what I can or can't do. I'd rather the fat arrogant man was in Philadelphia, because at least then I could throw something at him. We don't need London any more. We're grown up. We want liberty. You grew up, Sam, and you didn't want your parents telling you what to do all the time. You wanted liberty, and you got it. You joined the army, which only proves that even the nicest people will misuse liberty, but it's better to have it and misuse it than not to have it at all." Martha shook her head ruefully. "I sound like a cheap lawyer at a town meeting."

Sam, ashamed of his previous outburst, spoke apologetically. "I like to hear you talk, ma'am."

Martha stuck her tongue out at him. "But I wish you would go, Sam. For Jonathon's sake."

"He's all right," Sam said stoutly.

Martha scorned the words. "Jonathon isn't all right. He's a cripple with a wooden leg strapped to an uncertain stump. He's in love, which means he's febrile, and he's only going because he's a stubborn fool who has to pretend he's as good as the next man! Have you ever thought how hard it will be for Caroline to get him to Trenton? They'll have to drag the boat past some of the rapids, and Jonathon won't be any good! She'll have to do all the work, and he'll be limping along behind. That's why I want you to help them. You're capable!"

Sam shook his head slowly. "If they can't do it by themselves, ma'am, they shouldn't be going."

Martha smiled sadly at the truth. "Of course they shouldn't be going, but Jonathon's in love. I don't know if Caroline is, but he is." She watched Sam for a reaction, but his face showed nothing and Martha shook her head in exasperation. "Love, love, love. Have you ever thought what a better world it would be without that inconvenience, Sam?"

"I wouldn't know, ma'am."

Martha shrugged at his noncommittal tone. "But if it wasn't for Jonathon, Sam, you'd cross that river, wouldn't you?"

Sam said nothing. Jenny, leaning by the fire, watched him.

Martha pulled the naval hat towards her and ran a finger across the stiff bristles of its plume. "Let us think for an uncomfortable moment about Miss Caroline Fisher."

"She's made her promise," Sam said stiffly.

Martha made a face at him. "You wouldn't become an American for liberty, Sam, because you don't think we lack it. And you wouldn't become an American out of a republican conviction, because you can't even spell it, but you'd become an American for Caroline. That's what love is, Sam."

"I didn't say I would." Sam was indignant. "And she wouldn't change sides for me!"

"Of course not! She has a passion for something other than the man she loves." Martha grimaced. "And I don't speak of Jonathon. He's a Patriot because she is. Caroline won't abandon the revolution, so her man has to embrace it with her. What's your passion, Sam? That fat German King? Do you feel as strongly for ugly George as Caroline does for General George?"

Sam stared at the table. "I couldn't fight against my own side."

"For mercy's sake, whose side is that? Where do you think our families all come from?" Martha blithely disregarded Jenny's presence. "England! Caroline's as English as you are, except that she lives here and not there. My God, Sam! You want to stay in the army for ever?"

"I might not have to."

"Oh, yes! Caroline told me. There's a glimmer of a chance that you might become Sir William's groom." Martha's voice had been mocking, but now she turned and pointed eastwards. "There's a river out there, Sam, and on its other side is liberty. All you have to do is cross the water. No more floggings, no more sergeants, no more Captain Vanes." Sam said nothing, and Martha sighed. "Do you dislike us so much, Sam?"

"You know I don't." Sam spoke indignantly.

Martha shrugged. "You can cross the river, Sam, and there's a whole new world. There are more hills and valleys than you could dream of, and they're just waiting for the touch of a man's plough. There are rivers wider than your Thames and they still don't even have names. There are horses waiting to be bred, and there's grass to feed them. There's everything a man could want here, Sam, and if we win this fight, there'll even be liberty for everyone to misuse."

Sam looked up. "Maybe I will cross the river."

Martha understood his truculent tone. "But in your own time and in your own way, yes? Because you can't have Caroline?"

"Well I can't, can I?"

Martha paused as a wind rattled the kitchen door. "I don't know, Sam. Maybe you can, who knows? I only know one thing . . ." She paused, wanting Sam to respond. He did. "Ma'am?"

Martha stared down at the gaudy hat. "My uncle will tell you that the only thing worth following is money. Money, money, money, but it never brought a moment's peace to him. The army will tell you to follow, what? Glory? Victory? The flag? And at the end of it, Sam, there's a grave." She looked up at him. "I'm telling you to follow love, Sam. There's no reason in it, and a deal of misery, but it's the only thing that will give you happiness."

Sam had listened carefully and, more than anything he desired, he wanted to follow that advice. "But someone will get hurt, ma'am."

"And it most probably will be you," Martha said, "because you're all three impossibly young and impossibly honourable, but it's still the only thing to do. And it does hurt, Sam, I know!" There was such a sudden pain in Martha's voice that Sam frowned, and Martha, sensing his pity, hurried on. "Follow love, Sam, say your prayers and be a good boy. Then the Green Man won't gobble you up."

"Yes, ma'am." He smiled, stood, then plucked at his red coat. "But there's this."

"It's only a red coat, Sam, badly dyed and very ill cut."

"But I took an oath for it."

"To throw prisoners into flames?" Martha saw the hurt on his face, and smiled. "I'm sorry, Sam. I know it wasn't you. But if you stay in the army, you'll change!"

Sam remembered how, before his brother's death, he had so

admired Sergeant Scammell and had wanted to be like him. Now he blushed at the memory. "I won't, ma'am."

"I do hope not, Sam. I even pray not."

Later, when Sam was gone, Martha went upstairs and stared at her sleeping child. Lydia's face was so peaceful, so smooth, so pure, yet Martha felt as if a great presence threatened the city. The Green Man, she thought, had crossed an ocean to haunt dreams and bring fear. Martha told herself there was nothing to fear, but the terror, as inchoate, shapeless and unreasonable as any forest monster, was upon her. She feared for the future. She feared for her child and for the madness that was coming to the seaboard. She feared Sir William's departure because the man who replaced him might believe, like Captain Vane, in victory. She feared and, because she feared, Martha wept in the Philadelphia night.

THIRTY-SEVEN

The *Deirdre-Ann* dropped down river under topsails, staysails and driversail alone. The great mainsails which would power her across the Atlantic stayed furled on the yards. Captain Carroll, who seemed disposed to be friendly, explained to Jonathon that too much sail was dangerous in such shoaling waters and that the *Deirdre-Ann* would creep her way downstream and anchor at nightfall in the lee of Billings Island. Then, at dawn, they would be guided through the remains of the rebel obstructions that were still not entirely cleared from the river bed. "Open sea by noon tomorrow, Mister Jonathon, and then you'll see her lean to the wind."

Jonathon, cloaked against the evening cold, rested on the barrel of a small cannon that was lashed to the poopdeck. The American pilot stood by the helmsman, while Captain Oscar Carroll, contentedly smoking his pipe, stood with Jonathon. "Your uncle," the Englishman said, "tells me you're not overjoyed about this voyage?"

"No, sir. I can't say I am."

"You'll be homesick, no doubt, but London's a grand city." The captain's tic distorted his face in a grotesque series of flickering winks. "There's temptation there, but it's a grand city, especially for a young man of means."

"I'm sure, sir." Jonathon was staring at the low, greasy shoreline that slipped past in the fading light. Duck punts were being poled in the shallows, while, closer to the merchantman, oyster boats loaded with rakes and baskets beat upstream past the battered and blackened walls of Fort Mifflin. A British garrison manned Fort Mifflin now, its soldiers ever staring towards the stark ribs of the sunken *Augusta* which showed on the *Deirdre-Ann*'s port quarter. Beyond the sunken frigate, on a small and reedy island, an upturned boat had been made into a cabin for a fisherman's family. A wisp of smoke drifted seaward from a squat metal chimney that protruded through the old keel. The island was so close that Jonathon could smell the fish that cooked in the tiny shanty. Tarred nets were hung to dry beside a shabby, weather-beaten shallop in which a child shucked oysters. Captain Carroll grimaced. "I warrant they had a cold winter."

"It was bitter, sir."

Carroll saw Jonathon's wistful expression. "Thinking of swimming, lad?"

"No, sir," Jonathon lied. He was determined to escape, and it had to be this night, for tomorrow the *Deirdre-Ann* would dip her bows into the open sea.

Carroll's face twitched as he tapped out his pipe on the leeward rail. "You're no prisoner, lad, not on my ship. I said as how I'd take you to England, and take you I will, but not as a captive. But there's not one of my men that'll stand by and watch as you try to drown yourself."

Jonathon wondered what kind of message was being delivered in the contradictory statements. "If I want to go ashore, will you let me?"

"I won't help you," Carroll said, "so don't ask."

"So I am a prisoner?"

"You'll be my guest for supper, I hope. Perhaps we can have a game of chess afterwards?"

Night fell dark. The *Deirdre-Ann* was the last of a dozen anchored merchantmen that waited by Billings Island for the dawn passage past the half-sunken obstacles. The river lapped and gurgled at the ship's waterline, and reflected the lamps from the other moored ships in wavering darts of light on the black water. Captain Carroll offered a supper of bacon and lentils, followed by three games of chess, all of which Jonathon lost. He played badly, thinking only of Caroline and of the shoreline that, in the dusk and beneath the evening star, had seemed so tantalizingly close.

At midnight Captain Carroll checkmated Jonathon for the last time. "You'll have to practise, lad."

"Yes, sir."

The Captain peered into the darkness. "Tide's flooding. Time for bed." He reached for his bible and opened its well-thumbed pages. "Sleep well, lad, and count your blessings!"

Jonathon limped to his cabin which was nothing more than a tiny cubbyhole in front of Carroll's more spacious quarters. There was no window, just a wooden bunk crammed beneath the poopdeck's hanging knees. Jonathon stooped inside and sat on the bunk. His dunnage, two sea bags, took up all the floor space. There was no light.

He undressed, but kept on his shirt and linen. Over those small clothes he drew his topcoat. He did not unstrap the leg, but just sat on the bunk and waited.

He would not go to London. Three years before, perhaps two years before, such a lure would have tempted him. Even the rebellion, with all its fine promise, paled against the great temptations of London, but now Jonathon had met Caroline and a city ten times greater than London could not dim her allure.

Jonathon was in love. Yet he also sensed that the love was not entirely mirrored. He had imposed a duty on Caroline, and she had assumed it, but Jonathon was determined he would earn her heartfelt love. Till now, he knew, he had achieved nothing. He had ridden with the rebel army for a few days and fallen at the first smell of action. This night he would prove himself worthy of Caroline. He would escape.

He waited through the ringing of the watches. He waited till there was a period of silence outside the cabin. Then, taking his stick, he opened the door.

A seaman was standing by the ship's wheel. A lantern hung under the break of the poop cast the shadows of the spokes forward. "Going somewhere, lad?"

Jonathon winced. "My stomach."

The seaman laughed. "Captain's broth, eh? You'd best develop a seaman's stomach, lad. You want a chamberpot?"

"I'll use the heads."

"You want help?"

"No, but thank you." Jonathon limped for'ard. His wooden leg thumped on the deck past the cannons and past the two men who kept a watch for rebel gunboats. The galley fire still burned low as Jonathon limped past. At the ship's bows, where the great bowsprit reared up into the starlit darkness in a web of ropes, chains and netting, there was a low rail, beyond which and suspended over the flowing tide were the heads.

Jonathon flinched with pain as he lifted his wooden leg over the rail. He gripped a rope and edged his one good leg out on to the spar, then, just as he was about to topple over, he sat. He saw that the seaman who had been standing by the wheel had followed him down the deck and was now watching him. Jonathon supposed that, despite Captain Carroll's assurance that he was not a prisoner, he was nevertheless regarded as a rebel in need of watchful supervision.

Jonathon draped his topcoat about him, sat, and looked down to the black water. Beneath him was a spreading net to save men who might fall from the precarious perch, while to his right was the full-breasted figurehead of the *Deirdre-Ann*. Her great painted eyes glittered eerily in the starlight. Beyond her, dark through the tangle of rigging and crossed by the vast black anchor cable, Jonathon could see the shore. It did not seem very far away.

The seaman, perhaps out of delicacy, turned to walk towards the galley.

As soon as the man was gone, Jonathon unbuckled the wooden leg. One strap was round his thigh, the second about his waist. The cold made his fingers clumsy. The leather cup stuck to his stump, but he pulled it away and felt the blessed coolness of the night air on the chafed and bleeding flesh. He dropped the leg, with the stick, into the net. One glance to his left showed that the seaman was out of sight and, knowing that delay could be fatal, Jonathon shrugged off his topcoat, then reached out and grasped one of the bowsprit's shrouds with both his hands. He let himself fall, hung for an instant from the thickly tarred rope, then dropped.

He bounced in the fouled netting. One tarred strand of the net cut across his stump, almost making him cry aloud, but he bit the noise back as he found his wooden leg and stick. He struggled up the netting's side. It was harder than he could have dreamed possible. His one foot kept slipping through the netting's holes, but he reached for its top edge with his right hand, and, with the new strength in his arms, pulled himself up until he stared down at the black tide just six feet beneath him. The stick and wooden leg were in his left hand. He lay along the netting for an instant, then rolled over, but kept a grip on the bobstay with his right hand. He hung for a heartbeat, then dropped.

The water was like ice.

It was so cold it almost seemed to burn him.

He plunged under and bobbed up against the rough, harsh hull of the ship. He was sobbing with the cold, shivering and trembling, but he pushed himself down the hull and trusted that the stick and stump would give him buoyancy. He had never swum in his life, though he remembered how Caroline had once told him it was as easy as walking. He prayed she was right.

The tide carried Jonathon down the ship's side. He clutched the leg and stick beneath his breast and fended himself off the great hull. He dimly heard a shout above him, and knew he had been missed.

He braced his good leg against the hull and thrust himself away from the towering ship. Water slopped into his mouth, choked him, and he spat and spluttered as he flailed with his one free arm. He saw the reflections of light on the water and knew a lantern was being held over the ship's side.

"Hey!" The voice seemed very close. "Hey, lad!" A rope suddenly splashed close beside him and Jonathon, who was still only feet from the merchantman, kicked with his one leg and desperately dragged back with his right hand, feeling as he did so the surge of the tide lift and carry him away from the *Deirdre-Ann*.

He was swimming grimly now. He was clumsy, splashing and desperate, but the wood bore him up and his desperation gave him enough momentum to pass outside the lantern's small light. He could hear bare feet running on the deck, then a shout as someone ordered the gig to be lowered.

The cold was eating into his flesh. He wore only a shirt. He fought for every breath. He heard noises behind and when he twisted round to look, he was astonished at how far from the *Deirdre-Ann* he was. The tide was carrying him, sweeping him towards the eddies of the New Jersey shore, taking him into the dark swirls where he would be hidden by the shadows of shoals and mudbanks.

Blocks squealed as the gig was lowered. Jonathon still floundered onwards, swallowing water, choking, but somehow keeping afloat and grimly determined to escape the fate his uncle had ordained. The thick bulk of the wooden leg was his salvation, and bravery his inspiration.

He heard, faint behind him, the order to pull on the oars and a last flicker of good sense made him stop his frantic beating of the water. He hugged the leg. The stick was gone. He floated, turning in the eddies, sobbing because of the cold. He thought of Caroline, summoning her image like a spirit of the ocean that would save him and keep him. He wanted to say her name aloud, as a talisman, but he kept silent except for the chattering of his teeth and the involuntary frozen sobs. He could not hear the gig, and dared not look.

The surging tide, that could have swept him to a grave in the wide river mouth, saved him. It was at the flood and it carried him landwards to bump him, as gently as another current had once put Moses among the bulrushes, against a glistening bank of mud. For a few moments, in the agony of his cold, Jonathon did not even know he was safe, then, with the blind instinct of a man on the very edge of death, he crawled towards the darker loom of the New Jersey shore.

He crawled in thick sticky mud that coated him black. He crawled through a creek and up on to another mud bank where, exhausted, he collapsed. He looked up to see the line of the shore stark against the stars, then he heard the creak and splash of oars behind him. He turned cautiously to see the gig's shadow on the water, and, like a wounded beast, he slithered down to the edge of the last creek. He would lie there, hidden by the swell of the mudbank, till his pursuers were gone.

He did not know that he slept, nor that the cold had driven him into the refuge of dreams. He thought he was marching, with two sound legs, in a sweet-smelling meadow beneath a summer's sun. Around him, victorious, were men who sang beneath a striped flag. The enemy was dead, beaten, their colours surrendered and their guns quite cold. Afterwards, he dreamed of a girl with golden hair who would welcome the hero home from the wars, and he smiled as he thought of her arms reaching for him and of her smile rewarding him. Then the cold touch of the rising tide slithered him from dream into brute reality and his eyes opened to see, not Caroline, but the first flush of dawn touching the rippled ridges of the mud before his eyes.

And he saw two pairs of boots. Two men were standing just inches from his face.

Jonathon tried to raise his head to speak to the men, but one of the boots nudged his face sideways towards the water at the creek's edge. "Caroline!" Jonathon said, then the water was cold in his mouth and nostrils.

There was only two inches of water, but it was enough. One of the men put a seaboot on to the back of Jonathon's skull and held his face under the saltwater. It was as easy as drowning a kitten. Jonathon shivered and twitched for a few moments. His left hand clawed feebly at the mud, then went still. A little blood, seeping from the stump of his leg, had oozed into the creek.

Captain Carroll lifted his boot and saw that the boy was dead.

"An ungrateful lad." Captain Carroll shook his head sadly, almost as if he had been personally offended by Jonathon's predilection for the rebels. "Offered the world on a platter, and he throws it away." He spoke to the gig's bo'sun. The gig itself was a hundred yards away at the end of the mudbank.

"It's a miracle he lasted this long." The bo'sun stooped and turned the body in a vain search for any valuables. "He said your name."

"The Lord alone knows why. I've no love for rebels." Carroll rolled Jonathon's body into the shallow creek, then turned to walk back to the waiting gig. "It was better this way," he said calmly.

"I'd have tipped him over the side," the bo'sun grumbled as though he had been cheated of some anticipated pleasure.

"Money's the same." Carroll's face flickered with the uncontrollable tic. "And this way he'll be found and Woollard will know our agreement was kept."

The tide was almost at the full. The leading merchantmen were already hoisting their anchors to negotiate the cleared passage, but they had to wait as a naval sloop, sailing towards Philadelphia, warped past the obstructions first. The bo'sun, who had once served in the Royal Navy, shaded his eyes to see the warship better. "*Porcupine*," he said. "A fast sailor."

"A pretty ship," Carroll said grudgingly. The *Porcupine*, clear of the obstructions, loosed her mainsails and the water seethed white at her stern. Her sails were streaked and dirty, evidence of a long, hard passage. "Despatches from London?" Carroll wondered aloud.

"Most likely, sir," the bo'sun agreed, then shouted for the gig's oarsmen to back their blades and bring the boat's transom close to the mud.

Two hours later the river was empty. Jonathon's body drifted on the tide to the eddies about the sunken obstacles which the rebels had planted the previous summer. There his body snagged and stayed. Gulls found him and tore at water-whitened flesh.

While above him, and filling the sky with the glory of their wings, the geese skeined north.

THIRTY-EIGHT

Major-General Sir Henry Clinton arrived at the city by a frigate from which, as the vessel edged past the old rebel obstructions in the river, a sharp-eyed topman saw a body lying caught in the twisted black stakes. The frigate's captain, unwilling to delay so important a passenger, refused to stop. Instead a signal was made to a nearby sloop which lowered a boat as the frigate went on to the city.

Sir Henry was not welcomed in Philadelphia as Sir William's men had been greeted seven months before. Winter, Saratoga and the news brought by the *Porcupine* had done their work on the city's Loyalists. The *Porcupine* had done the worst damage to morale for, in its despatches from London, came news that France had declared war and that consequently a small rebellion had been blown into a European conflict; indeed, more than European, for fortresses as far removed as Florida and India were being warned and readied for battle.

And so Sir Henry rode through gloomy streets. They were also filthy streets, for the city's thoroughfares had become tips of stinking ordure. Standards, Sir Henry thought grimly, had been left to slide. Fewer parties and dances and more discipline would do Philadelphia a world of good. Sir Henry, thinking of the augean task ahead of him, had the face of a man come to kill shambolic uncertainty with force and decision.

Yet, before he could impose his will upon his new command, the due ceremonies must be completed and so Sir Henry rode to the Centre Commons that were filled with the panoply of eight thousand paraded soldiers. There were dark-uniformed Hessians, red-coated British, and cavalrymen in their rainbow finery hung with lace and gilded chains; and all paraded behind their colours to be inspected by their old and their new Commanders-in-Chief.

"Fine! Very fine!" Sir Henry, trotting down the ranks of the

40th, complimented their Colonel. If the city was filthy, then at least the men looked spruce and fit. Sir William, he allowed, had not let all standards slip.

It was clear, too, just how popular Sir William was. Sir Henry must listen to the cheers with which each battalion said farewell to Sir William Howe, and the sound confirmed to Sir Henry just how difficult a task he was undertaking. The men would resent his coming because they lamented his predecessor's leaving, yet Sir Henry was sure that there was no soldier's unhappiness that could not be cured by a day's fighting and the reward of victory.

The two Generals rode together to the western edge of the Commons. A massed band played "Yankee Doodle Dandy" and, as ever, the musicians extended the last note into a discordant raspberry to mock the pretensions of the Yankee enemy. As the music changed to the "Grenadiers' March", so the great parade began its own march past. Ladies, come from the city to watch the fine display, added the colours of their fringed parasols to the day's finery.

"I hear," Sir William leaned confidingly towards his successor, then winced because his back gave a sudden and sharp stab of pain, "that our enemies have done little else but drill training all winter."

"Then perhaps they'll give us better sport!" Sir Henry saluted the colours of a Highland battalion, all tough clansmen who followed their hereditary chieftains to war. With such men, Sir Henry thought, how could the war be lost? After the Scots came the 2nd battalion of the New Jersey Volunteers, then the green-uniformed horsemen of the Queen's Rangers.

Sir William nodded towards the Loyalist cavalry. "The best horsemen you have!"

"But not mine yet. It might be more convenient," Sir Henry saluted the colours of an Irish regiment, "if you retained effective command until you leave?"

"That's most kind of you, most kind." Sir William sounded astonished at the generous offer. "I won't hesitate to accept, but are you certain?"

"I'm certain," Sir Henry said curtly, not caring to say that he was nervous of stepping into Sir William's place. The troops' resentment at losing their popular commander might be lessened if Sir William retained effective command until the day he left. That way no immediate and odious comparisons could be made, and Sir

Henry would be granted a breathing space in which he could judge the men he was to inherit. "Though doubtless your departure will be soon?" Sir Henry did not bother to hide his eagerness.

"There's just the Meschianza to endure," Sir William said apologetically.

"Meschianza?"

Sir William smiled. "It's concocted of two Italian words. *Mescere*, to mix, and *mischiare*, to mingle. A very fanciful word to describe a small party which will mark my farewell." He waved at Lord Cathcart who led the Hussars in review. "Nothing too lavish, you understand?" Sir William added modestly.

"Indeed." The word Meschianza summed up all Sir Henry's derision of Philadelphia's famous social life of the past winter. Sir Henry had encouraged no such frippery in New York.

"And I'm still a Peace Commissioner, of course, so I shall stay in America for as long as is necessary." Sir William's old enthusiasm shone through. "You heard the rebels have agreed to meet us?"

"But not in Philadelphia?" Sir Henry sounded justifiably alarmed at the thought of his predecessor lingering in the city.

"I thought I'd request the meeting in New York," Sir William said happily. "Perhaps there'll be no more fighting?"

Sir Henry believed peace was as likely a prospect as pigs growing wings, but he said nothing on the matter during the parade, nor during the dinner which followed, as lavish as the one at which Sir William had announced his imminent departure. And again, as on that previous occasion, every available officer's servant was ordered to attend. Sam Gilpin, as he served slices of roast goose, heard a distant crackle of musketry. Heads turned towards the windows. Again the musketry sounded. Sir William smiled at Lord Robert Massedene. "Would you investigate, Robert? I'm loath to think the rebels are greeting Sir Henry so rudely, but I fear that must be the answer."

Lord Massedene returned a half-hour later to report that an enemy cavalry patrol had made a brief appearance on the Germantown Road to the north of the city redoubts. "It seemed to be a *feu de joie*, sir."

Massedene had spoken to Sir William, but Sir Henry took it upon himself to give a testy response. "In English, man! This isn't a whorehouse!"

Robert Massedene reddened. "The rebels are firing muskets in celebration, sir. They also saw fit to unfurl a French flag."

"God damn their insolence," Sir Henry growled.

After luncheon the two Commanders-in-Chief retired to Sir William's study. "I fear," Sir William said, putting Hamlet on his lap, "that the news from France will make your task hard. Very hard."

"It might." Sir Henry paced the floor between fireplace and table.

"Might?"

Sir Henry scowled. "London has ordered me to send eight thousand men to the islands."

"Are they sending you any replacements from England?"

"Two thousand if they can. They're scouring Hanover as well, of course."

"Good God." Sir William stared into the fire which, even though spring was warming the land, he still liked to find burning in his study. "Good God. One third of your troops going to the Caribbean?" His voice expressed all the relief of a man who no longer needed to pick at the Gordian knot.

"But it may not come to that," Sir Henry said brusquely.

"Indeed not." Sir William's voice became warm as he realized that his successor, like himself, believed in the peace negotiations. "I'm led to believe that the rebels will be prudent enough to see the generosity of our proposals and, if we can conclude a peace, the French will surely stay away."

"Peace!" Sir Henry sounded horrified. "I was born here, Sir William, I know these people. They're like spoilt children! Give them an inch and they'll scream for more. Saratoga ended any chance of peace, and there'll be none now that the damned Frogs have joined! They've only agreed to talk so they can lull us to sleep! Surely you see that? No, Sir William. You hold your talks, but nothing will be decided unless we hammer them on the battlefield first!"

"Always one more battle," Sir William said softly.

"One more battle?" Sir Henry frowned with misunderstanding.

Sir William feared that his successor was right, and that the peace proposals would come to nothing, but he could not surrender his dream so easily. "There are Whig voices in the city which are most encouraging!" He almost mentioned Martha Crowl by name, then decided that Sir Henry would be better served by a more gentle introduction to the exotic Widow. "The rebels will make some noise about surrendering their independence, of course, but I think they can be persuaded." Sir William shook his head chidingly. "Independence is a nonsense, and they must realize it. Where's the justice in it? It was not their money which settled these colonies, but ours. They're like tenant farmers demanding the freehold, aren't they? And there's no law nor reason in the world to take them seriously."

Sir Henry's irritation had visibly grown through this patient argument. "Damn law and damn reason," he growled. "My job is to hit them! If I do that, then they might grovel for peace, but I won't lift the hounds till they do!"

Sir William, realizing he had spoken in vain, sighed. "You'll find them most adept at dodging our blows."

Sir Henry appeared not to hear the calm response. "And if I can drive the rebels away from the city, then I see no need to relinquish a garrison on the coast. Five thousand men to hold Philadelphia and the same in New York. That should suffice."

"Indeed, indeed." Sir William was suddenly too tired to argue.

"And one savage blow at Washington before the French fleet can bring troops. If indeed it ever passes the Channel Fleet!" Sir Henry, as he spoke these optimistic words, had walked to the table where a pile of his papers sat alongside Sir William's documents. "But it seems to me, Sir William, that any blow we do aim at the rebels is first betrayed. . . ?" Sir Henry found the paper he wanted, and drew it out.

"Betrayed?" Sir William seemed startled by the word.

"Captain Vane wrote to me. I presume you saw a copy of his letter?"

Sir William closed his eyes rather than betray his bitter disappointment. For a second he was tempted to say that he had expressly forbidden Captain Vane to communicate with Sir Henry, but what good would such a protest make? Clinton was now the master of Vane's destiny, not Sir William, who, therefore, kept silent.

Sir Henry scanned the paper. "He says he has proof of a rebel organization within the city. One that has betrayed each and every one of our moves. He explains that you permitted its existence as a conduit for the discussion of peace?"

On hearing the accusations that he knew would be reported to London and whispered in Parliament, Sir William sighed. "It was never quite like that."

"But the French are in the game now. It made sense to treat with the rebels before, but not now, Sir William, not now! Now we must strike at all our enemies." Sir Henry, still holding the letter, went to the window and stared at the State House roof. "I like the sound of young Vane! He doesn't have a lot of nonsense in him."

"I'm sure he'll be gratified to hear you say so."

"I shall make him an aide, of course, then let him end this defiance." Sir Henry remembered that he had already asked Sir William to continue in temporary command. "With your permission, of course."

Sir William thought of contradicting the proposal, then realized that, in a week or so, he would be gone so his contradiction would amount to nothing. He shrugged. "The future command is yours, Sir Henry. You must make your preparations for the year's campaigning as you see best."

"Then I shall ask Captain Vane to put his ideas into practice."

"He will appreciate that." Sir William spoke absently, then, fearing he might be thought rude, tried to essay some small enthusiasm for his successor's eager plans. "The Loyalists will be gratified that you intend to stay in the city."

"They must be rewarded," Clinton said harshly. "For if they're seen to prosper then more of them may take up arms for our cause!"

"Oh, indeed!" Sir William made it sound as though he had never thought of such a simple solution to the nagging shortage of men.

"Let the Loyalists hold Pennsylvania and New Jersey," Clinton said, "and I can punish the French in the Caribbean."

"Then come back and complete the pacification of the colonies?" Once again Sir William achieved a tone of awed astonishment, just as if an answer, for which he had vainly sought through long and frustrating months, was suddenly, and too late for his own good, becoming clear.

"Exactly."

"It is gratifying," Sir William paused to put Hamlet on to the rug, then groaned as another backpain stabbed at him, "that you have brought such eagerness to the war's prosecution, Sir Henry."

Sir Henry preened under the praise. "It should never have been fought, of course, but we can't lose now! That way lies ruin. We're in it, and the damned business will have to be finished."

"We shall see you as Earl of Philadelphia yet!" Sir William said gleefully. "Now, will you forgive me? Hamlet does like a turn in the garden before dark."

Sir William, beyond caring now, walked through to the dining chamber where the orderlies were clearing away the long tables. He smiled vaguely at them, then tried to open the garden door, but a stab of pain from the small of his back made him first flinch, then fumble with the lever.

A red sleeve pushed past Sir William and the door was opened for him. "Sir," said a nervous and respectful voice.

"I do thank you." Sir William's back was suddenly extraordinarily painful, so much so that he had to clutch at the red sleeve for momentary support. "Do please forgive me."

"You want to sit down, sir?"

"No, no. It's a passing thing. My father suffered from it, you know, and the doctors never knew how to treat it! Never." Sir William, as he spoke these words, leaned on his helper as they went into the garden. Hamlet ran happily to the far shrubs, but Sir William was forced to hobble on the Redcoat's arm. He saw that his helper was one of the orderlies. "You're Vane's man, aren't you?"

"Yes, sir."

"Ah! Indeed." Somehow the recognition seemed to upset Sir William, but, as he still had need of Sam's support, he forced a smile. "It's really very foolish. I haven't had a twinge as severe as this for months. Perhaps there's wet weather coming?"

"It always seems to make it worse, sir, but a linseed poultice will have it beat."

Sir William's face lit up with a sudden and happy recollection. "Sam! That's your name, isn't it? You're the fellow who cured my bay stallion of the colic."

"Back in January, sir. Tom Evans fetched him to me."

"What on earth did you do?" Sir William, instead of being the Commander-in-Chief talking to a private, was suddenly an English squire talking of his favourite subject to an expert.

"Nothing much, sir. Just warmed his drinking water and gave him peppermint and honey."

"I must remember that."

"And some liquorice and powdered ginger after, sir."

"I think I could do with some powdered ginger myself." Sir William tentatively took his arm from Sam's and tested how his back felt. "It seems to be passing. Why on earth are you in the infantry, Sam? I'd have thought a fellow like you would be a cavalryman!"

"Dunno, sir." Sam, now that his support was no longer needed, felt embarrassed.

Sir William saw the embarrassment and, eager as ever to see men comfortable and happy about him, strove to allay it. "But you'd like to work with horses, wouldn't you?"

"Yes, sir."

"You should, you should. The world's not so full of experts as you'd think. Did Evans pay you for curing the bay?"

"Yes, sir."

"Quite right." Sir William nodded happily. "You met Captain Vane at Germantown, am I not right?"

"Yes, sir."

"Good horse country, that." Sir William sounded wistful. "Fine grass and good drainage. If it wasn't for this damned war, Sam, I'd as soon raise horses on those pastures as anywhere in the world."

Sam's voice was warm in answer. "It would be a good life, sir, so it would."

Sir William nodded. "It's beyond my power to have it now, Sam. The damned French have seen to that. I don't know why God made the French, they're no damned use to the world." He gave a small laugh. "But if I was a young man, and we hadn't been so damnably stupid, I'd be over here." He shrugged. "But it'll be back to England, and that's a good country, too. What will you do when you're back in England, Sam?"

Sam plucked at his good red coat. "I have no choice, sir."

"Of course you have! A man like you can name his price!" Sir William peered at Sam and decided that what he saw he liked very much indeed. "D'you want to come into my service?"

Sam was so astonished that he could not answer at first, and when he did he almost stammered. "Your service, sir?"

"Racehorses, Sam. Fast!" Sir William was eager suddenly. "Something to make Newmarket jealous, eh? Well, you think on it, and talk to Tom Evans before the week's out. I'll say you were invalided out of the army." Sir William laughed. "There's always a way, Sam!"

"I'm sure, sir."

"Talk to Tom. I'll see that Vane doesn't make a fuss." Sir William added the last words rather grimly, then saw Lizzie

Loring come on to the upper terrace. He waved her a welcome. "Talk to Evans, Sam."

"I will, sir."

"And thank you, Sam. Thank you!" The words came over Sir William's shoulder, and Sam, astounded, knew that he had achieved the Redcoat's dream; he could go home.

THIRTY-NINE

On the evening before the Meschianza, and in a graveyard where the rain spat from a grey sky, the Revd MacTeague read the order for the burial of the dead. "Man that is born of a woman," he intoned, "hath but a short time to live, and is full of misery. He cometh up, and is cut down, like a flower."

"Murderer," Martha Crowl said aloud, as she had said the word aloud in the pauses of every prayer. She stared at her uncle as she spoke, oblivious of the embarrassment she caused.

"O holy and most merciful Saviour," MacTeague raised his voice to drown the Widow's interruptions, "deliver us not into the pains of eternal death."

"Murderer!"

Captain Lord Robert Massedene took Martha's arm and drew her away from the grave. She went obediently, threading the gravestones and treestumps on a red-sleeved arm. Martha had so feared her own violent reaction to the news of her brother's death that she had asked Massedene to bring her to the funeral, leaving Lydia in the house with Jenny. The priest's voice faded behind her and the thin late-afternoon rain beaded the black veil that hung over Martha's face. She was cloaked in her widow's weeds. "Jonathon didn't go willingly, Robert."

"I'm sure." Massedene, even if he was not convinced by Martha's words, spoke with gentle sympathy.

"He's lying!" Martha cried the words as if in pain. "Jonathon was in love. He would not have gone to London if the very throne had been offered to him!" She led Massedene across the wet grass to where, beneath a broken pillar that marked an old grave, Caroline stood. The girl had sidled through the cemetery gate just a moment before.

"I couldn't come earlier," Caroline said, staring with seemingly empty eyes at the dark huddle of mourners.

"It doesn't matter," Martha embraced the girl, "I'm just glad the message reached you." Martha had sent a brief note across the river, but so hurried were the funeral arrangements that Martha had doubted whether Caroline would arrive before the coffin was obliterated by earth.

"What happened?" Caroline asked.

"They say he was going to London and that he stumbled overboard in the night." Martha's voice was scathing.

"They're lying." Caroline's voice was as bleak as the rain-soaked sky.

Martha drew Massedene forward and made a perfunctory introduction. "I want you to tell Lord Robert Massedene what Jonathon planned to do."

Caroline hesitated. Massedene politely took off his hat in greeting.

"It's all right." Martha had seen Caroline's hesitation. "He's one of the decent ones. Not like that murderer!" This was again directed at her uncle. "Tell him," Martha said again.

"Jonathon was going to run away," Caroline's voice was weary, "and we were to be married."

Lord Robert Massedene's face grimaced with pain. He did not know what to say, so fell back on the stilted and commonplace. "I am so very sorry."

"He would never have boarded that boat willingly," Martha insisted.

"I'm sure." Massedene's voice was very soft.

"Perhaps he tried to swim ashore, perhaps he was pushed, but it amounts to murder, Robert, murder!" Martha, in her rage, was vehement.

Massedene shook his head helplessly. "The ship's long gone, ma'am."

Martha turned to stare at the mourners. "God damn them," she said, then began to weep.

Caroline was weeping too. She was weeping silently and remorsefully, weeping because she had not loved Jonathon more. The priest's voice droned on. Despite the coffin, the smell of the body was rank and thin in the graveyard where the rain, stinging and sharp, slanted on the wind. The dark clouds threatened an early dusk.

A hollow rattling made Martha turn back towards the grave. Abel Becket had shovelled earth on to the coffin and now the sexton took the spade and thrust it into the pile of raw soil that would smother the cheap pine box. "Wait!" Martha's voice rang loud across the graveyard. "Wait!"

She took Caroline's arm and dragged her towards the open pit. Ezra Woollard moved to block their approach, but Robert Massedene hurried ahead and the big man, not wanting a confrontation with a British officer, stood aside.

The sexton, his spade loaded with earth, hesitated, while MacTeague, his damp robes fluttering, stepped towards Martha as though to offer solace to her grief, but Martha pushed past the priest. She opened her black cloak and took out a folded flag which she shook loose. Red and white stripes and stars on a blue field were bright in the drizzle. "He can at least be buried as he would wish to be buried," Martha said defiantly.

Abel Becket stepped forward and snatched at the rebel flag. "He had forsworn that nonsense! This is sacrilege!"

Martha plucked the flag beyond her uncle's reach. "He forswore nothing, you murderer!"

Becket looked at Massedene. "Will you permit this? On British ground?"

Lord Robert Massedene stepped gently forward and took the flag from Martha. Sensing the Widow's defeat, Becket and Woollard smiled.

But Massedene had only taken the flag so he could arrange it properly. He found two of the flag's corners, then gave the other two to Martha. He smiled at her, stepped back, and the flag was stretched between them. Massedene's red coat and golden aiguillettes stilled any protest that the mourners might make.

Caroline reached out to touch the flag with a tentative finger, then Massedene and Martha let their corners go and the bright standard fluttered awkwardly down to rest in ripples on the coffin lid. Lord Robert took off his hat in formal salute. "God rest his soul."

"At least it will rest in a free country soon!" Martha stared at her uncle. "Thanks to the French. And where will you run and hide, Abel Becket?"

"It was an accident," Abel Becket said. His wife plucked at his sleeve to draw him away, but Abel Becket was not a cowardly man. He looked at Martha. "I wanted Jonathon to go to London to learn his business, nothing else. There was no unkindness in such a wish, none!"

"It was murder, uncle."

"Grief speaks in you, not sense."

"And you?" Martha turned on Ezra Woollard. "Do you say it was an accident?"

Ezra Woollard glanced at Abel Becket as though for support, but none came. He shrugged. "A ship's deck, darkness, and only one leg. Yes, I'd say they were the ingredients of accident."

"And when," Martha asked in a clear and loud voice that carried to every mourner, "do you purchase a share of the trade, Ezra Woollard? There's no nephew in your way now, is there?"

"You're mad, woman."

"Enough!" Abel Becket had said his piece and had no wish to stay in a damp graveyard to bandy words with an hysterical woman. He led his wife and houseservants away. Ezra Woollard nodded at the sexton and, with a last grim glance at Martha and Caroline, he turned away.

"Murderers!" Martha shouted.

"Dear Mrs Crowl?" The Revd MacTeague hovered beside Martha, but she twitched away from the priest. The sexton began to fill the grave, shovelling fast as though eager to cover up the rebel symbol.

Martha walked between Lord Robert Massedene and Caroline towards a walnut tree that offered some small shelter from the stinging rain. Jonathon's body had been landed in the city the day before, just hours after Sir Henry's arrival, yet the corpse had not been named until this morning. "They buried him quickly enough!" Martha said vengefully, suggesting more wrongdoing on her uncle's part.

"I fear they had to," Lord Massedene murmured.

"I know. I'm told it wasn't pretty." Martha put an arm about Caroline's shoulder. "I tried to tell Sam, but Jenny couldn't find him."

Caroline shuddered. "I suppose I'll have to tell him."

"I will," Martha offered.

"He wants to meet me at six o'clock this evening," Caroline's voice was bleak. "He left a message with a sergeant on the wharf. I presumed he wanted to talk about Jonathon."

"Sam doesn't know from me," Martha said, "and I can't imagine who else might tell him. Will you go?"

Caroline turned to look at the grave. "I don't know if I should."

"It isn't your fault, Caroline. You didn't kill him!" Martha turned on Massedene. "Why was Jonathon even on a ship, Robert? He was supposedly a prisoner, wasn't he?"

"He was released."

"By whom?" Martha's voice was dangerous. "Don't tell me, Robert. Let me guess. Captain Vane?"

Massedene shrugged. "I don't know. Truly. Jonathon's name was added to a list of people who were to be given passes, and there's no way of knowing who contrived it."

"And there's nothing I can do, is there?" Martha was close to tears again. "A brother dead, men burned alive in a straw barn, and there's nothing anyone can do because the murderers wear red!" She almost screamed the last word at Massedene, then, in tears, she shook her head. "I'm sorry, Robert. That wasn't fair."

Massedene said nothing. The sexton, his job done, slapped the heaped earth with the flat of his spade, then walked away through the mossy stones. Caroline, staring at the newly shaped soil, broke the silence. "Sam wears red."

"A coat can be taken off." Martha said it scornfully.

Caroline still stared at the grave. "I won't see Sam," she said softly. "I can't."

Martha moved in front of Caroline and tilted the girl's face up to hers. "Why ever not?"

"Not today." Caroline stepped to one side, the better to see the grave down which the rain trickled to make puddles in the newly turned earth. "Not after this."

"Jonathon's dead!"

Caroline shook her head. It was hard to tell whether the drops on her face were rain or tears. "Not today."

Martha gripped the girl's shoulders. "Listen! Go to Sam! Tell him to cross the river. Tell him from me that he'll lose his soul if he doesn't cross the river!"

Tears were flooding down Caroline's face now. She said nothing.

Martha shook her. "You must go! Tell him to cross the river! He'll know what I mean! Tell him they killed Jonathon and that he must cross the river!"

But Caroline was not listening. She was sobbing and, in a sudden rush of horrid truth, she clutched at Martha. "I wanted him to die."

"Oh, God, child." Martha hugged her.

"I used to imagine him dead and I'd be free." Caroline's words, racked by huge sobs, tumbled out. "I hated it, I prayed to stop it, but I still thought it. I was wicked. Wicked."

"No." Behind their veil, Martha's eyes were shut. "I wished for the same once. You think that's so unnatural?"

"I wish I'd never met Sam."

"No, you don't." Martha held Caroline as tightly as she would hold her own child. "You're to go to Sam and you're to tell him to cross the river."

"Not today." Caroline pulled away and wiped her eyes on her sleeve. "I want to, but I can't. For him." She gestured towards the grave. "It's not very much, but it's something for Jonathon. I just won't see Sam today."

Martha, understanding and approving, nodded. "So what will you do?"

"I don't know." Caroline, who prided herself on not showing weakness, could not control her weeping now.

"Come to my house."

"I'll go home." Caroline hated to be seen this vulnerable, especially in front of a British officer. She sniffed. "You'll never forgive me for what I said."

"Jonathon loved you," Martha spoke softly, "and whatever happiness he enjoyed came from that love. You never spoiled it, so I thank you. But you and Sam were made for each other."

If Caroline understood the words, she gave no sign. She sniffed and cuffed at her eyes. "I'm going home."

"God bless you." Martha watched the girl walk away, then she seemed to slump with a sudden tiredness. "I wish I were a man."

"Why?" Robert Massedene stepped to Martha's side.

"So I could swear." Martha watched Caroline go through the gate, then shrugged. "She's in love with a Redcoat."

Massedene's eyes flickered towards the grave, understood, and went back to Martha. "Poor girl."

"Lucky girl. Jonathon would never have been strong enough for her, never. And her Redcoat isn't a weak man." Martha sniffed. "I do hate love sometimes."

"No you don't."

"Poor Robert." She took his arm. "So patient. Thank you for coming. It cannot have been very pleasant for you."

"I would have sought your company today, whatever happened." He walked beside her towards the grave. "I'm charged with a message for you, from Sir William. He desires me to tell you that Captain Vane has been given the licence to seek out traitors within the city."

Martha stopped and looked into his lordship's eyes. "Traitors?"

"Someone warned Fort Mercer." Lord Robert Massedene's voice was very soft, scarce audible above the rain that fell on the newly made grave. "Sir William thinks that Lizzie told you, and that you sent the message."

Martha gave a short, abrupt laugh. "That wasn't what happened. Lizzie said nothing! Tell Sir William that!" She shook her head. "Robert, it was servants' gossip, nothing else, just servants' gossip!"

"But it was you who – ?"

"Of course it was me!" Martha seemed irritated because he had needed to ask her the question, but she immediately became contrite. "I'm sorry, Robert. I suppose you'll have to become pompous now? Are you going to arrest me? I shall deny the charges, of course, but I don't want Lizzie in trouble."

"She isn't in trouble. Nor are you, least of all from Sir William or myself. But in seven days, my dear Martha, we shall be leaving the city. Sir Henry will be in command then, and Sir Henry is already much impressed by Captain Vane."

Martha shook her head sadly. "I understand."

"And Sir William is eager that you're protected," Massedene said. "He feels keenly that he was responsible for your brother's fate, and he's fond of you, as I am . . ."

"My dear Robert."

". . . and so he has charged me with this." Massedene took a piece of paper from his sabretache, but, because of the rain, he did not open it. "It's a pass for you and all your household. It enables you to leave the city with two wagonloads of property." He held out the pass to the reluctant Martha. "Please, take it."

Martha took it, inspected Sir William's red seal, then thrust the pass into a pocket of her cloak. "I really don't know why you're doing this. I'm your enemy, Robert."

"No woman is my enemy, you least of all." Massedene smiled shyly. "Indeed, I value your friendship and would make it more than a friendship."

"Robert . . ."

"No, hear me, please." He was blushing as awkwardly as any

schoolboy, but he looked into Martha's face and said his piece. "I would offer you my own poor protection, my dear, in the only way I can. I'm a younger son, not wealthy, but no man will dare offend you if you are to be the Lady Robert Massedene. I know these are inappropriate words in a place and on a day like this, but they are sincere."

"Thank you."

"I hope I have not offended?"

"My dear Robert." Martha walked in silence for a few paces, then offered her suitor a hopeless shrug. "Could you become an American?"

He thought about it, evidently seriously, then offered her a wry smile. "I'm not sure I'm brave enough. England's the place I know, the place where I have my friends, or most of them," he gave her a swift smile, "and it takes a brave man to surrender friendships."

"And a brave woman." Martha waited as Massedene opened the cemetery gate, then followed him into the small walk which went towards the city. "And one day, Robert, I'm going to see our flag up there." Martha gestured towards the State House spire. "And I have no wish to live under any other flag. Not even with someone as dear as you. There, I have been offensive, and you will think me ungracious."

"Never."

Martha smiled. "There was a time, my dear lord, when all I ever dreamed of was being called 'My Lady', and I thought I should die of a broken heart if I were forced to live in Philadelphia instead of London, but here I am, with a heart still beating."

"It isn't too late."

"Those dreams, dear Robert, were the dreams of a child. Perhaps I will see London some day, but I would rather, a thousand times over, see a free America. And I shall!"

Massedene walked in silence beside her until they turned north on to Seventh Street. His voice, when at last he spoke, was filled with a gentle curiosity. "Were you always this certain of rebel victory?"

Martha laughed. "Certain? I sometimes watch raindrops on a window and I tell myself that if the drop on the right of the pane reaches the sill before the one on the left, then we shall be victorious. I am reduced to praying for a raindrop to hurry." She grimaced. "That is the measure of my certainty, Robert."

"We're the same," Massedene said sadly. "We look for portents. Most soldiers do."

"Most? Not all?"

Massedene absent-mindedly returned the salute of a sergeant who led a file of men south towards the 2nd Grenadiers headquarters. "Most, yes, but not all. I rather think your General Washington has a certainty of victory in his bone, else he could not endure so much defeat. Such men aren't comfortable to live with, but wars aren't won without them."

"Do you have such men?"

Massedene smiled ruefully. "Not in this war. Instead we believe that God is an Englishman and, in His own good time, He will ensure our deserved victory. Till then we muddle along, not quite sure why we're here or whether we even ought to be here or, worse still, how to end the wretched business." Massedene, pacing slow beside Martha, suddenly frowned. "But we also have men who aren't content to muddle, men who will try to force God's hand."

"You mean Captain Vane," Martha said tonelessly.

Massedene stopped and turned to her. "I want you to promise me that you will not stay in Philadelphia. Captain Vane has changed. I cannot explain. I've tried to be kind to him, and still would, but . . ." Massedene shook his head. "He was brave in battle, so very brave. He made me jealous. But he cannot endure defeat, and I think he feels he has suffered too much defeat. He resents his birth. He thinks that to be called a lord would be the greatest gift this world has. I could tell him it isn't really worth a bent penny, but he'd never believe me." He sighed. "Do I assume, my most dear lady, that you have turned down my proposal of marriage?"

"Probably to your relief, yes."

"When this is over, my dear, and your new flag flies, I might try again?"

"I shall anticipate your return with pleasure," Martha spoke with genuine feeling, "but for now you leave in a week's time?"

"Till when you have Sir William's protection."

"Then I shall leave the day before you sail, and you will bring Sir William and Mrs Loring to supper with me on the Friday night. Will you promise me that?"

"With all my heart." Massedene felt an immense relief that Martha would leave the city, and the relief showed on his face.

Martha put her arm into his again. "I fear I won't see Sir William till that parting. Mourning has its duties."

"The Meschianza will be the poorer for your absence."

"But next Friday we shall part as friends." Martha looked again towards the State House spire and her voice was suddenly filled with a happy eagerness. "And one day, Robert, you will come back, and you will see my new flag in a blue sky, and you will know that I helped put it there."

"I think I shall." Lord Robert Massedene smiled at the thought. "I truly think I shall."

The minute hand of the clock which was built against the State House wall jerked with an audible click to mark the new evening hour. It was six o'clock, and Martha wondered if Caroline had changed her mind about meeting Sam, and hoped, for the sake of love, that she had.

FORTY

"It will stop raining," said Captain John Andre, waving his hand as though he wielded a magician's wand, "at midnight."

"I hope so, sir," Sam said loyally.

"Do not hope, young Gilpin. Trust me! I have spoken with the Deity, and he has harkened to my prayer. The rain will stop and tomorrow will be a day of the most sublime sunshine." Andre stared from the window across the wide lawn upon which, the next day, the Meschianza would blaze. "Plumes!" Andre said happily, sketching the air with his hands as he said the word to illustrate the size of the plumes. "Elaborate, beautiful, and magnificent plumes!"

"High plumes?" Sam had looked after the Captain's two horses during the winter and he was always amused by Andre's enthusiasms.

"Very high plumes," the Captain said firmly. "Black, red, green, white, and high plumes! Yes, high. Plumes for the Knights of the Blended Rose and their sworn enemies, the Knights of the Burning Mountain. The hooves of their steeds will shake the very earth with their fierce pounding." Andre imitated the pounding hooves with small clenched fists.

Sam nodded through the window. "But they won't get under those arches, sir. Not with plumes on their hats."

"I have no doubt," Andre said with a pained voice, "that when Almighty God suggested creating a heaven and earth, there was a gloomy angel who said it couldn't be done. Of course they'll get safely under the arch!"

"Not unless they're little plumes, sir. Or unless the knights duck."

"Knights don't duck! They strut! And they wear huge plumes!" Andre's hands again sketched his feathered fantasy in the air. "Enormous! Awesome!"

Sam laughed. Captain Vane had ordered him to Walnut Grove and given instructions that Sam was to stay at the mansion to help Captain Andre with last-minute preparations for the grand Meschianza. And grand it would be. The guests would come by water, serenaded by bands and escorted by nymphs of the sea-green deep who would be tastefully posed on the prows of decorated longboats. On shore the guests would be squired up the sloping lawn to where they would watch a grand tournament between the two bands of knights, and only then, when the tilting was done, would the doors of the mansion be flung open for dancing and feasting. "Perhaps, sir," Sam suggested, "the knights could carry their hats?"

"Under their arms, you mean? Like ghosts carrying their severed heads?"

"It will give you a chance to see their faces, sir."

"It would," Andre allowed, though not with any enthusiasm. "But they have to carry shields, Sam, and lances!"

"They could hang the hats from their saddlehorns?"

"They'd fall off!" Andre, distraught at the image of tumbling plumes, stared from the ballroom's shelter at the two offending arches. The one closest to the river was dedicated to Admiral Lord Howe and was decorated with Neptune's trident and a model ship, while the closer arch, in tribute to the departing Commander-in-Chief, was festooned with unfurled colours, drums, piled arms, and was surmounted by the figure of Fame who tomorrow would bestow her fickle laurels upon Sir William. "I think they're high enough," Andre said. "I think you just take joy in filling me with gloom, you wretch."

"They'll be trotting," Sam said darkly.

"Galloping, boy! These are knights, not farmers clumping to market."

"It'll add another two feet to their height, sir. Up and down?" Sam gently imitated a riding motion.

"I have ridden a horse," Andre said with fragile dignity, then turned to scan the whole garden. "A horse! A horse! My kingdom for a horse! How could the man write such clichés?"

There were no horses in sight. There were sailors building the scaffold on which some of the Meschianza's fireworks would be arrayed, and soldiers who carried boards and trestles into the mansion, but there were no horses. "You could use little horses?" Sam suggested helpfully.

Andre did not even bother to acknowledge the notion. "I shall prove you wrong, you wretched Gilpin. Find me a horse!"

"Yes, sir."

"A large horse, mind! Not some spavined pony. Find me a horse fit for a Knight of the Burning Mountain. Fetch two, and we shall rehearse this wondrous pageant ourselves!" Andre flung an imperious finger towards the rain. "Hurry, Gilpin!"

Sam hurried. He was looking forward to the Meschianza. Captain Vane was to be one of the Knights of the Blended Rose, in which obscure cause Sam had borrowed a cavalry breastplate, a dragoon's helmet and had burnished both. A shield stood in Vane's kitchen on which was painted a heart pierced by an arrow. In truth Sam was fairly sure that a plumed Captain Vane, and all the other knights, could negotiate the two arches, but both he and Captain Andre wanted to play at tilting, and so they had indulged in their disagreement which would mean Sam could spend the evening charging on Captain Vane's stallion with a lance couched in his arm.

Sam walked the length of Second Street, turned left on to Race, and felt the familiar pang as he passed the synagogue. The clocks in a watchmaker's shop told him it was twenty past six, and he hurried his pace so there would be time to couch the twin lances before darkness spoiled the enjoyment.

The door to the Lutheran church stood ajar. Sam pushed inside and clicked his tongue in his customary greeting to the horses. Their long faces turned towards him, then reached out as he walked up the aisle. He took off the sling on which his bayonet was scabbarded, and which always encumbered him when he saddled horses, and hung it over the stallion's door. Then he unlooped the stallion's headrope and stroked the white blaze. "You're going to be a knight's charger, boy."

The horse nuzzled him, then Sam turned away to climb the three steps to the tack room. As he reached the second step he saw a movement out of the corner of his eye and instinctively broke to his right, rolled down the steps, and seized the first weapon to hand – an empty water pail.

Sergeant Scammell was a believer in sudden and overwhelming force, but Sam's quickness had spoilt his attack. Scammell, stepping from the dark space behind the pulpit, had tried to stun Sam with a blow of a reversed musket, but instead Sam was untouched, crudely armed, and ready to fight.

"Stop!" The voice came from the back of the church.

Sam looked into the shadows and saw Captain Vane appear from behind the horsestalls. The Captain closed the church door, then walked up the aisle. A moment ago Sam had been exhilarating in nonsense, but suddenly the echoing church seemed a place of strange menace. Vane, whose face seemed feverish in the dull light, stopped by the stallion's stall. "Where is she, Sam?"

"Who, sir?"

Vane did not answer. Instead he stroked the stallion's nose. "I thought I told you to stay with Captain Andre?"

"He wanted his horse, sir." Sam nodded towards Andre's mare stabled halfway down the aisle. "And I was going to borrow yours, sir, because – "

Vane cut the explanation off with an impatient gesture. "Did you meet your girl today, Sam?"

"My girl?" Sam backed up the steps. "No, sir."

Vane smiled. "I don't think she likes you, Sam. She was supposed to meet you here a half-hour ago."

Sam said nothing and understood nothing. Scammell, below him, hefted the musket.

"Drop the bucket, Sam," Vane said softly. He waited. "I said drop it!"

Sam released his grip and the wooden pail rolled down the three steps.

"Did you warn her, Sam?"

"I don't know what you're talking about, sir. I wasn't going to meet her, sir! I came to fetch the horses."

Vane stared at Sam as though he was seeing his servant for the very first time. "No one can be that innocent, Sam, no one. You lied to me! You said she was a kitchenmaid. She isn't. She's a rebel. Did you know that Miss Fisher was a rebel?"

Sam thought the world had gone mad.

"Answer the officer!" Scammell barked.

"I knew!" Sam said. "Oh course I knew! She never made a secret of it!"

"Sir!" Scammell barked the correction at Sam.

Vane waved a hand which suggested Sergeant Scammell should keep silent. "You knew she was a rebel, Sam, but you never saw fit to inform me?"

"Why should I? It ain't your business!" Sam paused. "Sir."

"But it was my business, Sam." Vane stepped closer. "Do you remember the attack on the forts? We were betrayed, Sam! Betrayed! And who carried the message across the river?" Vane pointed at Sam. "Your girl!"

"No!"

"Oh, I don't know it for sure," Vane said, "but I'm going to find out."

"She wouldn't do – "

"Oh, shut up!" Vane snapped. "She wasn't your girl, and you know it! She was sweet on a rebel. So she used you. God knows what she thought you could tell her, but she used you! And whatever she learned, she told to her precious friends. We're going to find those friends, and stop their treachery."

Sam shook his head stubbornly. "She didn't use me."

Vane scuffed some fallen oat husks with the toe of his boot. "You're a fool, Sam. I like you, but you are a bloody, bloody fool. I've no doubt she murmured endearments in your ear, but all the time she was in love with a rebel!" Vane stepped another pace closer to his servant. "Your Caroline's clever, Sam, very clever. Too clever to be here tonight. Perhaps my message didn't work? Is there some special word you use when you want to meet her?"

"No, sir." Sam was indignant.

"But if she sees you at her farm tomorrow, Sam, she won't be suspicious, will she? She won't run away." Vane watched Sam's face for any reaction. "You can help me tomorrow, Sam."

Sam's silence made Sergeant Scammell heft the musket. "He's bloody useless, sir."

"Quiet!" Vane whirled on the Sergeant, then climbed the steps until he was just two paces from Sam. "Are you in love with her, Sam? Oh, it's understandable! She has that rude pretty look of the country girl, doesn't she? But she's a traitor, Sam, a traitor!" Vane saw the protest form on Sam's lips and hastened to still it. "Quiet, Sam! I want you to listen to me. I saved your life at Germantown, remember? You owe me loyalty and trust because of that. I want those things from you now. I want you to understand that there are some things in war which are hard to comprehend. That's why there are officers. Officers make those decisions, not men. Do you understand that?"

Sam stepped a pace back. "What were you going to do to her tonight, sir?"

"Just question her, Sam." Vane smiled reassurance. "Just question her."

"With him?" Sam nodded towards the Sergeant.

"So instead we must question her tomorrow," Vane said, ignoring Sam's question and talking instead as though what he proposed was the most reasonable course in the world. "We have to discover where she collects her traitorous messages, and I want your help, Sam. I've earned it!" Vane smiled. "So, are you going to help me tomorrow?"

But Sam understood that Captain Vane did wrong. Vane would not need Scammell otherwise. The realization startled Sam. Officers might be good-tempered or bad, strict or easy, but never guilty. Never at fault. Officers could be fools or wise men, but never evil, and it was evil that Sam felt in this desecrated church. Sam stared at Vane, seeing for the first time, not an officer, but another young man, and a man, Sam thought, weaker than himself.

Vane, when no answer came, shrugged. "Sam! You have to trust me! I want your help tomorrow. Caroline Fisher has betrayed us, and we have to stop the betrayal." His voice was confiding, even friendly. "She's gulled you, Sam, but she trusts you. Now it's your turn to gull her. If you go to the farm, she won't run away, but go with you. And you can bring her, quietly and calmly, to where I'll be waiting. Will you do that for me?" Vane paused a second. "Not just for me, Sam, but for your King. For England!"

But Sam was not thinking of England, but of an American boy whom Scammell had murdered before Germantown, and he remembered, too, his own pusillanimity when Sergeant Derrick had insisted the boy was a rebel. Nate had been brave, then, and Sam, to curry favour with Scammell, had swallowed the lie. Nate had scorned Sam for that, and now Sam imagined that his dead brother's spirit was somehow listening and judging him. His decision now, Sam felt, would be the weight in the eternal balance of his soul. He could choose good, or repeat the evil he had spoken at Germantown.

Vane had watched the struggle on his servant's face, and thought that no reply was coming. He sighed. "I shall ask you once more, Private Gilpin, and if you decline to help me, then you are no longer my servant. I shall return you to Sergeant Scammell's authority."

"I ain't your servant anyway!" Sam blurted out. "Sir William wants me to work for him, and I'm going! Going home!"

Vane shook his head as though he found Sam's defiance both pathetic and amusing. "Oh Sam, Sam, Sam! How little you do know of the world." Vane turned almost wearily to Sergeant Scammell. "I believe Private Gilpin struck you at Germantown, Sergeant?"

"Yes, sir, he did."

"And that offence remains unpunished?"

"Yes, sir!" Scammell was the very model of an efficient sergeant.

Vane turned back to Sam and his voice was still that of a reasonable and kindly man. "If you won't help me, Sam, then I fear you'll be under arrest on a most serious charge. I hardly think Sir William will have time to remember your existence before he leaves Philadelphia? So, Sam. Will you help me tomorrow?"

Sam hesitated again, not out of indecision, but to choose the proper words that would save his soul from perdition. "You can go to hell, sir."

Vane stared at Sam for a regretful second, then turned away. "He's yours, Sergeant."

"Dead?" Scammell's voice was toneless.

"I said he's yours!" Vane had turned away to stride down the church aisle, but he paused to loop the stallion's loosened headrope about a wooden pillar at the pew's corner. "Sam has resigned my service, Sergeant, and I return him to your authority. You must do with him as you see best." Vane reached the church door. He opened it, turned, and his eyes suddenly seemed very bright in the gloom. "Report to me in the morning, Sergeant."

"Yes, sir!" Scammell pulled back the flint of his musket. Sam, staring at Vane, appeared not to hear the click of the musket's lock.

Vane smiled. "Good-night, Sergeant." He slipped out of the church and pulled the door shut. He pulled it hard enough for the door to slam loudly, and Sam suddenly understood the click he had half-heard an instant before and, with the quickness of a cat, he dropped and rolled and scrambled towards the altar. The crash of the firing musket coincided with the banging of the church door as Vane left, but Sam heard both. He had survived, and the bullet was buried in the choir stalls. The powder smoke billowed and stank in the church as Sam slowly climbed to his feet.

Scammell chuckled. He felt behind him, drew out his bayonet, and twisted it on to the musket's muzzle. "Fast, aren't you, Sam?"

Sam did not reply. He was watching the seventeen-inch blade. He had seen how effectively Scammell used such a weapon on a battlefield, and a bayonet was a far more certain weapon than a bullet's vagary, and Scammell, slowly walking towards Sam, had a look of absolute certainty on his scarred face.

The attack was not sudden or frantic, but deliberate and slow. The Sergeant backed Sam towards the altar, judging the moment, and the killing thrust, when it came, was a short hard lunge that should have driven the blade into Sam's left lung.

Except that Sam attacked first.

He had stepped back in front of the blade's menace, but he had known there was no escape in retreat, only in attack, and so, a heartbeat before the bayonet was rammed forward, Sam had twisted and leaped beside the blade. His right hand clawed for Scammell's eyes, while his left gripped the musket's barrel and tugged with sudden and demonic force just as Scammell jabbed it forward.

Sam's tug and the Sergeant's thrust combined to unbalance Scammell. Sam felt the elation of success, butted with his head, brought up his knee, and still tried to twist the musket away with his left hand. He hit Scammell with his right, then used all his strength to drag the weapon away from the Sergeant. To Sam's astonishment, Scammell let the musket go and Sam, pulling now with both hands, tumbled backwards. He tripped, fell, and the weapon fell across him.

Scammell followed hard. The Sergeant was the more experienced fighter. He had been taught in a thousand gutters how to maim and gouge and cheat, and he had let Sam take the weapon so the boy would topple. Now Scammell would finish Sam.

Scammell kicked Sam's kidneys, then booted his unprotected ribs. Sam gasped, then Scammell's knee thumped into his belly and the Sergeant was on top of him, fist flailing on to Sam's face. Blood spurted from Sam's nose. "Bastard, bastard!" Scammell grunted the insult, then clawed with hooked fingers for Sam's eyes. His thumb slipped into Sam's mouth and Sam closed his teeth on it, clamping down, and felt Scammell's spasm of pain. Sam, abandoning the musket, rolled right, heaved himself to his knees, and drove his right fist into the Sergeant's nose. He felt the bone break, but feared his own was broken too.

Then a lance of pain seared up from Sam's groin, doubling him, and Scammell grunted in grim laughter. He whipped fists across Sam's face and, when Sam huddled behind raised hands, the Sergeant stood to kick Sam in the belly. Sam twisted towards the Sergeant, reaching for a boot, but Scammell stepped back so that Sam fell forward on to the flagstones.

Sam saw it coming and could do nothing, for his balance was lost. Scammell raised his steel-tipped boot and hammered it down on to Sam's right hand. The middle finger snapped in sudden agony, and Sam, on all fours, screamed with the pain. The horses, as though in sympathy, neighed in fear.

"I'll finish you, boy." Scammell's breath was coming in huge, lung-racking gasps. He plucked the fallen musket from the floor, aimed the bayonet, then drove it down at Sam's exposed neck. Sam, his vision blurred by the punches and by the pain that lanced up his arm, did not see the attack, but he heard the grunt of effort as the blade came and he skewed aside so that the bayonet stabbed past him. It clanged on the floor and the blade bent like a wattle under the impact.

Sam rolled, stood, and kicked. Scammell was still unbalanced from the massive thrust and Sam's boot smashed into the Sergeant's knee, then he followed it with hard, stinging blows of his left hand to Scammell's face. Sam's right hand seemed useless, but Scammell staggered backwards from the one-handed assault. Then Sam tripped on the discarded musket and Scammell used the opening to hit back. He split Sam's top lip wide and rocked Sam back with a crashing thump to his left eye. Neither man spoke. They stood like prizefighters at the scratch, trying to punch the very blood and bones out of each other, but Scammell had two fists, and Sam only one. Sam was rocked back again and he felt blood swill salty in his mouth from a loosened tooth. Scammell, now winning, was grunting through his heaving breaths.

Sam brought up his right hand, not clenched in a fist, but held with the heel of the hand uppermost, and he slammed it into Scammell's breastbone, jarring torture towards the heart, and the Sergeant stepped back. Sam kicked him, hit him with a left, then drove his right hand into the sergeant's solar plexus. The pain of the broken finger was like a red-hot flesh hook stabbing up his arm. Each time he hit with it, Sam whimpered, but if he tried to protect the broken hand he knew he would die.

Scammell swayed back from a punch, it missed, then the Sergeant bored in, head low, and his skull cracked on Sam's skull. But Sam had lowered his own skull to butt, and the crack of the meeting bones made both men stagger backwards.

For a moment neither man could fight. Scammell was hurting, but Sam was hurting more. He knew that if he went down now, he would never rise. The Sergeant, half dazed, stared from a blood-boltered face, then limped forward on his bruised knee.

Scammell ignored Sam's blows, reaching instead to grip and wrestle Sam down to the floor where his boots could finish the job, but Sam lunged with his clenched right fist and the pain of the broken finger made him scream like a stuck pig as the blow landed on Scammell's nose. Sam hit again. He was panting, half blinded by blood from his cut eye, but he saw the Sergeant make one last huge effort. Sam let the blow come, then swayed back so that the fist hissed past him. He hooked with his left fist and the blow had just enough force to drive Scammell down the steps, staggering for support on the front pew where the frightened black stallion was tethered.

Sam leaned on the choirstalls. Blood trickled from his eye and mouth. His stomach hurt, his ribs were bruised or broken, and his right hand was clutched to his belly as though he could cram the pain out of it. He did not want to move.

But nor, it seemed, did Sergeant Scammell. He stared at Sam with eyes as hard as an animal's in a blood-mashed face. He was taking huge breaths, as if summoning the strength to make one last attack. Blood ran from his mouth. He was fumbling behind him, and Sam suddenly understood and despaired, because Scammell had seen Sam's bayonet on the pew door, found it, and was now limping forward with the new weapon held like a long knife in his right hand. "I killed your fucking brother," Scammell said. "Now you, you bastard." Scammell slowly climbed the choir steps. "And tomorrow I'll have that girl of yours before I kill her."

Sam could not fight the bayonet, and he knew it. He backed away towards the altar that had been draped with a tarpaulin, and he pushed two fingers of his left hand into his mouth. He tried to whistle, but his swollen and bloody mouth would not make the sound. He spat blood on to a floor that was already spattered with blood.

The Sergeant came slowly forward, made wary of Sam's

strength, but confident that the bayonet, sharpened and bright, would end the fight.

Sam wiped his mouth on his sleeve, put the fingers against his tongue again, and blew. The sudden whistle shrieked in the church and, instantly, the black stallion lunged at his headrope. Hooves clattered and banged on the pew door.

Scammell, hearing the noise, turned. The stallion, eyes white, was rearing and thrashing.

Sam whistled again and again.

Scammell turned back. "You're dead, Sam. You're dead!" He came forward, limping, and Sam gave one last piercing whistle that threw the stallion into a final lunge.

The headrope snapped. The stallion jumped, and Scammell whirled to face the new threat.

"Up!" Sam shouted. "Up! Up!"

The horse, as Sam had taught it, reared, bright hooves flailing, and the Sergeant shouted at the beast, stabbed uselessly with the bayonet, and was forced backwards.

"Up, boy! Up!" Sam was staggering forward. The stallion, neighing and frightened, reared again as Sam picked up the discarded musket with its bent bayonet. The pain in his right hand had translated into a scream in his body, making him moan. Scammell turned, sensing the new danger, but Sam had swung the musket in one last despairing effort and the needle-sharp point, bent at right angles to the weapon's shank, hooked and tore into Scammell's belly.

The stallion skittered sideways. Sam, almost fainting from the pain in his hand, twisted the crude flesh hook to tear and rend, then dropped the musket which, like a harpoon embedded in its prey, hung from the Sergeant's belly.

Scammell's eyes were fixed on Sam. The Sergeant clutched at his belly with his left hand, staggered forward, and probed with the bayonet in his right hand. He tried to speak, but no words came.

Sam stepped back. Blood was dripping on the floor, puddling there, spreading, then, as if poleaxed, Scammell dropped to his knees. He looked in pathetic appeal at Sam, then fell forward. The musket clattered as he fell and as he moved and as he twitched in the sheeting blood.

Sam knew there would be no mercy now. He knew it dimly, through the red sheets of his consciousness and through the pulses of pain that came from broken bone and bruised flesh. Sam had tried to kill, and maybe had killed, and the army would demand his punishment, and Captain Vane would encourage the punishment, and Sam instinctively twisted away from the bleeding and moaning man and called the stallion's name.

There was no time to find a bridle or a saddle. There was no time left. There was only a horse, and a man scrabbling in blood, and Sam led the beast down the long aisle and dragged the church door open with his left hand. He was sobbing with pain.

And astonishingly, in the small evening rain, ordinary people beneath drab umbrellas went about their ordinary business in the ordinary street.

Sam slowly and painfully climbed on to the horse's bare back from the mounting block beside the church door. The first passers-by stopped to stare in astonishment at the bloody Redcoat who, ignoring them, slashed his heels into the horse's flanks. He gripped a handful of black mane as the stallion surged forward.

Sam was running.

FORTY-ONE

Sam fled the city. The alleys and courtyards would have offered a fugitive better hiding, but Sam was a country boy, at home where leaves gave shelter, and so he let the stallion take him through the western hovels, across the Centre Commons, and down towards the bare stumps where once the Neck had been so pretty with trees. He rode bareback, without stirrups or bridle, but he had learned to ride horses thus in his childhood and the stallion, trusting Sam, obeyed the pressure of its rider's knees.

Sam checked the stallion by hauling on the broken headrope. He had taken shelter among stakes that had been pushed into the soil to support the string beans which soldiers had planted to supplement their meagre rations, and he paused in the scanty cover, feeling the rain's spit on his bloodied face, and he tried to work out all his future in a moment's pain-racked thought.

He could ride to the city and throw himself on the mercy of Sir William, or he could cross the river.

Sir William, Sam thought, was a kind man, but Sam must needs explain a murder in a church before the General would offer protection. Yet the temptation of a stable in England, far from all Redcoats and rebels, was strong, and made stronger by the thought of parents and home.

Sam was wincing because of the pain in his right hand. He keened softly as he rocked back and forth in an attempt to dissipate the agony that lanced from his broken finger. The stallion shivered and Sam, without thinking, stroked its neck with his left hand.

His whole life, Sam thought, had come to this rain-soaked moment in a vegetable patch. Nate's moment had come on a battlefield, and Nate had chosen his freedom and taken a bullet in his spine as reward. That bullet was avenged now, but the vengeance meant that, unless Sam threw himself on the army's mercy, he would be a hunted creature for the rest of his life. He could escape the army and, by begging and tramping strange roads, go north to Canada where Redcoat rumour had it that ships' captains would offer a deserter passage home in exchange for work. But even if Sam reached his English village, his name would be posted in the church porch as a murderer and a deserter.

He stared wildly about the ruined landscape of the Neck, where ragged stumps, weeds, and straggling vegetable patches had replaced the once gracious parkland. A few officers, braving the rain, exercised their horses, and Sam knew he must move before he caught their attention. Yet he feared to move. A part of him knew he must run, but he could only run to a future that was far from home. He was a stranger in a strange land, and the girl who could have drawn him into that wilderness was to marry another man. Sam would be alone.

He would be alone with the knowledge that he had betrayed his red coat and his bright flag. At this moment, bareback on a frightened horse, Sam wanted to know what was the right thing to do. Captain Vane had done wrong, that much Sam knew, but Vane was not England. England was wintry mornings with the horses fretting to see the hounds unleashed after the fox. England was a line woven from horsehair that could tease a trout from a willow-shaded stream. England was laughter in the ale-house, and the sturdy friendship of villagers who knew, as surely as they knew the sun would rise, that they lived in the best of all countries. To Sam, England was the countryside, never the town with its grasping merchants and venal ambitions, and, after a winter in a great city, Sam suddenly yearned for the soft English countryside where the sun never sweltered and the snow never lay as deep as it did here. Sam wanted to go home.

But Caroline was across the river, and Captain Vane would go to her home and Sam knew that what the Captain would do there in England's name was wrong. And Sam did not believe he could stop the evil by going to Sir William, because the Commander-in-Chief, however kindly, could not listen to a private. The Private must make his own decision and, even if doing the right thing meant abandoning himself to loneliness in a strange wilderness, far from home, then it must be done. Otherwise a man could not live with himself. Sam could betray his flag, or he could betray the girl that he loved but who could never love him because there was another man.

He turned the stallion's head towards the south and clicked his tongue. Sam would miss England, so much that he could weep for the loss, but England would survive without Sam while Caroline would not. Sam would ride for love and perhaps, when his wounds were healed and the armies had marched on, he would risk the journey north to Canada and take his chances on a voyage home in the hope that his crimes would be forgotten. The stallion, its coat glossed by the rain, smelt other horses close by and whinnied.

Sam twisted to see a group of mounted officers approaching him from the city. They were suspicious because of the disarray of his bloodied clothes. One of them called for Sam to halt, and Sam, fearing all questions, kicked his boots back and gave the stallion its head.

The black horse galloped as though the Green Man himself were on its heels. It galloped with all the power and speed that Sam himself had put into the muscles with the long mornings of patient exercise, and now, beneath the rain, the stallion left its pursuers far behind. Sam rode south of the guardpost at Gray's Ferry and did not haul the stallion's head back until he had reached the undergrowth and shrubs which grew beside Schuylkill north of the Lower Ferry. There, and knowing he had bought a few moments' peace, he slid from the horse's back.

Sam was half crazed with pain. He crouched among new leaves and took deep, calming breaths. The bruises could wait, and the split flesh would mend, but the broken finger was a torment. He took a deeper breath and closed his eyes.

Slowly, gently, he closed his left hand over the broken finger. He squeezed till the pain was almost unbearable, then jerked the broken finger straight. The agony bent him over, misting his closed eyes with red, but at least the finger no longer stuck out like the bent bayonet that had hooked into Scammell's guts. Sam could still feel the bone grating, but he took the roller from about his neck and, ignoring the pain, strapped the finger to its neighbour.

He could hear the voices of the young cavalry officers behind him now. The army would search for him, for Sam had branded himself as a deserter, but these curious men, piqued by the strange sight of a bloody soldier, were just as great a danger as any formal search party. The inquisitive cavalry officers knew he was up to no good and would take pleasure in dragging a fugitive back to the guardhouse. Every man who had been Sam's friend was now his enemy, and the flogging triangle would precede his death. Sam looked west and saw, with relief, how the light faded from the clouded sky. A rent in the grey pall was edged with crimson and, in the dying light, a scarlet bird flew across the river. Somehow that sight gave Sam hope.

The stallion shivered and Sam muttered for it to be still. He could use the horse no longer, for now there was a river to cross.

He slithered down the Schuylkill's bank to the water's edge and headed south. He had ridden the Neck almost every morning, and he knew where some engineer officers, quartered in one of the gracious summer houses beside the river, kept punts for duck shooting. He prayed that the rain had kept the sportsmen indoors.

Sam clambered along the bank, slithering in the mud, forcing a way through brambles and careless of the poison ivy. He tried to understand what he had learned in the church – that Caroline had warned the fort of the Hessian attack – but he could not find it in himself to condemn her. Loyalty to England was confused by love, and Sam told himself that Caroline had never made a secret of her allegiance to the rebellion. She had not deceived Sam, even though Captain Vane had claimed that she had.

Sam felt a surge of vicious anger at Captain Vane. A man looked upwards in this world for his security, but if the master was rotten, what hope was there for the man? So now the man was alone, cut off from all that had inspired and sustained him, and Sam would be forced to take Martha's vaunted liberty for there was nothing else left.

Then, breaking the train of his fevered thoughts, Sam heard the cracking of twigs above him, followed a moment later by an officer's loud voice proclaiming the discovery of the stallion.

But Sam had made his own discovery: two duck punts that lay in a muddy cove of the riverbank. The boats were chained. There were no quant poles or paddles, just the two empty and shallow vessels and their strings of crudely painted carved decoys with which the hunters lured the waterfowl down to the marshes.

The chain was looped through iron fairleads that were bolted through the prow of each punt, then locked to a thick stake which was sunk in the soil at the bank's top. Sam tugged the chain and winced for the pain in his right hand. He tugged again, risking the clangour of the rusty links, but both stake and chain were secure.

He looked at the fairleads. One seemed loose, but not so loose that he could prise it off with his bruised left hand. He listened. He could hear the river running and the small rain falling, but no sound of horse or man.

He lifted his right foot, paused for a second in fear of the noise he must make, then slammed the heel of his boot on to the looser fairlead. The punt leaped under the blow. He slammed again and again, crashing and thumping at the rusted iron, but the bolts were stubborn and the fairlead stayed put. The chain jingled with every blow.

Hooves crashed through undergrowth above him. Sam, sobbing and gasping, ignored the pain in his right hand and seized the punt by both gunwales and, with all the strength left in his body, tugged it away from the stake.

"Stop!" A mounted cavalry officer burst through the low bushes six feet above Sam's head.

Sam pulled again, given strength by desperation, and the fairlead's bolts tore out of the wood so that Sam staggered backwards, the punt dropping, and he fell with the shallow craft into the river's margin where the current caught the light punt and threatened to swirl it away. Sam drove his boots through the clinging mud, and, with one last heave, threw himself across the punt's gunwale.

The cavalry officer turned in his saddle. "For'ard away! For'ard away!"

Sam had often heard that shout across the winter fields when a fox broke cover and the huntsman shouted to put the hounds on the trail as the horses clattered out of the brakes to follow the fleeing beast. Now Sam was the hunted beast, and the cry would bring the horsemen to his kill. Sam pulled himself into the boat and lay gasping with exhaustion on its bottom boards.

The officer watched the punt circle. He drew a pistol from his saddle holster and pulled back the flint. He held the gun at arm's length, allowed a foot for the ball's dropping and another foot for the wind, and pulled the trigger.

The bullet whipcracked over Sam's head and drove a splinter from the punt's gunwale.

There were whoops from the bank. A half-dozen officers had joined the first man and, seeing an obvious attempt at desertion, they dragged pistols and carbines from their holsters. This was more joy than they had any right to expect of a rainy evening.

Sam knelt and wrenched at a low shelf in the punt's prow which supported the duck hunters' aim. He tore it free and drove it through the water like a paddle. The Schuylkill was fast, its currents swirled and clashed, and he saw the speed with which the bank swept past. But the horsemen were faster, and their shots attracted more men from the houses on the riverbank.

Bullets flecked the water. The range was long and growing, but some of the officers prized themselves on their marksmanship with the long-barrelled pistols. One bullet slashed across Sam's back, tearing the red coat, while another cracked into the blunt bows to let a trickle of water leak into the shallow boat. One of the decoy ducks, struck plumb in its wooden belly, jumped and clattered on its tarred twine, but the laughter of Sam's pursuers faded as the current swept him faster and faster away.

Ahead now he could see the wide expanse of the Delaware, he could see the foam where the two rivers met to clash and break in tumbling waves. He pushed with his makeshift paddle, driving himself towards the great water, and only turned to watch the pursuit when the punt's bluff bow juddered and reared into the eddying whirlpools.

The cavalry officers had given up the hunt. Instead, in a splash of bright colours, they stood their horses by the battery at the Lower Ferry.

Sam knew what was about to happen. He paddled desperately, but he could not fight the surge of clashing waters, and the punt turned in the maelstrom, almost tipping him over. Somehow he kept hold of the makeshift paddle, then saw the billow of white smoke blossom mighty from the parapet.

Less than a second later the thunder of the gun crashed about Sam's ears. The sound alone hurt, but the roundshot missed his head by a clear yard. Sam saw the fountain of water rise and fall to his right.

He paddled again. The current was driving him downstream, but holding him against the Pennsylvanian bank. He forced his way eastwards, struggling for the calmer waters that flooded from the wider Delaware.

Another pulse of thunder hammered his eardrums. He ducked instinctively and heard the ball's passing like a second clap of thunder. The battery's second gun fired, but its barrel was cold and the gunners had overcompensated by elevating their aim too high. Sam imagined the artillerymen sponging out, then ramming the joined sabot of ball and charge down the warmed bore. He counted the seconds, then drove the broken wood hard into the water.

The two guns fired together. Their noise was like the banging of a door in hell, and the splash of water from the falling shot drenched Sam and added to the slopping coldness in the punt. But he was alive. He screamed a challenge for the joy of it, screaming that he lived, that he would win, that he would escape, that he would, God damn it, cross the river. He would not be beaten.

The current was carrying him south towards the islands where the British garrison manned Fort Mifflin, but Sam forced the pain aside to kneel and drag back with the paddle, and every stroke carried him across the currents, across the river, and towards the low, dull, and muddy shore of New Jersey. There was no garrison in the abandoned Fort Mercer, no garrison closer than the Cooper River, and that, Sam knew, was horribly close to Caroline's farm.

A sloop, far down river, heard the gunfire and turned, sails shivering. Sam watched it, then saw a great spume of water spray up ahead. The droplets thrown up by the gun's strike whipped across his face. But he was a small target, and getting smaller, and the gunners were losing him in the fading light. He felt the first elation of success, then Sam knew there could be neither success nor happiness unless Caroline was warned. Another young man on this same river had used the same girl as his talisman of safety, but Sam was ignorant of Jonathon's death.

The guns fired for the last time, and Sam watched a black cannonball skip across the grey water like a skimming stone. The splashes died and the gunsmoke skeined thin. The sloop, puzzled by the gunfire, had not fired.

Sam had been swept more than a mile downstream, far from Cooper's Point where Caroline lived, but second by second his frail boat closed on the New Jersey shore. He drove the paddle furiously, not realizing that he moaned with pain each time his right hand took the strain. It seemed oddly quiet now that the guns had ceased their fire. He dipped the paddle for the last time and felt the bow of the punt bump on to land. For a second he remained motionless, in danger of the current sweeping him back into the river's centre, then he collapsed over the low gunwale and let the cold river flow about his wounds. It was like the balm of Gilead.

He climbed to the top of the river's embankment. The dusk was thickening fast, making a threatening blackness beneath the trees which barred Sam's northward path. He began to walk, stumbled, then lifted his battered face to see, clear across the river and the Neck, Philadelphia spread like a magical city in the gathering darkness. A myriad of lights glittered pale as the sun's last light flared from wet roofs and windowpanes, and Sam, delivered from the river's threat, stared as if he were in a trance.

Then he shook himself free of the sight. Scammell's body might already be discovered, and Captain Vane could guess where Sam would flee. Guard companies would be rousted from their billets and longboats ordered from the navy, and now it was a race between Sam and his erstwhile master to reach a rebel girl.

The last sunlight went, and the clouds lowered heavy above the river. A dash of lightning, sudden and bright, stabbed at the far hills and the thunder sounded soft in the distance before the rain, with a careless malevolence, began to drive into Sam's face. He faced a journey across miles of wet darkness, not for Liberty, nor for a republic, but for love. Sam went north.

FORTY-TWO

After dark the rain became harder. It guttered the torches outside the guardhouses, and flooded the cellars on Front Street. The wind snatched at windows and doors, wildly swung the hanging signs above shop doorways, and flecked the river with hissing white-caps. An Irish sentry crossed himself and said the Shee were riding the night winds and that no good would come of it. Somewhere to the west, a sudden bolt of lightning stabbed bright to the ground and its blue-white brilliance revealed men gathering in the lee of a warehouse close to Painter's Wharf.

Two companies of Light Infantry had been ordered to the city's quays. Their musket barrels were stopped with cork, and their guns' locks were wrapped with rag as some protection against the driving rain. A naval officer, cloaked and shivering, crouched by the quayside and watched the black river for the promised longboats.

Lord Robert Massedene ran up the wharf. He was in dancing shoes, evidence that he had been snatched to this duty from a warm parlour, and his white silk stockings were soaked through to his cold skin. His cloak was sopping wet and his wig was streaked with the cheap dye that leaked from his cocked hat. "Captain Vane! Captain Vane!"

Vane, sheltering from the storm in a warehouse doorway, stepped forward. "Here!"

Massedene swerved into the doorway where, in a rage, he snatched off his hat and wig and threw them on to the ground. "What the hell's happening?"

"It's raining." Vane said with calculated rudeness.

"You know what I mean! What have you done to Mrs Crowl?"

The sentries' fires flickered on the quay. The rain hissed in the flames, but pitch-soaked wood kept the watch fires alight to cast a dull glow into the doorway. Vane could see the anger on

Massedene's face and, at this moment, he despised it. His lordship represented all that was most feeble about the British effort to crush a rebellion, and Vane could not hide the scorn in his voice. "I've done nothing to Mrs Crowl."

"She says . . ."

"Oh, I've no doubt she's said a great deal to you. Like every true Yankee, she screams for British help when something inconveniences her."

"You ransacked her house – " Massedene began, but again Vane interrupted him.

"I searched her house for a murderer and a deserter. Is there some new regulation that says rebel houses must be spared in such a contingency?"

"It was your servant who ran," Massedene said threateningly, as though it was a reflection on Vane that his servant should prove disloyal.

"Not my servant," Vane said airily, "but Sir William's. Or didn't you know that Sir William wanted him as a stable-boy?"

"He ran across the river," Massedene protested. "You know that! There was no call to search Martha's house!"

"A man was seen to cross the river." Vane's voice was cold, "But there's no proof it was Gilpin. I merely searched where I thought he might have taken refuge. Moreover I made the search on the authority of Sir Henry Clinton."

"Sir Henry should have sought Sir William's approval," Massedene argued weakly, and knew it.

"Sir William commands here by the courtesy of Sir Henry," Vane spoke the brutal truth.

"And did Sir Henry order you to destroy her house?" Lord Robert Massedene's voice rose in petulance, attracting the glances of the uneasy Redcoats who waited in the rain for the promised longboats. "My God, Vane! Her house looks as if it has been plundered by savages! Floorboards ripped up, panelling torn away, the child terrified!"

"I was told to make haste," Vane said. "There was no time for the delicacy with which you wish to conduct this war."

Massedene leaned wearily against the archway. The rain bounced on the glistening cobbles and hissed in the weak fires. "You're a bastard, Vane."

"For doing my duty?" Vane's anger suddenly erupted. "Gilpin killed a good man tonight! He did it because he's been seduced by some rebel woman to turn against his King. We can't love our enemy, Massedene! If we do they'll weaken us one by one, but not me! Not me, by God!"

"You're confusing vengeance with victory," Massedene said feebly.

Vane laughed at the accusation. "My lord, our attack on the forts was betrayed. It was done, I believe, by Mrs Crowl who communicates with a farm across there." Vane pointed through the seething rain to the blackness which hid the river's far bank. "Traitors, my lord, traitors. You think I should let them be? You'd lose the colonies out of a delicacy for women's feelings?"

Lord Robert Massedene shook his head as though he found the argument irrelevant. "You pulled Mrs Crowl's house into destruction! You'll keep the colonies by such barbarism?"

"I'll do whatever is needed to end this rebellion." Vane glanced angrily towards the river, willing the longboats to come. It was long past midnight, and he was finding it hard to curb his impatience. It had taken hours to roust the navy to their duty, and the Bluejackets had insisted that the expedition wait until the darkest hours were past before they would risk their men on the turbulent water. And every passing moment, Vane knew, could be taking Sam Gilpin closer to the Fisher house.

"You found nothing at Mrs Crowl's," Massedene said accusingly, as though it proved that Vane's actions this night were as futile as they were barbarous.

"I'll find the proof," Vane said. "By God I will!"

Lord Robert Massedene feared Vane was right, and he feared for Martha. If her guilt could be proved, then all her goods would be forfeit. Her furniture, clothes, jewellery, and house would be auctioned and she would be sent, penniless, into the country. Sir Henry Clinton, like any new commander, was eager to demonstrate his energy, and Vane had cleverly harnessed that desire to take his personal revenge. If Vane found proof this night, then neither Massedene's affection nor Sir William's kindness could protect Martha from ignominy.

"I'm crossing the river with you," Massedene said.

"By God, you're not!"

"By God, you have no right to stop me!" Massedene found a sudden spark of anger to shout Vane down. "You'll not fabricate evidence this night, Captain Vane! I have Sir William's orders to make certain of that!"

Vane's face was pale with anger. "You accuse me of dishonesty?"

Lord Robert knew that Vane was seeking a duel, but he did not care. "I accuse you, Captain Vane, of having the soul of a tradesman. You don't care for honour! Do you truly believe that by breaking two or three skulls you can make America loyal? America's lost, Vane! It was lost at Saratoga!"

"Then it must be regained," Vane said. "Not by your pusillanimity, but by soldiers."

A shout from the quayside announced the arrival of the longboats. Oars creaked and gunwales bumped against the wharf's steps. Vane, forgetting Massedene, ran forward to hasten the embarkation. The rain slanted red in the firelight which showed that the boats, prepared for the Meschianza, were ludicrously disguised as swans and sea-serpents, but, however ludicrous, the four boats could take soldiers across a wind-torn river to find Captain Vane's evidence.

Lord Massedene picked up his hat and ruined wig, then followed the soldiers down into the rocking craft. The eastern horizon was already edged with grey. Lightning flickered and a clap of thunder rolled its vast sound across the clouded sky beneath which, at long last, Captain Vane had been unleashed.

Sam Gilpin was soaked and chilled to the bone. He blundered through undergrowth and brambles that scratched his already-bloodied face and sometimes caught his broken finger and made him crouch in agony to let the pain ebb. His uniform snagged on twigs and thorns. The red coat was festooned with loops; loops to fix the crossbelts and loops to fasten to breeches, loops to make a man immaculate on parade, but in this night the loops clutched at every bush. Sam ripped the crossbelts away and tore the loops off, but kept the coat for what small protection it offered against the weather.

He had turned off the river path into the deep woods to avoid the small settlements on the New Jersey bank. He did not know whether the villagers were Loyalists or Patriots, only that every man could be his enemy, and so Sam forced his way through the woodland. Once, crouching because of the pain in his finger, he thought he heard the sloughing of vast footsteps behind him. He swivelled in terror. He heard the rain and the wind, the creak of huge boughs, then he was certain that a monstrous beast, green as the trees, dragged its huge limbs in pursuit of him. He forgot the pain and fled northwards, fleeing the Green Man that had come to haunt him in America.

He fled northwards, but he knew it could all be for nothing. Perhaps Caroline was already taken. Perhaps another sergeant, as hard as Scammell, questioned her in some stone cell. Or perhaps Captain Vane waited at the farmhouse in the knowledge that Sam would run there. Perhaps tomorrow Sam would be stripped to the waist and tied to the triangle, and the whips would be dragged through fingers to loosen the gobbets of Sam's bloody flesh from their lashes.

He stumbled on, always keeping the reflective sheen of the city's small lights to his left. Sam was putting his faith in the delays he knew must attend any man seeking permission to cross that river. He had been an officer's servant long enough to know that Captain Vane could not instantly command boats and men, but the night was passing, and every moment put more fear into Sam's already terrified soul.

He was terrified for Caroline, he was flinching from the great thunder, and he feared the Green Man that prowled about him in the darkness. He feared his future. He could save Caroline, but he could not have her love, and Sam knew he struggled towards a strange life in a foreign wilderness. He was a fugitive. At home his name would be posted as a criminal, while here, if the British won this war, he would have to flee far from their justice. Yet love drove him through the wet darkness. Nothing else mattered; neither King, nor country, nor regiment, nor home; only love.

He climbed on to a shallow ridge of sandy ground where there were fewer brambles and on which he could travel faster. He ran, stumbling and panting, tasting the blood that trickled on to his broken lips. He feared now that he would not be able to find Caroline's house; he had only ever seen it from the city's wharves when Caroline had pointed over the water. In the winter, when the ice had thickened on the Delaware, Sam had stared forlornly towards Cooper's Point, and he knew where the wooden house stood in relation to the river's bend, but he had no certainty that he could find the house in this rain-soaked darkness. He imagined failure, he imagined Vane striking Caroline's face to force a confession, and he sobbed with the pain of his bruised body and because he feared he would be too late.

He came to the ridge's end and he saw the sky's first pale

greyness in the east. The rain still sheeted down and Sam, to his surprise, found himself regretting that all Captain Andre's hopes for the Meschianza would be spoilt. Sam laughed at such a stupid regret, then knew that if Captain John Andre had been his officer, and not Vane, then this would never have happened. God damn Vane, Sam thought, then, in the dazzle of a fork of lightning that slammed towards the river, he saw the boats closing on the New Jersey shore.

He ran. Thunder cracked over his head, loud as a cannon's hammering, but Sam did not hear it. He forgot the rain, he forgot his fears, and he ran instead towards the place where, in the stark brilliance of the sudden lightning, he had seen the wooden house. He ran as if his whole life depended on this one moment. He ran for Caroline.

He stumbled across pastureland, cannoned into a fence, but forced himself onwards. There was enough light in the east to silhouette the soldiers who climbed from the river's bank. There was still time, Sam knew, but only a sliver of time.

"Caroline!" He shouted her name as he ran. "Caroline!"

A dog barked in the house, then more thunder drowned the noise as Sam climbed a last fence and staggered over a patch of wet grass. He hammered on the farmhouse door, beating his bloodied fist against the wood and provoking the dog into a paroxysm of noise.

More thunder smashed the heavens above him and a streak of lightning, smelling of burning, seared into the orchard. Sam had an impression of soldiers beyond the orchard, soldiers who were already too close, and he drove his fists against the locked door. "Caroline! Caroline!"

Sam knew the soldiers would be frightened because the metal on their muskets might attract the lightning. They would be running for the house, seeking any shelter now that the storm was directly overhead. Sam beat his fists on the wooden door, sobbing with the frustration, suddenly convinced that Caroline was gone, or that this was the wrong house and he would be captured here and flogged to death. Yet he would not leave the locked door, for there was still a slim chance that Caroline was inside and ignorant that the Redcoats had come from the river to find her. "Caroline! Caroline!"

Sam shouted her name in despair, then suddenly the door was snatched open and the dog strained at its leash to snap at Sam's face. An old man, a blunderbuss in one hand, the dog's leash in his other, demanded an explanation.

"Soldiers!" Sam cut the man short. "Soldiers! Get out! Get out!"

Light flickered in the room as an old woman opened the stove-door and blew the embers into flame. The dog still lunged at Sam, but the old man hauled it back. "Soldiers?"

"They're here!" Sam gestured towards the orchard where the Redcoats advanced.

The old woman lit a spill from the stove's flames and, in its bright light, Sam saw Caroline who, standing at the foot of a wooden staircase, stared at the bloody apparition in the doorway. "They're coming to get you," Sam said. "Run!"

"Sam?" Caroline, swathed in a great woollen robe, stared in disbelief at the Redcoat. "Sam?"

"They're here! Get out! Get out!"

The old man, who must have been Caroline's grandfather, turned. "The keep bag, Anna! Use the back door! Go!" The old woman snatched at a bag which hung beside a door on the far side of the room. In the bag, Sam knew, the family would keep its valuables that could be plucked to safety if fire or danger threatened. "Go, Anna!" Caleb Fisher shouted it, then hefted the ancient gun in his right hand. "I'll teach them to wake Christian souls in the night. I'll – "

"Go!" Sam pushed the old man past the kitchen table and towards the other door. "Go! Leave me the gun. Now go!" Sam took the ancient gun from the old man. "Caroline! Go!"

But Caroline, instead of fleeing, had slipped round the kitchen table to drag at a heavy dresser which stood beside the front door. "There's a letter I need!" She spoke with a hissing determination as she pulled at the huge wooden dresser. Her grandparents were already gone. "Help me! It's hidden here."

"Damn the letter! Go!" Sam pulled her away from the dresser and thrust her towards the table. He could hear the soldiers outside, then he saw the terror flood on to Caroline's face and he ran to protect her as a huge voice filled the small room.

"Don't move!"

Sam whirled round. A sergeant, huge in a dripping greatcoat, filled the front doorway. Other men pushed in behind the sergeant. They had bayonets bright on their guns. The rain, Sam knew, could have turned the black powder in the musket pans into porridge, but Sam could not be sure. He watched the men tear the rags from their flintlocks and he pushed Caroline behind him so that, should a musket fire, she would be protected. Caroline pulled

Sam towards the back door, edging him round the big kitchen table.

"Stay there, lad!" the sergeant cautioned.

Sam backed away. He pointed the blunderbuss towards the Redcoats, watching the soldiers' eyes, and when he was clear of the obstructing table he pushed Caroline towards the back door. "Run!"

"I think not."

Captain Christopher Vane suddenly stood in the back door. He had a drawn sword in his hand that he whipped left and right, as if to free it of water, and the steel made a hissing noise in the air. "Well done, Sergeant. Very well done." Vane had lost his hat in the darkness and the rain had plastered his fair hair to his narrow skull. He looked dangerous and tough. He also looked pleased. "Put the gun down, Sam."

Sam did not obey. He stared in shock at Vane, while the officer looked in awed fascination at the bloody marks on Sam's face; wounds that told of the desperate struggle in the church. Vane knew Sam was cornered and desperate, but he feigned an insouciance he did not truly feel. "Put the gun down, Private!"

Sam raised the blunderbuss and aimed it at Vane's mocking face. The sergeant, who had started to edge round the big table, checked. There was silence in the room. Two more men appeared in the doorway behind Vane and looked appalled at the great weapon which threatened the staff officer.

Captain Vane glanced at Caroline, then looked back to Sam. "You're a deserter, Sam, and a murderer, but I can find reasons for all you've done. Truly I can!" Vane spoke with the glib reasonableness that Sam knew so well. "Scammell persecuted you," Vane suggested, "and you were frightened. So you ran. I can explain all that, Sam, all of it! But if you pull that trigger, Sam Gilpin, then all the kindness in the world can't help you. You'll be a rebel, boy. You'll be an enemy. You'll be nothing."

"Get out of my way," Sam said.

"Don't be foolish. You think I give way to peasants?" Vane laughed, then threw a scornful look at Caroline. "Are you doing it for her, Sam? Has she convinced you to become a rebel?"

"Move!" Blood trickled down Sam's chin to drip on to his red coat.

"She's trapped you here, Sam." Vane said. "So put the gun down." He paused, then snapped the words again. "Put the gun down, Private Gilpin!"

All Sam's old instincts were to obey. He was a Redcoat. He had been trained to obedience. But those chains of obedience had been broken by Vane and Sam, staring at the sleek face across the bell-mouthed weapon, did not move.

Vane seemed to sneer at Sam's defiance, then he looked past Sam at the sergeant. "Take him, Sergeant. And his whore." Vane spat the last word, then sensed that he had made a mistake. He saw the sergeant open his mouth in warning, then Vane looked back to Sam just as the gun's trigger was pulled.

The recoil slammed at Sam's broken finger, making him scream, but the scream was lost in the blasting thunder of the gun which spat flame and smoke and its filthy charge of broken metal and bent nails at Vane. "Go!" Sam shouted it, dragging Caroline behind him, and he did not hear the clicks as the flints fell on damp musket pans that did not fire.

He charged into the smoke of his gunfire and he saw one Redcoat lying in the doorway, another crawling into the night, and Sam had an impression of blood as though a man had been flensed alive by the screaming metal scraps, then he shoulder-charged the third man, sending him reeling, and leaped over the threshold. Caroline was with him. There were more soldiers in the farm's yard, men who were dragging open the barn-doors and who now turned with raised bayonets towards the fugitives. Sam knew that all was lost, that he was truly trapped, but the madness of battle was deafening him to reason and he whirled the empty gun as though he would fight a regiment before he would surrender.

"Stand back! Hold your fire!" Sam heard the shout and thought he must have dreamed it. He was running hard, dragging Caroline with his broken right hand, sobbing with rage and pain, then Caroline twisted away, dragging Sam into the darkness of the shadows beyond the barn. Suddenly Sam was cloaked by night and the rain was cool and blessed on his bloodied face. He stumbled, but Caroline pulled him onwards, and Sam realized that no one pursued them or shouted after them.

They stopped at the treeline. Both were panting, but Sam heard Caroline say his name aloud, heard her say it again and again, and he held her close in the greying darkness where he could not tell whether the wetness on his face was his own blood, or the rain, or tears of joy because, with a whole army set against him, he had not failed.

FORTY-THREE

The rain stopped. By full dawn the clouds were in ragged retreat from a blue sky in which the sun shone as sweetly as any man might have desired. The Meschianza was saved.

The crowds gathered early to throng the wharves which had been hung with bunting that steamed dry in the warm sunlight. Other spectators took to river boats to watch the grand procession which, at half-past three on the afternoon of 18 May 1778, launched the great event. The Meschianza, for which Sir William's officers, out of loyalty and love, had collected more than three thousand guineas, had begun.

A fleet of longboats carried the guests south from Knight's Wharf. A larger pinnace carried the two Commanders-in-Chief beneath a gaudy silken awning. The *Roebuck*, a frigate which had spent the long cold winter in Philadelphia, fired a nineteen-gun salute as the pinnace passed, and the spectators cheered the gallant sight. Surely, the Loyalists reasoned, the British did not fear defeat if they could mount such a spectacle as this. The French could come, yet this display of confidence suggested that, come what may, Philadelphia was safe.

The guests were landed on the wide lawns of the Wharton mansion that was far enough from the city's streets to be spared the stench of rotting effluent. Seven young ladies, unmarried maidens all, were led to a pavilion which had been specially built on the north side of the lawn, and another seven were guided to an identical spired booth to the south. The girls, chosen for their beauty, were the ladies of the knights this day. The maidens wore turbans edged with silver lace and hung with pearls and golden tassels. Veils hung from the turbans. Their white dresses, fashionably slashed to reveal silk petticoats, were encircled by sashes which each girl in turn presented to her chosen champion.

Those champions, at full gallop and with plumes erect, came

safely beneath the twin arches. Each of the fourteen knights was an officer, but never, even in an army that loved its uniforms, had officers been so gorgeously arrayed. They wore doublets of white satin, sleeves slashed to show coloured silks beneath, and boots of silver leather. The Knights of the Burning Mountain challenged the Knights of the Silver Rose to a tourney to decide which pavilion held the most beautiful girls. Gauntlets were thrown down, lances raised, and the mock fight could begin.

It was all such happy fun. The knights charged, tossed away their coloured lances, then hacked at each other with blunted swords. The ladies gasped their admiration. The knights drew pistols charged only with powder and the small explosions reminded the spectators of the real war that waited on these diversions, but today the knights fought, not to contain the foul creed of republicanism, but for their ladies. At the battle's end, happily without a drop of blood to mar the day, it was declared that each band of knights and each group of ladies were as brave and as beautiful as the other.

Sir William applauded the judicious decision, but his mind was far off. At last, at long last, the rebels had agreed to send Peace Commissioners to New York where they would discuss the war's ending and, while there were those who averred that the rebels merely played for time until the French forces arrived to tip the balance, Sir William was trying to persuade himself that peace could be attained. "Willie?" Lizzie Loring leaned towards him.

"My dear?" Sir William seemed to start awake. He blinked, then waved a dutiful hand at the bedecked garden. "It's very beautiful, isn't it?"

"We're supposed to lead the procession, my dear."

"The procession? Ah, of course. Just so!"

The guests, now that the mock battle was done, walked in pairs between a hundred musicians and, as the day faded into a perfect evening, they entered a silk-hung hall lit by a galaxy of milk-white candles. Musicians played and guests danced.

Sir William surrendered Lizzie Loring to the arms of John Andre and walked with Lord Robert Massedene in the twilit garden. They strolled to the great arch which celebrated Sir William's triumphs and which was decorated with piled arms, unfurled colours, and surmounted by the figure of Fame who carried a laurel wreath in her outstretched hand. Sir William, standing beneath the proffered honour, chuckled. "It's all nonsense, Robert, all nonsense."

"You did win the victories, sir," Massedene chided. "You've not been beaten here."

"True, I wasn't defeated, but I suspect that lady," and here Sir William glanced up at the goddess with her outstretched laurels, "I suspect she won't reward victory over Mister George Washington with undying renown. And victories or not, Robert, we still have our backs to the water, don't we?" Sir William looked towards the *Roebuck* which, moored in the stream, was lit by lanterns that cast shivering reflections on the dark river. "Is Mrs Crowl safe?"

"She is now, sir. Her house is damaged, but . . ." Massedene shrugged.

"Houses can be repaired. And the papers you found across the water?"

Massedene shook his head dismissively. "There was merely a letter from Charlie Lee, sir, offering Mrs Crowl's brother a post with the rebel army. Hardly a treasonable document, I think?"

Sir William smiled. "Not treasonable at all. But in the search for it, Robert, Captain Vane was killed."

"Indeed." Massedene's voice was quite toneless.

"Sir Henry says he must have a hero's burial." Sir William's voice was equally without expression.

"A very apt gesture, sir, if I might say so."

Sir William turned to his aide. "Sir Henry also says that you prevented his killer from being captured?"

"He does, sir?" Massedene sounded faintly surprised.

Sir William smiled in the darkness. "One of the light company captains says you ordered his men to hold their fire?"

"It was raining, sir. The muskets couldn't fire. Besides," Lord Robert Massedene shrugged, "it was dark. There was no way of knowing what damage might have been caused by indiscriminate fire."

"Quite so, quite so." Sir William began strolling across the lawn. "It was Vane's servant who fired the killing shot?"

"I wouldn't know, sir."

Sir William appeared not to hear the disavowal. "Mrs Crowl will be pleased."

"She will?" Massedene pretended surprise.

"She told me she was rather fond of . . . whatever his name was."

"I'm glad for her sake, sir." Voices called from the house and Lord Robert gestured towards them. "I rather think your presence is needed for the fireworks, sir."

"Ah, yes, indeed! Fireworks for my victories! How very nice. And Lizzie will be pleased. And well done, Robert. Well done."

Massedene checked, astonished. "Well done?"

"That's what we're here for tonight, is it not? To congratulate ourselves?" Sir William smiled, then laughed. "So, well done, my dear Robert, well done indeed."

Rockets exploded into stars of crimson that fell like jewels into the river. Chinese fountains spewed white fire to make the night seem like day. Twenty separate displays launched their dazzling flames into the darkness to astonish a city.

Sam watched from across the river. He sat on a grass bank with his arm around Caroline's shoulders. Sometimes he stole glances at her face which, lit by the brilliance of the fireworks, seemed so very beautiful. He felt tears in his eyes. His brother, whom he had loved, had never found his American paradise, and Jonathon, whom Sam had befriended, he now knew lay dead beneath this soil. But Sam lived and he must now live for both the dead men.

"What are they celebrating over there?" Caroline asked.

"Victory."

She laughed softly, then flinched from the glare of a brighter rocket that exploded above the river in feathers of white light, casting stark shadows from the warehouses on the city's wharves. "I never liked the city," Caroline said suddenly.

"Nor I."

"I would have lived there, though."

"You'd have had to," Sam agreed. He held one of her hands in his left hand. Their fingers intertwined.

"I didn't want to live there." Caroline's voice was soft with regret.

Sam understood what she was saying. "You never let Jonathon down."

"I did in my dreams."

"That's what dreams are for. Things that aren't real. Things like the Green Man." He smiled because he had confessed to Caroline how scared he had been in last night's darkness.

Caroline looked at him. "Dreams can become real, Sam."

"We did nothing to make this one real."

"No." Caroline's voice revealed that she took comfort from that truth.

They had hidden in the woods all day. In the morning the soldiers had searched the Fisher farm, slaughtering the livestock for rations and taking away the precious stores from the barn. The farm had been plundered for food, but the family was safe. Caleb and Anna were now with neighbours, waiting to make certain that the Redcoats would not return, while Sam sat with Caroline beside a dark river.

Caroline leaned her head on his shoulder. "What were you planning to do, Sam?"

"After I'd warned you?" Sam thought for a moment. "Go far away, I suppose. Somewhere where no one could find me."

"And raise horses?"

"Like as not."

She smiled. The night was riven with fire, and made beautiful by the falling sparks that hissed as they fell into the river. Caroline's voice was scarcely louder than the sound of the fire's dying. "You can raise horses here, Sam."

"It's a good country for horses," Sam agreed. He paused, not because he feared to say the next words, but to savour the pleasure of uttering them. "And children."

"Yes." Caroline felt a surge of joy which was so strong that it astonished her. There was no explanation for love, she thought, but only a fool would want one.

"But children need peace." Sam sounded wistful.

Caroline said nothing. Their last exchanges, as stumbling as they may have sounded, were the declarations of love that would last their lifetimes, but Sam was a Redcoat, and she a rebel, and Sam had now hinted at the unasked question that lay between them.

"Children need peace," Sam said again, but this time more firmly, "so I suppose we'll have to fight for it."

Caroline turned her face up to Sam's. "We?"

"We," Sam said, and for a moment Caroline thought he would say no more. She expected nothing more, for Sam was not like Jonathon who would have wanted to spin words around this moment. Sam thought the simpler an assertion was, the firmer it was meant, but then, to Caroline's surprise, he did offer an explanation. "A man must fight for his home, mustn't he?"

"Is this home, Sam?"

"Home is where you love. And where you are loved."

Caroline stroked his hand. "This is your home, Sam."

The fireworks died. The dancers' music played on, coming thin over the dark water, but Sam and Caroline walked away. They walked home, and on the bank they abandoned the coat which Sam had spread on the muddy grass to keep the damp from Caroline's dress. It was his soldier's coat, his red coat that he had worn at Paoli's Tavern in that night when he had carried a red blade to the killing, but now the coat was left in the mud and a new flag would dazzle Sam's eyes.

Because the Redcoat was free.

HISTORICAL NOTE

I have taken some liberties with the Revolution's chronology; thus the skirmish at Paoli's Tavern occurred on the night following the panic in Philadelphia, rather than, as the chapter order would suggest, on the previous night. The explosion which destroyed HMS *Augusta* is here brought forward by one day to coincide with the failure of the assaults on the river forts. Similarly the news of Saratoga reached Philadelphia a few days before those failed assaults, but it seemed apt to inflict all the bad news at once on Sir William. I fetched General Charles Lee early to Philadelphia, then delayed his return to Valley Forge by one week so he could witness the aftermath of the action at the Crooked Billet.

The only characters drawn from history, besides the obvious and famous names, are the General Officers, Admiral Lord Howe, John Andre and Lizzie Loring. The rest are fictional.

The British had troops in Philadelphia for only one more month after the Meschianza. Then, needing the city's garrison elsewhere, they abandoned Philadelphia to the rebels. The Loyalists fled, some to Canada, some to the islands, a few to Britain. The occupation of the city had lasted a mere eight months.

Redcoat is drawn from many sources, but I must acknowledge an extraordinary debt to John W. Jackson's *With the British Army in Philadelphia, 1777–1778* (Presidio Press, San Rafael, California, 1979). To Mr Jackson's splendid work and fine research *Redcoat* owes much of its accuracy. The inaccuracies that remain are, of course, my own.

Frustrated by the quality of books available at Exeter station for his journey back to London one day in 1935, Allen Lane decided to do something about it. The Penguin paperback was born that day, and with it first-class writing became available to a mass audience for the very first time. This book is a direct descendant of those original Penguins and Lane's momentous vision. What will you read next?